Phantom Madness

Sadie Montgomery's Phoenix of the Opera Series

The Phoenix of the Opera

Out of the Darkness: The Phantom's Journey

The Phantom's Opera

Phantom Death

Other Phoenix of the Opera Novels

Phantom Madness

Phantom Murder

Phantom Madness

Sadie Montgomery

iUniverse, Inc.
New York   Bloomington

Phantom Madness

Copyright © 2009 by Sadie Montgomery

All rights reserved. No part of this book may be used or reproduced by any means, graphic, electronic, or mechanical, including photocopying, recording, taping or by any information storage retrieval system without the written permission of the publisher except in the case of brief quotations embodied in critical articles and reviews.

This is a work of fiction. All of the characters, names, incidents, organizations, and dialogue in this novel are either the products of the author's imagination or are used fictitiously.

iUniverse books may be ordered through booksellers or by contacting:

iUniverse
1663 Liberty Drive
Bloomington, IN 47403
www.iuniverse.com
1-800-Authors (1-800-288-4677)

Because of the dynamic nature of the Internet, any Web addresses or links contained in this book may have changed since publication and may no longer be valid. The views expressed in this work are solely those of the author and do not necessarily reflect the views of the publisher, and the publisher hereby disclaims any responsibility for them.

ISBN: 978-1-4401-6248-0 (pbk)
ISBN: 978-1-4401-6249-7 (ebk)

Printed in the United States of America

iUniverse rev. date: 8/4/2009

To Doug and Zach

We are never so defenseless against suffering as when we love, never so forlornly unhappy as when we have lost our love object or its love.
\
Sigmund Freud

There is more wisdom in your body than in your deepest philosophy.
\
Friedrich Nietzche

Every normal person, in fact, is only normal on the average. His ego approximates to that of the psychotic in some part or other and to a greater or lesser extent.
\
Sigmund Freud

Only passions, great passions can elevate the soul to great things.
\
Denis Diderot

CHAPTER 1

❈

The Case

What if it tempt you toward the flood, my lord,
Or to the dreadful summit of the cliff
That beetles o'er his base into the sea,
And there assume some other horrible form,
Which might deprive your sovereignty of reason
And draw you into madness? think of it:
The very place puts toys of desperation,
Without more motive, into every brain
That looks so many fathoms to the sea
And hears it roar beneath.
      Hamlet, William Shakespeare

20 May 1888

Dear Dr. Klinen,

  I have been in Rome for several weeks. The staff at the asylum has facilitated my installation, and I am comfortably at work on my project. The volumes of the illustrious Maakstrek that you so kindly posted to me have also arrived. His treatise on the electrical stimulation of organisms and their reactive properties has given me several avenues to explore during this sabbatical.

My letters of introduction were received warmly by your former colleague, Dr. Castanella, and as promised he has escorted me personally through his asylum. His experiments with selective punishment and reward have had great results on those patients who are at times responsive and show an occasional lucidity, although he does not pretend to return his patients to society. I have no doubt that the transitory cruelty of withholding food and water in exchange for more appropriate behavior, as well as periods of isolation, the use of restraints, and the careful administration of moderate doses of pain to remove negative behavior, is justified if it saves any of these poor souls from a perpetual life of confinement in an asylum.

Dr. Castanella also has an interesting theory in regards to the housing of his patients. He rates the inmates according to a complex scale that gives a numerical value according to the individual's behavior, responsiveness, degree of violence, and prognosis. Patients who score in a similar fashion are housed together in the same wing and are expected to spend their days in a common room.

In marked contrast to most asylums that encourage inactivity among the patients, Dr. Castanella's hospital veritably sparkles with industry. The esteemed physician holds that his patients prosper when they are kept busy. Appropriate activities are encouraged, including work. The articles fabricated by the inmates are held in high esteem among the gentry who pay exorbitant sums of money for the most bizarre pieces—fantastical carvings of nonexistent animals, articles of clothing in bright colors, baskets, pieces of pottery, and rough sculptures that reflect the most traumatic horrors of a sick mind. Dr.

Castanella firmly believes that these patients must be socialized, so the only outlets for individualized expression are the products they make. Isolation is used punitively or in limited cases to calm an overwrought patient, but otherwise no patient is allowed to remove himself from the common area or to seek out privacy of any kind. This arrangement has allowed the doctor to observe his patients in situations in which they must interact constantly with others.

This visit with Dr. Castanella has been most productive. I imagine that I will be able to write several articles based on our interviews which should be of interest at the university.

Your humble colleague and constant student,
Dr. Richmond

26 May 1888

Dear Dr. Klinen,

I hope this letter finds you recovered from your recent bout of rheumatism. Have you tried hypnosis? I know that unfortunately you do not personally respond well to opium. It is curious how different individuals react to the distillation of the poppy. I myself find small doses of opium to be effective in managing some pains, but an excessive amount renders the patient passive and lethargic. I use it only sparingly in my own practice given what we know about its addictive properties.

I continue to settle in here in this glorious city of antiquity and splendor. I have indulged myself in the past week as if I were not pursuing work but, like the thousands of pedestrians across which I come daily, merely on holiday. The highlight of my recent foray into the treasures of the city was, I have to say, the Cerasi Chapel in Santa Maria del Popolo. I was particularly impressed by the scene of Paul's conversion by Carravaggio. The figure of the saint, cast to the ground and in ecstasy, hands raised, eyes apparently lowered or turned within by some powerful delusion, struck me as an apt depiction of something akin to madness. As a man of science, you won't be shocked by my interpretation. I overheard the most amazing nonsense coming from passing groups of admirers. I wonder what they would say of miracles if they spent even one afternoon at Bragant. The pose of the figure in Carravaggio's painting reminded me of more than one poor soul locked behind the institute's doors.

As you can see, even when I pretend to be on holiday I cannot easily leave my professional concerns behind me.

In an effort to introduce me into society and to pull me away from my endless reading, Dr. Castanella has taken it upon himself to invite me to several dinner parties. Although at first I might have preferred to remain in my rooms reading the materials that I have amassed, it is fortunate that I have given in to Dr. Castanella's kind insistence.

His wife, Donna Ilaria, is engaged in many philanthropic and cultural societies, including one dedicated to historical preservation. Many of her associates, who are artists and benefactors, have also attended these dinner parties. What most intrigued me was not the remarks my hostess made about the frescoes and paintings, but her insistence on disclosing personal information about the patrons and artists with whom she came in contact via the many societies of which she is a member. It was difficult for her to distinguish what was nothing more than gossip from any discussion of substance. She assumed that I knew one school of architecture from another and went on at length easily changing subjects, first remarking on one or another historical landmark and then without rhyme or reason whispering about the particular proclivities of a curator at one of thousands of museums until she must have noted my silence, whereupon she asked me what I had as yet done in Rome in the way of culture.

After I listed for her my recent excursions, she studied me as if she found me lacking in some necessary ingredient. I extricated myself as politely as I could and mingled with the guests whose private lives now lay open before me regardless of my efforts to disregard them.

I found myself speaking with several gentlemen involved in architectural recovery and preservation. They spoke of the deplorable condition of many buildings and monuments. In their discussions the name, Sig. Erik Costanzi, surfaced time and time again. He appears to be a consultant, and both men defer to his opinion whenever a controversial subject cannot be resolved. Evidently this Sig. Costanzi has drafted blueprints for the reconstruction of a particularly deteriorated section of the Coliseum, as well as segments of the Roman aqueducts and baths. The same name now cropped up in a different conversation about dramatic structure. Subsequently another gentleman I overheard extolled the same Costanzi for the composition of a recent opera.

Realizing that Donna Ilaria was assuredly my most complete and obliging source of information, I sought her out and engaged her once more in conversation. I asked her if she had any knowledge of this Sig. Costanzi.

"Which? Do you refer to Costanzi, senior or to his son, Don Erik?"

"I believe the latter," I replied and then, eager to meet such an accomplished individual, asked, "Is he not here?"

"Oh my, no!" Her answer struck me as odd. She laughed as if the question were somehow foolish. Seeing my consternation, she was good enough as to explain, "Don Erik is a strange man. He attends few social events and only those that his…father holds."

I noted her hesitation before the word "father."

"Don Marcelo," she continued, "lost a son. Don Erik has been taken into the Costanzi family." She edged nearer and lowered her voice before she added, "No one knows where he came from. Some say he's Don Marcelo's bastard son come to demand a share in the inheritance."

"You don't sound convinced."

"Don Marcelo is a well known man, and a secret of that sort usually has a way of circulating among those of us who know how to listen. It would be a hard secret to keep for so long."

"Especially from someone of your discernment." I encouraged her to go on.

"And it's not as if he looks like Don Marcelo. But then again it's impossible to know what he looks like under that mask."

"Mask?"

"Yes. Oh you've not met him. You must accompany us to the opera next week. Sometimes one can catch a glimpse of him at the theater. He's the artistic director at the Teatro Dell'Opera."

"I assumed he was an architect from a conversation I overheard between Sig. Adamo Valerio and Sig. Ettore Locascio."

"Don Erik is a Renaissance man. I had the dubious pleasure of meeting him at a dinner party last season for the opening of one of his operas." Donna Ilaria grew unusually reticent. "He sat to my left, and I made every effort to be sociable and to draw him out. All to no avail. And it was quite disconcerting to look at his mask, wondering all the time what horrible disfigurement it must be hiding. But that wasn't the only thing that unsettled me. When he turned his eyes upon me, at one point in the conversation, I felt…in danger."

"In danger?"

"Yes. As if he might…attack me." She had brought her hand, unconsciously, to her throat. "And it wasn't as if I had said anything offensive. All I said was that the aria Signora Costanzi had sung was a sweet little song. But he looked at me as if I had offended him!"

"Artists can be sensitive."

"I suppose that's true. Well, if he said five words to me it would be amazing. Afterwards, he simply disappeared. At one point Don Marcelo—who is one of the most dashing men I know—went to search for him. Evidently he found him skulking around in one of the side parlors, hiding away, and brought him forward to mingle with us. Someone asked if Don Erik would play. The man turned as if to rush off again, but Don Marcelo and Don Erik's wife, Donna Meg, a marvelous singer, escorted the reluctant performer to the piano. He played, and she sang a wonderful little melody from the opera."

"He sounds like an interesting man," I said, for I was intrigued by the obvious discomfort that the man displayed in the context of society.

"Interesting? I don't know how one would know! He is impossible to engage in conversation. I spoke of many of the best families, but he had not one word to exchange about them. He does seem to converse easily with Don Adamo and Don Ettore, but then all Don Adamo talks about are struts, beams, arches, and foundations."

I had not thought this conversation of much

importance until I sat to write you this letter. Indeed Donna Ilaria's gossip has most probably exaggerated the character of this artist. I have no doubt that he may be a talented man, but I imagine that his reclusive behavior has endowed him with a mystery that Donna Ilaria enhances with her considerable talent at confabulation. I have consigned it to paper in an effort to give you an accurate depiction of the society with whom I am in contact here in Rome. However I foresee little time for socializing and intend to devote myself assiduously to my investigations.

Your humble colleague and constant student,
Dr. Richmond

29 May 1888

Dear Dr. Klinen,

Your kind note and suggestions for other readings have come at a fortuitous moment. I had been impressed by Dr. Castanella. His institute is far more advanced and progressive than many of its kind. As you know, I have my own private clinic in Austria which boasts a select population of patients—all unfortunately suffering from severe and irreversible maladies. They have been invaluable subjects in my research. However I may have learned all that I can from them. I find myself drawn more and more toward an issue that your own work raises. I refer, Dr. Klinen, to a lecture you delivered in Austria in 1878 on the subject of the nature of genius and obsessive drives. I found it fascinating at the time. Recently it has been much on my mind. Your theory that extreme talent arises from mental conditions not dissimilar to various illnesses that, in the common man, lead to antisocial and nonadaptive behavior has taken on renewed relevance for me.

If one could only find the genesis of the one, could it possibly lead to the understanding and alleviation of the other? "Do madness and genius walk hand in hand?" Such a question as you proposed in your lecture must haunt you with potential remedies for the insane and their ramifications for the future of mankind. Might we cure the ill and nurture genius at the same time?

The cases you presented at that conference strike me as similar to a peculiar case that has come to my attention. You may recall the conversation with Donna Ilaria, Sig. Castanella's wife, that I related in one of my previous letters, a conversation concerning a reclusive, eccentric composer whose work is highly esteemed here in Rome. He is widely accepted as a master composer, an expert in several fields including architecture and engineering, with an exaggeratedly excitable artistic temperament. His behavior manifests a morbid revulsion for all society, a pathological misanthropy that keeps all but a select few at bay. His past is clouded in mystery, but there are rumors that he is horribly scarred or disfigured and had experienced some great trauma before he found success in the opera houses in this ancient city. The man wears a mask. But this mask is only the outward sign of the distance and reserve he practices on a daily basis.

Having more time than I had expected, I allowed my curiosity to persuade me to seek out this peculiar man. I have now attended several performances at the Teatro Dell'Opera, where he reigns as artistic director. The opera happens to be one of his works, a stirring and daring piece of music and drama. Unfortunately,

I have only caught a glimpse of the man himself and this, only in passing. As Donna Ilaria has suggested, Sig. Erik Costanzi is morbidly reluctant to come into contact with his public. Knowing of your interest in talents such as those of Sig. Costanzi, I thought I would mention his case.

On the subject of redirecting and channeling energy, which is a theory worthy of further investigation, as well as your thoughts on the excess of energy and its distorting effects on character, I find that it most plausibly explains the frequent combination of a nervous and excitable personality with an artistic temperament. Would that we could isolate a specimen, such as this Costanzi, in order to study further the connections among a heightened intellect, the excitability of the nervous system, and the tenuous line between sanity and insanity. In all honesty, it strikes me that genius is no more than a kind of madness of which we stand in awe. How often do such men suffer from the very nature that lifts them above the masses! Would it not suggest that genius is yet one category of mental illness similar to those that plague our inmates? If that be the case, is it not our duty to seek a way to alleviate such extreme behavior?

Dr. Castanella is to call on me within the hour. I must prepare. Again I most fervently thank you for the books and papers you have sent and for your letter of introduction, which has opened so many doors for me.

May you accept my fond wishes from your student,
Dr. Richmond

10 June

Dear Edward,

I lapse into my old ways of addressing my pupils. I should, I daresay, address you as Dr. Richmond, but forgive an old man his small delights.

It is with great interest that I read your recent letters. It happens that I have returned to the subject of rare manifestations of talent among a population of patients here at the Bragant Institute. As you know we have among us several interesting subjects such as a young man whose mind is obsessed with mathematical quotations and formulae. Given any accumulation of objects the young man can tell one, with great exactitude, the quantity with merely a glance at what to any normal person would be an indecipherable chaos of objects.

Upon entering a room, our patient will immediately commence to count the number of people, the number of chairs, the number of each and every object of which he becomes aware, including the random smudges on the white wall. He cannot stop categorizing and quantifying his environment. Of course, we at first assumed that the numbers he recited—when he finished summing the obvious objects in any given room—were simply random numbers flashing into his mind at the moment. However, we recently put him to the test.

We filled several transparent containers of differing volumes and sizes with odd objects. In one we placed small pebbles gathered from the bed of the creek near the western border of the grounds. In another we placed coins. In yet a third we placed buttons. My assistant Frederick counted the items in each case and was the only one who knew precisely the quantity in each of these round jars. The first container was brought to my patient Gustavo who fell upon the jar, as if compelled, and turned it round in his hands and mumbled unintelligibly for a matter of no more than two minutes. Then once he tired of his examination, evidently satisfied with the results, he left the jar of pebbles on the table and would have stolen away to count the tiles along the wall in our corridor had we not stopped him. Of course he detests any physical contact, so we simply stepped within his path and asked him directly how many objects were in the jar. He stared at a point beyond our faces as if to find the number written in the air or on the wall of the room. Then, in a flat, emotionless tone, as if it were not he who spoke but the number, he gave us the exact quantity as written down previously by Frederick on a sheet of paper in his notebook.

The same procedure was repeated with the coins, with equally precise and correct results. When presented with the third jar, the patient gave a figure that was off by one. We were puzzled by the error. However the nearness of his answer to the correct sum was nonetheless remarkable. Indeed we could not help but be disappointed to find evidence of his fallibility. It was only later when Frederick returned to his study that he discovered, on the floor near the edge of a carpet, one shiny button which he must have included in his calculations and which had dropped before it could reach the jar. This missing button, added to the others in the jar, would make up the difference between the answer of 247 which Gustavo gave and the expected answer of 248. Not to let simple conjecture go without proof, Frederick enlisted me, along with Dr. Grafton and Dr. Krause, in counting the buttons in the jar. After several attempts and recounts, we all arrived at the same number—247—that my patient had correctly calculated, without the one button that had fallen to the wayside.

How this is possible, we cannot imagine. No one else in the clinic had come close to guessing the actual number of objects in one jar, much less in all three. Yet some peculiar turn of this young man's mind has allowed him to develop one faculty to an extraordinary level at the detriment of his other abilities.

Dr. Grafton and I have come to believe that there must be a way to block the energy that flows inexorably into the development of this peculiar talent and redirect its course into behaviors that have been stunted through lack of exercise. For this reason, we have placed him in a room that is perfectly square, without any colors except whitewash, windowless, and bare. He is kept naked, although I do fear our lack of means to heat the cell may endanger his health if the treatment lasts longer than a modest few days. Shielding him from all stimuli, we hope to stanch the endless flood of numbers and allow his energies to find other avenues of release.

I will keep you informed of our progress with the young man.

As far as your reference to a certain musical genius, that is, a man who is also functioning in society, even if imperfectly, one who could discuss his own case, who could comment and reveal the inner workings of his obsessions and react and respond to treatments, such a specimen would perhaps teach us more than the woeful specimens who, already broken and incapable of expression, find their way to our hospitals. You mentioned a troubled past and a disfigurement or handicap of some sort? This, too, intrigues me, for it is a theory that I hold that some event must give rise to the unnatural concentration of energies that leads to such an intensification of skill or talent in a single area.

Edward, I see no harm in your investigation of this man, Sig. Costanzi. He's obviously a complex case. I will be most curious to know more of him. Your mention of this genius, this man who hides behind a mask, has re-energized me. It strikes one's imagination, does it not? I don't wonder that you should find him an intriguing case study. Perhaps you might conduct some interviews with the gentleman during your tenure in Rome? Do keep me abreast.

Although the case studies here at the Bragant Institute for the Insane are interesting, they do not hold my interest as they would have in the past. I have long postponed a sabbatical. A colleague has been trying to convince me to come to Edinburgh. However, I think I might prefer to rest for a month or so and then to tour the continent. If time permits and you are willing to host an old teacher like me, I would enjoy visiting with you at your clinic in Austria. Let me know when you mean to return to it.

Your friend and colleague,
Dr. Klinen

18 June

Dr. Klinen,

I would be honored to host you at my clinic. Indeed I hope that we might collaborate on the questions that have so recently occupied my mind.

As you have urged me to make inquiries and to conduct some observations of the subject, Sig. Costanzi, I have diligently sought out an introduction to the Costanzi household through the Marquesi De Tello. I have also subscribed to the Teatro Dell'Opera and, as an acquaintance of the Costanzis, am allowed to attend and observe the rehearsals at the opera house itself. Unfortunately, my interaction with the subject has been limited—a more reclusive and wary patient I've not met. Indeed it is a marvel to realize how this man has managed to be as successful as he is in an industry that depends on the avid response of so many people. Had he chosen to be a scholar, say, or confined himself to musical composition, he'd have been able to eschew human contact of any sort but the minimal. Yet he functions, selectively well, among the peoples with whom he must work.

I believe you are correct that he would make an excellent case study. Of course, at this stage, I need not make my intentions known to the Costanzis. I have spoken with Don Marcelo, the patriarch of the household, and his lovely wife, Donna Madeleine, as well as the subject's wife, the famous diva, Donna Meg, Il canarino. The subject himself made a brief appearance a few nights ago. I observed him with his children—they have five—before he realized that there was a guest. He was quite tender with all of them. His oldest boys are nearly as tall as he is, but slight of build as befits their youth. His youngest are twin boys, and although he took special pains with them, inspecting their efforts at building with multicolored blocks, it was the daughter—the only female of the five offspring—that seemed to hold his attention most. The child hung upon his arm. Only when his wife approached did the girl reluctantly leave her father's side and then only after he gave her a kiss on her upturned brow. I was not meant to witness this private scene, so I stepped back from the partially opened door when I noticed Donna Meg start to lead her husband to the parlor where I awaited. However in the next moments, Donna Meg alone came to usher me to the dining room, making all sorts of polite apologies for the absence of her husband. Of course, it was obvious that he had refused to join us for dinner because of my presence. This is the third time that I have dined at the Costanzis' and on no occasion has the maestro deigned to join us for dinner or even for after-dinner conversation.

My subtle inquiries among the household staff have given me scant information. I've had somewhat more success at the teatro in spite of the fact that most of the personnel tend to speak only reticently about the maestro. Indeed the information I have managed to collect has been painstakingly sifted from fragments and overheard snatches of conversation; few of the facts have been imparted to me willingly or directly. I have found opportunities to mix with even the lowliest paid workers, as well as the orchestra director; a rather obstreperous aging diva, Carlotta Venedetti; Sig. Costanzi's assistant Rinaldo Jannicelli; the tenor Grimaldo; and the other artists in the company. The chorus is the source of many a rumor, but the information in this instance is highly suspect. Most of the women in the company seem to suffer from a juvenile infatuation with our subject and tend to explore a number of evocative fantasies woven around the object of their affection.

It is risky to sift fact from fancy in such a situation, but I have deduced the following minimal information where rumors seemed to bear out the same facts and where plausibility was not too thinly stretched. As you recall, our subject wears a mask. This mask evidently covers a partial disfigurement. I myself have noticed that Don Erik wears masks of varying sizes and shapes which suggest that it is not his entire face, but a portion thereof that suffers from the disfigurement. I assume he was born with the affliction. Given scant remarks about his parents, I infer that he was not raised by them. Rumor has it that his mother died early, details unknown, and there is no information on the father except that he died under mysterious circumstances. It is likely that the subject was treated badly from his earliest days because of the facial disfigurement. The usual ostracism and abuse would surely have resulted in the subject's violent withdrawal from society and an intense focus on his own inner fantasy world. Not surprisingly there should also be a tendency toward misanthropy and paranoia. These symptoms seem to be manifest in the subject to a modest degree. Given the fact that Sig. Marcelo Costanzi adopted Sig. Erik Costanzi as his heir, I deduce that the latter was an illegitimate offspring abandoned early in life. There was mention of a gypsy fair. From his swarthy complexion, I would judge that he may well be of the Romany race, and his placement among his people in an itinerant fair would be logical. As mysterious as the origin of his disfigurement is the source of his musical training. It appears he took up residence at an early age—still in a formative period—in an opera house in Paris where I imagine he worked with the artists and received his musical education. Evidently his fortune took an adverse turn at some point because more than one person relayed the same "rumors" concerning his encounter with Sig. Marcelo Costanzi. Most hint that he was hiding in Sig. Costanzi's smaller opera house, the Teatro Argentina, impoverished and in need of refuge. It has been Sig. Costanzi, senior, who has raised the subject above his station, out of poverty and obscurity, by giving him a name and legitimate position in society. Evidently our subject had already married and was a father, for his new life in Rome as a Costanzi is more recent than the birth of his oldest child.

 His history before coming to Rome is a mystery he guards closely. There have been several strange events recently in the Teatro Dell'Opera, but the staff is curiously reticent—almost protective in their silence—to comment on what happened.

As far as his personality and his genius are concerned, it was easy to glean from my own observations and from remarks at the theater that he is respected and admired by all but feared by some. He has been known to fly into a rage when the company does not live up to his expectations. Although I was careful to stay well out of the way and sit discreetly in a section of the auditorium where my presence would not be unduly noted, I have watched him interact with the artists during rehearsals. He and the older star of the opera Donna Carlotta have a relationship built on alternating calm and turbulence. He sent the tempestuous singer to her room after a particularly thorny bout and vowed to lock her in for the entire season. From the reaction around them, it seemed that this was not an unusual encounter, for no one was upset or worried by their vehement exchange. With others in the company, he apparently maintains a margin of distance. I would like to observe him more in this milieu. He drives everyone hard, including himself.

He shows classic symptoms of an obsessive personality. He demands more of his artists than any other director in Rome. (Evidently he's willing to pay for excellence; no one in Rome matches the salaries the staff and artists earn at the Teatro Dell'Opera.) He is prolific, has a memory for music that is astounding. More than once was I told that he composes often in his head and that once he plays or hears a piece, no matter how complex its arrangement may be, he can reproduce it down to the last musical notation. He seems capable of playing any instrument placed before him. Apparently, at one time, he had an excellent singing voice. Although it might not be as exceptional as it was, he evidently has sung in his own operas on at least one occasion to much critical acclaim. (I managed to find clippings related to several productions in the past and have transcribed them for you.)

Besides his fits of temper, he suffers recurrent migraines. Of course his most obvious symptom is his agoraphobia. Nightmares, it was mentioned, are frequent, but less so in the last couple of years. No explanation was forthcoming, and I had the impression that his lovely wife Donna Meg was sorry to have said anything about the matter. He periodically seals himself away from everyone—supposedly in fits of creative frenzy—coming out only when the obsession has been satisfied. His wife is the only person who dares approach him during these episodes or fits.

Dr. Castanella is becoming curious about my interest in the Costanzis. I hesitate to bring him into my confidence. Too often have we discovered that a colleague has published premature results based on another's meticulous and incomplete research. As my mentor, you are beyond suspicion. I would never withhold details of my study from you. Indeed I would be honored to have your guidance in the course of this case. Perhaps we could collaborate.

I regret to mistrust our esteemed associate, but I find myself jealously guarding the object of our interest. I remain vigilant and as always

Your pupil and colleague,
Edward

La canzone di Costanzi?
Paolo Ricci

In a season plagued with mishap, the current production of La canzone di cuore *opened last night to a mixture of mayhem and applause. The reader will not be forced to read a tedious review of this latest opera composed by the mysterious masked genius of Rome—need I say his name?—Signor Erik Costanzi. Give me leave to admit that, as in other productions, the composer-director has succeeded in surprising and challenging our expectations. Those of you who faithfully follow this humble reporter's reviews will know that Sig. Costanzi continues to set precedents. We have long known his jealous control of the Teatro Dell'Opera. Not only does he compose the majority of the operas staged at that venue, but in recent seasons he has even taken charge of the artistic direction of the works. Now it would seem he intends to star in his own compositions! Lest the reader ascribe this new turn of events to megalomania, we must confess that the unfortunate collapse of the tenor, Sig. Grimaldo Tessari, required that someone step forth on the boards. But are we to think that there is no understudy for such an important role? Whatever the circumstances, Sig. Costanzi evidently did not trust anyone but himself to adequately interpret the role of the hero. Of course, he managed to do a respectably good job on the stage, in spite of his insistence on wearing the mask. Ah, such showmanship! Is there no end to this man's talent? Indeed it appears he would suggest there is not!*

La Signora Macbeth
Paolo Ricci

Ah, so rare it is that the masked genius of the Teatro Dell'Opera permits any but his own work to grace the stage! One can only imagine our delight to hear the strains of Giuseppe Verdi revived for the public in this version of Shakespeare's Scottish play, Macbeth. *We can only guess as to the motives of Sig. Costanzi in allowing the performance of a lesser light. Perhaps it is the exuberant mayhem itself of the original tragedy that sparks a kindred flame in our maestro's soul? Let us not question too closely his motives, for the result has been delightful. Not only does Verdi refresh like a cool breeze over the desert sands, but the surprise of casting a mature, forceful Amazon such as we have not seen for many a season in the role of Lady Macbeth, I reluctantly admit, was inspired! The enthralling power of Carlotta Venedetti, who once ruled the opera houses of Europe as Carlotta Giudicelli, has not lessened over the years. She wears Lady Macbeth as if the role were written expressly for her! Indeed I would suggest that, under Sig. Costanzi's direction, Signorina Venedetti has refashioned the tragedy, which henceforth for this humble reviewer will bear the title,* Lady Macbeth. *The company worked seamlessly around the principals. Among the supporting performers shone the talent of our chanteuse, the inimitable Meg Costanzi, Il canarino. The music was—let us be frank—Verdi. Who could ask for more? And let us bring this modest review to a close by congratulating our masked genius for the show of an unusual amount of restraint and self-sacrifice in his choice of Verdi's masterpiece for the current season.*

25 June

Dear Edward,

    I have been called unexpectedly to Edinburgh and must go. Dr. Holtz has most fervently solicited my assistance at his school and clinic. I most likely have to commit to a series of lectures. One of his instructors unfortunately has retired from the academy due to ill health. Mine continues to be robust in spite of my seventy-five years.

    Your observations are fascinating, and I would give anything to be free to join you in Rome and to meet this specimen. We could learn so much from a wise handling of such a case. I caution you, my dear Edward, to take care. I well recall your enthusiasm in your student days, and you have been known to get carried away. We doctors, regrettably, often suffer disorders similar to those of our patients, and your particular challenge is obsessive involvement in your work. I know that you are aware of your own foibles and will wisely keep an eye on yourself as well as on this enigmatic opera person.

    If you do manage to get him to agree to some regimen of treatment, a careful record of the process may be of untold value. I want you to keep me abreast of your progress in the case.

Your friend and teacher,
Dr. Klinen

7 July

Dr. Klinen,

    Finally I have met our subject. I had nearly given up hope, but last evening I again received an invitation and was contentedly chatting with Don Marcelo and Donna Madeleine about the new pharmaceuticals that are coming out of the East. Several distillates of the poppy, I was saying, have great use in the treatment of some complaints.
    As I was describing their effects and administration, the parlor doors swung open and in the doorway stood this tall ominous figure. At his side was Donna Meg. The ominous figure was without doubt Sig. Erik Costanzi. If nothing else had convinced me, the white mask covering three quarters of his face would have confirmed it. I had only seen him at a distance on the stage or imperfectly when I observed him surreptitiously through the narrow crack in the door. Nothing could have prepared me for this unexpected meeting.
    Don Erik is an extraordinary man with an intensity that compels. It is remarkable how he manages to convey such power and emotion with so little of his face visible. It was as if he exuded something almost animal. You remember those lectures on magnetism? Well, if it could but be proved, I do believe that this man hums with some force that is simply produced by his body or his will. He is a tall man, well above average, with a powerfully athletic frame, slim in the hips, broad in the shoulders. His bearing is regal, almost predatory. He reminds one of a sleek panther. The similarity is borne out by a natural grace in the movement of his body. His eyes are intense as if he could see through walls. I'm afraid they quite

unsettled me. It was as if he knew of my interest in him and what I would say and do without my opening my mouth.

I almost thought he would come and strike me, but he did not. Instead he walked into the room with an almost feline elegance and greeted me with all the decorum one would expect of a properly born gentleman. Of course the thought of his origins and racial constitution made it difficult for me not to find something distasteful in his aping such civilized ways. Even so, I have to admit he was dignified and impressive.

Throughout dinner, my host and I took turns studying each other, but while the others made sure that the conversation did not flag and that I was a regular participant, our subject spoke fewer than three or four sentences the entire evening. He was perfectly polite, but the party evidently was accustomed to his ways and never placed him in a situation in which he would either be forced to converse at length or to be unreasonably rude.

I gleaned from the after-dinner talk that Don Erik was intrigued by my profession and the advances in our science. The longest conversation of the evening took place at that point. Knowing your penchant for detail, I have set it down with as much detail as I can recall.

"Pain is a phenomenon of the mind in most cases of hysteria and mental illness. Dr. Charcot has demonstrated that hypnotic suggestion can actually relieve patients of the chronic syndrome of pain, as well as other ills such as hysterical blindness, when their cause lies in the psychology of the mind."

"Would you propose that pain that arises from a bodily injury can be dealt with in this manner?" It was the first time Don Erik had entered the conversation. I was struck by his voice. It was deep and sonorous, a voice that one enjoys listening to. I was amazed that I could not hear any hint of his French background in the flawless Italian he spoke.

Unfortunately so many of the lecturers we listen to—whose ideas are riveting—have voices totally inadequate to their uses. But I digress.

"Actually, even pain, whose etiology is completely physical, can be managed through certain psychological exercises and chemical compounds. We've had success with some patients through therapeutic…"

"What manner of exercises?" he interrupted. I took note of his impetuous tendencies.

"Exercises of a mental nature. There are those colleagues of mine who believe that all illness arises from an emotional imbalance in the mind. This imbalance is seen to have its basis in trauma, usually deep seated trauma related to early childhood experiences. There are all manner of symptoms that can keep a man from leading a normal, happy life, and these invariably have their origins in catastrophic childhood events." As I concluded my statement, a hush descended on the entire room, unbroken by any of the company present. There was something ominous about it. I grew immediately uncomfortable, feeling I had overstepped my boundaries and been too direct in my allusion to our subject's mysterious past. Evidently I touched a raw nerve.

"Can one be cured of a bad childhood?" Our uninformed patient came forward on his seat and asked me this question with an edge of sarcastic skepticism. Even so, I sensed a reluctant urgency in his question, which I found sad.

"Cured is perhaps too strong a word to use, Don Erik, but my colleague Dr. Klinen has brought comfort to many patients who have unsuccessfully tried to bury their demons. It is only by bringing these demons to the surface that we have any hope of arresting their cruel hold on our lives."

This seemed to give him some pause. I swear I've never seen any two eyes that were more expressive than this man's. I noted in equal proportions hope and skepticism, doubt and interest.

Although I tried to draw him out further, he didn't speak another word the rest of the evening. Indeed he seemed not to be attending at all to the conversation. I saw that each of the others often stole concerned looks his way, in particular his wife who appeared anxious for the evening to end. Just as I thought I should make my excuses to depart, Don Erik sat at the piano and began to play.

It was a lovely piece that I was not familiar with. I asked Signora Madeleine, Don Marcelo's wife, what the melody was, and she smiled at me in a manner that could only be described as proud and said that Don Erik was composing. I have no experience with the creative process in music, but I cannot imagine that a complete score bursts forth at the initial moment a composer sits at his instrument. And yet no one but I was the least surprised by Don Erik's accomplishment.

A more apt specimen could not be found, Dr. Klinen, and a daring—if not scandalous—idea has begun to form itself in my mind. Do you recall a rather heated argument in which Drs. Grafton, Krause, you, and I discussed the ethics of our profession as impediments to necessary study and experimentation? Not too long ago, medical science was unduly constrained by the superstitious prohibition against dissecting the human body. The results were that physicians had partnered with villainous criminals in order to steal corpses for vivisection, a practice without which we would still be ignorant of the internal workings of the human body. As appalling as that episode was—for we know some unscrupulous grave robbers brought specimens too recently deceased to have been exhumed from proper graves—it was a necessity. Are we to stand by and allow the workings of the human mind to lie in shadows? Only through close examination and experimentation will we unlock its mysteries.

Don Erik is obviously a curious case, plagued by an exquisite and volatile mind, gifted in many ways. But he will not willingly submit himself to our study. If I could devise some stratagem by which to secure the man as a patient, we might learn much. It would be a sacrifice. The world will have lost a musical giant, his family a loved one, for there is a risk that Don Erik would never be able to return to his current life. Unfortunately our need to study might not allow us to cure our patient. He would be perpetually confined. His family would not allow this, I'm sure, so we would need to transport him to a private clinic across the border, beyond the reach of family and friends.

Of course it would not be easy to convince his family that he should be committed to our care. Without some critical episode, a breakdown or fit of some dramatic sort, I cannot hope to convince them to part with him. His symptoms are manageable—they are even seen as "normal" to his artistic temperament—and are not so difficult that his family requires their elimination. Indeed, his obsessive nature feeds his creativity. Why would they wish to treat a condition that is apparently the bedrock of who he is and what he achieves?

Yet perhaps circumstances can be arranged to push him to an extreme reaction. I am placing my seeds of doubt and concern with his wife and father. I have suggested on more than one occasion future dangers. I exaggerated the fate of that sculptress who applied the tools of her trade to her lover's sleeping body one night in their own bed, because he loved another, and who used his blood in the clay she molded to create a life-sized replica of him, all the while convinced that she created a living, breathing being. I have the compounds I need to unsettle the subject, making him susceptible to suggestion and misapprehension, as well as the necessary tranquilizers to make him manageable, should Donna Meg decide him ill or dangerous enough to submit to treatment. She would not need to know that the treatment would not be brief, limited to a few days or weeks of care in a nearby sanatorium. The clinic in Austria would be the perfect setting for our experiments. Don Marcelo would not easily find us, and if he should, what would he be able to do?

My dear Dr. Klinen, you have been my mentor, friend, and colleague over these past fifteen years. I value your judgment in this as in all matters. If I should embark on this path, I would not wish to do so alone.

Your humble student and fervent colleague,
Edward

16 July

My Dear Edward,

Your attention to detail is admired and appreciated. Indeed the subject sounds remarkable. He manifests many symptoms that could lead to tragedy. Yet I cannot, in all good conscience, accept a diagnosis of madness. He shows a number of interesting coping strategies that keep at bay the most egregious forms of obsessive disorders common to our patients. Although you correctly identify his agoraphobia, as well as a personality that is at the extreme on a spectrum of behaviors, he is functioning moderately well. Of course, his family and his milieu compensate for his temperament. Indeed, I cannot imagine him functioning as well under any other circumstances.

I am intrigued not only by his genius but by his ability to rise above certain proclivities that would have—in another specimen—led to madness and failure. This Erik Costanzi is a success in more ways than one. The theoretical questions involved are myriad. I understand your enthusiasm for his case, Edward. Like you, I would give my right arm to study such a man. But I must caution you.

You and I have taken an oath to ease suffering and to do no harm. I have gently warned you before about your tendency toward unrealistic ideas and fantastical plans. I'm afraid your consideration of absconding with the subject is just that—a flight of fancy. Not only do our ethics restrain us, but our compassion should also impede us in any course that would lead to this man's unnecessary confinement. As you know, our successes, so far, are meager. Condemning Sig. Costanzi to a clinic, submitting him to our experiments, would most probably guarantee his madness and permanent institutionalization. If he is not 'mad,' our treatment would certainly make him so. What would we learn? Probably a great deal. And I know, Edward, that the potential for further knowledge is what drives you to consider such a cruel and unethical act. But we won't dwell on what surely was no more than a hypothetical construct.

On the other hand, should the subject experience a critical break with reality and lose his ability to control his adverse behavior and symptoms, then we would certainly be compelled to intervene for his family's sake and for the benefits we might achieve in his treatment, as well as for his own sake. Your reference to the lovely sculptress Celeste is a sad reminder of the tragedy of a creative temperament when the rational mind gives way and can no longer control such impulses as jealousy and rage. She should also remind us how limited our powers have been to allay suffering. She is still confined at your clinic in Austria, is she not?

I'm afraid, my dear friend, that you must content yourself with observations. Perhaps you will discover something that will lead you to an insight that might aid in your treatment of your other patients.

However, if Sig. Costanzi's situation should deteriorate enough to justify institutionalization, I would be most anxious to be kept informed of his treatment. I am flattered that you refer to the subject as "our patient," but the case would be entirely yours. Even so, you can always count on me as a consultant. But I would not dream of interfering with your treatment or study of the patient. In the meantime, please continue to share your observations and thoughts with me. I find them most interesting.

Your humble teacher and friend,
Dr. Klinen

CHAPTER 2

❁

To Fall

O, let me not be mad, not mad, sweet heaven
Keep me in temper: I would not be mad!
                    King Lear, William Shakespeare

time, he wanted more, time to write, to compose, the notes were cutting him, pounding away at him, razors, blades insistently punishing him, driving him in his waking hours, haunting his dreams, sounds blocking speech, leaving him incapable of following the empty discourse after dinner, drowning out the words of his children, keeping Meg's endearments from his ears, a wall of music between him and life and his loved ones, the hours wrestling with a barrage of images and sounds, Carlotta's missed notes, orphans crying for succor, incapable of letting them slip into silence, he gathers them with their unborn siblings, collecting them, gathering them, sweeping them from the floor of the stage where they have fallen unsung, crippled by the company's mishandling, the off-key dross of violin and cello, the mutilated chords from the untutored chorus, all the poor victims of their endless approximations to the score in his mind, he insists and explains and corrects, waiting for the impossible moment when all the notes will link together into a pristine expression of the sublime

her hand, her voice, her lips, her gentle laughter break through the morass of wounded sounds and unborn scores to touch him, to cool his fevered despair, and bring him back, back, back, back to the hard dead reason of wood, stone, iron, only she fills the sonorous gap and anchors him to the pitch and sway of life

memories of Francois's hands on his, the boy's large green eyes, too familiar not to be painful, a false mirror to himself, play and play his father's score, achingly he hears it in the notes from his son's hands, now the boy plays, there it is, the sylvan warmth of a fairy wood, the magic incantation, it eases his mind, it feeds his hunger, it promises, it promises, it soothes the ache, his notes merge with sparkling surprises forged in another's mind, the mind of a young adolescent on the verge of awakening

he draws back, afraid, afraid to know, there are dangerous, milky shadows he fears to find mirrored in the innocent landscape of his young son's mind, he will not follow the slope to see too deeply where a burgeoning sexuality lies waiting, waiting

thoughts like ice slivers sap the loving warmth, the ghost touch of his fingers on Francois's as they dance across the polished keys of the piano, no, not thoughts, shades from the past, chained and locked away in slimed stone tunnels, the echo of sodden water drips its one, lonely, unforgiving note on damp floors, the smell of mold, underground chambers, the half-light of closed channels under the opera palace

the other boy, deep brown eyes, olive complexion, dark brown hair, a smile that knows too many dark brown secrets, eyes that have seen into the darkness inside men's souls, his eyes meet the boy's, can't sustain his gaze, too sad to see the pain that has made its home in those eyes, eyes too young to be so old, eyes that remind him of his own damnation, his own desperate needs

the little angel's fingers tug at his limp hand, cherry smile, brown softness of her mother's eyes stares into his, unflinching, unwavering love and trust, violin strings, variations on the same melody, playful nursery songs, abrupt changes, stops, restarts, crowned by the quivering glory of one perfect chord, she lays the instrument irreverently down on the settee, he catches it before it slips to the floor, bites back the chiding, the sharp warning, rubs his fingers across the polished wood, still vibrating from Laurette's practice, lays it like a bleating babe in its velvet-lined case

he watches them—two hearts born of the same love—as they build their towering city of cut blocks across the hearth stones, two boys, fruit of his unbounded love for her, she flicks a gold curl from her brow, scowls as one child Raoul in a fit of pique crashes into the palace his brother Etienne has built, a word spoken draws both boys—faces identical, expressions the same, as if the action of one belonged equally to the other, two sons, the last gifts of his body, treasures of their mother's womb, he watches, mesmerized by the life around him

yet he trembles, knowing happiness like this is fragile, and rare, and beyond his control

the music draws him from them, the notes, implacable, insistent, angry, impatient to be given life and substance, urgent to flow through his fingers to the instruments that link the world of desire to the world of substance realized, to be heard, to be written down and fixed, to leap from potential to actual…he closes the door to his study, he sits and plays and dips his pen in the inkwell, to set it to paper, to relieve the insistent demand, the unending cascade of sounds that fill him to bursting

His headache had returned lately with a vehemence difficult to bear. In pain, but unwilling to worry Meg, Erik's nerves had begun to fray. His forbearance, of which he had rightly been proud, was harder and harder to sustain as he found himself enmeshed in unending complications at the theater. Home was a refuge except that he struggled against his family's demands for his attention, needing to lock himself away with his music. It was beginning to feel as if he were bound to disappoint everyone, including himself, for he was unable to satisfy everyone's expectations.

Meg had glimpsed him as she came backstage. He quickly dropped his hand from his forehead and attempted a reassuring smile.

"Why are you hiding, Erik?" Meg teased. As she saw the drawn look to his eyes, she stopped short. Concerned, she asked, "Do you have another one of those headaches?" She slid her arms gently round his waist. She tilted her head up at a sharp angle to look at him. Erik was aware of her soft eyes as they examined him.

"It's just a twinge," he lied. He didn't wish her to worry. He only wanted to see her carefree, happy, safe.

Rinaldo, his assistant, approached with the latest revisions in hand. He was a handsome young Italian with dark sensuous eyes and velvet black curls, nearly as tall as Erik, lithe and athletic. Rinaldo hung back for a moment, giving Erik and Meg time to conclude their conversation. Meg nodded for him to come. She kissed Erik lightly on the cheek and returned to the stage.

Erik could hear Carlotta practicing the scales, her voice powerful, rich, and deep. She no longer sang the soprano that had made her the toast of Paris. Her voice, like her figure, had matured into a beauty overwritten by life itself. She was in good form and had stopped complaining, at least within Erik's earshot, that she was not to sing the leading role in the opera they were currently rehearsing. Meg was the heroine.

Rinaldo handed Erik the score upon which several marks had been added, bowings had been simplified, instruments rearranged, a phrase moved and modified. Following Erik's instructions, Rinaldo had noted the adjustments. Erik perused them, pleased.

"Yes. This is better." He paused and glanced at the assistant and added, "The bowing is more elegant."

Rinaldo had made the suggestion to rework the bowings. It was rare for Erik to incorporate anyone else's suggestions, so Rinaldo was pleasantly surprised at the maestro's favorable judgment.

"Carlotta sounds rested. Did you not accompany her last night?"

Color rose to Rinaldo's cheeks at Erik's allusion to the affair that he had been conducting, on and off again, with the diva. It certainly was no secret that he had become Carlotta's lover. But periodically they would argue and separate for days or weeks at a time only to fall into each other's arms in a tempestuous reconciliation that was difficult for the theater company to ignore. As a reminder of his independence, Rinaldo still rented rooms in a fashionable hotel, but in effect, when they were not fighting, he lived with Carlotta.

"I made sure that she retired early last night, Don Erik," he answered noncommittally.

Erik smiled to imagine how Rinaldo might have enticed the older woman to forego dancing and drinks at several of her favorite haunts in order to go to an early bed.

"You've been good for her, Rinaldo. But has she been good for you?"

If anyone else had asked him that question, the young Italian might have been offended. But Rinaldo knew that Erik was perfectly serious, his concern sincere.

"I can manage her."

"That wasn't what I asked."

"I can't explain." He hesitated as if the conversation were awkward. "I know it makes no sense, yet I can't imagine not being with her."

Erik's expression was intense and direct, his green eyes even more striking in the context of the alabaster mask he wore. He examined his assistant.

"Be cautious, Rinaldo. Carlotta can be dangerous."

Suddenly, Erik swiveled on his heel and stared off toward the back of the stage.

"Did you hear that?" he asked, straining his ears toward the sound he thought he had heard.

"No," answered the assistant who had heard nothing unusual, nothing different from the ambient noises from the rehearsal.

Erik paused. "I thought…I heard…bells."

Rinaldo couldn't imagine the significance of such a sound for his employer, but he felt the short hairs at the back of his neck rise as he was drawn in by Erik's intensity. There was something unpleasant about the tense regard Erik threw down the dark passageway of the theater in either direction.

Just as Rinaldo was about to ask Erik why the bells might be significant, they both saw two young chorus girls winding their way toward them. Each was chatting and laughing in an intimate tête à tête. The sound of tinkling bells grew as they approached. One of the girls waved her arms to draw attention to some aspect of the story she was recounting to her companion. On each of her wrists were bracelets with silver charms and brass bells that filled the air around them with multiple, thin, tinny vibrations.

Rinaldo heard Erik sigh and saw him visibly relax as the girls smiled at them and walked past. Before Rinaldo could ask him about his peculiar reaction, Erik turned and marched down the hallway to the stage.

"Bells? What the devil was he so worried about?"

"You really should have come down to meet our guest, Erik. I was embarrassed by your lack of courtesy." Meg slipped easily onto the soft brocade cushion next to the piano where Erik was playing.

He didn't answer her. Instead he focused intently on his fingering. The cascading sounds intensified until the subtle notes that were like tinkling glass became a torrent more like the rumbling presage to a summer storm. He could feel her gaze on him, but he pursed his lips solidly shut and ignored it.

"If you could hear him talk of his patients, you'd be surprised. All those horrific images of asylums must be gross exaggerations, or at least Dr. Richmond and his colleagues are more enlightened, more advanced than doctors who have treated mental problems in the past. And the patients he described are actually remarkably normal. They simply have specific problems of an emotional or mental nature that need addressing in a professional way. Weren't you impressed, Marcelo?"

Marcelo caught Erik's glance out of the corner of his eye, but when Marcelo turned toward the piano Erik tilted his head toward the keys. "Dr. Richmond seems a compassionate, earnest physician. I have no doubt that his patients are far more fortunate than those poor devils you see locked up in insane asylums."

"Remember that one man who wouldn't come out of his room for days because he was afraid his father's ghost was waiting on the staircase to kill him?" Marcelo nodded reluctantly. He kept his eye on Erik as Meg continued to speak of the successes Dr. Richmond had described at the dinner party the previous evening. Meg pressed on. "Dr. Richmond used what he calls a diagnostic history to find out why the young man had such irrational fears. It had something to do with his past, memories that he had squirreled away, and once he brought the memories out to the surface, the young man was able to face his fears. Then the doctor used hypnosis to plant a suggestion that he and his father had made amends. Anyway, Dr. Richmond says the young man is home now and quite relieved."

Madeleine sighed heavily. She had been the only one who had expressed disagreement when they had spoken about Dr. Richmond's successes. When Meg suggested that they try to get Erik to meet the doctor and to consider some modest treatment, Madeleine had refused to be a part of it.

"You cannot play with his life, Meg. He is who he is. Either you accept him or you don't."

Meg had angrily countered that she thought it no crime to try to mend what might be broken, to help Erik overcome some of his problems. Madeleine had given up, shaking her head and rubbing her hands compulsively together.

"Then there were the nightmares that plagued a little boy. The parents were beside themselves, but after spending a few nights at Dr. Richmond's clinic the child was sleeping like an angel."

The mention of nightmares brought Erik's music to an abrupt end. He looked up at Meg as if he were trying to understand something about what she had said. He studied her intently for a moment.

In a voice deceptively soft, he asked, "Am I to be Dr. Richmond's patient, Meg?"

Meg stopped, taken aback by Erik's directness. She hadn't been prepared to address the question so baldly, so she hesitated.

Her failure to reassure him, to discard the idea out of hand, appalled Erik. His gaze riveted to her stunned expression, he carefully veiled his rising sense of panic. In her hesitation, he read her doubt. *She wasn't sure that he was sane. Was he?* He had always thought his doubts were his alone. He had found comfort in Meg's confidence in him. *Why had she changed her mind?*

"Perhaps I should meet the doctor one of these nights." Erik carefully kept all emotion from his voice. He looked away, unable to bear the relief he saw on his wife's face. He felt his fingers turn to ice on the keyboard. The feeling had quite disappeared from them, and he could do no more than play the simple melody of a Brahms lullaby. If he agreed to meet the doctor, perhaps they wouldn't push him for more. Perhaps the doctor wouldn't see madness surging underneath the surface of his control.

Vaguely he could hear Marcelo and Meg speaking now in relaxed tones. They were marveling at the accomplishments of modern science and basking in the certainty that Erik, the mad Phantom, could at last be cured.

5 July 1888

My dear friend, Raoul,

I can't say how much I enjoyed the account of your recent trip to London. I am delighted that you and Christine were able to find time to be alone. Our children are wonderful, but exhausting. I speak from my own experience. The twins have begun to roam independently about the estate and are now in need of constant vigilance. It is a wonder that our species has survived given the lack of common sense and self-preservation of our young. The other day, Etienne fell headfirst into a vat of new wine that my steward had left open in the wine press. We still don't understand how he crawled to the top of the barrel. Regardless of how Etienne managed to tip over the side and into the vat itself, if Raoul hadn't sent a shriek to wake the dead, he might have grown up sans twin.

My recent production, "The Willow," has been received with accolades. An impresario from London insists that we allow him to mount a production in

London this season and has asked me to direct it. I flatly refused. He astounded me by his knowledge of my repertoire. He is a frequent reader of the cultural journals from Italy and visits several times a year. Evidently he has seen a number of my operas, including, *Don Juan Triumphant*! I was speechless, I'm afraid. Perhaps he'll think me an idiot and withdraw his invitation.

I regret that you have to delay your visit to us again. I practice my fencing daily in the expectation of being able to humiliate you in the hall that I've had built for that purpose and that alone. Meg thinks that I am joking and calls it the Raoul versus the Phantom hallway. It may be in bad taste to mock our past, but I am determined to beat you soundly at a good match with the blade. At any rate, your suggestion of late October will only give me more time to perfect a few of my recently acquired strokes. We look forward to your visit and insist that you stay for several months. The Christmas holidays in Rome are spectacular, and I can't imagine a better way to spend the time than with my friend. For you are my friend, at least I hope that I may always call you so. I swear that I will forever be in your debt and you can never doubt my sincere friendship and respect.

I used to write brief missives to the owners of the Opera Populaire. M. Lefevre, in particular, would practically swoon whenever he ran across one of my letters sealed with the death's skull. I enjoyed watching him fall into the nearest chair in an apoplectic fit, frantically searching for his handkerchief to wipe his brow. But alas, such devilish delights are no longer appropriate or useful for such a respectable businessman and artist as myself. I have no one to write to. Except you!

If anyone had told me, years and years ago—I do feel old when I put it that way in spite of the fact that I am actually feeling quite fit and youthful for a man in his late forties—that I would be carrying on a correspondence with the Count de Chagny, I would have thought them mad! On the other hand, if the same people would have said that I'd be a happily married man with five children and successfully making my living as an artist in Rome, I would have also thought it as likely that the dead would rise and the lame walk. Well, the dead have risen, haven't they? Like the phoenix, I am reborn, am I not, dear friend?

When I think back to my life, before my many deaths, I shudder. How could I not have realized how devastatingly miserable I had become? It is as if that man, that shadow, that ghost, were not I. And yet, in the wee hours just before dawn, I am that man again. I can recall how I felt, what I thought, the myriad fantastic dreams I entertained, while I listened to the roar of the applause above my head, the strains of the flute and oboe, the vibrato of the soprano. I lived in the beat of the giant heart that was opera. I was not who I was, a starved and lonely fugitive, a pariah, a hideous creature that had been destined to die in a cage or in the gutter. I was so much more than that miserable child. You will not understand how a child like me could grow to manhood in the dark. I fear I have allowed myself to digress along a path that is both painful and wasteful.

Do you find yourself drawn back to your past more frequently as you become older? What memories do you return to? Let me see. I recall spying on you in Christine's dressing room—surely this is no surprise to you now—and hearing you and my pupil, my dear sweet Christine, reminiscing over holidays in the country and on the coast when Gustave Daaé was still alive. There was mention of chocolates, the violin, and stories of monsters. Monsters! Looking back on that day, I know that the look Christine gave you when you entered to congratulate her on her debut—a debut made possible only by your humble monster, that is, servant—was the look that I had been painfully waiting to see in her eyes for me. It still hurts, sometimes, my friend. I had given her so much, all the better part of myself, and I could not help but love her then.

I have been tormented by memories. Those of Christine are bittersweet but are not the ones that most torment me. Please accept my apologies for bringing up a subject that you can only find distasteful and disturbing. I am happy that Christine and you have one another. I have no desire for any but my canary! She is almost more than I can handle. Her belief in me, her determination that I be happy, her enthusiasm for my art, her impossible resolve to fight to keep me whole and safe fill me with joy and concern. Joy, because I am overwhelmed by her love for me. Concern, because I know how far I fall short of her view of me.

A physician who specializes in illnesses of the mind has recently visited us. Marcelo and Meg have encouraged me to make his acquaintance, but I resist. They say that he believes that madness can be cured. I hesitate to continue, but I trust you more than any other man I know. Indeed, apart from Marcelo, you're the only man I truly call friend. I sometimes fear that I am mad. I would much prefer to think that the Phantom committed those violent acts and died the night of the fire or certainly on the scaffold when he was hanged. Or that Erik Fiortino simply expired one night in his wife's ghostly embrace. Or even that Erik Costanzi died immolated in a fire to rise again eventually as himself. That is, I would like to believe the madmen in my soul have all been purged, but you, my dear friend, understand the difference between such conceits and reality.

I fear that my wife thinks me ill. I hope that she is wrong, but I have such misgivings. Can someone experience what I've experienced and still be sane? If I am sane, it is because of Meg. You have also contributed to my sanity on more than one occasion.

I must conclude this rather long and rambling letter. I need to review the notes before tomorrow's rehearsal. We are practicing a particularly difficult aria that Carlotta is to sing, and this is always a rather sticky process. I will post this letter within the day and wait for your reply,

Your friend and sometime monster,
Erik

6 July 1888

Dearest Christine,

We have met a most interesting gentleman, an English physician who specializes in the mind; a psychologist, I believe is the term he prefers. Marcelo heard him lecture at the university and met him at a reception shortly thereafter. He didn't hesitate to invite Dr. Richmond to dine with us. Since then, he has been a frequent guest. I can guess as to why Marcelo was excited to have him come to meet us. In point of fact, I'm sure he was thinking of Erik.

Dr. Richmond is not a great conversationalist; his interest in gathering information is too obvious, but he is fascinating to listen to. He seems quite confident that we are close to unraveling the mysteries of the mind. We have invited him to several dinners and his tendency to speak to us as if he were in an auditorium of students is not unpleasant. He obviously enjoys the attention he's receiving while here in Rome. He's become something of a celebrity.

Erik, of course, refuses to dine with us, saying that he has no intention of airing his personal problems before a stranger who thinks he understands something as complex as the human mind.

Is it wrong of me to want to find some help for Erik? It's not that I think he's insane, for goodness' sake. But you know him, Christine. You must have sensed that his demons are not laid to rest. He falls into such despondency at times, in particular when he is between projects, that I worry about him. I can't shake the fear when I remember we found him hiding, waiting to die, talking to people who weren't there, and ready to fight us as if he didn't know who we were. When we carried him away, he didn't speak for several days, not to me, not to Maman, not to anyone. He'd been down in those underground vaults for days with that dead man—a man who had hounded him and tortured him, a man who had threatened our son—as his sole companion. Raoul told me that Leroux had not died in the chamber where we found him. Erik had carried Leroux's corpse through the maze to that final chamber. He had washed the body with his own hands and laid him out as if to keep vigil over him. I'm sure Raoul shared these details with you. I needn't say more. But I still find it puzzling that Erik would have treated Leroux so kindly, so respectfully, when Leroux would have executed him and thrown his body to the dogs.

If I had been in Erik's place, I'd have wanted Leroux to suffer as he had made Erik suffer in prison. I'd have crushed his fingers and flogged him, kept him naked and cold and hungry, exhibited him to the mob!

And when he had died, after many, many days of pain and hopelessness, I'd have left him to rot in one of the abandoned tunnels under the opera house.

Is what Erik did saner than I had at first thought? He certainly wasn't in his right mind when we finally found him, Christine, and it was only short of a miracle that Raoul saw the hint of light that led us to him. Oh I can't go on when I remember how easily we might never have found him. He'd be dead, and there would have been no one to tend his body, to close his eyes. I can't continue down that road. It's too frightening, even now.

I had seen him "mad" before. You can never know. You weren't there. He had let you slip away with Raoul. He had released you and told you to forget him, to forget everything. Would you have been able to forget him, if he had disappeared at that moment? He had not been willing to forget you. He escaped through the mirror into another branch of the subterranean world under the Opera Populaire. This, too, was part of his hidden kingdom. As you know, I followed him. He was mad with grief at having given you up. With his own hands, he had destroyed the only world he knew. I don't like to remember those first days. He didn't want me to follow him. If circumstances had been other than they were, he would have frightened me away and buried himself alive in those cold, dark rooms. Maman, even weeks later, after he had forced me to leave him, found him distraught, intent on self-destruction. He had slashed his face with broken glass. She got to him before he could do himself irreparable harm, but he was not in control.

Does a sane person do what Erik has done?

Don't mistake my intentions. I don't believe he's a lunatic that needs to be locked away in one of those atrocious asylums we hear of! But I do believe that his mind is wounded. It makes me cry to think how brave he is to be able to function as well as he does. Even if he can't change, even if he can't heal any more than he has already, I would be content to stay by his side. I watch him struggle sometimes to face the day, to brave the host of people in the theater or on the streets. Actually he's become stronger and more adept at his role in the theater. There are moments when I believe he forgets his torment and walks among the chorus and musicians as if he were merely one of them. In the theater, busy at work on the music, and with us, he is most at peace and most himself. Even with Carlotta, he sometimes enjoys respites in which he accepts who he is—the better part of himself—as whole. But I see the other times, too.

Lately he's plagued by headaches, and I fear there might be something seriously wrong. His nightmares have returned as well.

If Dr. Richmond can help him, wouldn't it be remiss on our part not to urge Erik to submit to some treatment? The physician speaks kindly of his patients, seems sincerely interested in returning them to health. He has hinted on several occasions that he is in awe of genius such as that which Erik has and speaks of the artistic temperament as one that is by nature plagued by an imbalance in the other mental aspects. It's so tempting to me to ask Dr. Richmond to take Erik on as a patient.

Can you see Erik submitting willingly to treatment? Can you imagine Erik speaking of his past, recounting his feelings, reliving them with a total stranger? Impossible! And yet I worry. It pains me to recognize that I worry that Erik might worsen. He can be so passionate, so irrational! He has killed!

Meg dropped the pen on the smooth surface of the desk and stared through a haze of tears at the words she had just written. Her hands grasped the sheets, still wet with ink and tears, and savagely crumpled and tore them. She let the pieces fall to the desk.

his dark eyes hide the horror of abandonment, he too wears a mask, his smile, his cheerful teasing too readily assumed, Erik watches Mario at the desk as he pours over the figures in a ledger, the young man, only a year or so older than François, but aged by a tormented childhood, a childhood like Erik's in kind, Erik hangs back in the doorway, watches, watches, watches, and he wonders if Mario is healed, can anyone heal a soul so early wounded?

"Papa, I didn't hear you." The young man at the desk was still a boy, only fourteen perhaps, but his eyes, when he was alone, were filled with a lifetime's experience. He had been kicked and cursed, had found his bed in the gutters of Roman streets, had stolen and begged, pretended to injuries he never had and masked those that he suffered.

Erik studied his son. Since Mario had come to live with Erik and his family, he had grown several inches. His limbs had straightened and strengthened from the diet rich in proteins and fruits. His dark eyes and hair glistened with health. His body was slim yet toughened with the recent development of muscle tissue. His smile was still quick, and Erik wished he could make it real.

"Have you gone over last month's expenses?" Erik asked, even though it was only a habit. He knew Mario had carefully examined every figure and checked each calculation.

They had realized soon after Mario came into the family that the child was not likely to become a performer in the opera. Erik and François took turns trying to teach him the piano. Mario, an intelligent and eager pupil, was determined to please, but Erik surmised early on that whatever he achieved in music would be in spite of the lack of talent. Mario learned to play without luster, without passion, more with the thought to obey his father than to enjoy music. Erik encouraged him, nevertheless, to continue.

When the children staged their own operas, Mario's voice was pleasant, but little more could be said of it. However, his ability to act was far more impressive than the other children's overwrought mimicry. Etienne and Raoul were too young to have significant roles in these operettas. They were messengers or would add sound effects, often at inappropriate moments. But Mario was mesmerizing as the Arabian prince or frightening as the mad pirate ghost or sweet and tender as the tragic lover who rescues his stolen bride from the cave ogre. Yet, without the voice, Mario would not find his future as a performer in the opera.

His talent was quickly discovered in running the business.

Erik had dismissed the latest bookkeeper when he realized that the man was the source for several published stories about the "masked genius of the opera," as the journalist Paolo Ricci had christened Erik Costanzi. Mario had curiously examined the columns of numbers Erik had brought home with the expectation that Marcelo's steward would be able to check them for the moment until he could find a replacement for the dismissed accountant.

The numbers, which had only succeeded in making Erik's head spin, fell into perfect order when Mario perused the categories and entries. While Erik and Marcelo discussed the need to make repairs to the theater, Mario picked up a pen and corrected one of the calculations. Interrupting his elders, he tentatively called attention to a long list of additions and debits and suggested that he could do the work.

Seeing the misgivings on both men's faces, Mario explained that he had spent a year at a law firm as an errand boy of sorts. He immediately turned scarlet as he met his father's inquiring gaze. It had been less than a year before he met Erik, then Erik Fiortino, and he didn't like to remember the solicitor who had "taken him in." He had done what he could to learn something from the experience, something besides staying away from men with large hands and cruel smiles. When he was first brought to Erik's study and presented to him, he'd feared Erik might be like the solicitor, but there was such a pitying and understanding look in the man's eyes that Mario understood immediately that Erik saw a child when he looked at him, not the other thing that the solicitor had wanted.

"You can make sense of all that? Count receipts, keep track of bills and accounts, register and calculate salaries?"

"Oh, yes, Papa. If we have the correct forms, I'm sure I can do it. It's actually quite easy."

Ever since, for the past several months, Mario had managed the accounts for the opera. He was particularly adept at finding funds needed for infrastructural improvements, the replacement of equipment, or whatever Erik and the technicians thought necessary. He had also managed to streamline expenses, work out deals with local tradesmen and suggested increasing salaries among the lower paid staff.

Now Erik smiled proudly at the child he'd rescued. Mario could easily have died on the streets if Erik hadn't decided to protect him. Children like Mario became thieves or prostitutes. Either option led most often to an early grave. Of course, Erik took the clever boy in for his own comfort as well. Mario had eased his loneliness when he lived as Erik Fiortino, a man who had lost all memory of his past.

"The profits from *The Willow* have exceeded those of the previous two operas. The exciting news is that subscriptions are up by 22%." Mario pointed to the figures in the ledger, but Erik didn't even glance down. He was unconcerned about profit and loss. He requested that a specific amount be set aside for his own use. This was the only money he directly siphoned off the theater. He never spent it. On the contrary it was, without fail, placed in a special account known only to him and Meg. This "salary" was no more and no less than the sum that he had extorted from the owners of the Opera Populaire when he lived as the Phantom in the underground tunnels under the Parisian opera house.

Madeleine had given him shelter in those subterranean vaults to protect him from the police who would have taken him to prison and to the gibbet, even though he was only a child and the man he had murdered had treated him like a beast in the traveling fair. Erik had known horror. He had lived with it until it became a part of who he was. It was Madeleine Giry who helped him invent the identity of the opera ghost or the Phantom, as most remembered him, and who told him to demand a monthly salary, which she carefully managed and invested for him.

That was a long time ago. Erik was a successful composer, the artistic director of the Teatro Dell'Opera, adopted heir to Don Marcelo Costanzi and wealthy in his own right. But Erik could not quite feel safe without the monthly stipend. It had become a talisman for him. Sig. Costanzi indulged him. The amount was set aside monthly. Erik never touched it.

"Mario, put the books away. Come. It's time to go home."

10 July 1888

Dear Erik,

As always I read your letter with trepidation and delight. I correspond with several old friends from my days at the Université, but we discuss philosophy and politics in a rather dull and conventional fashion. Their letters are never as interesting as yours. I cringe to think what you might have been like if you'd had my advantages—the best tutors, travel abroad, university, a title, and my library. It humbles me to realize that I regret so having taken such opportunities for granted. I was an able student, commended by my teachers, but I never applied myself with the passion that you, my friend, have always directed toward music. My achievements—a fair and general success in many subjects, but mastery of none—came easily to me, and I thoughtlessly understood them to be my natural rights. I daresay the only struggle worthy of the name that I've had to make was to win and keep my wife from blindly following you to your underground fantasy world. It may surprise you, but there have been moments when I feared Christine would choose to run off with you. The night of the chandelier still haunts my dreams. I don't think you realize how close you came to success. I think I'd have rather died that night, strangled or drowned, than have left without Christine. And there have been other moments.

Even so, I have made her happy. You must grant me that. It hasn't been solely my fear that she'd abandon me for you or my concern that I'd have to deal with your wrath if I made her unhappy that has spurred me on. I simply delight in seeing her smile. She still sings, you know. If I feel guilty about any of my decisions or actions, I suppose it's the fact that I kept her from the stage. In my circle, it would have been scandalous for a count's wife to sing professionally. I guess we all live, to a certain degree, hampered by invisible bars.

Perhaps that's why your friendship has been a revelation to me. You are more real to me than my esteemed peers. You force me to delve inside and find strength that I wouldn't have known that I had. You can't imagine how difficult it is sometimes for me not to tell my friends about the things that I've seen and done because of our association—yours and mine. Who would have thought that I could work out the details for an escape on the very gallows itself or be a "grave robber" and exhume an executed criminal? I've worked under disguise as an investigator, been involved in brawls, spent weeks in an inn of ill-repute. I've learned more about theater, music, and bohemia than even my most scandalous peers who, from time to time, indulge in less savory and more revolutionary activities than are permitted to those in my station. Indeed, Erik, you've made it seem rather dull to be a count.

The business that keeps me here is a nuisance that I soon hope to resolve. Your invitation to extend our visit to include the holidays is very generous. Christine and I—not to mention the children—will be delighted to spend Christmas with the Costanzi household. My parents are deceased, and Madeleine and Meg have always been family to Christine.

By the bye, Erik, I thought you might like to know that the case of Leroux's unexpected disappearance has been officially put to rest. The police assume he expatriated to Italy where he met an unfortunate death. No one has thought to look closer to home, and in their usual bumbling, hypocritical way they've officially awarded Leroux a posthumous medal for his service. That is how I came upon this information. The official ceremony was reported in the gazette. I've enclosed the clipping. Perhaps you could risk returning to Paris someday. The story of the "Phantom" has begun to recede from memory. Indeed I believe most who've heard it think it no more than a fiction without basis in reality.

I can't close this letter without remarking, even briefly, on your trust and the fears you have confided in me. You have led a strange life, Erik, and I confess that I have thought you mad. Perhaps it is the nature of sympathy that one learns to understand one's friend in such a way that all actions that once would have seemed irrational are partnered to a cause. Such is my conclusion in our case, for I now cannot help but see why you acted as you did, even when I believe you acted unwisely, foolishly, or mistakenly. You have made serious errors, but since you left France, your actions have always been motivated by the best intentions. Your life is difficult. I sometimes sit before a mirror to examine the scar my encounter with Leroux left on my face. It has faded a bit, but it's still evident. Your scars are visible and hidden, my friend, and I know you struggle with them every day of your life. You are not mad. You are the sanest man

I know. You are more in touch with reality than any of the silly men and women in my class who strut about as actors in a farce created in their little minds, a farce that has no foundation in anything but their vapid desires.

Christine sends her love, as always. See how well I do with my own possessiveness? Victor and Elise are chomping at the bit to see Mario, François, and Laurette. Erica and Elise are squabbling over who should take care of the twins. Our youngest Roland wants to see the Pope, who he thinks is able to grant any of his desires. He wishes to have wings and fly! Needless to say, we keep a close eye on him and keep him well away from the edge of the balcony.

I have recently contracted a fencing master, so I look forward to your challenge. I intend to thoroughly humiliate you in our hall. Until October, I remain, as always,

Your affectionate rival and friend,
Raoul, Count de Chagny

"Mario, put the books away. Come with me."

The boy did as he was told. Erik led him through the corridors to the side door. The light of the afternoon sun was softened by the trees along the avenue. Erik walked down the street ignoring the curious glances, Mario by his side. The boy on occasion threw an impertinent pedestrian a scowl as he accompanied his father. They walked in silence until Erik came to a graveyard by a small church. He recognized it immediately as the one in which Meg and he had parted when he thought he was Erik Fiortino. The memory had lost its sting unlike those that still haunted him from his days in Paris. He wondered if they would ever lose their ability to hurt him.

"Papa? Are you all right?"

"Yes. I'm sorry, Mario. I'm all right. I've just been full of memories. When I finish an opera, I often feel…at loose ends."

"*The Willow* was tremendously popular. Even that journalist Ricci had to admit it was a success."

The reference to Ricci sobered Erik. The journalist had taunted him from season to season. It was his acerbic reviews and commentaries that had led Carlotta to him, and Carlotta had foolishly brought the police officer Leroux to his doorstep. Leroux had vowed to capture the Phantom again and make sure he was properly punished for the deaths Erik had caused in the Opera Populaire.

"Ricci is no idiot," was all Erik would say on the matter.

"Papa, was there a reason you wanted me to come with you? Did I do something wrong?"

"No, nothing wrong. I just wanted to spend some time away from the theater and thought you needed to get out for some fresh air. You're still young, Mario. You do not have to work."

Mario's smile fell. The accounting was something he enjoyed and was good at. "I like working in the office with you. I've rearranged the ledgers so that accounts are easier to track. I'm proud of the work I do for the theater."

"I know, but François doesn't work in the theater and nor do you have to. Marcelo and I were selfish to put you in the situation of an accountant. It's a fulltime job, and I want you to have a childhood."

Was it too late? Erik wondered. Mario seemed to be considering his words. The boy took a seat next to his father on a bench.

"Did you have a childhood, Papa?"

Erik scowled at the question. He knew that François and Mario had only a sketchy idea of his past. He had pleaded with Meg to keep his secrets for yet a while longer. But François knew that he had killed. The policeman Leroux, who had carried out a vengeful manhunt for the Phantom of the Opera Populaire, had told the boy as much. Embedded among all the lies Leroux had sincerely laid at Erik's door were the true crimes Erik had committed when he'd lost control and brought destruction even to his own world.

"No, Mario. I don't believe I ever had a childhood." Perhaps one might say the elaborate tricks and masquerades he perpetrated in the Opera Populaire were a manifestation of the lost child in him.

Hidden in the bowels of the opera house, he had played at heroes, villains, princes, and thieves. Well into his adult years, he had created fantasies and played them out—alone and unwitnessed. But had he ever been a child? He had a handful of memories. They were pathetic and few, overshadowed by the memories of the cage and the years of solitude and madness in the vaults under the city of Paris.

"You've seen a lot of bad things, haven't you, Papa?"

"Yes."

Mario saw the cautious veil drop over his father's eyes. He had tried to explain to François that their father had dark secrets that he couldn't share with them. Mario certainly had his own secrets.

"You've seen your share of horrors, too, haven't you?" asked Erik.

If anyone could understand the evil things he'd been a part of, Mario reasoned that it would be Erik. But he couldn't force himself to speak. If he opened his mouth, such vile memories would come spilling out. What if he were wrong? What if his father were disgusted by him? By what had been done to him? By what *he* had done?

"When Luigi first brought you to the apartment, you were wary of me, weren't you?"

Mario couldn't help but look up at his father in surprise. He'd always prided himself on being able to fool everyone. "Wary? Why would I be wary of you, maestro?" Mario gave him a crooked smile and tried to laugh off the serious air that surrounded them.

"Yes, you were afraid of me. It wasn't the mask, though. It was something else. It was because I was a man, a grown man, a man who could hurt you."

Erik fell silent. He saw the effect of his words on Mario's downcast face. The smile and teasing manner had vanished. Erik was sad to know that he had surmised correctly. There was no doubt in his mind as to what must have happened to the boy.

"A child should never know such evil, Mario. It…wounds the very soul."

"I…I'm sorry, Papa."

Erik scowled at the boy. He was on the cusp of adulthood. At moments, Erik could see the young man Mario would soon be. At others, he was struck by Mario's vulnerability. *Was there still time?*

"Never feel guilty for what others have done to you. When you are a man, you will have to accept the guilt of your mistakes. A child is not responsible for what others do to him."

"I thought you might want to do what the other man did. I knew you weren't like him almost immediately. I saw it in your eyes."

"This other man beat you?"

Mario blushed and turned away. Erik could barely hear him when he spoke again. "That wasn't the worst of it. He made me come to his bedroom."

Erik stifled a groan and tensed against a wave of rage.

Mario rushed to add, "But I might have run away sooner. I stayed because…"

"You stayed because you had no other options that didn't terrify you. You stayed because the man told you to stay. You submitted because not to do so would bring down on your head consequences of which you were woefully afraid. You suffered because you were alone and lost and unprotected."

They sat silently for a long time. Mario fought back stinging tears. Erik drew near enough for his son to know he was there without actually touching the lad. They let the pain dissipate in its own way, in its own time. Eventually Erik could feel Mario relax. Carefully he draped his arm across the boy's shoulders and patted him reassuringly.

They were about to return to the theater when Erik glimpsed a boy running down the street. In the next moment, the young boy darted sharply toward Erik and Mario, reached out his hand, and ripped off Erik's mask. Mario ran after the boy. A second boy, who had been sauntering along the path, rushed up to take Erik's purse, as his accomplice ran down the block. However, he came to an abrupt stop when he caught sight of Erik's disfigurement. A passing couple gasped and took several steps back in shock at the strange sight of a man with half his face deformed. Erik glared at the stunned boy, daring him to attack. No longer interested in stealing the man's purse, the second boy turned and fled in the opposite direction, away from the path his partner had taken. Instead of chasing the would-be thief, Erik dashed down the street in pursuit of Mario. The first assailant had been slowed by a number of pedestrians casually strolling along the avenue. He had barely disappeared round a corner as Mario sped close behind him.

"Mario!" Erik called out as he saw his son turn onto the next street and vanish. Ignoring an increasing number of men and women who stopped to stare at him on the street, Erik made his way to the intersection. As he neared the turn, he heard the grinding squeal of iron and wood, a frantic neighing of several horses. Voices were raised in alarm, and somehow he knew what had happened before he turned the corner.

The crowd parted to allow Erik to rush forward into the middle of the avenue. The path they made, as they fell back from the disfigured man, led to a twisted shape in the lane. The figure of a boy, legs turned, head pressed awkwardly to the side, lay under the wagon. Mario's eyes were closed, and there was a rivulet of blood flowing from the corner of his mouth. Erik fell to his knees and pulled the child from the bloody pool into his arms. The crowd kept up a constant murmur. Above it all could be heard Erik's breathless sobs muffled by the boy's coat. No one saw the white mask drop from the boy's pale fingers.

The strangers tried to take Mario away. Erik saw the hideous grimaces among the crowd—revulsion, shock on their strange, naked faces. *Why weren't they wearing masks?* Surely nothing could be uglier than the scowling and heavy brow, curved and twisted mouth, beak-like nose, and blotchy cheeks of the average person. The sea of faces, as if boneless, bobbed up and down around him. Hands ripped at his child. Hands jutted out of dark cloth and grabbed and pulled. They tried to take Mario's broken body from him, but he growled like a wounded dragon at them, spewed forth fire and sulfur, and held the child to his heart.

They made noises like magpies, jagged, inchoate sounds that made no sense. Nothing made sense anymore. He held broken bones, inert flesh, pooling blood in his arms. This had been a child!

Erik, the dragon, would not surrender his child to these monsters. No more harm could be done to him. Erik had not been vigilant. He had let the child escape his care, but not again.

The bobbing faces, jagged cacophony, clawing hands surrounded him in an ever tightening circle.

He'd kill if he had to. They would not take his child from him.

Meg could not move. She had been standing in place for an eternity. Her feet were fixed to the tiles as if she wore chains. Strange men had brought the bloody bundle of her adopted son through the foyer and up to the bedroom. She felt the back of her throat spasm as she stared at the irregular droplets of blood on the black and white tiles of the entrance hall.

Don Marcelo had pulled her to the side out of the way of the urgent servants, the attendants, the physician who had happened by the scene of the accident, and their own family physician as they rushed to and fro, from the upstairs bedroom to the street below. Maids carted containers of hot water, brought fresh, clean linens up the stairs in an unending parade of purposeful activity.

"Where's Erik?" she had asked in a panic. She refused to think of what was happening upstairs. They would have unwound the bloodied sheet and laid the body on the bed. They would be examining Mario. They would be calculating the likelihood of his survival. They would be piecing him together, if God willing, this could be done. "Where's Erik?" she repeated, her lips pale, her heart fluttering against her ribcage as if her chest, too, had been crushed under the horses' hooves.

The accident had been explained. She remembered the chain of events even though nothing seemed to make any sense to her at the moment. A flutter of shouts and calls had made its way from the scene of the accident to the theater. Jacopo had brought several workmen with him to the intersection. There they had helped the crowd wrest the child from his father. The physician that had stopped to help the victim followed his patient as several from the theater carried the poor boy to the Teatro Dell'Opera and from there handed him into a carriage for transfer to the estate.

Once the child had been removed, Erik had gone mad, lashing out at everyone within his grasp. Among them all, they had managed to restrain Erik but not before the latter had pummeled several of the men in the crowd. Jacopo tried to reason with him, peeling his fingers from the throat of a hapless young man who had been the one that dared to wrench the child's body from a mourning father's arms.

Police whistles had savaged the air, sending several witnesses on the periphery down the street and away from the violence. Breaking their way through the crowd, the officers had come upon the grotesque figure of a man whose face was disfigured by physical deformity on one side and by excessively violent emotion on the other.

"Erik is on his way. Jacopo sent word. They thought it best to keep him at the theater until they could calm him down a bit." Over Meg's shoulder, Marcelo spied his wife's approach from the upstairs landing. He nodded at Madeleine. Her expression was somber, and she descended the stairs as if unsure of where she should be. Seeing Marcelo's serious expression and the grip he had on Meg's hands, she found a new determination and approached them. She lightly embraced her daughter and faced Marcelo as he continued, "He lashed out at several of the bystanders."

Meg's brows furrowed in puzzlement. "What do you mean?"

"Erik was nearly carted off to prison. He tried to strangle one of the bystanders with his bare hands. He wasn't thinking clearly."

"Thinking? Did he hurt anyone?"

"Nothing too serious." He consoled Meg with a faint hint of a smile. "Jacopo and some of the staff had heard the commotion and came in time to help. The police were sympathetic once they realized what had happened. No one wanted to press charges against Erik."

Meg could see the recognition of a danger narrowly escaped in Marcelo's eyes. He couldn't make light of this. Erik had meant to kill someone. How could he have lost control so thoroughly? To risk prison? To murder?

"Meg, he was beside himself. He's convinced that Mario is dead."

"Oh God, no! Don't say that word!" The mention of her greatest fear unraveled the little control that she had left.

"Sssshhh. It's all right, ma petite. He's alive. The doctors are with him," soothed Madeleine. Even the thought of Mario's death was unbearable.

Marcelo could tell that Madeleine, too, was unsure that Mario would survive his injuries. The child was not dead. Not yet. But the weight of doom lay heavily upon them all.

Suddenly Meg wrenched free of Marcelo's fatherly hold. She was angry, desperately angry, she knew not at whom, but the hot, white blaze found focus on one possible target. "Dr. Richmond is right! He's mad! God help us, he's insane!"

Police Log 7 August 1888

Accident involving driver and wagon pulled by four and one pedestrian on Via Nazionale near intersection with Via Firenze at 15:44. Victim: fourteen-year-old male, Mario Costanzi. According to several witnesses (names and domiciles noted in the report) a young man ran out directly in front of Cosimo Maggiore's wagon just seconds before the victim, in apparent pursuit, grabbed and struggled with the first young man (description: indeterminate age, 12-16, dark hair, dingy and torn dark coat a size too small, brown pants too short for the boy). This boy pulled away just before the horses and wagon trampled victim.

Given that the incident was unprovoked by Sig. Cosimo Maggiore, he was allowed to claim his horses and vehicle and to leave. Officers have been alerted to watch out for the first young man. Witnesses confirm that he most likely fled after a failed attempt at purse snatching. The victim was injured while in pursuit.

Although the father of the victim, Sig. Erik Costanzi, assaulted several well-meaning citizens at the scene, he was allowed to leave. No charges were brought against him as those involved refused to press the matter.

Erik had tried to strangle one of those who were trying to help. Several of the staff from the Teatro Dell'Opera had taken him to the theater to calm him down. They had not yet brought him home.

Meg knelt on the black and white rectangles. She gripped the handkerchief in her right hand and set her palm against the cold, slick surface of the black marble. Wet. She pulled her hand back and stared at the red stain on her fingers. She wiped it—thick and sticky—against the skirt of her gown. Settling back upon her heels, she leaned over the trail and soaked up one rounded drop with the lace edging.

Blood. Mario's blood.

Soaked, her handkerchief only smeared the next ellipsis made by the stippled drops of blood.

They had not brought Erik home. They had kept him at the theater. *To calm him. Wild, violent.* They had needed to wait. *Unstable. Volatile.* Richmond's words dropped one by one into her ear, heavy, hot, and thick. *Unpredictable, erosion of control, fits of violence.*

Meg had dropped the bloody handkerchief and was rubbing against the slab with the hem of her gown. Her tears diluted the deep crimson clots. She shrugged away the solicitous hands of the servant who tried to lift her to her feet.

"Leave me," she shouted, wrenching her arm free. "It's his blood." She redoubled her efforts.

How could this happen? An accident? Why hadn't Erik prevented it? Where had he been when the carriage wheels ran across Mario's body?

Another hand wrapped round Meg's upper arm. She reared back on her haunches to rebuke the servant only to look up into pale blue eyes—Dr. Richmond's.

"Donna Meg, let the servants clean this up."

His voice was so calm, so rational, so soothing. She let him help her to her feet. She held her hands out as if to show him. They were bloody.

"Our son," she began to explain.

"I heard the news. We must clean you up."

Suddenly everything seemed to fall into place. Dr. Richmond snapped his fingers, bringing to the fore one of the servants. Meg listened as instructions were given and carried out.

"He's upstairs," she said, at a loss as to what else to say.

"Sig. Costanzi?" When she looked at him as if confused, he asked, "Your husband?"

"Erik? No, he's…he's…" Her voice faded. She told herself that she should not lean her weight against this man's chest. She barely knew him, and yet she felt comforted and safe with him. "Erik flew into a rage."

"Where is he?"

"At the theater. They…" She could not tell Richmond that her husband had had to be carried away from the scene, that he might still be out of control. But Dr. Richmond must have guessed.

"Would it be helpful were I to go and see your husband?"

"I…I…"

"I could bring him home. Would you like me to do that?"

Recovering herself, Meg answered, "No. No, Dr. Richmond. It won't be necessary. They sent word. They're on their way by now, I'm sure. He was upset. He was…not himself."

"Has Sig. Costanzi ever been violent before?"

Meg stepped away from the doctor, turning so that he could not see her face.

When she didn't respond, Dr. Richmond let the question drop. Instead he said, "I think I should stay. Just in case. I have something that can calm your husband down should it prove necessary."

Meg glanced over her shoulder at Richmond. She nodded, mutely. She looked at her hands as if she'd only just noticed them. Then she looked at the hem of her gown stained with blood.

"I better go change."

A servant had brought a bucket of soapy water and had bent to clean the trail of blood. Meg was about to step around him when the door slammed open on its hinges and Erik rushed into the vestibule. When his gaze fell on Dr. Richmond, he pulled himself up short.

"What the hell is he doing here?" he shouted. Then he stared, mouth agape, at the blood on his wife's hands and gown.

"Don Erik, I think you should calm down. The boy…"

Richmond had made the mistake of stepping into Erik's path. He made it worse when he attempted to steer Erik to a side parlor, placing his hand on Erik's arm.

"Get the bloody hell out of my house." Erik pushed Richmond to the side. "He's dead. He's dead. Mario." He rushed past Meg who grabbed at him. Barely had he reached the stairs when he heard Meg crash to the floor. Calling to a servant, Dr. Richmond went to help Meg up from the marble floor. She had fallen when Erik pulled away from her grasp. Erik stood, hands fisted, indecisive. Dr. Richmond held Meg by the elbow. He stood between Erik and his wife.

"Don Erik, the physician is with your son. There's nothing you can do for him, and your current behavior is making matters worse."

"Erik, please, listen," Meg pleaded, her voice barely a whisper.

Erik scowled at Meg. The signs of carnage were blazoned on her hands and gown.

"That's better," Richmond said. He spoke in a cautious and level tone as if he were attending one of his patients. "Let's go to the drawing room where we can await word from the physician."

The moment he had seen Dr. Richmond, Erik had known what Meg and the foreigner were thinking. *Mad.* Well, perhaps he was.

He had found Mario, a broken body, trampled in the street. All he had wanted was to protect him, but what protection could he offer now?

Someone had said the boy was dead. Another had said there was still a faint heartbeat. Then Mario had been taken from him.

He had gone berserk. It had taken a lot to convince Jacopo to let him return home. He had managed to hold himself in check until he found Richmond standing in the entryway to his own home. But it was the startled and frightened look on Meg's face that had made Erik wonder if indeed he had gone mad.

"It's only natural to be upset, Don Erik." Richmond lingered. The intruder had suggested that Erik join him in the parlor where they could discuss the situation rationally. Had it not been for the frightened look in Meg's eyes, Erik would have told him to go to the devil.

Richmond spoke. A dull string of sounds without emotion, the intruder's voice droned on and on. Erik wasn't listening. He paced from one end of the room to the other. His mind was elsewhere, out in the streets, at the crossroad where a boy lay bloodied on the stones. How could a child's body withstand the weight of wagon and hooves? Why did they lie to him? Why were they keeping Mario's body from him? He longed to hold the child. The pain in his own chest seemed a pale reminder of his son's.

Still the man spoke. Erik ignored him. Richmond thought him mad. So much the better. Let him beware the mad dog. Erik would have liked to howl and run on all fours if there were any hope that this might dull his anguish.

Dr. Richmond stepped outside the room, leaving Erik to his dark thoughts.

Dr. Richmond blocked Meg's advance.

"Before you see him, you must be prepared not to find the man you know."

Meg stared open-mouthed into Dr. Richmond's concerned face.

"What are you saying?"

"He's not himself. The tragic events of the day have broken his hold on reality. I took advantage of the moment to speak with him.

It's my professional opinion that your husband needs help—medical attention—immediately."

"Mad?"

"Let's be cautious, Donna Meg, in the use of such words. With the proper intervention, if done quickly, we may prevent further—and permanent—deterioration."

"What can I do?"

"First we will calm him down, then remove him to facilities where we can more properly treat him."

"I can't…"

"Decisive action is required. If you want to avoid a complete breakdown, you must act." Dr. Richmond steered Meg to a side room. "May I?" He indicated a small desk where paper and writing materials had been left.

Meg nodded.

Sitting at the table, Richmond took one clean sheet of paper, dipped the stylus in the ink, and wrote hurriedly.

"There, that should do it." He blotted the sheet and indicated that Meg should approach. "Sign here, Donna Meg." When she hovered over the paper, stylus in hand, Richmond rushed to add, "It's just a formality. It authorizes treatment. We must hurry. No need to read it now."

His urgent tone woke her from what had seemed a trance. With trembling hand, she signed the paper.

"You can't take him away," she said.

Richmond considered her for a moment. "No. No, of course not. We would only need to take him if he proved a danger—to himself or to others."

She breathed a sigh of relief.

"We do need to calm him down, don't we, Donna Meg?"

"Yes."

"He's agitated, violent."

"But he's waiting in the parlor. Surely that means…"

"Yes, I know. It seems as if he might be regaining some control, but I don't wish to distress you by repeating the wild things he said. I had great difficulty convincing him to wait in the parlor. He's not in touch with reality. He swears that Mario's body has been stolen away and that we're lying when we say the boy's upstairs being attended to."

"We'll take him up to see for himself," Meg suggested. She headed for the door.

Richmond outstripped her and stood, barring the way.

"That wouldn't be wise."

"Why not?"

"I tried to explain. He became horribly agitated. He…he said the blood in the hallway wasn't human. I'm afraid that even if you were to take him to see the child, he wouldn't accept the truth. He could even do something dangerous."

"Oh my God, it can't be that bad, can it?"

Richmond relaxed when he saw Meg retreat a step.

"First we must calm him down. You asked the servants to prepare tea as I instructed?"

She nodded.

"Have them serve it in the parlor. Act as if nothing has happened. Humor him. Don't talk about the accident. Put this sedative in his tea." Richmond opened a small flat pouch that he extracted from his inside vest pocket. From this he removed a paper envelope and opened it to show Meg the small, glittering crystals inside. "Harmless. These dissolve immediately in hot liquid and will soothe him. Once he's relaxed, we can talk to him together and convince him that there is hope that the child will recover."

"Will he? Will Mario recover?"

Richmond scowled. "We will hope for the best. Otherwise I'm afraid such a confirmation of your husband's wild fancies will firmly lock him into this violent episode."

Meg bit her lower lip in an effort to stop the trembling.

"He won't want to be drugged."

"Then we won't tell him, will we?"

Meg's eyes fixed on the doctor's steady gaze.

"Remember, Donna Meg. This is just to calm him down so that we can help him."

Once Meg and the servant disappeared inside the parlor where Erik surely still paced like a caged animal, Dr. Richmond approached the doorman.

"See that this message is delivered immediately."

The servant bowed and took the note.

The wagon should arrive just as the drug took effect. The symptoms varied according to the subject. It was perhaps a bit risky to administer such a large dose to a subject who was already agitated. In extreme circumstances it had been known to cause infarctions. The heart rate could sore to a critical level. But Costanzi was a large man. He was also healthy and strong. Richmond was fairly confident that the drug would produce only the effects he required. Once Meg saw her husband's agitation increase, she would deliver him gladly into Dr. Richmond's care.

Why was she lying?

She cleaned the blood from his face with the coarse cotton dipped in soapy water. He watched the blood as it swirled and spread throughout the cloudy liquid. He couldn't feel the sting, only the pressure and movement of her hand. He'd failed. The bodiless faces with their ugly grimaces and the rough hands had taken the child—his child—from him.

She lied!

Mario wasn't hers! Never hers! Mario was his. Only *he* understood the deep hunger in those brown eyes. Only he knew what it was like to be a child cut adrift, unwanted, unprotected, stealing food, surviving by his wits, using lies and stealth when required, watching from the sidelines as others enjoyed a secure, loving life. Only *he* could understand Mario, for only *he* had felt such pain, such loss.

Meg cleaned the wounds. She bit back the recriminations. Something in his eyes frightened her. She felt torn. She should be with Mario, but Erik had only stopped his frenetic pacing when his gaze fell on her.

Now, as she tended to his cuts and bruises, reminders of the insane rage when they took Mario from him, she watched and worried over the flash of vertiginously changing emotions that roiled over his features. The wildness in his eyes was terrifying.

The doctor was with Mario. She calmed herself with the mantra. The doctor was with Mario. Surely he would be able to mend his broken body. Erik didn't believe her when she said Mario would be all right. Why should he? She didn't believe it herself.

She lies! She sits cleaning cuts that mean nothing! If Mario were alive, she'd be with him. He would need her, but a dead child needs no mother. A dead child! My child!

She dropped the bloody swabs onto the tray. She glanced at the cup of tea. *Not yet. Not yet. Wait until he's calmer.* If he threw the tea in the fireplace, she would need to take more of the crystals Dr. Richmond had given her and make a fresh cup. She didn't want to leave him alone. *Wait.* Soon she could offer him the tea. Soon he'd take it and drain the cup. She would get him to drink it. He was already calmer. The wild angry look he had was softening into despair. His body was visibly releasing the tension that kept him perched on the edge of the chair, turned obliquely away from her. He no longer glared at her. She reminded him again that Mario was in his room. The doctor was with him.

Don't leave me. I must find something to fill the empty gaping hole left by Mario's body. They took him from me. I failed to hold on to him. I failed. I didn't bring him to safety. Other hands took him. Meg, forgive me! Forgive me for failing to protect our son!

Now. Now he was ready to accept the cup. The crystals would taste bitter, but the tea was strong, a dark brew. She drizzled it with honey and added heavy cream, prepared it the way he liked it, sweet and rich. *Now. If she were to do it, it were better to be done quickly.* If she handed it to him, he'd take it. He'd trustingly accept the cup from her hand. She stared at the swirling, milky liquid. She stirred it again, far longer than she needed to. Now, he would drain the cup. Then perhaps he would slip away into a calm, semi-dormant state. Would he know that she had drugged him?

She would not see him come to harm! Not for the world! But what he did today, what he did in the street was not sane.

She's holding back her tears. For me, she is holding back the pain. She thinks I'm too weak to bear hers together with my own. Her hand trembles slightly. She disguises it with a smile, attempts to distract me from her hand, from the cup she is offering me, the cup from which she wants me to drink. She doesn't want me to see her hand tremble as it offers me the cup.

He would calm down. They would talk about what must be done. There were treatments, Dr. Richmond had reassured her. This was only a temporary measure—to calm him down, to bridge the crisis. But she knew Erik would not willingly accept treatment. Not in his present state. To calm him. The drug was harmless. Meg swallowed the rising sob in her throat as she watched Erik drain the cup.

If Meg hadn't seen it with her own eyes, she would not have believed it. Erik's hand began to tremble. As he moved to set the cup and saucer on the edge of the tray, his hand slipped and they toppled to the floor. The crash brought him to his feet. Meg slid forward and picked up the larger shards of porcelain.

Never mind. She would prepare another cup.

No, he didn't want another damn cup of tea. He wanted to see his son. Why was she keeping him from him?

Erik became more agitated, insisting that he would go upstairs to the boy's room. Dr. Richmond had slipped inside the room. Erik strode forward as if he would walk through the man if he had to.

Dr. Richmond tried to reason with him.

The doctor was with the lad. They would be in the way. Wasn't it best to allow the physician to carry out his examination and begin his treatment?

She heard only bits and pieces of their discussion, a discussion that spiraled out of control and became an argument. Erik pushed the doctor to the side where he toppled a small table with bric-a-brac from several of Marcelo's exotic voyages, smashing the figurines against the floor. The doctor then rose and struggled with Erik. Meg called for help. The servants pulled Erik, cursing, off Dr. Richmond.

Even then, Erik continued to shout obscenities at the doctor. His eyes were wild. Dr. Richmond took Meg to the side. In a whisper, he advised her not to interfere. That was when several large strange men came into the room, men that Dr. Richmond had summoned.

"Why is he acting like this?" Meg clutched the fabric over her heart. The strange men wrestled Erik to the ground. One placed his knee hard against Erik's heaving chest, while the other grabbed and bound his wrists. A third lay across Erik's legs to lessen his efforts to kick them. There was no other way to describe Erik's behavior than to say he had gone berserk.

Dr. Richmond inspected the binding around Erik's wrists. He must get him into the carriage before Signora Costanzi had time to change her mind.

"Regrettably, Signora, this episode was easily predicted. I'm afraid that his hold on reality has been slipping, and this latest tragedy has unloosed his grip completely."

The men that Dr. Richmond had summoned to the Costanzi mansion jerked Erik from the ground. Erik's cries were muffled by the heavy cloth band tied across his mouth. In spite of their efforts, Erik arched his back and writhed under the restraints, nearly toppling the brawny men to the ground.

Dr. Richmond could see that Meg was beginning to balk. He urged the attendants to remove the patient as quickly as possible.

With great difficulty, they managed to lift Costanzi to the wagon, a special wagon from the asylum made for the transport of violent patients. It was a miniature cell block forged from steel, completely cut off from the outside world once the heavy door was closed and secured by bolts. The enclosure had no windows, only two narrow slits for fresh air over which were metal covers that could be clamped down, sealing the inmate entirely from the outside world. The wagon was made to transport the patients only a short distance with the minimum of disturbance to the decent citizens of the city. No one would be bothered by the screams, kicks, and banging from inside the wagon as the wagon proceeded through the city streets. Given that the trip was not meant to be long, there was little fear that the person inside would die of asphyxiation. Once outside the city limits, the slits could be opened to allow a minimum of fresh air.

"But you said that the medicine would calm him. You said he'd calm down so that you could speak to him." Meg trailed behind the doctor as he started toward the front compartment where he would ride comfortably behind the driver in a semi-open carriage.

Dr. Richmond turned, reluctantly, and forced himself to assume a reassuring demeanor. He couldn't risk her suspicion. His plan might even now unravel if they hesitated.

"Signora, you must be brave. The fact that the crystals did not tranquilize him is a sign of the extent to which he has had a mental breakdown. I've seen men like your husband bend iron bars in an effort to run amok. I regret you've witnessed the disintegration of his personality, but you must be brave. I can't delay any longer. I must get him under proper conditions so that the treatment can commence. Call on us tomorrow at the asylum."

Meg watched the driver speed the horses down the street toward the asylum, her husband, in the dark metal box, bound and tied. She wept openly, her hands covering her mouth. In spite of the gags, in spite of the airless chamber, Meg could still hear Erik screaming!

CHAPTER 3

❈

Walls

'Tis the times' plague, when madmen lead the blind.
King Lear, William Shakespeare

Private Clinic, Austria 10 August 1888
Transport of patient Erik Costanzi completed.
Patient: Male
Age: Exact age unknown, approximately late forties.
Height: 6'3"   Weight: 190-200 lbs.
Eyes: green   Hair: light brown
Previous Domicile: Costanzi estate, Rome, Italy

Distinguishing characteristics: Disfigurement that spans most of the right-hand side of his face, continuing an inch or so past the hairline to include his right ear, reddened and irregular surface, origin of deformity unknown. Evidence of burns, not recent, on palms of both hands, across upper back, between shoulder blades. Faded scarring apparently from lash across back, less discernible across buttocks and back of legs. Several small scars on body, one on right shoulder, the other in soft tissue of left side just above the hip bone. The latter appears to be from a knife or sword wound. Index and middle finger on left hand, little finger, ring finger and index finger on right hand have been broken and have mended poorly, leaving index finger on left hand, in particular, with reduced flexibility. No birth marks or moles except the aforementioned facial deformity.

Condition: Severe dehydration, bruising, mild aftereffects from drug induced stupor, semi-conscious, confused, violent when approached.

Patient taken to cell "c" on the third floor due to possible violent and unpredictable behavior. Patient momentarily calmed as he was taken through the building. Once in the room, when he was restrained to the bed, he began to react violently, showing a mixture of confusion, fear, and anger. Patient continued to struggle even after restraints were tightened until several minutes passed at which point the patient collapsed, exhausted. Patient did not call out or shout.

Diagnosis: Preliminary evaluation of Patient finds that he suffers from violent tendencies, denial, agoraphobia, paranoia, psychic disassociation leading to breaks with reality, recurrent migraines, occasional nocturnal terrors, an obsessive fixation on music, and an inner fantasy world based on "artistic" flights of fancy which, unfortunately, those around him have encouraged. In addition, it is likely that his unusually strong sense of his own superiority masks an intense level of self-loathing. Caution is to be taken with subject at all times. Strong likelihood of violent behavior.

Attending Physician: Dr. Richmond.

Patient 579, cell c, floor 3, Erik Costanzi. 12 august

Patient pretended to be calm and cooperative until restraints were removed at which point he broke away from the attendants, struck one unconscious to the ground, then shrugged off the other. He reached the locked doors at the end of the corridor before several other attendants—including Himmel, Audrich, and myself—finally wrestled him to the ground.

Dr. Richmond has instructed us to keep Patient manacled until he gets used to his new surroundings and has prescribed a mild sedative. Further medications to be determined over the next several days. W.--

Patient 579, cell c, floor 3, Erik Costanzi. 13 august

Upon his initial physical examination of the patient, Dr. Flescher insisted on treating him for dehydration. Liquids were administered. Dehydration has been corrected. Patient has not eaten since arrival. Patient is uncooperative, will not speak. Violent behavior has abated due to medication and physical weakness. Dr. Richmond has instructed us to keep a log on the new patient, recording his reactions and behaviors while in the common room. He has also ordered continuous observation, through transparent mirror, while Patient is restricted to his room.

At present separated from the community, Patient gives in to alternating bouts of struggle, angry vituperation, and weeping. Suspicion that Patient understands that the mirror in his room is transparent, allowing staff to observe him without his knowledge, is based on his frequent inspection of the mirror in his calmer moments, an inspection that does not seem to be narcissistic for his eyes never seem to look directly at his own image but rather search the surface and edging of the mirror as if to study it instead of his reflection. He also directs his anger at the mirror, yet during bouts of anguish, turns away, or tries to hide from the mirror's vantage point. Medication has recently been increased to maximum level without risking unconsciousness or dire side effects. If other strategies are not found to restrain the patient, there is a danger of long-term addiction. H.--

Dr. Richmond's Journal. 16 August

I daresay that some will say I'm mad to have taken such drastic steps in the name of science. They may even discount the advances we will surely make here by harping on the cruelty perpetrated against one man and his loved ones. It's not without some regret that I take on this challenge. Even Dr. Klinen has cowardly removed himself from direct involvement in the case. He has made it clear that he is only available for consultation and only with the understanding that the patient has indeed required intervention and treatment. To protect my mentor, I will not disabuse him of such a mistaken assumption. Yet I sincerely think that the subject may have eventually suffered a psychic breakdown, even without my interference. Should this study lead to his perpetual confinement, I will mourn the loss of an individual. But I will glory in knowing that his sacrifice will benefit many others in the future. I have to steel myself against compassion. Of course, there is a chance, unlikely though it be, that this treatment and study might draw to a close at some distant point in the future and that the patient might then end his days with a measure of calm and resignation.

Costanzi insists on fighting us. I've not seen a more obdurate patient. He refuses to speak and will not understand that it's for his own good, as well as the good of science, that he's been committed to this clinic. Signora Costanzi by now has realized that her husband is beyond her reach, out of the country, and legally under my care. My private clinic is known only to a handful in the field, so it may escape her efforts should she be as tenacious as her husband and persist in searching for him. The papers are legitimate. Should she have second thoughts—which I fear is quite likely given her state of mind when I took her husband into my custody—she has no legal rights. For that matter, nor does her husband. Only the attending physician or the court can annul the commitment act. I can easily transfer our patient to any number of other institutions before Sig. Costanzi, his father, even arranges for a hearing in court. Of course, it might be risky, but once I publish my findings, no one will question my methods. Indeed I will be judged a champion who fought to protect his patient from the fickleness of a guilt-ridden wife. Albeit unwittingly, his wife did sign the papers. She committed him to the treatment. Perhaps we may eventually release the patient. If too much damage is not done, in time, we might understand the workings of his mind and be able to cure his violent tendencies. However, we must be clear on our goals.

Sacrifices must be made.

17 August

Patient is much weakened. But whatever drives him, the man is as vehemently opposed to being in the clinic as ever. If he won't submit to our experiments, we might be forced to do something drastic. It's imperative to subdue him so that he is more manageable. I have not begun the initial conversations, I confess, for cowardly reasons. This morning we decided to introduce food. He hasn't eaten for slightly more than a week—since we left Rome. A simple, watery gruel of oats and honey was set before him. The attendant said that the patient hesitated as if he'd refuse to eat but set upon it avidly once he was left alone. He's stubborn and proud. I watched him from the other side of the mirror. He was indeed ravenous. After breakfast, I decided to start his history. I would not have had the courage to be in the same room had he not been manacled still. Keeping a careful distance, I sat down with the notebook and tried to establish what Dr. Klinen terms the "contract." I addressed him by his given name to establish our relationship as intimate. He did not respond, so it was not yet necessary to instruct him to address me as Dr. Richmond at all times. Patient must recognize the doctor's role as one superior to his own. I explained that we must start with some understanding of who he is and for that we would conduct several interviews—this being the first—and that he must be truthful and forthcoming if he expected to be cured. He glared at me with such malice that I felt my professional demeanor slipping. He was silent and refused to answer my question, until finally he blurted out, " He's dead, isn't he?" It took me a moment to recall the child's accident.

Here Dr. Richmond scowled and twirled the pen between his fingers. It was a new invention, a cylinder of ink embedded in the long stem and attached to a sharp, steel stylus. He liked new things. For science, he must be thorough. This of course was his own journal and would be read and studied in future generations. Did he have to explain what had happened and who the child was? He decided it was unnecessary. The official log would complement his own journal. He resumed writing.

    The question was curiously ambiguous. It was simultaneously an attack—his tone was belligerent—a statement of fact, and a plea for contradiction. I was amazed by the depth of emotion he conveyed in the brief utterance. I didn't answer. I believe the ambiguity is useful for his submission to our therapy. His demeanor, and I admit his disfigurement, disquieted me greatly. It was obvious that he thought me a fiend. Had I not supped with his family? Had I not presented myself as a friend? He fights against the knowledge of his own mental state, refuses to understand that he's ill and that I'm his only hope. I explained the situation as best I could. His cold silence was testament to his skepticism. He hid his anxiety behind a grimace of contempt.

Patient 579, cell c, floor 3, Erik Costanzi. 19 august

    Patient is calm. Still refuses to speak. Dr. Richmond allowed manacles to be removed. Patient ate well. Dr. Richmond gave permission for the patient to eat in his cell, but insisted that he be introduced to the population on the second floor, in the common room. Patient briefly resisted being led to the common room. Dr. Richmond suggested that the lack of a mask might make him reluctant to enter the population. This seemed to be borne out by his pulling back slightly and his attempt to keep his disfigurement turned away from the other inmates. His introduction into the room frightened several of the more responsive patients. Lisbet screamed repeatedly and clutched her face in a curious sympathetic reaction to the new patient's deformity. It was as if she wished to hide it. Lisbet's reaction was particularly disturbing to Patient who searched about the room for a means of escape. His agitation further increased the anxiety among the other patients. Franz and Gertrude rushed away to hide in a corner. Patient 'X' intensified his repetitive tick of clawing at his arms and had to be restrained. As would be expected Laurent laughed and heckled him, throwing out his usual rant of vulgar words at our new patient. When it was obvious we meant him to stay and we were retiring from the room, Patient 579 followed us to the door and pleaded to be taken back to his room.

Further observations: Patient "Erik" attempted to escape Laurent who dogged his steps, laughing and cursing at him. Lisbet eventually found a safe place and quieted. Patient kept his distance from the girl. Several other patients "woke up" and were mildly startled by Patient's face as he passed by them in an attempt to escape Laurent's heckling. After traversing the entire space more than once without shaking off Laurent, Patient 579 turned aggressively on Laurent and screamed at him to stop. The unexpected violence set everyone off again. The usual behaviors were intensified by the addition of the new inmate. However, as ordered, the attendants did not interfere except in one case where Patient 'Y' threatened to bash himself a second time against the wall. 'Y' was removed for his own good.

As a response to the renewed cacophony, Patient clasped his hands over his ears and squatted against the wall closest to the doorway. He remained there in the same position until several hours later when he was taken back to his room for the midday meal.

Afternoon was similar to the morning. Patient was returned for dinner and allowed to remain in room for the rest of the evening. H.--

Dr. Richmond's Journal. 25 August

I have repeated my request that Dr. Klinen join me on Erik Costanzi's case, explaining the unfortunate—but not unpredicted—breakdown of the patient. Although Dr. Klinen protests his inability to extricate himself from his present commitments, I sense a reservation on his part. Perhaps he has his suspicions. I confess that

I'm not as disappointed as I thought I might be. Dr. Klinen's rejection of my invitation will allow me full control over the treatment.

Each day that Erik has been brought to the common room, he has caused a good deal of unrest among the others. It has been interesting to see what the addition of such a unique specimen will do to a society as rigid as the one created among our permanent residents. Only those like Ludwig and Frieda, who are classic catatonics, were unmoved by the introduction of our composer. The population's first reaction was, of course, to his disfigurement. The ensuing chaos triggered a flight reaction in our new patient. Unable to escape, he collapsed into a protective pose similar to a fetal position near the only exit known to him. Curiously his response has been to hide his face and shrink his presence by bending his body in upon itself. It was as if he were trying to regress to an infantile, separate, and protected realm. He has not lashed out, nor has he seemed particularly fearful of violence from the population. If he feared violence, his face would not have been turned to the wall. Rather, he'd have maintained vigilance and kept his face forward to keep an eye on the others. So either he did not fear assault or it mattered little to him if anyone meant him harm. Thence I deduced that his principal fear was to be observed. He did not want the others to look upon his face. Was this to cause them the least discomfort or was this a response to some inner pain of his own?

These patterns have recurred on a daily basis among the other patients, and Erik has assumed his spot near the door and waited to be taken to his room. However, today and the previous two days, the patient has abandoned his crouching position near the door. There are signs that he is observing the others. Today, for the first time, after an hour of inactivity, Erik gradually explored the room. He avoided eye contact with the other patients and eventually arrived at the series of windows that overlook the south gardens. He skirted around all the individuals as if he feared contact or proximity might upset them further.

Laurent, who had settled down after fifteen minutes of ranting and cursing at the new man, was set off again by Erik's change in behavior. 'Y' defecated in a corner and was quietly removed. Erik was curiously quiet and watchful while the attendants had to deal with

'Y' and clean up after him. Heinrich started toward the exit and had to be taken to his seat several times before he finally settled. Lisbet began to scream when Heinrich scooted his chair too close to hers.

Himmel has proved exceptionally helpful with his detailed record of events in the common room. Given that he has some medical training, I may recommend him for further study at the Bragant. On the other hand, the other attendants are literate but untrained in the matters of mental health. Even so their reports are useful. I am concerned about Gunter. He has been accused of employing excessive force to subdue the patients. I may have to dismiss him. However I'm reluctant to do so. He is not an unintelligent man, and the fear and respect he inspires among the population can come in handy. At any rate, I have no proof that he has crossed any limits that we have set.

Returning to my special subject, our mad musical genius, he eventually came to the windows and stood staring out over the gardens for the rest of the morning. Most certainly he entertains vain hopes of escape.

Later in the afternoon, Erik repeated his same journey round the perimeter of the assembly room. (We kept 'Y' in his room after the noon meal. He's been very difficult since the arrival of the new one.) The patients were lazy and less excitable after their meal. Most lounged around the room or quietly soothed themselves. Heinrich, who walked to the exit and knocked on the door, needed to be taken to his chair only once. Patient 'X' had to be restrained for inappropriate touching of himself. I am considering castration as a treatment. It has been known to help in cases where subject is oversexed. Erik stood, as before, for quite some time at the window. Even if escape were not his interest, suicide would not be possible. The bars on the windows are not wide enough even for someone as slight of build as Lisbet to slip through. Attendants noted that Erik did not remain at the windows but began to walk round the circumference of the room, repeating the same pattern.

Repeated behavior is, of course, a symptom common to many mental illnesses. Repetition, whether it be of movement or speech, seems to be a natural means of self-gratification. It tends to calm the patient and substitute peaks in negative behavior. Even so, we must watch carefully in order to avoid calcification of such behavior. Indeed if we wish to delve into the patient's psyche, we may have to suppress all such compensatory activities. Only then will we see the true workings of his mind.

I've decided Celeste can rejoin the population in a day or so. After the last episode with the sharpened stick, she seems to have calmed down. I had once believed that her case study would lead me to some insights into the relationship between madness and genius. Of course as a woman, she has by nature a weak grip on her emotional state. Her nymphomaniac tendencies have made her treatments difficult, and any progress in her therapy has stalled. The best we can hope for is management in her case. Given her cooperative manner this evening, I believe I can reward her with reintegration into the population.

"Erik, you must resign yourself, sooner or later, to the situation."
"Where is my wife?"

Dr. Richmond tried to mask the sigh with a cough. The pen and tablet lay impotent on his lap. Polyhedrons and Kabalistic symbols decorated the edges. He resisted awareness of the clock whose regular ticking grew louder in the chilled silence between him and his patient.

He had taken the subject off all but a mild drug; the latter he thought advisable given the strength of the patient and his amazing stubbornness. Frustrated, he forced himself to sustain Sig. Costanzi's angry glare. It had been weeks, and there was still no sign of adjustment on the part of the patient.

"I've explained all this to you several times, Erik." He purposefully used the subject's given name. For one it suggested the role the patient was to assume. The physician expected Erik to recognize the unequal relationship between them. There was nothing the physician did not control. Erik would eat or sleep only if the physician allowed it. Erik must recognize his dependent status. For another, use of the patient's first name created an intimacy that eventually would assure the patient's attachment to and emotional reliance on the physician. "I've even shown you the document with Meg Costanzi's signature. She has commended you to our care. She wants us to help you."

There it was, again—the flash of anger followed by a blistering agony in the man's eyes. Without the mask, the subject consciously controlled his facial expressions in an effort to disguise his reactions and feelings, but his eyes sometimes escaped his efforts to appear impassive. Erik looked away. Dr. Richmond smiled at the momentary victory.

"You were going to tell me about your childhood," Richmond lied. Erik had flatly refused to speak to him, limiting his speech only to demands and questions of his own.

Given the patient's lack of cooperation, Dr. Richmond made his decision. He had heard claims that hypnosis placed the subject in a state in which he not only would obey but could not lie. Dr. Charcot had demonstrated amazing control over his patients under hypnosis, making them perform acts that seemed nearly impossible. They also would confess to truths regardless of their embarrassment. Charcot maintained that patients would go on at length concerning events completely forgotten when they were not under hypnosis. The potential use of the technique was staggering.

Of course Erik was hardly a willing subject. Inducing the hypnotic state might be difficult. Tranquilizing drops might sufficiently undermine his resistance, but the patient was already on a mild sedative.

"Erik, we're here to help you." Dr. Richmond refused to allow the man's open smirk to rattle him. "I know you distrust us, but the sooner you learn to cooperate the sooner your madness will be cured."

The smirk disappeared. The physician resisted delighting in his subject's misery. After all, he had no intention of being cruel. Whatever he did was in an effort to break down the patient's resistance to treatment. The word "madness" had had an instantaneous effect. Erik's defenses momentarily crumbled, and Dr. Richmond noted, with satisfaction, that his patient was not as confident as he liked to pretend. Indeed, it was as if he'd been able to lift the veil on one of the patient's own fears. Erik, too, thought himself mad, feared it, at least.

Pressing his advantage, Dr. Richmond sat forward in his chair, his elbows anchored on the desk, his hands folded together in reverential concern. "Cooperate, Erik, and someday you will return to your family," he said with a comforting tone. It was important that the patient not lose hope of walking out of the clinic, cured, one day, even if such a hope was without foundation.

Without the mask, Erik was naked, vulnerable. Even so, Richmond could see the battle in his restless eyes as he struggled to find some way to hide. The patient was beginning to understand that he was at Dr. Richmond's mercy.

Impassivity returned to Erik's face. Richmond was momentarily surprised by Erik's control.

"What do you want?" Erik asked cautiously.

"Just relax." Dr. Richmond gestured toward a narrow couch along the wall. Reluctantly Erik sat on the soft leather. "Lie back. Relax and let me ask you some questions. Relax and let all your cares fall away." As Dr. Charcot had demonstrated, Dr. Richmond sat near the subject. As if it were simply a meaningless personal habit, he pulled the gold watch from his breast pocket and gently swung it back and forth, catching Erik's gaze. "That's it. That's it. Calm. Relaxed. Soon we can begin to talk, talk about what is important to you, what you've lost and forgotten." Erik's eyes began to close.

Richmond's voice was soothing. He spoke of the past—Erik's past—suggesting that he cast his mind back in time. Knowing only the broad strokes of the patient's history, guessing at others, he told Erik to think of the time before he became the artistic director of the Teatro Dell'Opera. Then he directed him to recall the period before he came to Rome. He didn't allow Erik to linger at any particular moment. He wanted to take him as far as he could, to his deepest memories. He was prepared to push Erik until he met resistance.

"You have secrets, Erik. You have memories that you have locked away." Once he knew the patient's secrets, he could begin to unravel the connections between the unstable aspects of his personality and his genius.

"A door."

Richmond scowled. Erik had taken him literally. The deepest memories were locked away behind a door, a door of Erik's invention.

"Do you see the door, Erik? Is it closed?" Erik barely nodded. "It has a large, shiny key in its lock. You see it, don't you, Erik? Are you sure you see it? Good." Erik's breathing accelerated. "Are you afraid of the door, Erik? Don't be. Don't be afraid. Doors are meant to be opened. Put out your hand, Erik. That's it. Take the key. It feels hard and cold in your palm. Turn it. Turn it, again. The door is opening, Erik. The door is opening. Now, let go of the knob. Let the door swing open. It's all right. You're safe. Nothing on the other side of the door can hurt you. They are only your secrets, secrets that have made you who you are. Step over the threshold, Erik. Step inside. Erik? Erik? What do you see?"

Dr. Richmond replaced his pocket watch and grimly studied the subject. Erik had begun to tremble. His lips drew back from gritted teeth, and a high, plaintive keening escaped. The doctor took Erik's wrist between his thumb and index finger to find his pulse. It had risen to a dangerous rate. His skin was cold and clammy.

"Erik?" He studiously kept the urgency from his voice. "Erik, do you hear me? You must not be afraid. Tell me what you see?" Inevitably his own nerves had caught the panic from Erik, and his voice had increased slightly in volume, taking on an air of command that he hadn't expected to need.

Erik's teeth parted slightly as he tried to push out the words. An explosion of air—a single word—was barely comprehensible, but the doctor understood it.

"Erik, take one step backwards. Erik, listen to me and do what I say. Take one step backwards now. Step away from the door. You see the door quietly close. The lock clicks into place. There is nothing to be afraid of. What you saw is now behind the door. You're calm now." He checked to find that Erik's pulse had indeed begun to decelerate. "Now I will count backwards from five and when you hear one, you will open your eyes and wake. You will feel refreshed. You will not remember the image, nor will you remember the fear. Now listen to me, Erik. Five, four, three, two, one."

The subject raised his hand to his face and wiped the wetness from his cheeks. He kept his gaze averted from the doctor's.

Dr. Richmond walked to the door and called for the attendants to take the subject back to the common room. They helped Erik to his feet. The patient was unsteady for a moment but quickly stiffened against the men's grip on his arms. Dr. Richmond nodded slightly at one of the beefy attendants, and they released their hold on the patient. Erik gave the doctor only a fleeting glance before he set off, on his own, toward the large room at the end of the corridor.

The physician sat at his journal and began to jot his notes. Round and round his mind circled the word the patient had managed to say. It's starkness alone unsettled him. He hadn't expected an image so blatantly violent, yet still cryptic. It certainly suggested a powerful resistance against seeing the actual memories behind the figurative door; however, it was equally certain that the formative experiences of the patient had been traumatic and violent. Dr. Richmond ended his notes with the one word the subject had uttered.

"Blood."

"Cock! Cock! You cock-sucker! You eat shit. Shit, shit, shit, shit. You don't belong here. Fuck! You don't—FUCK—you shouldn't be here. Shit, shit, shit! Cock! Fuck my… You—ugly fuck—don't—fuck, fuck, ugly, shit, shit, shit."

Laurent balled his fists and pressed them hard against his eyes. He forced himself to take several steps away from the new man in the room. There were enough men in the room. There was not enough air for another man to be in the room. There should only be ten. Eleven was an ugly number. It was misshapen and awkward. It could not be used to complete anything. It could not be arranged. There were fourteen chairs and five tables. Eleven left three chairs vacant. Three was a good number, thought Laurent; momentarily he was comforted. Three could balance. A three-legged stool would not fall over. But a four-legged chair was by far superior to one with only three legs. If you sawed off one leg on the three-legged chair, it would fall over. There was no room for mishap with three. Who ever heard of eleven legs? Laurent thought of ten men, one at each end of a long table and four on either side. One man had three legs. "Shit, shit, shit. Fuck!" But that made no sense. There was an eleventh man. An extra leg did not solve the problem of the eleventh body! Laurent imagined the eleventh man lying prone on the ground under the table. No, on top of the table was better. But which end would he face? The man at the north end of the table or the one at the south end? No, it would not work.

"Cock! Eat my shit, my shit, my shit, you cock-sucking fuck, fuck, fuck!" The new man had only half a face. He imagined the man as if he were only a face in the middle of the table, on a spinning disk. The disk spun to one side, then the next, back and forth on the table.

Laurent calmed down. He bit down hard on his tongue to stop the flow of offal that forced itself to his mouth. He had vowed to be silent, anything to keep from spouting the words that had a will of their own. The anger, the painfully tight explosion of ugly filth, burned as it fought its way to the surface. It had not been so bad, not until the new man had come.

Laurent watched the patient with the garbled right side. At first he'd been afraid of him. The man was much taller than he was. He was strong looking, too, not as large and fleshy as the attendants but muscular in a sleek, elegant way. Laurent had been relieved to see that the new man tried to keep to himself. It had helped to note the man's discomfort at being in the room. The stranger didn't like that the others could see his face. Laurent was helpless in his curiosity. He drew near enough to see the terror in the new man's eyes. And as he recognized the despair, he couldn't stop the torrent of filth from spilling out of his mouth.

The man with half a face had turned on him sharply, anger in his eyes and told him to leave him alone. Laurent's fear made the flow of curses rush even more quickly from his mouth. If only he could turn away from the eleventh man! Then he might be able to bite off the snake of words. Perhaps he could turn the words to meaningless barks. Sometimes he barked. The sound was less offensive to his own ears than the steady flow of obscenities that shocked and frightened even him.

He had expected the new man to strike him. That was what usually happened. He had taken a step away, crammed his neck deep between his shoulders, and hunched his back to better protect himself from the force of the blow. But the blow never came. The rough demand to be left alone rang in the space between them. Then comprehension flashed in the new man's eyes. He had understood Laurent's inability to restrain his invectives. The man went to the doorway, crouched down, and turned his face to the wall. He was making himself small, so small that he'd become invisible.

The new man's name was Erik. He no longer hid against the wall. Laurent tried to ignore the fact that Erik was the eleventh man in the room. He still didn't like Erik's intrusion, but over the past several weeks he'd come to think better of the man himself.

Something had changed when they brought Erik to the room this time. Laurent saw that his eyes were bloodshot. Slowly he edged close to Erik who had, uncharacteristically, dragged a chair to the farthest corner of the room and sat, his back to the others.

"Cock, cock, cock, cock-a-doodle-do, cock, cock, doodle, doodle, doodle, eat…eat…eat my shit…shit, shit, shit." Oh God, would he never be able to stop his tongue? Laurent gritted his teeth and tried to hum to forestall the curses. Erik sat very still, his disfigurement turned toward the edge where the two white walls came together. Laurent was so near he could hear the soft trembling breaths the man was painfully trying to disguise. The slight shaking of his shoulders brought a new wave of panic to Laurent, but he knew it was not his own turmoil he was feeling. He reached out a hand toward the gray shirt that they all wore as patients in the clinic for the insane. As he stretched out his fingers to touch the shirt, Erik turned sharply toward him. Laurent withdrew his hand quickly and stuttered, "So…so…so…sorry…ry…ry…so, so, so, shit, fuck, damn, sorry, you cock-sucker. Are you—fuck, fuck, shit, shit, damn, damn sweet cock—all right? Sh…sh…shit!"

Erik turned so that his entire back was to Laurent, but Laurent heard his voice softly answer. "Please, go away. Leave me alone."

Laurent couldn't believe his ears! He had spoken to the man, and the man had understood! Erik had spoken to him, had answered him. It didn't matter to Laurent that it was a rejection. It was a response—a clear response—to him, to what he had so imperfectly tried to say.

"Sh...sh...sh... Damn, damn, damn it. Cu..cu...cunt, penis, prick, cock. Sad, sad, weeping, sad, so... I'm...cock-sucker...sorry, shit-face, fuck, asshole, asshole, prick. So...so...sorry."

Erik bowed his head, his back still shielding him from Laurent's observation. "I'm all right."

Laurent nodded, not trusting his mouth. He edged backwards, his eyes trained on the broad back of the eleventh man, his friend. This man didn't belong here. He had no business being locked up inside with them. Not because he was an awkward unwieldy number, but because he was not mad.

Patient 579, cell c, floor 3, Erik Costanzi. 28 august

Patient continues to move his fingers along the edge of the table at the far side of the room. He's done this same thing on and off for days. The movements are never quite the same. Sometimes he's fast, sometimes slow. Himmel says that he's pretending to play a piano and that the patterns are the notes and rhythms of different songs. Today the patient must have been playing something lively and dramatic. His hands moved so quickly, I couldn't see the fingers. He bent over the edge of the table as if he could hear something no one else could hear. The "playing" keeps the patient busy for the greater part of the day. It also lets him avoid interacting with attendants or inmates. The regularity, according to Himmel, suggests what Dr. Richmond calls "an entrenched, compulsive behavior." Attempts to make him stop so far have been useless. Patient starts up again as soon as we leave the room. W.--

Patient 579, cell c, floor 3, Erik Costanzi. 30 august

Patient's "playing" has stirred up the inmates. Lisbet got up from her seat today after watching the patient for nearly an hour and began to "dance." Her strange behavior set off a reaction among the others. Himmel went inside the room to try to calm Lisbet, but she kept slipping away from him. Franz and Gertrude watched Lisbet and began to clap their hands. The noise startled Erik. He stopped for a moment but started again as if to fit his playing to the racket Franz and Gertrude were making. "X" began to moo and had to be removed. Laurent's mumbling got louder and louder until we could all hear his string of curses. Lately, since Celeste's return to the common room, Laurent's obscenities are all related to female anatomy. Lisbet, her eyes closed, came too close to "Y" who reached out to touch her breasts as she twirled by. Lisbet fled screaming to her chair, Laurent began to yell at the top of his lungs, "Fuck, damn cunt, bloody pussy, etc.," while Franz and Gertrude, terrified, stopped clapping and began to moan. Heinrich scurried under the table to hide. I called Himmel out and sent him to find Gunter. W.--

Gunter and Wilhelm went in to handle the inmates while I remained at the observation desk. Gunter seized Lisbet by the arm, meaning to force her to quiet. Her shrieks were upsetting everyone else. Erik rose from his seat—even though Gunter clearly instructed him to remain seated—and approached Lisbet. Gunter pushed him forcefully back toward his chair. Erik flushed with anger and struck Gunter a blow to the face. I think it might have broken his nose. The blood splattered "Y" who ran to the far wall where he began to beat his head against the surface. Wilhelm sounded the alarm. Audrich rushed in to restrain "Y" and to assist in dealing with Erik.

Uncharacteristically, Laurent came forward as if to intercede while Gunter tried to subdue Erik who lashed out indiscriminately at each of the attendants. Although they finally managed to subdue the patient, Gunter, Wilhelm, and Audrich received minor injuries in the fray.

The only patients who did not seem adversely affected by the scene were Ludwig, Frieda, and Celeste. Celeste was intensely entertained by the whole performance. She never once moved from her reclining pose on the couch, but she nevertheless watched the scuffle with evident delight.

Patients were kept in their rooms for dinner and the rest of the evening. Erik was taken to the infirmary. H.--

Infirmary 30 August

Treated:
Attendant Gunter Wassler, broken nose.
Attendant Wilhelm Eggert, dislocated shoulder, cranial contusion. No sign of skull fracture.
Attendant Audrich Blocher, blow to groin, broken third finger on right hand.
Patient "Y" suffered severe contusions to forehead, self-induced. Administered pain medicine and tranquilizer.
Patient 579, Erik Costanzi, multiple contusions about face and torso. Wrapped ribs. Nose bled profusely as well as cut over right eye, but patient's disfigurement impeded proper examination of nose. Severe contusions over left kidney. Must watch for blood in urine. Left arm wrenched, tendons strained but not torn. Several blows to the groin suggest excessive violence from guards. Have made official complaint. Dr. Flescher.

Patient 579, cell c, floor 3, Erik Costanzi. 1 September

    In keeping with Flescher's orders, Patient remained in infirmary last night, returned to private room for the day. Uncommunicative. Ate porridge late morning, apple sauce in evening. No blood in urine. In spite of the doctor's recommendation that he remain in bed, Patient rose and paced room for several hours in late evening after lights were turned off. G.--

Patient 579, cell c, floor 3, Erik Costanzi. 2 September

    Dr. Richmond says Patient's hands are to be bound with gauze and wrapped with bandages except when dining or relieving himself. Attendants are instructed to report any activity which seems remotely "musical." G.--

Patient 579, cell c, floor 3, Erik Costanzi. 3 September

    Patient returned to common room. In spite of recent injuries, his energy seems high. Unable to sit quietly, he spent entire morning walking around the edge of the room. The regularity of the patient's activity soothed the inmates who went back to their own activities after a brief tense pause.
    Bound hands make "playing the piano" impossible.
    Patient remains sullen and uncommunicative. Refuses all interaction with other patients and attendants. G.--

Patient 579, cell c, floor 3, Erik Costanzi. 5 September

    More active than usual. Paced room. Abruptly stopped by window, fell to knees, cursed loudly, and began to gnaw at wrappings with his teeth. Useless effort abandoned shortly after. Patient was threatening. He confronted Gunter and demanded that he take the bandages off his hands. Other patients started to shout and move about. Attendants went to restrain Patient 579 who dropped to the floor and refused to rise. Had to be dragged to his room and manacled to the bed.
    Patient kept up constant screaming for thirty minutes before Dr. Richmond could be found. Patient quieted slowly upon seeing Dr. Richmond enter his room.
    An hour later, sedative was given (see medication log for doses and instructions for the next forty-eight hours), and patient slept.
    Bandages were removed.
    Standing Order: Replace bandages upon waking. W.--

Dr. Richmond's journal 5 September

    The patient exhibits a deterioration in his capacity to cope. Binding his hands so that he cannot "play" his nonexistent piano has led to a surfeit of energy that has not found a viable outlet. The creative drive, being thwarted, has led to compensatory behavior, in particular, an automatic locomotion throughout the common room. The constant, rhythmic pacing has been only partially successful as is proved by today's breakdown. Pent-up rage exploded, and patient lost all sense of control, dropping to the floor, biting at his bandages in a vain attempt to free his hands, and shouting invectives. Anger eventually turned to despair.
    When I came to his room, I found him thrashing about wildly on his cot. It took several moments for the patient to recognize my presence and to calm down. He demanded that I free his hands. The imperative form—he did not beg, nor attempt to reason with

me—demonstrated as well as anything else in his behavior how out of touch he has become with his circumstances. I pointed out as much. Patient held his tongue but glared at me with the ferocity of a caged animal.

"Do you wish me to treat you like an animal, Erik?" I asked, careful to keep all emotion from my voice.

The question had a more drastic and immediate effect than I could have hoped. He visibly calmed himself and shook his head, obviously unable to trust his voice to make a satisfactory reply to my implied threat. I could not shake the intuition that I had hit on some threat of personal import.

"We must stop the music, Erik. It is part of your psychosis. If you wish to be healed, you must fight your impulses, including your obsessive enslavement to your art."

I could see his resistance to my diagnosis and treatment. As I explained the excessive energy produced by his drive to create and how it was twisting his mind, he grew more and more desperate.

I went on to explain—in spite of his obvious agitation—that he must trust me. I insisted that he let me inside his mind. I need to know the history of his illness, and for that he must not hold back any of his secrets, no matter how painful.

Eventually I wrung from him a reluctant acquiescence. This is the first positive sign that I have seen in weeks. It doesn't matter that it has been coercively won. Once he begins to unfold his past, he will find it impossible to hold back. We will find the roots of his genius, and there, too, will reside his madness.

We will begin in earnest tomorrow.

Patient 579, cell c, floor 3, Erik Costanzi. 6 September

Gunter brought Patient to common room after morning session with Dr. Richmond. His hands were unbound. Order: Watch for signs of regression. Should he begin to use his fingers again as if playing the piano or any other instrument or even tapping out a rhythm, we are instructed to bandage hands again.

Patient was curiously quiet. He didn't even acknowledge Laurent's "greeting." Laurent is obviously fixated on Erik in spite of the deformity. He practically fawns over him. Normally Patient suffers Laurent up to a point then tells him to back away and leave him alone. Today it was as if Erik were unaware of his surroundings. Instead of pacing, he held his hands in a fist, as if praying, and sat as far from the others as possible. Eventually it became apparent that he was rocking just slightly back and forth in his chair, similar to the more obvious coping strategies of our two catatonics, Ludwig and Frieda.

Curiously, Lisbet approached him. She came within a meter or so of him and reached out to touch him before she panicked and ran back to her usual corner. We were all surprised by her unexpected desire to draw near someone else. Celeste, too, reacted somewhat bizarrely to Erik's new behavior. She sat up on her couch and stared at him the whole time as if studying him. At one point she brought both her hands up to her face and between them formed a rectangular opening through which she observed the man.

Erik's behavior has shown a dramatic change. No longer agitated or violent, he has become passive and nonresponsive. He seemed oblivious to all about him. Gunter had to shake him to get him to rise for lunch. He ate slowly and meagerly, barely touching the sausage and dumplings.

In the afternoon, he seemed to have shaken off the malaise of the morning. He began to pace again, but without the frenetic tempo of previous days. He kept his hands cosseted under his arms, buried nearly in his armpits or by his side in tight fists. H.--

Dr. Richmond's journal 11 September

I was urgently called to the common room to witness the commotion wrought by Erik. Before I reached the room, I could hear it. The scene I found was amazing. "X" and "Y" were singing. Laurent was slapping the table and humming. Ludwig and Frieda were rocking back and forth in a matching tempo. Heinrich was imitating a violin or some other stringed instrument. Lisbet was singing a combination of what seemed three or four notes in a high clear soprano. Erik was going from one to another giving instructions to each. The only one who wasn't participating was Celeste. She lounged, like Cleopatra on her barge, with an unapologetic smirk on her face as if enjoying the folly of the lot. From time to time, she laughed out loud until Erik came to a stop in the middle of it all and began to sing.

All their attention was riveted on Erik's voice. Lisbet began to dance around the room, still singing her accompaniment. Laurent missed several beats and shouted out a couple of obscenities—"four fingers fucking Figaro"—before settling down again to the required percussion. "X" came up behind Erik and began to imitate his body movements, gestures, and his voice, a half step after Erik's performance, creating a strange echoing effect. What sounded at first like cacophony began to emerge as something ironically melodic.

I noticed the effects even on the attendants. Himmel, who has never shown any affinity for the arts, was swaying in tempo with the music.

Of course, I had to stop it. I can't allow a patient to disrupt the treatment of the other inmates. Regrettably, I hoped Erik and I were making some progress. This is a setback I hadn't expected.

Patient 579, cell c, Floor 3, E. C. 11 September

Forcibly removed patient from common room as ordered by Dr. Richmond. Bound hands, manacled to bed, gagged mouth.
Order was difficult to restore among the rest of the patients. Laurent had to be taken to his room and locked in for the rest of the day. "X" was given medication to keep him from hurting himself. Lisbet continued to dance and sing, growing more and more excited until Gunter offered to take her to her room. Unexpectedly, Lisbet

became hysterical the moment Gunter took her by the arm, screaming and pulling away from him. Refusing assistance, Gunter picked her up bodily and took her to her room. It was several minutes before the others calmed down.

Of the patients in the common room, Celeste was the only one who hadn't been a party to the concerto Patient 579 put together. However, when Himmel and Audrich returned, after dragging him from the room, Celeste walked over to Himmel and slapped him hard across the face. Although she showed no signs of continued violence, she, too, was taken to her room. W.--

"Why is it dark, Erik? Where are you?"

The patient moaned in discomfort. The scowl on his face only made his reluctance more infuriating to Dr. Richmond. The doctor sighed audibly and looked down at his pocket watch. Twenty minutes had already passed, and the subject had only repeated a handful of words that told the doctor nothing, nothing useful.

"Cold," he muttered again. His teeth began to chatter in response to the vivid fantasy he was experiencing.

Dr. Richmond would not lose his patience. He'd spent more time with cases where the rational mind had deteriorated to a mere shell and yet had managed to persevere until some outline and shape of a life could be discerned. Erik was not destroyed. His mind might be obsessed, but this was a man who had not lost his grip on reality. It should be simple to break into the traumatic episode in such a case. Somehow Erik was resisting the deep hypnotic suggestion.

"Erik, look around you. Tell me what you see."

A sound of distress exploded from Erik's pursed lips. This was not the way it was supposed to go. The patient was supposed to face the buried memories, divorced from the emotional impact they had originally inspired. Why was nothing as it should be with this man?

Exasperated, the doctor leaned back in his chair, closed his eyes, and counted silently to himself. He jerked forward when he heard the subject begin to murmur.

"Cold. Bars. The straw smells foul."

"Erik, where are you?" Had he gone back far enough? Bars suggested a prison. Perhaps not. Might the young Erik be on an excursion? A stable would not have bars, would it? It occurred to the doctor that Erik might remember an outing to a zoological park.

"Home."

"What is your home like? Look around and describe it to me. You're outside."

"No," the voice interrupted him. The doctor wasn't sure of the tone. Erik added, "Inside."

"Tell me what room you're in, Erik."

Silence.

"Is it a room where you eat?"

The patient nodded. Finally, they were getting somewhere.

"Then it's a dining room?"

The patient scowled and shook his head.

Swallowing his annoyance, Dr. Richmond pushed further. "What do you do in this room, Erik?"

"Sleep. Eat. Live."

"It sounds like more than a bedroom. Perhaps it's a small house?"

"I have no house."

"Erik, you must help me understand."

"Bars. Long, thick, rough to the touch, cold. My skin snags on the round surface. It hurts to lean against them. I need fresh water. There are bugs floating in the water from last night. One is swimming. I picked it out and laid it on the straw. I can touch the top now. I'm a monkey. I grab the bars overhead and lift my feet. I can hang upside down. I like feeling the blood rush to my head. I swing, but I have to watch for him. Everything's upside down. I want to watch him fall from the earth and fall and fall into endless sky. I can almost bend as well as Belle."

Dr. Richmond sat helplessly enthralled by the strange images in Erik's ravings. He examined Erik's face. The former pain and fear had faded as he described a moment of playful exuberance. He seemed almost content. But he made no sense.

"Erik, tell me where you live."

"I don't know," he said petulantly, as if he were annoyed to be interrupted.

"How old are you?"

"I don't know. I think I'm as old as Gregoire."

"Who's Gregoire?"

"The tiger."

Dr. Richmond rose from his seat and took several long strides to avoid shouting at Erik. "Who are your parents? Describe your parents."

Erik's contented placidity gave way to an anxious grimace.

"No."

"Erik, listen to me. I need to know who you are."

The subject seemed to be struggling with himself. Slowly resistance ebbed, yet the answer came haltingly. "No one. I'm…no…I'm… The letters on my cage. They say my name. They say who I am."

Cage? "What…?" The doctor paused. As unlikely as it seemed, he had heard of cruel cases where mental defectives and the severely deformed were kept under conditions little better than those for animals. "Tell me the letters, Erik. Read off the first letter to me."

"I can't read." The doctor could hear the prevarication in his excuse.

"Yes, you can, Erik. Tell me the first letter."

Reluctantly, Erik whispered, "D."

Richmond was pleased. "Now the next one."

"The bug is dead. I pushed him with my finger, but he won't move."

"Erik, leave the bug alone. Look at the sign. Read the second letter."

The patient was trembling slightly. His voice was paper thin as he complied with the doctor's demand. "E."

"Good. That's wonderful, Erik. You can see the next one, can't you? Tell me each of the next letters."

Erik barely nodded, and then the letters came rushing forward. "L, S, C, V, I, D, H, I, L."

Dr. Richmond wrote the letters down in the sequence given: DELSCVIDHIL. Nonsense! Sternly he addressed Erik, "Are you trying to make a fool of me, Erik?"

The subject lay still.

"What does this mean?" Then it dawned on him that the patient had complied, but he had jumbled the letters. He didn't want to see the name. The first two were surely correct. He had specifically asked for the first, then the second letter. After that, the doctor had not demanded the letters be given in order. Now more precisely, the doctor requested, "Give me the third letter, Erik."

"I."

The patient's sly hesitation registered. Richmond wrote the "I" on the sheet of paper, but he placed it third from the end.

"Is this one name or two?"

"It's what I am."

"Is it two separate words, Erik?"

Reluctantly, "Yes."

D E _ _ _ _ _ I _ _ _. "What is the last letter?"

"D." There was no hesitation. Perhaps it made sense. Whatever he was spelling began and ended with "D." He further reasoned that the "C" and "H" were likely together. Suddenly it came clear. "CHILD" most certainly was a possibility for the second word. Then the first had little or no choice. The "V" struck him as painfully clear! "DEVILS" was the only thing that made sense. Made sense? Surely he had wandered with Erik into a complex fantasy, a nightmare that was so vivid for the subject that he couldn't tell the difference between it and his own history.

"Who is Belle?" The doctor changed tactics.

"Tinkle, tinkle, tinkle."

"Who's Belle?"

"Belle, ma belle, ma cherie, ma femme petite qui me besse, qui me touche."

"Erik, I prefer that you not use French. Is Belle your mother?"

A lewd laugh erupted from the subject's mouth. His whole body convulsed with the suddenness of it.

"Belle? Belle bends her back and licks her heels. She presses her ankles against her ears and smiles. She smells of straw and wet darkness. She likes to play with toys. She likes to play in my cage when he's not looking. She's soft, so soft, not like the bars. She's strong, but small. She makes the bars disappear."

Richmond was momentarily shocked by the obvious arousal in his patient's voice and could see the effect, even now, of the images as Erik turned his body and writhed uncomfortably against the fabric of the couch.

"Erik, I want you to tell me how old Belle is."

Erik shook his head as if unwilling to let the images shift.

"How old is Belle? Is she young or old?"

"Young."

"Younger than you?"

"No. No, she's old."

Exasperated, Richmond tried again.

"Is she younger than thirty?"

"Yes."

"Is she younger than twenty-five?"

"Yes."

"Is she...?"

"She's seventeen. I remember. She told me on her birthday. She brought me some of her pastry. She smeared the cream over her body and let me lick it off."

"Erik, do you have a beard? Are you old enough to have a beard?"

Erik scowled and shook his head. "No."

Incredulous still, Richmond understood that the subject was not lying. A horrendous picture began to form in the doctor's imagination, a picture of a child in a cage, a deformed child, a child introduced to the complexities of passion too early. *Was this also the source of his obsession with music?*

"Where is the cage, Erik?"

"Inside the tent. Abel's tent."

"Who is Abel, Erik?"

Silence. The patient clutched his arms about his chest and drew his knees sharply into his body until his chin practically rested on his knees. A tremendous rush of sound came from his depths, one long note of grief or terror or pain. Dr. Richmond could not tell which.

Quickly the doctor brought Erik up from the deep layers of his mind until the man's body unfolded and his eyes snapped open. In the deep green of his eyes lingered the memory of that inner path. The residue of emotion was unavoidable. The patient remembered fleetingly where he had been, but his mind—given the post-hypnotic suggestion—could not hold it. Within seconds, he lay on the couch, exhausted, yet empty, as if he couldn't even recall having lain down.

CHAPTER 4

❈

Needles and Pins

Before the beginning of years
There came to the making of man
Time, with a gift of tears;
Grief, with a glass that ran;
Pleasure, with pain for leaven;
Summer, with flowers that fell;
Remembrance, fallen from heaven,
And madness risen from hell;
Strength without hands to smite;
Love that endures for a breath;
Night, the shadow of light,
And Life, the shadow of death.
　　　　　　"Atalanta in Calydon,"
　　　　　　Algernon Charles Swinburne

After Dr. Richmond took Erik away, Meg knew she had made a horrible mistake. She decided to go and demand that Erik be allowed to return home with her. To her dismay there was no word of Erik at the sanatorium that Richmond had mentioned. Neither did the staff have any information regarding Dr. Richmond. He had used the facilities for a short time, but he had vacated them. Fortunately, Meg recalled the name of a colleague at the university with whom Dr. Richmond had discussed his research. Without delay, Meg and Don Marcelo set out to get an appointment with Dr. Castanella.

However, the physician was unavailable, away at a conference. A grim awareness that she had lost Erik seized her. She sat and wrote to Raoul, pleading with him to come.

As soon as Raoul read Meg's frantic letter, he and Christine set out by train for Rome. On a warm, sunny morning in the third week of August, the Chagnys arrived. While Christine settled into their rooms at the estate, Raoul, crumpled and badly in need of a bath and shave, travel-weary and irritated, insisted on accompanying Meg to the university to speak with Dr. Castanella, who was supposed to have returned from his conference.

Raoul escorted Meg into Dr. Castanella's office.

"Please, sit down." Dr. Castanella was a squat man with a barrel chest and protuberant belly. He might have once been imposing, but years sitting behind his desk had not been good for his physique. "Signora Costanzi, I've long admired your work on stage."

Meg smiled curtly, having little patience for such nonsense at the moment. "Dr. Castanella, this is a friend of the family, the Count de Chagny."

"It is an honor, your grace."

Raoul bowed grimly and addressed the doctor. "We've come to see Sig. Costanzi. We mean to take him home."

From the puzzled look on the physician's face, it was painfully obvious that it was not going to be easy to get Erik released.

The count had no patience for flattery or delay. "Dr. Castanella, we are prepared to go to the police. It has been more than a week since Sig. Costanzi was taken from his home by your colleague, Dr. Richmond. Supposedly he was to be transferred to the asylum for treatment. Signora Costanzi has been told that he is not at the asylum."

"I'm sorry, but I don't know what you're talking about."

Meg stopped Raoul with a light hand on his sleeve. "Dr. Castanella, my father-in-law, Don Marcelo Costanzi, has gone daily to the asylum in search of news about my husband, Erik Costanzi. He was to be committed for a brief assessment and treatment, and I have had no word of him. They insist he's not a patient. Dr. Richmond promised me that I would be able to visit him daily, anytime I wished." Meg could see the same closed expression on the doctor's face that she'd seen at the sanatorium. The futility of her search overwhelmed her. She rose abruptly and shouted at the man, "I've changed my mind! I want my husband released. I have no idea what you're doing to him in that so-called hospital of yours, but I want him released."

Raoul tenderly urged Meg to sit back down. He had been observing the physician's obvious lack of concern. Dr. Castanella listened as if he were more interested in studying Meg's emotional outburst than in answering her questions.

Switching tactics, Raoul followed his hunch. "Perhaps there's been a mistake. Evidently Don Marcelo was told that there was no patient listed at the sanatorium or the hospital under the name of Erik Costanzi. Would he have been listed under a different name? Or might he have been transferred to another institution? We want to ascertain his condition. Surely his family has the right to…"

"My dear Count, did Don Marcelo sign any papers?"

"I did," Meg answered. "I signed the papers Dr. Richmond brought." There was a desperate guilt in her confession. Woefully fearful of what she'd done, she couldn't refrain from a weak defense. "My husband had been under a tremendous amount of pressure. He was acting…strangely. Dr. Richmond insisted that the situation was serious and offered to treat Erik. But…but…he…took him away… and there's no word… It's as if both of them have disappeared." She had been frightened since the men took Erik and locked him in the windowless wagon. She had been angry at everyone, but mostly at herself. She had not given in to despair except at night alone when she allowed herself the comfort of tears. She did not want to lose control now. She had finally gotten an interview with the head of the clinic, and surely he'd be able to help her.

Calmly, as if answering a student's foolish question after a lecture, Dr. Castanella disregarded Meg's tears and set about instructing her on the consequences of her actions. "Signora Costanzi, I'd no idea that Dr. Richmond had taken your husband on as a patient. I'm sorry you've wasted your time and energy at the asylum. You won't find either Sig. Costanzi or Dr. Richmond there. He was a visiting doctor, working on sabbatical. We had several interesting conversations, and I allowed him access to my facilities for the time he was here."

Raoul scowled at the impersonal position Dr. Castanella was taking. The hollow sensation in his gut was expanding as he realized the physician was disavowing any knowledge as to Erik's whereabouts.

Dr. Castanella saw the dawning of recognition on both his guests' faces. He, too, was puzzled and worried by a niggling suspicion that the young doctor he'd met may have embarked on an unethical course of action. Castanella was not a cruel man, nor was he overly courageous. He feared the power of the Costanzis should Dr. Richmond's brash actions become associated with his own practice.

"Then you're saying Sig. Costanzi is not one of your patients?"

"No, he's not. I was completely unaware that Dr. Richmond was considering taking on any patients while in Rome. And I'm afraid, Signora Costanzi, that there's little you can do to secure your husband's release if you signed any papers the doctor gave you. You most likely signed over any of your or your husband's rights to the doctor in charge. Only Richmond can release your husband from treatment. Madmen have no rights."

Meg rose to protest, but Raoul held her back. In a voice that masked his own concern, he asked, "Where is Dr. Richmond?"

"I wouldn't know."

Raoul spanned the gap between the doctor and himself in one long stride. Reaching across the desk, Raoul pulled the doctor roughly by the collar over the cluttered surface to within inches of his face.

"Dr. Castanella, I've not rested for the past two nights. I just arrived, haven't bathed or even eaten, so I'm not very comfortable. My patience is nonexistent. My friend has been kidnapped, and we've no idea where he is or how he's being treated. Dr. Castanella, I've visited asylums. I've seen the squalor, the neglect, the cruelty with which the 'insane' are handled. Now you're going to tell us everything you know about Dr. Richmond so that we can find Signora Costanzi's husband."

In the end, Raoul had to force Meg into the carriage and demand that the driver take her directly home. From Dr. Castanella's office, Raoul proceeded to the solicitor's. After several hours' conference with the lawyers, he returned to the Costanzi estate.

When Christine heard her husband's voice in the foyer, she came down the stairs to meet him and accompanied him silently to their rooms. She could tell that his news was not good.

An hour later, Raoul entered the parlor, refreshed, shaved, bathed, and dressed for dinner. Christine entered on his arm. Don Marcelo greeted his guests warmly, but everyone was obviously subdued given the circumstances of the Chagnys' visit. Madeleine asked the servant to inform her daughter that they were about to dine. Upon returning from the university, Meg had gone to tend to Mario. Within moments, anxious to hear what Raoul had discovered at the solicitor's, Meg joined them in the parlor where they had gathered.

"It's worse than we thought," said Raoul. "The papers you signed, Meg, in effect consigned Erik to Richmond's sole care." Although he would have liked to soften the blow, the situation was critical and no time could or should be wasted. They must face the facts, even those that were most upsetting. "Even if Erik asks to return, the decision lies only in Dr. Richmond's hands. Erik has no rights, nor do we."

"Oh, my God!" Madeleine rushed from the room. Meg blushed scarlet and dropped to a chair behind her. Her mother's tearful reaction brought home to her, more than Raoul's explanation, the extent to which Meg had imperiled her husband.

"Unfortunately, Dr. Richmond could be as far away as England. He's associated with the Bragant Institute. They treat the insane, cases of hysteria, all manner of mental illness. However, there are a number of other clinics—both private and public—with which he's associated. The solicitors have been charged with making inquiries. There's little we can do until they report back."

Sobbing, Meg slipped from the seat of her chair and fell to her knees. Christine came swiftly to her and pulled her roughly to her feet. Instead of comforting her, as Raoul had expected, Christine shook Meg. When Meg continued to cry hysterically, Christine slapped her across the face. Stunned, Meg's hand flew to her cheek.

"Now that I have your attention, Meg, I think you need to listen." There was no pity in Christine's voice. "You did this. You sent him away."

Raoul was shocked by the anger in his wife's tone. "Christine," he warned.

"No! Someone has to say it. He's not here to defend himself." Christine challenged them all. Then she turned her baleful gaze back to Meg. "You might as well have let him hang. It would have been a mercy. Oh, Meg, how could you?" Anger waned, and sadness took its place. Fiercely she embraced Meg. "What have you done?" At first Meg stiffened, but unable to break Christine's determined hold, she wrapped her arms around her friend and clung to her.

Raoul drew Don Marcelo aside and spoke in a low whisper. "Once we know where Erik is, we've no choice but to get him out by whatever means we have. I'm afraid the law can do nothing for us. As a matter of fact, it is entirely on the side of the medical profession in this instance. Even if we had the law on our side, it might be risky to involve the local authorities."

"What do you suggest, Raoul?"

"I think we might have to ignore the law."

Christine and Meg had overheard the men talking. Meg broke away from Christine and faced the men.

"I'll do anything to get my husband back. Anything!"

Meg helped Mario to the chair by the window. His leg was broken in several places, and it was urgent that he change positions frequently to keep the circulation healthy. It was a miracle that he had survived the accident. At least Meg had saved Erik the painful vigil over Mario's suffering. The days of waiting to find out anything about Erik were only bearable because she dedicated herself to working with her son. She worked with him daily, forcing Mario to do the exercises prescribed by the physician. She had to be strict even when it tore at her to put him through such pain. After only a couple of weeks, she'd seen an improvement, the movements were more fluid, he complained much less, and she could see the strength returning to his limbs. He'd even begun to smile and tease her the way he used to before the accident.

When the children had asked where their father was, Meg had told them as much of the truth as she could bear. "Dr. Richmond thinks your father needs to go away for a while. He'll be back as soon as he's feeling rested." Mario had been ill, unconscious for days. When he called for Erik, Meg could only say that he was gone and that he'd be back soon.

Now with Raoul and Christine at the estate, the children understood the adults' sullen, worried expressions and their hushed whispers. They knew something was wrong. Raoul had offered to speak with the boys, but Meg knew it was her obligation. She explained to them that she had made a mistake and allowed a doctor to take their father away for treatment. She asked their forgiveness and said she'd never stop until she brought him back.

All but Mario were silent. "Maman? Was Papa upset when I had the accident?"

"Of course, Mario. He was very worried for you."

"Why did you think he was sick? Why did you believe the doctor?"

François scowled at Mario and told him to stop hounding his mother. "She didn't mean to do it! He was acting like a madman."

Meg gasped to hear François describe his father in such an unkind light. But it was true. He had not been rational. He'd been distraught.

"Acting like a madman? What did he do? Can you tell me what he did that was so crazy? Did he forget who he was? Did he think he could fly? Did he try to hurt you?" In spite of his clumsy cast, Mario stood. He was somewhat shorter than François, but that didn't stop him from coming face to face with him. Both boys were angry.

Meg squeezed between them and told them to sit down and keep silent. She reluctantly turned to Mario to explain, "Erik thought you were dead. He…he…was violent with those who tried to take you away from him. Even I couldn't convince him that you were not dead. The doctor who had visited us said that he could help your father. He said that he might lose his mind and do us and himself harm."

"He'd never hurt us! Never!" Mario rarely raised his voice to Meg. But he was incapable of disguising his distress and anger. "I don't care what happened, he'd die before he'd hurt any of us!"

François lowered his face to his hands. The memory of Leroux washed over him. The police officer had kidnapped him. Deranged, the man had threatened to kill him and his father. François knew what madness looked like. But Leroux wasn't the only image that came to mind.

"You didn't see Papa the night he killed Leroux."

Mario was about to speak, but François was right. They weren't supposed to know all the details, but they had overheard the adults talking about their father's determination to bury himself, along with the other man's corpse, in the underground tunnels of the Opera Populaire. Erik had not been himself.

Laurette had begun to cry quietly, and Meg held her tightly. "François, you're right. Your father was devastated. I'm afraid that the accident with Mario pushed him over the edge. But he came back to us that time, and he'll come back this time, too. I know him. I know how…how…strong he can be. He loves us. He knows we love him. It will bring him back to us."

11 October

Dear Maman,

Raoul, Christine, and I arrived in Austria just a week ago. We're near Linz, in a small hamlet in the valley. This is the last clinic on our list on the continent. My greatest fear is that Dr. Richmond may have taken Erik to England or America. Raoul has spent the last few days investigating the clinic.

The people with whom Raoul has spoken say that the patients at the madhouse, as they call it, are not from the area. A man who works on the grounds says there are only a few patients and three to four doctors. The clinic draws on the city for most of its employees, and there's a bit of resentment here in the town for that reason.

Apparently the patients remain on the premises, as do the staff. The rumor is that once a patient goes inside, he never comes out again. Raoul intends to go tomorrow and ask for work. This has proven the best way to find out, with any certainty, if Erik is a patient. If we're fortunate, we should know in a couple of days if Erik is here.

Kiss my babes for me, Maman, and tell them that we are determined to find their father. I can't bear the thought of failure. What will they say if I come home without Erik? I think I shall die if we don't find him. But I will keep my courage up. I must. More than one of the physicians with whom we spoke in Vienna mentioned this clinic, and they knew Dr. Richmond by reputation. So I will trust that it is only a matter of time now and I'll have Erik back with me. I won't think of anything else but that.

Your loving daughter, Meg

"You can start by cleaning out the latrines. Afterwards, you can take the early shift."

Raoul didn't need a disguise. He and the doctor had never met. All he'd required were the appropriate clothes. Meg made sure he'd removed his jewelry—especially the ring Christine had given him on their last anniversary. She regretted his finely manicured hands, but she gave him workmen's soiled gloves. They would effectively hide the fact he'd not done manual labor.

Gunter sneered at the count. Herr Raoul Gilbert didn't seem somehow to be the type they needed at the clinic. He was strong enough, he supposed, but his attitude was peculiar. He stood too stiffly—as if he had a board up his back, and he looked everyone too directly in the eye. Proud. Too sure of himself.

"Tomorrow, if you're still here, you'll help with the baths."

Raoul choked back a feeling of dread. Perhaps he'd find a way to locate Erik and get him out before he had to subject himself to that particular humiliation.

Unfortunately, cleaning the latrines had been far worse than any embarrassment he might have suffered giving a madman a bath.

"I saw him." Raoul ripped the gloves from his hands and threw them on the floor. If Meg had not been in the room, he'd have stripped naked and washed himself inch by inch using the drinking water on the small bar. But Meg was keeping vigil with Christine in the tiny parlor that adjoined each of the two bedrooms at the fashionable inn. Christine stared aghast at the state of her husband's attire. They had rented a very modest room above a tavern closer to the clinic where Raoul was to change into his disguise. That room would be his address for work. He was supposed to change his clothes there before returning to the stately rooms at the inn.

"Is he all right?" Christine spoke before Meg even had a chance.

Raoul could see the fear and shame Meg barely held in check. Softly, he addressed his answer to her. "He's well."

Christine heard the reticence in those words. Raoul glanced at her meaningfully, and she understood that there was something that he was holding back.

"Did you speak with him? Did you tell him we were here to get him out?" Heartened by Raoul's success, Meg was overwhelmed by a need to know everything.

"No."

Meg masked her disappointment. They had found him. After weeks and weeks of travel and innumerous dead ends, never certain that they had turned the last stone, dreading coming to the end of possible destinations, they had finally found him at a private clinic in a small town in Austria. Erik had been distraught when they had carried him off. That had been in August, and now it was October. How could he have endured abduction and confinement with no ill effect, no crippling injury to his mind and soul?

Meg needed more details. Was he thinner? Had he shaven? Did he wear his mask? In what condition were his clothes? Was he alert or drugged? Did he seem…insane?

Raoul cautiously shared as much as he thought wise, enough to satisfy Meg's demands without troubling her further.

With some difficulty, Christine convinced Meg to retire so that Raoul could bathe and rest. He was expected back within six hours to cover the late shift.

Once the door to their bedroom was locked and Raoul lay back in the steaming bathwater, Christine turned on him and demanded, "What's his true condition?"

"I told you," he said, his voice flat. He rinsed the lather from his long, dark blond hair. The tension had just begun to ease, but now he stiffened at his wife's tone. She rarely addressed him with such a fierce attitude. He almost smiled at the way she stood. She was so thin and delicate, yet she had taken up a pose, her hands on either hip, her feet slightly spread, her jaw thrust forward, as if she were the town bully.

"I heard the pretty lies you told Meg so she'd not fall apart. I want the truth." When Raoul didn't answer, Christine wrestled the bar of soap from his slippery grasp and lathered his back. At first her strokes were rough and vigorous but abruptly she lightened her touch and drew large, soft circles, starting at his shoulders and slowly winding her way down below the surface of the water. Raoul let out little groans of pleasure as he bent over the water, stretching to give her full access to his body. Christine could feel him relax under her constant, gentle pressure. "Tell me how it went. Did they actually believe you to be a worker?"

"I peppered my speech with a few choice expressions from conversations I've heard at pubs and country inns. They didn't expect me to sound natural. I'm a foreigner. They think all us Frenchmen are odd, so I was convincing enough."

She moved her strokes along his arms and waited.

"You can't imagine the literal 'shit' I went through today." He shuddered at the memory. He forgot what he was saying when Christine leaned over him and began to soap his chest. "You'll get wet."

"Never mind," she purred in his ear as she drew larger and larger circles of soap across his chest and down his abdomen. "Tell me more."

"More? Oh, you don't want to know the manual labor I did today. I know what you want."

Her hand disappeared below the soapy surface of the water. Raoul's former fatigue gave way to desire. He encircled her waist with his arm and would have pulled her to the water except that she knew what he was up to and slipped away from the tub.

"Oh no you don't. My gown may not yet be ruined." She worked at her buttons with anxious fingers. Keeping her eyes on Raoul, who lay back in the water and watched her with pleasure, she slipped the gown from her shoulders and began to unlace her undergarments. "I think I might lie down to take a nap."

Raoul reached over the edge of the tub for the towel that had been set aside for him. He stood. Water cascaded down his limbs. He wrapped the thick, plush towel about his hips and stepped out onto the rug.

Having slipped out of her own clothes and under the covers, Christine smiled at Raoul and patted the empty place next to her, inviting him to come.

"I think a nap would be just the thing at this moment." Raoul let the towel drop to the floor and strode to his side of the bed.

Later, when the angle of the sun had crawled along the surface of the wall, Raoul roused from his slumber to see Christine's face hovering over his in the bed. Refreshed and deeply content, he judged that he must have slept for hours.

"Now. Tell me the truth. How is he?" Christine insisted, picking up the thread of their previous conversation as if nothing had intervened between that moment and this one.

Raoul sighed. He recognized her determined look. He understood that she was worried. "He's all right, really. In every important sense of the word."

Christine scowled at the puzzling response. Her silence demanded he continue.

"He's alive. He seems to be uninjured." Raoul fought to hold back his own misgivings. He knew details would be disturbing, that Christine would glimpse the truth behind the reassurances.

"And?"

He swallowed before adding, "His hands are wrapped in bandages like mittens." He saw the glint of fear in her eyes and rushed to explain, "His hands are fine. They remove the wrappings when he eats, for example."

"Then why?"

Raoul could think of a hundred reasons, not least of which was simply the intention to take from Erik the ability to perform even the basic minimal actions, to humiliate him, to keep him from touching... But such general reasons seemed empty. "I can't say, Christine." Raoul lifted his hands, fanned his fingers, and wiggled them as if somehow they'd reveal their secret power to him. "I don't understand it. It's really his fingers that are bound. What do they want to keep him from doing? If he'd tried to strangle someone, wouldn't they have simply put him in isolation or chained him? Why remove his ability to use his fingers?"

Watching the curious movements Raoul was making, Christine sat up on the bed. The thought struck both of them at the same time.

"Do they have a piano or any other instruments?" she asked.

"No. Nothing. That's it, isn't it?"

They had observed Erik playing his silent concertos. If he couldn't play a real instrument, he would certainly have played an imaginary one. The first time they'd witnessed the strange activity, not only had his fingers danced across a wooden table, but he'd actually taken blank sheets of paper and written a score for a lovely little piece.

Later, when they had returned to the Costanzi estate, Erik sat and played the piece on the piano. Whenever they were sedentary or if he was bored, he'd compose in his head, his fingers miming the sounds.

"Why would they take his music from him? It's so…cruel."

"I don't know," whispered Raoul as he comforted Christine. The sadness of it had not struck Raoul until he saw his wife brush away her sudden tears. He smoothed her long brown hair away from her face.

In a small voice, moist and warm at the base of his throat, she urged him. "Don't tell Meg."

14 October

Dearest Maman,

We've found him, Maman. He's here at Richmond's private clinic. Raoul went in disguise seeking work at the clinic. We rented a small room over a tavern near the clinic for Raoul. There he is to change his clothes and spend some time to keep up appearances. However, yesterday, without changing from his workmen's clothes, he came directly to our rooms, he was so anxious to report his news.

Erik's safe. He's alive. Raoul caught only a glimpse of Erik, but he could reassure us of his general wellbeing. I was so thankful, Maman, that I couldn't ask anything more. I just wanted Raoul to repeat over and over again that we've found him.

It's so hard to wait. Raoul insists that we move slowly. He has ascertained that Dr. Richmond is indeed in the clinic. I must stay out of sight so as not to alert him of my presence or our designs. Raoul fears he'll do something drastic—remove Erik to another institute or worse. I can't think of what Raoul is suggesting. It's too monstrous. But Raoul argues that Richmond has acted most heinously, and even if the law is on the doctor's side, his actions have been unethical. He may, if challenged, wish to erase all evidence of his connection to Erik.

Maman, I have a confession. I'm frightened. I'm elated that we've found Erik, but what if we can't rescue him? What if he's really ill? Oh, Maman, I know I was wrong to do what I did, but he's been locked away in a madhouse for months now. What have they done to him?

Whatever his condition, I'm determined to take him away from there. We will do what we can to heal him, but it will be in the heart of his family, not among strangers.

I will write again as soon as I can.

Your loving daughter, Meg

Meg couldn't sit by and do nothing.

"I'm determined to do this, Christine. So either help me get these buttoned up properly or get someone who can."

The uniform stretched tightly over Meg's bosom. She had had little time to get her disguise together. It took Meg considerable time and an exorbitant amount of money to convince the seamstress to sell her one of the uniforms from the order commissioned by the nearby clinic. It was a standard nurse's uniform, starched white and unadorned, stiff lines that bespoke the honesty and determination of one who comes to the aid of the suffering.

"But Meg, you're not a nurse. You haven't any training."

"No, but I'll get the position," she retorted.

"How will you manage that?" Christine snapped, incredulous.

"My interview with Dr. Flescher. I'll use whatever I have to in order to convince the good doctor that he wants me around."

Christine's mouth fell open at Meg's provocative smirk.

"What are you thinking of doing, Meg?"

Meg's complexion darkened before she turned again to the mirror to pin her blond hair tightly against her scalp. Her silence appalled Christine, for she understood how desperate her friend was. Meg grimaced as she drove in the pins as if she meant to punish herself.

"You wouldn't. Meg, tell me you wouldn't do anything you'd be ashamed of. Erik would…"

"Stop, Christine. Don't, please, don't say another word."

"What if you become pregnant?"

Meg rose so violently that she toppled the chair. "I know how to protect myself, Christine. There are ways to be… Anyway, I don't think it will come to that!"

"But you expect you might have to!"

"I want to be prepared for any eventuality. I'll do what I must!" Meg lowered her voice, which had risen to an angry pitch. She couldn't involve Raoul; he'd stop her. She hissed at Christine, "I'll flirt with the doctor, nothing more. I'm a novice, so he'll instruct me and won't be surprised by my inadequacy." Seeing her friend's ambivalence, Meg pushed on. "I've heard that he's a kind man, an honorable man. I don't think he'll make improper demands on me."

"But…"

"You said it, Christine. I signed the papers. I helped them take Erik away. And if I have to lie with a stranger to get Erik free of that clinic, I'll be the most wanton whore you can imagine. Dr. Flescher can do with me what he will, but I'll have Erik back in my arms."

"Erik would…"

"Erik will never know. Promise me."

Meg could see that Christine was thinking of her own experiences with Erik's jealousy. Could he bear to know that Meg had willingly been intimate with another man? It was a question that had dogged Meg's own thoughts, filling her with misgivings. Yet, knowing him better than Christine ever had, Meg was sure that he'd forgive her, but would he be able to forgive himself? If she did this to rescue him, he'd berate himself. He'd loathe his inability to protect her.

In a small voice, but clear-eyed, Christine wilted before Meg's resolve. She promised. Erik would never learn the truth from her lips. But she still didn't think Meg had thought her plan out.

"What good do you think you'll be able to do? Do the nurses even come into direct contact with the patients unless they're ill or injured? With his constitution, do you imagine Erik a frequent visitor to the infirmary?"

"There are medications to dispense. There might be ways to get word to him. Eventually, perhaps I can persuade Dr. Flescher to help us."

Christine pursed her lips, torn by the need to hope in the face of such improbabilities. "If you go with Dr. Flescher on rounds, you may well run straight into Dr. Richmond. What then?"

"Surely the uniform and this hideous monstrosity of a hat will protect me from easy discovery should Dr. Richmond happen to see me passing in the hallway."

Meg pinned the winged wimple in place. It covered her glorious blond hair and framed her heart-shaped face. In the cold flat surface of the mirror, her eyes seemed disproportionately large.

"Doe eyes," she whispered.

"Come again?"

Meg turned away from the stranger mocking her from the glass. "Oh, just something Erik used to say."

"I shouldn't have blamed you, Meg." Christine laid her hand on Meg's arm. Only when Meg ceased her nervous fidgeting at the pleats in her uniform and returned Christine's earnest gaze did the latter attempt a reassuring smile. "You thought you were helping him."

"Well, yes." Gone was Meg's former confident demeanor. "I did believe that Edward—Dr. Richmond—was a good man." She didn't mean for it to sound like an excuse. She couldn't deny her own complicity, for she thought of her role in the affair as nothing less than a betrayal of the man she had vowed to love—the man she still loved. "I thought he'd take some of Erik's pain away from him."

"I thought you were both happy. I thought he'd finally laid his demons to rest."

"Will Erik ever be truly free of them?"

Christine couldn't think of how to respond. She had never heard Meg sound so defeated, so utterly hopeless.

"Please, don't look at me that way. It's all well and good for you. You aren't with him day in and day out. Even if you were, he'd never show you the face he shows me. And you know I'm not referring to his mask or his disfigurement. When Dr. Richmond described the symptoms that he treated in his practice, I began to see some of Erik's behaviors in a new light. Then, after Mario's accident, Erik was acting bizarre, more than panicked, less and less like himself. I was frightened. But I was wrong. I was wrong to do what I did. I should not have signed those papers. It doesn't matter that I didn't understand what they were. Richmond lied, manipulated us. We should have waited. Erik might have calmed down. I think he was calming down. Until I gave him the medicine Richmond prescribed. Oh, Christine, I'm so frightened. Something is horribly wrong. Not to inform us of the location of the clinic? To have left the country with Erik? And to tell no one? He lied to us. And I trusted him—a complete stranger—more than I trusted my own husband. And every night I crawl into bed alone and wonder what Richmond is doing to him. Now I can see it clearly. He doesn't know Erik. He saw a madman, someone to dissect and study. I don't know how Erik will bear it."

Christine didn't have the heart to argue. Instead, she slid her arm around Meg's waist and waited for her friend to calm.

"He's always needed your faith and hope, Meg. Have you given up on him?" Christine's and Meg's eyes met in the mirror.

"No, never." Meg batted away at the tears trailing across her cheeks. She turned and took Christine's hands in hers. She sniffled loudly and smiled. "He's impossible. He's terrible and wonderful. And nothing will ever destroy him. I know that, too. I just forget sometimes."

"That's why I'm here, to remind you."

Meg took Christine's hand and kissed it hard.

"I can't go looking like this. He'll think I have some awful disease." Meg took the handkerchief Christine offered and wiped at her face roughly. She stood and examined herself again in the mirror. "Almost done."

"I suppose I should help you into those hideous shoes." Christine bent and retrieved a pair of mannish black shoes with laces. "Then your costume will be complete."

Meg smiled and grabbed her friend's hands in hers. "You'll never guess what name I'm using. Remember the old dragon in the laundry at the Opera Populaire that always made us wash our own underclothes?"

"I haven't thought of her for years!"

"Lucky you! She embarrassed me on a number of occasions. You're looking at the widow Boncoeur, Constance Boncoeur."

"Oh, you can't!"

"Oh, but I can."

October 20, 1888

My dearest Meg,

I hope this letter arrives. I have posted it to the address on your most recent letter. We are relieved to know that you have found him. My heart weeps to think of what he's been going through. Our anxiety and fear cannot rival what he must have felt when they tore him from his home.

I know you are heartily sorry for the mistake you made. Although I never agreed with it, I understood your reasons and know that you only had Erik's wellbeing in mind. But I must caution you that Erik might not understand. And it may be difficult for him to forgive you. You must prepare yourself for his initial rejection and anger. Be very careful. Do not put yourself in harm's way. I don't believe he'd mean to hurt you, but we can't know what this experience has done to him. We can only pray that he has not truly gone mad. I beg you to allow Raoul and Christine to handle this. He will not see them as threats. He will understand they are there to help him. He may not know how to interpret your presence. You must give him time.

Would that we could call the authorities and have this Dr. Richmond put away for a thousand years. I might have changed my mind about the treatment had Dr. Richmond done what he said he was going to do. We might have visited Erik. With the evidence of our own eyes, we might have judged whether or not he was being helped by the treatment. Had they remained here, we could have elicited the help of our friends, many of whom are very powerful. He would not have been perpetually condemned to the asylum had we insisted on his release. But this physician had no intention of healing him. We must ask why it was necessary to kidnap him and transport him to an undisclosed location. We must ask what he has meant to do to Erik.

Take my words to heart, ma petite. I do not want you to be in danger. I couldn't bear to lose you. And Erik, too, would ultimately be destroyed if you came to harm at his hands. If he were to act rashly and hurt you, how could he ever face your children? Be safe and take good care of yourself and your husband. I pray that soon you all come back to us.

Your loving Maman

"Frau Boncoeur, I can't see how you expect me to hire you without references. It's clear from our conversation that you have no training." Dr. Flescher was struck by the strange woman seated across from him. "This is a nice letter from the Countess de Chagny, but it only proves that you attended a sickly uncle of hers through a lingering illness. It's hardly the experience we require."

"I know, Dr. Flescher, that my credentials are wanting. I wouldn't have to work as a nurse, then. I could clean or I could organize your papers. I have a good hand and am quite able to transcribe documents or file them for you."

"But there are people on staff who clean for us. And as to my papers, I do them myself. There aren't so many that I need help with them. What I need is someone who can suture wounds, give injections, lance boils, empty bedpans."

"I can empty bedpans!" Meg rushed to say. "I can also wield a needle, even if it's only been through cloth. I imagine it's not so difficult to stitch up a bit of loose skin."

"Oh do you?" laughed the doctor. He liked the woman. She had spunk. But he sighed and shook his head.

Meg rose from her seat and walked around the desk to stand intimately close to the young doctor. Flescher knit his brow in puzzlement at the woman's closeness. She was small, perfectly proportioned. He knew that most men would appreciate her generous bosom. It was striking in contrast to the dainty smallness of her waist, the length of her neck, the delicate shape of her arms. He imagined that most men would lust after her. He was not most men. Had she been flat-chested and in trousers, her taut body might have enticed him. Nevertheless he was made uneasy by her obvious appeal to his masculinity.

"Frau Boncoeur, I must ask you to step away." He used his kindest, most patient tone with her. He didn't want to spurn her. She had admitted she was recently widowed. She might be lonely, desperate for someone to be gentle with her. Perhaps she needed money.

"Please, Dr. Flescher." Meg leaned even closer toward the young doctor. He was comely, his straight chestnut hair was swept to the side, off his forehead. Only a stray lock fell over his eyebrow, brushed his long lashes. He had large, brown eyes with a touch of gold to them. Meg willed herself to see him as a lover might. She imagined herself in an opera singing a love song to the man. She would seduce him if she needed to. "I would do anything to have this position. I need this position."

Dr. Flescher had not been approached so brazenly by a woman since the sister of a lover had tried to seduce him, to convince him that he should prefer women's soft bodies instead of the hard muscled bodies of men. He had lain with her, begrudgingly, perhaps to prove to himself that he could. But never again.

"Please, step back before you embarrass us both." He stood and took Meg by the elbow and escorted her to her seat again. "I have other proclivities, my dear." He knew that it was risky to be so direct with the young woman, but he wanted no misunderstandings.

Meg paled visibly and sat hard in the wooden chair. She couldn't look at Dr. Flescher for several moments so deep was her despair. She had no leverage with this man. How would she convince him to let her stay?

"Would there be any hope of a position somewhere else in the clinic?" she asked feebly, grabbing at straws.

Dr. Flescher studied her hands. They were delicate and soft. Those hands had not done manual labor, had not spent hours in hot soapy water, had not scrubbed floors with bristle brushes. "You need this job that much?" he asked. He leaned one hip on the edge of the desk and studied her.

Meg nodded, unable to trust her voice. She had to be here. Erik was here, somewhere in the building. Somehow she'd find a way to get word to him, to see him.

"Well, I suppose I could take you on as a kind of apprentice." Dr. Flescher smiled at Meg's upturned face. She was really quite charming, he thought.

"I'll do whatever you want."

"Yes, I already know that," he chuckled. "But don't worry. We won't ask you to do anything too horrid." As an afterthought he asked, "You don't faint at the sight of blood, do you?"

Meg thought of blood, of Erik's blood when she visited him in the prison cell, of Raoul's blood after Leroux's attack, of Mario's blood when they carried him to his room. "Oh, no, Doctor. I'm quite used to blood."

"Jesus, Mary, and Joseph!"

Meg saw the drops of blood on the floor as she came out of the pharmacy to see what the commotion was about. Hilda was still muttering under her breath as she led the men to the surgery. One of the men, obviously attendants at the clinic from the look of their uniforms, shouted out for her to get Dr. Flescher. Among them, they were carrying a body.

Meg turned quickly on her heels, set down the box of morphine she'd been about to store in the locked cabinet next to the surgery, and set off for the adjoining apartment where the doctor retired when not on duty.

She knocked several times before she heard someone rouse on the other side. Eventually the doctor opened the door and peeked out. The moment he saw Constance Boncoeur, he gathered the edges of his robe even more tightly together and ran a hand through his chestnut hair.

"There's a patient, Dr. Flescher. He's bleeding."

"Get started. I'll be right there."

Meg quickly returned to the infirmary. A half-formed thought clawed at the back of her mind, making her pulse race. The blood led her to the surgery. Hilda's broad back impeded Meg's view of the patient. The nurse was already cutting away the poor man's clothes.

Silently Meg prayed she'd not faint if Hilda asked her to do anything.

"Get some hot, soapy water, Connie." Without a glance in her direction, Hilda instructed her.

She went to the basin and poured the soap powder into a basin. The angry tones of the attendants' voices distracted Meg. As she prepared the soapy water, she could hear them talking excitedly about the attempted escape. She felt her ears twitch as she strained to hear them.

"He can bleed to death as far as I'm concerned," said one.

"You should have called the dogs off, Gunter," whispered one of the others.

"Keep your mouth shut, Himmel," said the first man. All but one of the attendants filed out of the room.

"Come on Gilbert," barked Gunter. "He's not going to give us any more trouble," Then more sharply, he snapped, "What you waiting for? Let's go!"

When she heard the name, she looked up to see Raoul reluctantly follow the others out into the hall. He slipped through the door before she could catch his eye. She turned toward the table where the wounded man lay. But before she could step close enough to look over Hilda's shoulder, the nurse sent her for gauze and wrappings.

This was a crisis. A man's life might be on the line. Meg was supposed to be a nurse. She prayed God she didn't do more harm than good.

"There. That's better, isn't it?" Hilda straightened and turned to smile at Meg who was rummaging through the cabinet at the far end of the room in search of gauze and bandages. "I'll be needing that pan of water soon, Connie."

Meg brought several stacks of cloth of various sizes to a nearby cart. She rushed to the counter to get the basin of water.

The nurse had removed the patient's clothes and thrown a sheet over him. Giggling wickedly, she held up the edge of the sheet and turned a sly smile toward Meg. "Oooooh! You want to see this, Connie! This one's a real stud, he is. Should be in a stable, this one."

When Meg looked back over her shoulder, Hilda dropped the sheet and spread her hands as if to measure something.

"Hilda! Give the man some respect," Meg chided as she tried to carry the heavy basin of water without the liquid sloshing over the sides. She placed it next to the stacks of bandages on the cart and returned to the cabinet to get a second basin and the instruments she assumed the doctor would most likely need.

"Oh, I'd like to give the man more than a bit of respect. I think I could get past the face. The rest of him is so sweet!"

"What?" Meg dropped the pan that she had just pulled down from the shelf. It clattered noisily to the floor.

"Jesus, Connie. He's not dead yet. No call to bang the pan to raise the dead." Hilda came and picked up the metal basin and the instruments it had held. Meg's hands were shaking as she bent to help. Misunderstanding Meg's reaction, Hilda kindly scolded, "Ah go on now. You've seen worse, sure you have. Go on over and take a good look and shake the jitters out. He just takes a bit of getting used to. He's been in before."

Meg gratefully rose and approached the table. Part of her was overjoyed at the possibility it was Erik; the other, horrified to find him unconscious and bleeding in the infirmary, prayed it wasn't her husband.

On the table, still dirty and bloody, lay Erik, his face lolled to one side. Meg bit her lower lip hard to quell her reaction. Glancing behind her, she saw Hilda remove the basin and reach for a clean one. No one was around so she quickly reached out her hand to caress his cheek. His skin was cold and clammy. Meg's heart lurched in panic, but she could see his chest rise and fall. He was not dead. There was blood everywhere. For a moment, she was lightheaded and thought she'd faint. Disgusted with her own weakness, she fought back waves of dizziness. She'd not let him out of her sight.

"What's the condition, Hilda?" Dr. Flescher marched in, the sleep forcefully shaken from his body. He washed his hands roughly in the small basin Hilda had prepared for him.

"Dogs got him. Mostly his forearms. Looks like Gunter had to knock him about a bit, too."

Anger, hot and white, blinded Meg for a moment. Dogs! They'd set the dogs on him as if he were an animal. Then they had beaten him! She wanted to wrap him in her arms and sing to him.

"Connie, he needs to be cleaned. Damn! Hilda you know better than to leave a wound bleeding like that."

Quickly, Dr. Flescher grabbed a large swatch of cloth and circling around the table wrapped Erik's arm. Only then did Meg see a small pool of blood on the floor on the opposite side of the tall, metal table. All business and apologies, Hilda rushed to assist the doctor. She took over the wrapping and applied firm pressure over the gash.

The next several moments passed as if in a haze. Meg heard the doctor's comments, followed his orders in spite of her trembling hands, and watched him stitch and bind her husband's wounds. After the more pressing ones were dealt with, Dr. Flescher pulled back the sheet to inspect the contusions on Erik's torso. Except during the examination, he carefully kept the patient covered. Hilda's demeanor, too, was strictly professional as they worked on Erik, no hint of the risqué teasing in her serious and competent handling of the patient. When Dr. Flescher gently pulled the sheet up to hide Erik's nakedness and Hilda had removed the bloodied swabs, Meg could barely restrain her need to thank the doctor and his nurse. She swallowed the stuttering impulse to weep.

"When he wakes, give him only small amounts of water. I'll need to check his urine so keep the bedpan nearby and wake me when he passes any liquids. I'm going back to bed." He washed his hands while Meg and Hilda struggled to put a nightshirt on the patient. "I gave him something for the pain. Call me if he wakes and requires more. Otherwise, I'd like to get a full four more hours if possible." As an afterthought, he addressed Meg. "Good job, Connie. Shouldn't you be on your way home? It's well past your shift."

Startled by the idea of leaving Erik, Meg asked without thinking, "Will he be all right?"

Both Hilda and Dr. Flescher were taken aback by Connie's intense interest. Dr. Flescher answered, "Yes. He's a beautiful specimen of a man. Healthy as a horse. You can run along now, Constance."

With a dismissive wave of her hand, Hilda added, "He'll shake this off like the other times."

"The other times?" Meg stepped to the side to allow Hilda to reach the instrument tray.

"Should we send for Dr. Richmond?" asked Hilda, ignoring Meg.

"No, let him sleep. We'll inform him in the morning."

Seeing that Meg had not yet departed, Dr. Flescher gently took her by the arm and started to escort her out. Meg resisted.

"Perhaps I could stay and…and…help Hilda clean up. I'm not tired."

Dr. Flescher hesitated. For a moment, Meg feared that the doctor could see straight through her and understood why she was there.

"I need the money," she lied. She lowered her eyes as if ashamed of her situation.

Apparently satisfied by the excuse, the doctor released Meg's elbow. Slowly, he relented. "Well, I suppose Hilda wouldn't mind the company. And if Erik wakes and needs help, it might be easier if there were two of you."

Meg was strangely comforted by the way the doctor said Erik's name. It also occurred to her that the doctor must not consider him dangerous in the least if he had meant to leave Hilda alone and in charge. Meg gathered these proofs and cradled them. He was not violent. He was not mad.

"Thank you, Dr. Flescher."

It took an annoyingly long time to convince Hilda to stop sneaking peeks at Erik's body and to accept Meg's offer to sit vigil over the patient.

"Ah, I know what you're up to," said Hilda, in a sarcastic stage whisper. Meg's heart was in her throat until Hilda went on to explain, "You want him to yourself, don't you? Well, you can look all you like but don't touch. That is, don't touch *him*, if you catch my drift. He could wake all of a sudden, and you don't want to be caught with the evidence in your hands. And believe me, I think it'll take both hands, my dear." Meg felt a tremendous desire to pull Hilda's blond hair out by the roots. No one should be on such a familiar footing with her husband's body! Even Christine had not inspired Meg with as sharp an edge of jealous anger as Hilda had unwittingly done with her lewd references to Erik's manhood.

After Hilda was safely gone, Meg pulled a chair up to Erik's bed. She listened to his smooth, even breathing, studied the cut of his jaw and chin, considered the length of his hair. It was sorely in need of a trim. It lay tangled and dirty on the pillow. They had washed him, first around the wounds and later the rest of him, all except the hair which lay matted against his skull. She had detested watching Hilda rub the wet, soapy cloth over his body even though, in her role as nurse, she was coolly objective and professional. Meg had wanted to rip the cloth from her hands and insist on cleaning her husband herself, but it would have been thought peculiar by both Hilda and Dr. Flescher. She had had to bite her already bleeding lip to keep from screaming.

Now he smelled of disinfectant with a slight hint of blood. She couldn't resist leaning over his lips and tasting his breath.

Raoul had been among the men who had carried Erik, wounded and unconscious, into the infirmary. So he knew where Erik was. Would he come back? Would this be the moment to get Erik out of the asylum? Suddenly alert, Meg rued that Erik had been drugged. Should she rouse him? No, what would she alone be able to do? Erik may not even be able to walk out of the infirmary on his own two feet. He was too big for her to handle. Even Raoul and she together might not be able to remove him unless Erik was able to bear some of his weight and help them.

In that instant Meg recalled Hilda's reference to 'other times.' He'd been in the infirmary before, often enough that Hilda had grown accustomed to his face and bold in her treatment of him.

Reluctantly, Meg left Erik's side and went in search of Hilda. She found her fellow worker, curled up on one of the unoccupied beds in the general room. This is where they'd move Erik come morning. Meg gently shook the woman who turned grumpily on her side away from the annoyance.

"Hilda? Hilda, wake up."

"Uhhhhh," she groaned.

"Hilda, the patient? When did you first meet him?"

CHAPTER 5

❀

The Dancer in the Dark

*O heavens! is't possible, a young maid's wits
Should be as mortal as an old man's life?
Nature is fine in love, and where 'tis fine,
It sends some precious instance of itself
After the thing it loves.*

Hamlet, William Shakespeare

12 Sept 1888

Dr. Klinen,

You must forgive my delay in answering your last several letters. I've been sorely disappointed that you've been unable to extricate yourself from the pedagogical duties at Edinburgh in order to join me here, at my clinic. I have taken a bold step, perhaps a dangerous step, and fear that it may be something that I come to regret. I'm in sore need of your help and counsel in the matter. I'm sorry to say that I have lost my way.

Everything had seemed so clear while I was in Rome. Even you recognized the opportunity Erik

Costanzi offered. It took little to convince his family that Costanzi was ill and that I had the knowledge and skills to make him well again. Once I sowed the seeds of doubt, his wife and his father saw everything Costanzi did through the filter of misgivings. But that would have been insufficient for them to conclude that he was mad. Unfortunately I was forced to manipulate events to a certain extent. Without entering into detail, let me say that Costanzi is now a patient at the clinic, and his family has no idea where I've taken him nor any means of getting him back.

I was invigorated by the unbridled opportunity to study this man. I imagined he would eventually open up to me and between us we would begin to understand how to tap the power of the mind. We would see the means to separate madness and genius and find the key to unleash in all men the power that lies untapped. We would create a world filled with mental giants, scientific and artistic geniuses, men of vision and wondrous capabilities and talents.

Little did I know what I might find when I delved into this subject's secrets. He has been uncooperative, refusing to speak. He was force-fed in the first weeks. I had no choice but to use hypnotism in our sessions, for he could not trust me. I've also had to medicate him in order to make him tractable. His stubbornness has forced me to resort to means that strike me as extreme. He has so strongly felt the absence of music that he has begun to pretend to play the piano, making empty gestures across any flat surface within his reach. I have had to bind his hands. His reaction was immediately violent.

The sessions I've conducted so far bring up bizarre fancies that obviously are inventions of a deeply disjointed mind. I would that I could share them with you. Perhaps you could see some path to follow through the chaotic nightmare of his delusions.

Not one shred of sanity have I unearthed. How is it possible for him to have functioned if the bedrock of his mind is a maze of horror? He sees himself as an animal, a supernatural entity. He believes that he is the son of Satan…the Antichrist. This he's said to me under deep hypnosis, Dr. Klinen.

I'm loath to admit it, but I wish I had not taken the steps I have to bring the man here. His madness is well beyond my means of dealing with it. I have no idea how to help him, and yet I'm afraid that I have unleashed some dire beast in him that he had somehow miraculously kept under restraints. If he wasn't mad before, I fear he now is.

I beg you to find some means to draw your term to an end and to come to my assistance. You were right to caution me against my obsessions. If there were a way to restore him to his family, I would. But the deeper I delve into his case, the more horror I find. I despair that I'll ever find the way out.

Your humble student, Edward

Patient 579, cell c, floor 3, Erik Costanzi. 12 Sept.

Patient has been lethargic. Remained the entire morning staring out the window. Celeste rose from her couch and approached Patient. She seemed to be speaking with him. We couldn't hear. Apparently Erik was unresponsive until she reached out and touched his face. He batted her hand away. Gunter was ready to subdue Costanzi, but Celeste stepped back only slightly and burst into wild laughter. It seemed directed at Costanzi. Since Patient remained still, not reacting to Celeste, Gunter restrained himself.

Celeste was agitated the rest of the day. She kept stealing glances at Costanzi who rigidly maintained his distance from everyone in the room. Celeste demanded that she be given clay, any material that she could work. When Gunter told her to sit down and be quiet, she started to shout and demanded to speak with Dr. Richmond. Gunter threatened to tie her down if she didn't stop shouting. Celeste spit in his face. I was at the station, keeping an eye on things, when unexpectedly Costanzi left his place by the window and stepped between Gunter and Celeste. I rushed in at once. Although it looked as if Costanzi might attack Gunter, the two men faced each other for several tense moments until I managed to convince Celeste to back away.

Costanzi didn't return to his seat by the window until Gunter withdrew.

Laurent uncharacteristically stepped into Gunter's path and cursed at him belligerently. Gunter pushed him aside, and Laurent made as if he might strike Gunter. Before anything could happen, Costanzi shouted at Laurent to step away. We were all so surprised to hear the patient's voice that no one, at first, made a move. A moment later, Laurent eased his way to the opposite side of the room, mumbling obscenities compulsively under his breath. He is slavishly obedient to Costanzi.

Curiously everyone else, including Heinrich, was subdued. "X" was the only one who seemed to react negatively to the scene. He wet himself and was removed.

Lisbet refused to come out of her room today. Gunter offered to check on her. H.-

Patient 579, cell c, floor 3, Erik Costanzi. 13 Sept.

Celeste worked frenetically the entire morning on the clay.
Lisbet sat in a corner biting at her nails. She has bitten them to the quick and still she continues to gnaw at the raw, tender flesh. Perhaps Dr. Flescher should examine her.
After his morning session with Dr. Richmond, Erik was brought to the common room. Since bandages have been removed, Patient

often keeps hands buried between his thighs or under his armpits. Lethargic, the first hour. Later, Patient rose to walk perimeter several times. The third or fourth turn round the room, he stopped near Lisbet. He seemed to study her for several moments. Afterwards, he stood at the window and stared out. Celeste shouted at him repeatedly, trying to get his attention. He ignored her. H.--

"Why are you crying, Erik?"

"Stop, please. Please, don't do that." Erik's voice was high, almost childlike. Tears flowed unchecked down his face. He had curled into a ball on the couch.

"Erik, what is happening?"

...

"Erik, are you in the cage?"

...

Dr. Richmond scowled at the patient. Perhaps he should bring Erik forward, forward to some point in his memories where he was more articulate.

"Erik, step away from the door. You are older now."

"No, don't." The childlike voice keened.

"We will come to a door, Erik. Not the door that you fear. A door that will bring you forward. Do you see the door?" Erik's breathing calmed, the violent emotions subdued. "Open the door and step across the threshold. You are older now. What do you see, Erik?"

"The walls are glowing. It's as if candles were flickering across the walls." Erik's voice had matured, become deep and sonorous.

Dr. Richmond sat up on the edge of his chair in anticipation. Finally, he had gotten the subject away from his persecution fantasy.

"Describe your surroundings, Erik."

"Dark. It's very dark, except for the tiny lights. Stone, mossy stone."

"What other senses can you use to tell me about where you are? Can you hear anything?"

"Yes, yes, yes!" Erik stretched out his legs and relaxed his body. His contentment was obvious. His voice was lush, charged with pleasure.

"Good. Erik, this is very good. You're comfortable. What do you hear that pleases you so?"

"Sshhhh." Erik scowled at the doctor's voice that interrupted such beautiful sounds.

"Erik, you must tell me. I can't hear what you hear. Tell me."

Reluctantly, Erik turned his ear toward the doctor's demand, his eyes still shut, attending to inner sounds and sights. "Such a sweet voice."

"Who? Whose voice do you hear?"

"The child, the girl."

"Whose child is she?"

"No one's. She's alone. She's an orphan. She's alone, so lonely, poor child."

"Is she in the room with you? Do you see her?"

"No, no one comes down here."

"Where is 'down here'?"

"Down, down, down. Hundreds of steps, across the black lake, to my world."

"Your world, Erik, what is it like?"

"Cold. Damp. Filled with flickering lights, full of echoes."

"Go on, Erik."

"My world. Endless night. The water drips from the stone ceiling. Things scurry along the narrow channels. My boat rocks across the liquid blackness, scrapes against the stony shore. Hollow and scratchy and slick. But none of these sounds survives when I play my music. Months it took me to bring the organ to my rooms. I had all that I needed—an entire world that I stole from those above and carried down the stairs and across the lake. I built my world, piece by piece, here in my caverns of endless night. Everything, everything I needed was here. Until…"

"Until what, Erik?"

"Until I heard the child singing. No, not singing. It was when I heard…her…crying."

"What is the child's name?"

The patient was so enmeshed in his delusions that Richmond knew his question had gone unheard.

"I was her angel. I sang to her, but she thought I didn't exist. She called me her angel, so that's who I became." Erik paused. The skin around his eyes tensed. His lips turned down in a frown. Dr. Richmond noted a distinct change in the patient's mood. With a voice that simmered low with unspent anger, Erik continued, "But they won't let me be her angel."

Slowly Erik raised his knees to his chest once more as if to comfort and protect himself. His hands closed tightly into fists. Dr. Richmond could see in Erik's body the battle between anger and despair.

"Why won't they let you be her angel?" the doctor asked.

"Angels are beautiful. Angels work miracles. They have no desires but to please, to comfort, to teach, to protect. Angels…Angels…are…not…men. They don't feel…what I… I can't be an angel. Angels live in the air, in the sunlight. They float on warm breezes and sing of joy. The weight of the earth crushes down around me." Anger had won the battle.

"Who are they, the ones who won't let you be the child's angel?"

"They live in the light. They lock the doors. They nail boards across the passages."

"Who locks the doors? Why do they lock the doors?

"To keep me in the dark."

"Why?"

"To keep me away."

"Why?"

"Angels are beautiful. I am not an angel."

"Who keeps you in the dark, Erik?" Richmond could feel the rising fear in Erik. His breathing had become rapid and shallow. His skin had paled. "Who…?"

"He says that I'm a monster."

"Who are you afraid of?"

…

"Who says that you are a monster and locks you away?"

"He will tear my wings and nail me to the rock."

"Who is this person?"

...

"Describe him."

...

"Erik, you must answer me."

...

Dr. Richmond clenched his jaw, swallowing his urge to demand that the subject answer. Instead he turned the questioning again in another direction. "Erik, let's move around the room. What else do you see?"

"Mirrors," came his voice, quiet and frightened.

"Why are you afraid, Erik?"

"Not afraid. I can bear to look at the monster."

"What monster, Erik?"

"The one I see in the mirror. But I fooled him. I disguised myself. The monster hides when he sees me in the mirror. Someday, I'll go above. I'll walk onto the stage, and I'll sing. The monster will die. The music will kill it."

"Erik, look in the mirror and tell me what you see?"

"No. No, I don't have to."

"Tell me what you see in the mirror." Dr. Richmond lowered his voice, his tone stern.

"The sewers are full of rats. During the rainy season the smell of raw sewage backs up even to my rooms. I have to go up to the opera house to escape the fumes. I sleep in the hallways, the hidden corridors, between the walls. I slip into their rooms and steal small comforts—a pillow, a warm coat. I...I...go up into the special box and listen to the rehearsal. I study the score M. Reyer marks."

"Erik. The mirror. Look into it. Tell me what you see."

"I...I...I see his...face... His eyes are dark green and bloody... his face is...purple...his head lolls on his shoulders...his tongue is thick, dry, swollen and won't fit back inside his mouth."

"Who is it you see? Who, Erik?"

"Him. The one who beats me."

"Who is it? What's his name?"

"The man who feeds me, beats me, feeds me, beats me."

"Erik, you are avoiding the question. Who is he?"

"He keeps the key to the cage. He throws water at me to clean the filth. He throws water across the floor of the cage. The straw is wet and smells. He beats me when I'm bad."

"His name?"

"Abel."

"What have you done that he keeps you in a cage?"

"I'm bad." Erik's voice had sunk to a mere whisper.

"What have you done?"

...

"Why does he keep you in a cage? Why does he beat...?"

"I AM BAD." The shout was angry and anguished.

"Erik, what have you done that is bad?"

...

"Why does Abel punish you?"

"He despises me."

"Why?"

...

"Erik, you're at the door. Everything bad is locked away behind that door. You can walk away from the door. You can wake up. Now. Wake up."

Patient 579, cell c, floor 3, Erik Costanzi. 14 September

Patient was allowed to stay in his room today. Celeste seemed ill at ease. Laurent was a bit more vocal than he has been in the past several days. He kept vigil at the door as if waiting for Erik to be brought to the common room. The others carried on as usual with their routine.

Patient slept the entire morning after his session with Dr. Richmond. H.--

Dr. Richmond scanned his notes again. Was the man more psychotic than he'd originally thought? Several sessions of hypnosis had afforded an accumulation of nightmarish images. They were obviously delusions. Yet somewhere in the horror of the cage and subterranean tunnels there must be some key to Costanzi's past. The only other possibility was too horrendous to contemplate. Could Erik be recounting actual experiences—memory and not delusion?

If such were the case, then Erik Costanzi may have already committed several violent acts.

The doctor jotted down the images Erik had described in the last session even though they were nothing more than fancies of a sick mind. Hidden memories were what he sought, memories the patient had not allowed himself to recall, buried deeply behind all the lies and nonsense that defended him from the truth. The persecution complex was obvious in the scenario of the cage. Such a preposterous fantasy suggested a need on the part of the patient to be singled out. His disfigurement no doubt formed the basis for such a negative notoriety. His true suffering became amplified via the fantasy of torture and abuse and raised the subject's pain to monumental scale. As if he were a martyr or Christ himself, the patient luxuriated in his vilification and suffering.

Music, on the other hand, provided another means by which the patient would be singled out. Unlike the scenario of suffering, the route of genius had its pitfalls. To rise to prominence and gain the world's attention by excelling in some area—such as art—required constant energy, work, inspiration, and the possibilities of failure were many. To suffer as the target of hatred and violence took little energy—given the boy's disfigurement and disadvantages in race and class—and was infinitely more within the child's grasp. It was gloriously foolproof. Indeed his fantasies suggested that continued persecution was always within one's grasp if one were prepared to strike out on occasion with violence. Erik embraced his pain for it made him unique and powerful. It justified even murder!

Dr. Richmond tapped the pen on the opened page of the journal. The black scratches on the page stared up angrily at him. Something did not fit. The trauma of the cage did not have any connection to his music. Except for the lone reference to a charm bracelet whose tinkling notes had struck his attention, there was no mention of music in these fantasies. Did the subject create a bifurcated fantasy in which his attraction and focus on music was safeguarded from an equally or more powerful fantasy of his persecution?

Music was his salvation. What would he be like without it?

Richmond scowled. This line of thinking didn't corroborate his thesis. On the contrary, it suggested that genius was, at least in Costanzi's case, a move away from madness, a path that sought a positive outlet for the patient's unhealthy tendencies. Music was the counterbalance to his wild fantasies of violence. It kept the door closed, the door behind which the patient saw only blood.

Denying the patient the means to express his energies in music might eventually unlock that door. It could perhaps unleash the patient's violence at the same time. The patient would not be able to repress the originating trauma should his defenses be taken from him.

Once this trauma is revealed, will the patient no longer be compelled to compose?

"Erik, who is the monster you see in the mirror?"

"Me, of course." The vulnerability and cooperation Dr. Richmond had witnessed in the prior session had disappeared.

"I could hypnotize you and get the information I'm after, but it would not lead you to any self-awareness. There's no reason for you to hide secrets that you've already told me."

"I don't want you to waste your time, Dr. Richmond."

"Do you think you're beyond help?"

Refusing to speak, Erik looked away.

"I see. You're resigned to live here the rest of your life, a madman."

That shocked Erik into attention. Even though the look in Erik's eyes was searing, Dr. Richmond did not lower his gaze.

"You're angry. Why?"

"Because you stole me from my life!" The dam had broken. Erik sprang from his seat and glowered at Dr. Richmond. "You took me away from my grieving family! I didn't even have time to say goodbye to him before they buried him. You took me and threw me in a box, like an animal. I couldn't…breathe." Anger threatened to give way to despair. Erik choked back his tears and towered menacingly over the doctor's desk. In spite of his distress, rage seething just below the surface, Erik reasoned with Richmond as if there were nothing more important than convincing this man—who had robbed him of everything—that he had existed. "I have done wondrous things. I…I have lived like a man. And you came…you put out all the lights. You extinguished even the lights of heaven. You sent me back to hell!"

Slowly Dr. Richmond felt for the small button under the lip of his desk and pressed it. A tiny alarm rang in the adjoining room where the doctor's clerk immediately responded by calling the waiting attendants. Himmel and Gunter rushed into the room.

Startled by their entrance, Erik whirled to face them but didn't move. Gunter was poised to spring upon the patient, but Dr. Richmond raised his hand to indicate that the attendants were to stay where they were and wait for his sign.

"Erik?" The doctor's voice was calm as if nothing had happened. "Will you calm down and take your seat again?"

Slowly Erik turned to face Richmond. He leaned over the desk and whispered, "Have you ever looked, Dr. Richmond, in a mirror and asked yourself these questions? What do *you* see? I know what lies in the mirror when *I* look. I know. I can tell you that it isn't always good to know. I don't look in the mirror anymore. It can't show me anything that I've not already seen."

"Gunter." Dr. Richmond couldn't mask his disquiet as he called out to one of the guards standing attentively just inside the doorway. "Take the prisoner to the common room."

Himmel and Gunter both approached Erik at the same instant. As they reached out to take him by the arm, Erik wrenched away from them and walked to the door. Careful to keep an eye on him, the attendants allowed Erik to go unassisted down the long corridor to the common room.

"Who is the monster you see in the mirror?" the doctor had asked him.

One monster stood behind another, an infinite regression of monsters in the slick, cold surface. The man had kept him a caged animal—a prized exhibit at the fair. Only many, many years later had Erik learned that the man had sired him. But Erik had not been a child. The man had cursed him as a beast. And as a beast, Erik had often been beaten. But the man had never been so cruel as to lash Erik with a whip and humiliate him before a crowd. The boy had momentarily lost all sense as to what was expected of him. The spectators were particularly vicious, except for a handful of angels who stood among the hardened customers. The crowd jeered and threw bits of refuse at him, calling to him to perform for them as if he, like the ragged doll he clutched tightly to his bare chest, were a monkey. The angels were soft, delicate creatures, with pale skin and long, flowing hair. One stood too close. The crowd jostled her, pushing her up against the side of the cage itself. Her thin, delicate fingers gripped the bars in sympathy. He was watching the tears spill over the rim of her eyes and course down her cheeks when the man yelled at him. He felt the sack pulled roughly from his ugly face. The man tossed it into the corner of the hay-strewn cage.

The first lash surprised more than hurt him. He would have scurried away from the pain except that the man had grabbed a fistful of his hair and savagely shook him like a wet rag. The boy writhed on the dirty straw, all visions of angels cast out forever. The crowd's raucous shouts increased in proportion to the man's cruelty. Over time, the child had hardened himself to the blows, requiring the man to impose ever sharper, longer, and more vicious punishment to elicit the cries for pity that the man thrived on. The pain was different this time from all the other times the boy had been beaten. It threatened to kill something inside him, something the man had never touched before. Finally, the boy lay still. He had not begged for mercy. Yet another lashing of the whip ripped his flesh. The leather cut across a raw wound, and at last he felt the man's grip lighten on his scalp. He lay limp and bleeding, waiting for the torment to abate. The jeers of the crowd dissipated as his fingers clutched at the bloodied straw. He slowly opened his eyes and saw the man's back in the opened doorway of the cage. The man's shoulders were bent over the coins the crowd had left for the exhibit of the Devil's Child. The tent was rapidly emptying. The angels, too, were abandoning the boy to his torment. With them went all hope.

Something felt as if it had broken inside him. He crawled to a corner of the cage and brushed the straw aside from the base of the last bar. He forced his fingers to unwrap the short length of rope, and without remorse or hesitation, he encircled the man's throat, twisted, and pulled with all his strength until the towering mass of flesh fell and twitched no more.

Beyond the man, the Devil's Child glimpsed the slim figure of an angel who, being the last to depart, standing transfixed in the narrow slit of the tent, had turned and watched in horror as he murdered his keeper. She rushed forward and took his hand in hers, and he nearly collapsed with the warmth of it in his dirty palm.

Erik didn't want to remember his crimes. He had no need for more detail. The images had dulled over time. Suddenly the doctor was demanding that he breathe new vigor into the dead play of shadow and light, that he infuse the scene with jarring sound and fresh color, that he feel the lash across his body. Father, his father, he had banished the word as well as the memories. Along with them, he had blotted out the grimace on the dead man's face. Erik didn't want to see the tongue swollen with black blood, two dark green eyes jutting out from the spongy flesh. Father, the word lied. He tried to evoke some feeling that wasn't twisted and evil. He resisted the voice of the doctor, his insistence that he recount again and again the scene of horror. *What did he feel?* Would the doctor not leave him anything?

These were his crimes, his torment, his scourge, and he wanted them locked away deep and forgotten in the farthest and darkest corner of his soul.

Dr. Richmond's journal. 16 September

As incredible as it seems, I believe that the incidents the subject recalls and describes under hypnosis are not delusions. If they are, they are incredibly consistent and have completely eradicated any other experiences or memories.

Yesterday's session was particularly difficult. I decided to forego hypnosis, but Erik was uncooperative and belligerent to an extreme. I could see that my questions were dangerously close to sensitive ground. Today I was resolved to question the subject directly about his past, using the information that I had collected during hypnosis. I was no longer confident that the fantastic scenes he described were delusions.

When I asked Erik to tell me about the Devil's Child, he turned ashen. The unguarded moment of shock confirmed for me his recognition. He tried to discount the allusion, saying at first that he didn't know to what I was referring. I persisted, and finally he broke into a thousand pieces. He was no longer able to maintain a false bravado. He lowered his gaze, as if ashamed, and confessed that he had been raised in a cage and put on exhibit at a traveling fair. Then I asked him—point blank—who Abel was. The answer shocked me, for he had not revealed as much under hypnosis.

Abel was evidently not only his tormentor, the man who kept him in a cage and displayed him as a monstrosity. He was Erik's father. I feared the answer, but I asked him what happened to Abel. I had before me the horrific image of the man's face in the mirror. Gripped by ill defined emotion, the patient confessed that he had murdered his own father. Whatever my previous motivation in bringing the subject to the clinic, this revelation has erased any of my previous doubts. If not here, this man should certainly have been in prison.

Patient 579, cell c, floor 3, Erik Costanzi. 20 September

This is the first day since his return to the common room that Erik Costanzi has moved from his seat near the window. Dr. Richmond cut his medication in half for the past two days, and there are finally signs of the patient's return to some awareness of his surroundings.

Celeste keeps asking for more clay. She is evidently working on a bust of Erik. She is intent on her work, yelling and lashing out with whatever is at hand, even throwing wet clay at anyone who interferes or distracts her from her goal. She continually reworks the surface of the bust which now has the distinct form of a man's shoulders and head. Evidently, she is more pleased with the sculpted contours of the shoulders and neck than with the features of the face, for she has left these parts of the object untouched for days. On the other hand, the face and shape of the head are continually fashioned, destroyed, and reconstructed. Whenever her attention is not on the bust itself, Celeste observes Erik.

Patient (Erik) spent a good deal of time near Lisbet. Although he studied her, as if he had placed her under a microscope, Lisbet stared out into space and paid him no attention. Since she cannot abide anyone being close, no one was seated on either side of her. Erik, however, took a spot by the window only a few meters distant from the girl. He remained still for some time, looking out at the grounds. We thought it peculiar because, after awhile, we couldn't help but think he had drawn closer to her. Yet he stood in nearly the same position as before, and we had not noticed him move. We watched carefully and soon perceived that he was speaking. But he must have been speaking to himself, for he was so quiet we couldn't hear him and there was no one nearby except the girl. Of course, Lisbet doesn't respond to anyone, and this case was no different.

There was no change in the situation over the course of nearly an hour, except that we were convinced that Erik was slowly, almost imperceptibly, approaching the girl. Lisbet remained huddled in the chair until close to sunset when the light was suffused with an orange glow and shone in from the farthest windows on the southern side. Erik was practically standing next to her chair by then, and Lisbet stretched her limbs as if waking from a long sleep. She rose from the chair and began to sway and then to dance in soft, sensuous movements, stretching and bending her body. She never left the band of light that streamed through the windows. When Erik turned to watch her, it was evident that he was singing very softly, for we could see the muscles of his face and throat move. Gunter protested that Erik should be restrained. Dr. Richmond's orders stand. However, the moment we came near, Erik faced us, his song silenced. Unfortunately, the interruption sent Lisbet hiding behind the sofa where Celeste was pounding and kneading savagely at her clay sculpture.

Gunter suggested Lisbet should be taken to her room again. Erik seemed poised to intervene. But before he could, Gunter had rounded the sofa and taken Lisbet by the arm. Lisbet went limp. Gunter was forced to pick her up and carry her. As Gunter was about to carry the girl off, Celeste threw herself on him. Her hands covered in clay, she jumped on Gunter's back and raked her fingernails across both sides of his face. I rushed to Gunter's assistance, pulling Celeste off and pushing her down onto the sofa. My back was turned so I saw nothing. I only heard the thud of a body slamming against a wall. When I turned around, Gunter lay in a heap, unconscious, by the door. Erik held Lisbet in his arms, her head resting against his shoulder. He carried her to her usual chair and set her down.

I called for assistance. Although the rest of the population was disturbed by the strange events, everything had happened so quickly that the other inmates settled down almost in the same instant. Even Laurent mumbled his litany of curses quietly to himself, watched from across the room, and did not get involved.

Gunter was taken to the infirmary. Based on the general calm of the residents, it was decided that we would take no action. Lisbet roused after Gunter was carried away. Unusually alert, she alternately watched Celeste who had returned to her sculpting and Erik who stood still and quiet, his face turned toward the setting sun. H.--

Patient 579, cell c, floor 3, Erik Costanzi. 23 September

Erik had to be subdued today again. Gunter insisted that he was inciting the others to disorder. When asked to step away from the window where he had insisted on standing, he refused to cooperate.

Gunter called for Audrich and Wilhelm to subdue the patient by force and to remove him to his room.

The moment Audrich and Wilhelm wrestled with Erik, taking him from the common room, Lisbet became hysterical. Gunter volunteered to take Lisbet to her room so that she could rest.

When Gunter returned to the observation desk, he reported that Erik had continued to resist the attendants' efforts to restrain him in his room, but the attendants finally managed to manacle him to the bed. Neither patient is to return to the common room today. H.--

Infirmary 27 September

Treated: Patient, cell c, floor 3, Erik Costanzi for broken nose and various contusions.
Notes:
Patient was brought in with bloody nose. Guard said patient fell as he was being taken to his room after an emotional outburst in the common room. Nose was broken. Reset with some difficulty given that the underlying structure on one side was already abnormal. I have tried to set it to rights, according to the alignment if the nose had been normal. In the course of my examination I found several other bruises. Although these injuries are not serious, I will keep Patient here for a day or two of observation. I must protest the brutal treatment given to this man. There are bruises and several raw wounds that have ulcerated round his ankles and wrists. He has never shown any signs of violence when under my care. I have asked him to tell me why he has had difficulties with the guards. He won't speak of anything related to himself. However, he insists that I examine one of the other patients in the ward, the young girl, Lisbet. He believes that there is something physically the matter with her and that she needs treatment. When asked for details, he would not speak.

Dr. Flescher

Infirmary 28 September

Treated: Lisbet Schneider, cell f, floor 3, female, approximately fourteen years old. Routine examination.

Subject is a fourteen-year-old girl. She has been institutionalized for more than two years. Parents committed child saying that she experienced seizures and had visions. Stepmother complained that Lisbet tried to smother her four-month-old half brother in his crib. Father deceased, stepmother signed the commitment papers. While resident, she has shown no signs of violence.

Lisbet is slender, too small for her age. Had she not come from a prominent family, I should say she had suffered from neglect as a child, specifically from lack of proper nutrition. Given her general lack of development, her cycles have been irregular. Girl stopped speaking at onset of menarche, according to her stepmother, some ten months before she was brought to the clinic.

I examined the girl in the presence of my nurse, for the child was very frightened. I found bruises on her ribs and upper arms consistent with violent restraint. Although there is no record in the daily log, I was told that she had to be restrained on several occasions. However, there were bruises on other parts of her body that would not arise from restraints. In particular, her inner thighs, as well as her buttocks, have several large bruises. Other bruises under her chin, behind her jaw, and along the soft flesh of her neck seem possible only if someone were to have tightly gripped and squeezed her face and throat.

Her general health is good, but I found the tissue around her vagina to be swollen and raw. Her breasts, too, are swollen and tender. She has recently been sexually abused. Evidence suggests that it was not consensual. I daresay that there have been several incidents since the bruises I noted above are from different moments, some being fresh and others having already begun to fade. Although I regretted putting this child through the shame and discomfort, I have examined her internally and have found that she is at least three months pregnant. When I asked her who had done this to her, she sobbed and flailed as if in great fear. She will not tell us who has raped her.

There are few in this clinic who have access to our patients and opportunity to molest a child like this one with impunity. Although I have my suspicions, there is little chance that I can prove it without a witness.

Dr. Flescher

Dr. Richmond's journal. 2nd October

A trying session with Costanzi. I have not put him under hypnosis for several days. Instead I have tried to get him to confide in me his history. In particular, I have asked him what happened after he killed his father and what he felt when he killed him. It appears that he was not aware at the time that Abel was his father. This he learned later.

Instead of answering my questions, he demanded that I tell him why his wife had him committed and if she has asked to see him. He refused to accept my answers, which were terse and to the point. First I reminded him that he had assaulted several individuals and that he had acted bizarrely the day we removed him from his home, and second I told him that his wife has not asked to see him. In point of fact, these answers are true. He was very quiet for several moments. I sensed he was waging some inner struggle to quell his emotions.

I was very surprised by his next statement. It was a request, not a question. He asked if he might have a violin or access to a piano or organ. Instead of answering him, I asked him to talk about his music.

I thought he was going to decline, as he had with so many of my other demands, but he didn't. In a completely different tone of voice he started to describe how music had come to him.

He said, "I heard sounds as if they were not isolated, separate units, but rather as if they were plotted on a score and played in harmony or counterpoint. I heard them linked sometimes and at others rendered in a staccato chain whose rhythm I would also find. The first sounds at the fair were strange tinny noises from pipe organs, whining notes from accordions, the sharp blare of the barker, the endless jumbling, rolling notes of crowds of people passing to and fro outside the tent where they kept my cage. When I listened intently to those sounds, I would bead them together until they made a necklace of notes and melodies that I could play and replay in my mind. I passed much of my time listening and reordering the notes and memorizing them. The bars would disappear. When Abel would come to the cage…"

Here I interrupted the patient and forced him to say "my father" instead of Abel.

"When my…father…came to the cage, I sometimes would not hear him. It made everything else less real, less bright, less sharp, less…" I encouraged him to continue. "I took the music with me when I left the cage."

Here I pressed him to tell me where he had gone after he murdered his father. Again, as before, I insisted that he say the words.

"I can't tell you where I went after I killed my father. It's not my secret alone. Those who protected me have every right to have it remain a secret."

I reluctantly held my tongue. Instead I asked him to tell me what music came to mean to him, later as a young man, and how he became aware of his extraordinary talent.

"I learned by watching and listening to other musicians and to a musical director at an opera house. Once I learned how to read music, I was able to write down all the melodies that I heard inside my head. There was not a moment that I did not hear some strain, some melody, some string of notes that were mine. I knew they were mine. I sometimes hummed the tunes I heard the director play, but I could tell which were mine. I didn't only hear them, I felt them. They were tied to my flesh, almost as if they were anchored deep inside my gut. Sometimes it hurt to feel them rise to my throat or ear, as if they were stretching their roots, threatening to rip live tissue inside me. Music was warm. It wrapped round me and held me together inside the notes."

I asked him if the music made him feel anything specific. Did he feel protected, joyful, hungry, violent? Or did the music awaken his lust? I could see that my questions disturbed him. Again I thought he would not answer me. He made me wait for several moments. It seemed an impossibly long time to wait, but I felt that we were on the verge of a confession.

"It made me feel powerful."

"What is power, Erik? What does power mean to you?"

His eyes turned sly and heavy-lidded. I considered calling the attendants in. He seemed to have grown several inches in the chair. Even the air about us was charged somehow with an intensity that had not been there. I am not a susceptible man. I have retained my equilibrium with vicious madmen who have committed the most heinous crimes, but for a moment I must confess that I was afraid.

"Power? Power is bending and breaking the bars of that cage. It's stopping the black heart of the man who tortured me. Power?" His eyes became luminescent with excitement as he spoke. He had slid forward to the edge of the chair. "Power is raw. It makes the colors vivid, the sounds clear and pure. Objects seem alive to your touch. Everyone bows down to power. It drowns all pain, washes away all fears. It feels…it…feels…like a woman's mouth on your cock."

"Is it like making love to your wife?"

He drew back and scowled, as if genuinely unsure. "No," he answered, barely over a whisper. "No and yes. I don't want to remember that."

"But you asked me about Meg just a while ago."

"I want to go back to my room now."

"Do you miss her, Erik? Do you feel the urge to masturbate?" Erik glared at me. The temperature in the room plummeted. But I refused to let him intimidate me. "Which do you miss more, Erik? Music or sexual intercourse with your wife?" When he didn't answer, I continued, "You've masturbated, have you not?"

"There is no privacy, as you well know."

"That doesn't stop most of our patients. Only the catatonics fail to indulge in self abuse. Laurent does it repeatedly, each night, without fail."

"Do you enjoy watching him, Dr. Richmond?"

I refused to rise to his bait. "Which do you need more, Erik?"

"I can't live without the music."

Surprised at the ease of his choice, I pushed on, "What did you feel when I had your hands wrapped in gauze?"

"Why did you order that? Why did you forbid me to use my fingers to make music?"

"But you didn't make music, Erik. The table is not a piano."

"It hurt no one. Music cannot hurt anyone. Why would you try to take my music away?"

"We don't indulge flights from reality, Erik."

"You're wrong. The music is real. I played the notes as I heard them in my mind. Why would you forbid my music?"

"Because it is tied to your violence, as well."

"No! You're wrong." He sprang from the chair and leaned his weight on my desk, his hands splayed across the surface. "It's what I fled to. If it hadn't been for the music, I might have kept on killing, killing them all."

"Sit down, Erik. Even now, you're becoming upset."

"Upset? I'm furious because you insist on depriving me of the only beautiful thing that is mine! I need my music."

I steepled my fingers in front of my face and leaned back in my chair. I waited.

"Erik, sit down."

An audible exhalation seemed to dull the sharpness of his anger. He wiped his hand across his face as if to rid himself of his frustration. Then he pulled the chair to the side and sat at an angle to the desk. I was relieved not to fall under his direct gaze.

"What if I allowed you some privacy? Say, once a week?"

"What do you mean?" he asked, a hint of wary curiosity in his tone.

"What if I allowed you to occupy a room in which I had no means of observing you, for an hour, once a week? You could relieve yourself in private, no one watching."

"Relieve myself?"

"Yes."

"The conditions?"

"Only one. You would give up music. You would have your hands bound if necessary. You would swear to silence the music. Even inside your mind. Even if only you can hear it. Silence, Erik. Silence the music."

"No."

"Is it so easy for you to choose between these two drives? Don't you miss your wife's touch? Her kisses? Her lips on your lips? Or do you prefer the image of her mouth wrapped round your…?"

I thought he would rip my throat out. Fortunately the loud banging of his chair as he leapt across my desk and grabbed me by the neck was heard in the next room. Gunter and Wilhelm came to my assistance. They managed to pull his fingers away, but they had to wrench them, one by one, from my throat. I fell sputtering and coughing to the ground. I felt the spasms of the forceful intake of air and the subsequent choking as if his fingers still clamped down on my airways.

There is no doubt in my mind that Costanzi is a maniac. He could easily kill. Music may indeed be what has saved him from committing horrors, but it is linked, too, to his needs. It masks his other impulses, but it doesn't eradicate them. Even though he chooses music over his sexual impulses, his loss of control in my office is directly tied to his lust. He is frustrated by more than the inability to play his music. He has a murderous desire for his wife. He may well not be able to distinguish his need to possess her sexually from his need to kill her for her betrayal and abandonment.

I may have to hypnotize the subject again. I know this man must have killed more than once.

Patient 579, cell c, floor 3, Erik Costanzi. 12 October

    Lisbet remained in her room. For the first hour or so this morning, Erik was agitated, glancing often at the door, pacing. We wondered if he was waiting for Lisbet to be brought to the common room. He stopped when Gunter finally entered to make his rounds. Erik refused to move out of the way when Gunter arrived at the windows. Gunter seemed ready to challenge the patient. The two men were very close as if involved in a conversation. I couldn't make out what transpired between them. Later Gunter brushed it off as unimportant. After a tense moment or so, Gunter turned and retraced his original path.
    Erik was restless, avoiding Laurent's attempts at conversation. He sat at the table and began to move his fingers rapidly across the blank surface. Given Dr. Richmond's orders, Wilhelm and Audrich forcibly restrained the patient while Gunter bound his hands. Erik didn't move from his seat the rest of the day. H.--

"You must protect Lisbet."
"Erik, you're avoiding my questions."
"And you're not listening, Dr. Richmond."
"You've killed. How does it make you feel?"
...
"Silence won't protect you." Dr. Richmond had allowed Erik's hands to be unbound during the session. He noted that the patient was softly tapping out notes of a silent melody. "Nor will your music." Erik closed his hands, folding his fingers in a protective cocoon.
    "Dr. Richmond, would it make a difference if I begged? Please. She's just a child. You must get her away from Gunter. Get rid of him. He's…"
    "You don't like Gunter, do you? You've had several confrontations with him, haven't you?"
    "I'll…I'll…tell you what you want to know. I'll tell you what I've done."

I failed to keep my face impassive. Erik could sense my interest.

"If you keep Gunter away from the girl." He laid his terms upon the table.

"What have you done, Erik? Something worse than killing your own father?"

In a quiet voice, Erik answered, "Yes."

"I'm listening."

"I lived in the vaults under a Parisian opera house. I pretended to be a ghost. I extorted money from the owners and made them do whatever I wanted. When they tried to capture me, I engineered an accident to hide my escape. The grand chandelier fell in the house during a performance. People died."

"Did you enjoy killing them?"

"No."

"Surely you must have felt something. You 'engineered' it, so you meant for it to happen. You meant to kill."

"I…I…didn't think about the people, about where the chandelier would crash."

"What were you thinking about?"

"About…getting away, getting underground."

"What do you mean you lived under a Parisian opera house?"

"I made my home in the caverns several floors below the surface. The vaults connected with a labyrinth of tunnels. These eventually led to the sewer system under the streets of Paris. I had to hide from the police."

"Why did you choose to live underground?" Erik stared at the doctor for a moment as if trying to gauge if he was serious. Seeing this, the doctor went on to say, "You live a rather public life in Rome. When did you realize you could come out of hiding?"

"I began a new life in Italy, a different life."

"When under hypnosis, you sometimes talk of being confined in dark places. What is that image?"

"I couldn't say. I didn't like being without light. I always kept lamps and candles lit. Some of the tunnels, the natural ones that connected to the vaults, were luminescent. Otherwise, it was like being buried alive."

"So for how long did you have to take refuge in these underground vaults?"

"I spent nearly twenty years underground."

"Twenty? You said twenty years?"

Erik studied his hands and didn't reply.

"Erik?"

"Yes! Yes, I lived in the tunnels under the streets for twenty years." Erik raised his voice but kept his eyes fixed on his quiet hands.

"But how could you survive underground?" Dr. Richmond chuckled at the absurdity of what Erik had said.

"I've always survived. I have a resistance to death. But others are not so fortunate. Dr. Richmond, I have to insist. I can assure you that, if you don't act now to protect Lisbet, that child will *not* survive!"

"It's not your responsibility, Erik. The running of this clinic and the welfare of the patients are my concern, not yours. Now, Erik, how has it made you feel to be without your music?"

The silence was absolute. Richmond found it difficult to witness Erik's raw pain. He put on the spectacles that he wore only when reviewing his notes. The movement allowed him to look away as Erik squeezed his silent hands between his thighs, rocking back and forth. The doctor cleared his throat, hoping to have given the patient time to recuperate his calm.

When he looked up, he saw no change. So he decided that he would best bring the session to a close. As Himmel and Audrich escorted Erik out the door, Dr. Richmond reminded them to replace the bandages on the patient's hands.

Did she twirl in ever increasing pirouettes round the flat of the roof under a star-dusted heaven? Did she think she could fly? When she danced, her tread was light, her body glided as if buoyed by the air. Was there a soft breeze from the south? Was it warm, caressing her, as it swung by? Or was it the cool northern slap that stopped her, sending her careening off in the opposite direction? Did she imagine a dark lover taking her by the waist, lifting her, settling her down on pointed toe, swinging her round and round, ready to catch her as she bolted off into the blackness? Did she dance? Did she dance as she fell? Did she open her eyes at the last moment? Did she see the cold constancy of death instead of her dark lover's embrace? Did she hear the music as it guided her body, pulsed inside her veins, enclosed her in an orchestral fancy? Did she dance until the last note sounded?

Infirmary 20 October

Patient: Lisbet Schneider, aged 14 years, 8 months, died from injuries sustained in a fall from the roof of the building. Incident happened shortly after 3:00 a.m. Internal bleeding in the cranial and thoracic cavities was extensive. Death would have been instantaneous. Unborn fetus crushed in the fall. The condition of the body makes it impossible to prove prior abuse. Given circumstances, a preliminary finding would suggest suicide. However, given the mental condition of the patient, such a finding is conjecture. Equally possible would be that the child found herself on the roof of the building and unfortunately came too near to the edge and simply fell.

Dr. Flescher

Dr. Richmond read the physician's report again, stalling for time, grasping for an appropriate reaction. Dr. Flescher sat, his stone face riveted on his employer's, waiting for Dr. Richmond to act.

"I suppose an autopsy would be redundant, Dr. Flescher?'

"I've already examined the body. The injuries are consistent with those induced by a fall. Unfortunately she was already bruised. She was in my infirmary just days ago for a routine examination."

"Routine? Since when do you call patients out of the common population to give routine exams?"

"She had not had her monthly cycles for several months. It came to my attention, and I thought I'd better examine her."

Dr. Richmond knew he was flushed. The subject of the pregnancy was not going to go away. Dr. Flescher would not be discreet and let it fade into the background. "Very well, Dr. Flescher. So you reported that the girl was pregnant. Did she say who the father was? How did she manage to have a lover under these circumstances?"

Dr. Flescher was momentarily stunned by the psychologist's willful obtuseness. "You can't be serious."

Dr Richmond cleared his throat and looked again at the various reports Dr. Flescher had turned in to him over the past month. There were reports of abuse, complaints of neglect of several of the catatonic patients who were allowed to sit in the same position day after day until large ulcers broke out on bony hips, a demand to investigate violence on the part of the guards—Costanzi's name stood out in several of the documents. Now this. Dr. Richmond held in each hand a report from Dr. Flescher on the poor child that had wandered onto the roof and fallen over the side.

When was the last time he'd tried to speak with Lisbet? In the first months of her confinement, Dr. Richmond had spent several sessions with her without success. He had passed her on to Dr. Vernon who had made little progress with her after nearly six months of regular sessions. Dr. Vernon and he had had a professional parting of the ways over a year ago. They had argued about the mission of the clinic. Altruistic, Dr. Vernon had taken exception to what he considered Dr. Richmond's misguided handling of the inmates. In particular, he had accused Dr. Richmond of experimenting with his patients instead of trying to heal them. Since Dr. Vernon's resignation, Lisbet had not been reassigned. Her case had fallen to the wayside.

"Dr. Flescher, the girl is dead. Her family won't even collect her body. She'll be buried in the cemetery on the grounds."

"And what about the man who abused her?"

"We have no proof that anyone abused her."

"I suppose you believe in the immaculate conception in this case?"

"Dr. Flescher, I'm tired of your sanctimonious attempts to undermine my efforts!"

"I am not concerned about your efforts. I am concerned about the physical wellbeing of the patients under my care! Lisbet was raped. She was raped repeatedly. She had no lover."

Dr. Richmond pulled himself back emotionally. Adopting a demeanor of objectivity, he made the dismissal clear in his tone. "I'm investigating your charges, Dr. Flescher. That is all."

Dr. Flescher wanted to strangle the man. Richmond had far too much power. The other physicians under his charge were young, inexperienced graduates from second-rate universities. There was no one who could oppose his will. Flescher left the office more frustrated and less satisfied than when he had entered. He was convinced Richmond would do little or nothing to investigate the poor child's death. It was painfully obvious that the man wanted the problem to be buried along with the broken corpse of the girl. As to the other charges of abuse and violence perpetrated by one or more of the guards, Flescher sensed that Richmond not only knew but condoned the authoritarian and sadistic bent of his employees. The guards that threatened violence were successful in keeping the patients in line. That was their function. As long as things didn't get out of hand. As long as… The image of Lisbet's bruised and smashed body would not leave him.

"Here, clean yourself." Dr. Richmond threw the wet towel he had used to wash himself to the naked woman on his couch. He had spilled his seed on her stomach. He looked away as Celeste wiped his cum from her skin and rose to gather her clothes from the floor.

This is the last time! He would keep the promise this time. He had only given in to Celeste because she thrust herself at him so flagrantly that he'd have had to be a saint to resist her. But he had taken her quickly, allowing her little or no pleasure, withdrawing at the critical moment, rushing to ejaculate on her soft white belly.

Celeste rubbed her hand across the swollen ache he'd left unsatisfied. Emptiness and unfulfilled yearning pulsed between her thighs. Even so, the doctor had filled her for a moment. For the time he had crushed her under his hard body. Though he had removed only the essential clothing, not even allowing her to feel his skin against her naked breasts, she had felt the pain recede. She had held pleasure inside her.

Edward saw her frustrated gesture. He almost relented. He felt small and mean to have used her, once again, without assuring her own relief. But he wanted, needed, to punish her. She had tempted him. But he would not give her what she wanted. This had to stop.

Lisbet. A child. A young girl. She had barely developed. Her breasts had been hard knobs under the uniform. Her menstrual cycles were irregular, painful, sometimes lasting a day, sometimes stretching out to more than a week. But she was still only a child. The report had reminded him. She was fourteen. Who could have taken her?

The patient logs that he had required the attendants to keep on Costanzi also included cursory information on the others. The attendants whose job it was to record the major incidents in the day were to register in detail Costanzi's behavior and to note any significant change among the population. Lisbet's name appeared with some frequency.

"Celeste?" Richmond studied the woman as she dressed. She pulled the starched dress over her head and down across her generous dark nipples. No corset, no fancy lingerie in the clinic. But basic undergarments were given out to each patient. Celeste hadn't even worn the modest chemise that was standard for the women in the clinic. When the attendant had told her Dr. Richmond would see her later in the day, Celeste had known the undergarments would only be in the way.

She didn't answer him, but she did finish pulling the gown past her hips to let it fall nearly to her ankles. Once she was covered, she waited for him to speak.

"Did Lisbet interact with anyone in particular among the male patients?"

"She didn't sneak out of her room and get up to the roof and throw herself off."

Richmond was annoyed at Celeste's mocking tone. "Her room was unfortunately left unlocked. She must have wandered out. We'll never know if she just stumbled and fell or if she jumped."

"Ha!"

"Answer my question, Celeste."

"She was quite taken with the ugly one, the one with half a face. He was able to get closer to her than anyone else."

"Costanzi, you mean."

"Isn't his name Erik?"

"Yes." Richmond didn't like the intensity with which she said Costanzi's given name. "Did he ever touch her?"

"You must be joking!" she laughed. "Seriously, Edward…"

"I told you not to call me…"

"Except when you're inside me. When you're inside me, you like me to do a lot of things I shouldn't do, don't you, Edward?"

He felt himself grow hard. Damn her! Damn her smoky voice and those hands. They had run over his body as if she were forming him from wet clay. He sat down behind the desk to hide his arousal.

"Do you think Costanzi was her lover?"

Again Celeste laughed, but it was a hard sound without mirth. "When and where would he have been able to give her cock?"

"Don't use that language, Celeste. It's not becoming."

"Even when I whisper it in your ear?" Celeste lifted the fabric of the hospital gown up over her hips, sat on the chair facing Edward, and slid her hand over her mons. Edward watched her fingers disappear into the dusky curls and begin to move. "I'd take his cock, Edward. I'd take that beautiful monster's cock and ride it until it sweat blood inside me."

"Stop it!" he hissed. But he didn't move, mesmerized by the wet, opened-mouthed gasp of pleasure he saw on Celeste's face as her limbs stretched and stiffened and her hand drove her to the edge and over into shaking orgasm.

He let her sit, breathing in deep, swift gasps as she relaxed and lay back in the chair. Her gown had fallen over her thighs again. He was glad of the fact that he would not see her wet and sated. After a few moments, Celeste sighed deeply and spoke, as if nothing had happened. "He watched her. He got her to dance. He sang so softly that almost no one but Lisbet was aware he was singing at first. God, that voice! She was different when she danced." She paused, lost in thought or captured by the image she'd evoked. "Oh you can't honestly think Costanzi fucked that child! He's constantly being watched. Where would he have done it? You even watch us while we sleep, don't you?"

Richmond, of course, knew how ludicrous the suspicion was. But the only other option was to accuse one of the attendants or Dr. Flescher himself. "You can go now, Celeste," he said in sign of dismissal.

"If you really want to know who might have dallied with the child, you should ask Gunter why he thought it necessary to check on her so often."

Gunter! Of course, it would be he.

Richmond scanned Celeste's clothing. "Button," he said as he pointed at her bodice. "Your last one is undone."

Celeste grinned at the doctor. As she fastened the last button on her bodice, she kept her eyes fixed on him. "You've no idea what you're doing to us, do you?"

Richmond didn't respond to Celeste's baiting. He swiveled his chair away from her. "Himmel is waiting to take you back to the common room."

CHAPTER 6

The Escape

As flies to wanton boys, are we to the gods.
They kill us for their sport.
                      King Lear, William Shakespeare

Erik couldn't remember a time when terror had so completely disarmed him. Panic took hold of him, stripped him of every defense, turned him into an animal driven only by the need to escape or to destroy. His pulse had reached a rate that barely allowed him to breathe. Meg's face—a look of shock—receded as the doors slammed shut. He pounded, with his entire weight, against the metal doors. He tensed his shoulder and drove himself against the cold steel, unable to feel the pain in bone and muscle. As if he were trapped inside a bell, a hollow repercussion echoed deeply around and through him. The wagon jolted forward. He lost his balance, glanced against a wall, and fell to the floor. He tasted the metallic salt of blood in his mouth as he licked the lip his teeth had lacerated. He leaned back, his palms flat and his arms locked to steady him, and pounded with both feet at the doors. Deep waves vibrated round him, making his ears ring, his muscles jerk. Only when he collapsed and gave into despair did he hear his own ragged cries. Eventually he found there were no more tears in him. He lay in darkness so thick that it entered his lungs and threatened to drown him. The silence was deafening.

Not even during his flight from the gypsy cage had he felt so frightened. Madeleine had taken him by the hand and led him through the unfamiliar streets of Paris. In the warmth of her touch, he had felt the promise of protection; he was not alone. Not during the lonely nights in the vaults—when he had not yet grown into the mastery of his kingdom—had he suffered such torment, for the cold, dark bowels were also sanctuary. Not even in prison had the terror been this unrelenting, for he had surrendered himself to his fate. And he had understood then what lay in his future.

Why? Why had she done this to him?

He had felt the effects of the drug almost from the moment he replaced the china teacup on the lacquer tray. He saw guilt in her eyes. An irrational desire—no, a compulsion—to flee had seized him. An irritation urged him to lash out, to break something, to destroy and remove from his path any and all obstacles. He had wanted to scream, to shout, to run until the fire in his gut extinguished itself. Too late he saw her plan. The men had been waiting all along to take him away. Away to where? What would they do to him? What had Meg done to him?

Hours of suffocating black heat. Hours he lay on the floor, buffeted by the steady progress of the wagon. He slept, woke, ranted, quietly gave in to weeping, and slept again.

He couldn't tell how long it had taken. He knew he was exhausted. His lips were cracked, and his mouth, dry. He went over and over the events of the last several days. She was punishing him, castigating him for bringing death to their door. He had always known this day would come. He had always feared she'd see him for what he was. And having seen him, she would not have stomached being chained to a loathsome creature of darkness that had dared to crawl from the black pit of the earth to sleep on cool, white sheets in the arms of a golden-haired angel.

But it made no sense, none at all. He wasn't that creature. Had he ever been? He could swear that he'd kept that creature buried, chained. He had fought him. Hadn't he won? She had told him she loved him. She had called him a man, not a monster. She had lit his way, and now he lay in darkness so thick it suffocated him. There was no road, no path he could find out of this torment.

The stillness of the wagon, the rush of muffled voices outside his prison wall brought chaos again to his thoughts. No sound was familiar. He strained to hear *her* voice. It was not among those he heard. The scrape of raw metal on metal screamed as the doors came free.

Before him the jeering faces of the crowd. The tinny music of a hand organ, the guffaws of the men, the shrieks of feigned horror from the women, the high-pitched chatter of startled and delighted children. Children! He had been a child then. The delusion gave way to rough, meaty hands that grabbed and pulled at him. Tall, heavy-set men in uniform, not policemen, restrained and led him from one hell to another. And there, standing at the mouth of the inferno, stood the demon, the avenging angel, the wrathful god that she had invited into their world. The sounds and images of the fair dissipated, crushed by the terse orders delivered by the one who had tricked them all.

Erik would not think. He would not see. He would not listen to them. The fight had left him. He went coldly limp in their determined grasp. He squelched the pitiable cry for Meg that sounded—he prayed that it had been silent—in his mind. There was no soft-skinned, doe-eyed angel. He had lost his angel. He called up around himself a protective film of oily black silence. He went deep inside his mind and lay in the soft warm cavern, drawing his arms around his shoulders, digging his knees into his chest to keep what was left of his heart from breaking.

How long would it take to die?

Days passed. Weeks. He learned the trick of moving his body through space and time, all the while lying in that black protective womb. He fleetingly noticed other bodies—all in pain—filling the spaces around him. A strange blond man pursued him round the cage, speaking filth, yet his eyes implored. Bodies without souls ruminated passively. Figures stolen from a hellish landscape of the underworld by Hieronymus Bosch accompanied him. The smells of unwashed bodies, the smell of urine and feces, the angry scent of vinegar and ammonia assaulted him.

How long did damnation last?

Oh yes, he recalled now. *Forever, toujours, forever.* The other word, "l'éternité," teased him with its seductive beauty. *Damnation, never-ending.*

Slowly he found his control weakening. Back, he forced himself back to the dark, safe hollow, but each day the images about him became brighter, crisper, blocking his retreat and pulling him inexorably forward until he found himself incapable of evasion. The repetition of daily routine dulled the pain, but it brought no consolation. Hopelessness took hold of his soul.

At night, they shackled him to his bed. He yearned to fold his arms across his chest, to allay the loneliness and hunger. Darkness had always been his refuge, but they controlled even the nighttime. He became aware of the mirror. He knew they watched him even in his dreams. He lay awake as long as he could to watch for them, waiting for them to come for him. But sleep would eventually win, dragging him down to hell or torturing him with lost happiness. Meg sometimes came to him in his dreams, and he learned to fear her. Whether in joy or sorrow, her presence soothed him only fleetingly, and the rush of pain and anger upon waking from her visitations only intensified the betrayal.

He couldn't remember the first time or so that Richmond—that was the name behind which the wrathful god hid—summoned him to his office. Eventually this torture, too, became a regular feature of his hell. The demon, the avenging angel, the wrathful god meant to plunder his very soul. Erik protected his secrets, knowing they were his only possessions. He asked, at first, for his wife. But the god who now enslaved his body and threatened his soul had no pity. The demon reveled in his power over Erik. He showed Erik the papers that condemned him to this torment. He brought Erik's unwilling attention to the bottom of the document. There, in her own hand, was the name, "Meghan Giry Costanzi." There was no doubt in Erik's mind after that. She had cursed him, forsaken him, withdrawn her love, broken each and every promise to him.

He would go to the doctor's office, prepared to defend himself. He would not speak, would not let the man drill a hole through his skull to suck out the marrow of his mind. Oblivion would wash over him, strange sensations and dreams, a feeling of helplessness and distance. Then he would wake, knowing that the doctor had stolen a piece of his soul. The doctor's preening, self-satisfied smirk enraged Erik. Impotent, he swallowed his anger, tightened his jaw against speaking.

Slowly Erik came to realize that this was his life. He could no longer retreat from it. That was when he began to notice his fellow victims, to watch and listen to them. At first that was the limit of his power; he could do no more.

Then the music returned!

The notes had stolen in one night as he lay staring glassy-eyed at the mirror. Tiny, sweet sounds as if a flute were playing. Then he heard the strings filling his mind with rich vibrations. His fingers twitched as he imagined the accompaniment of the piano. An oboe joined them, a French horn. He closed his eyes to better hear the swirl of sounds that rolled over his mind, filling the gaping wounds left by the wrathful god who only wanted to cannibalize him. He was a failed creation. The wrathful god would reuse his parts to make another monster. The sounds drowned the ache, wrapped warmly round him. He felt loved and cherished by the music. It called to him. It knew his names. It had found him even in hell.

The days were bearable. He walked in music, melody his constant companion. He rehearsed old songs, familiar rifts, listened and performed entire operas. The room swelled with his orchestra. Heavy crimson and gold curtains hung from the three story ceiling. Hard, varnished oak spread beneath his feet. Those shadows around him became Figaro, Don Giovanni, Beatrice, Camille. When the last note of his last opera died, Erik was ready to compose again. He sat at the piano, the keys wavered only for a moment. Then he set his fingers on the slick surface and began to play the score he heard inside his head.

Music had again saved him. He would go deeper this time. He had no choice. He could not change this world. It wasn't his. He could not live here. He would go deeper and deeper into the music until one day he would be safe.

Even that they took from him.

The bandages. They had put them on again. The avenging angel would smother the seraphic chorus. But Erik screamed in defiance! It would not stop the notes. He prayed they could not stop the music. His hands, swollen and bulbous, lay impotent on the piano. The drive to flex and move them across the keys beat at him without mercy, without pause.

Erik shivered. They were watching through the glass. They had freed his hands from the wraps and no longer manacled him to the bed in the night. They thought they'd won. They believed him resigned. He turned away from the mirror and touched himself. The sounds were far off. He could still hear a plaintive chord softly playing. Its notes came intermittently from far, far away, so far that he wasn't sure what instrument had struck the notes. It might only be the echo, the reverberations fanning out after a last note. He began to work rhythmically to soothe himself. His mind tried to summon the notes of his last opera to mind. He envisioned the black notes on paper. He didn't want to read the score but to hear the orchestra perform those notations. The miracle! He wanted the miracle of those sounds. Desperately he caressed and then rubbed his hand along his shaft. Silence brought fear, loneliness. He raced to finish before fear consumed him. The whimper escaped before he closed his lips tightly against it. His shaft pulsed, hot and heavy, in his hand. He pulled harder, trying to block the sensation of loneliness. The knot in his chest loosened. Meg's fingers brushed his aside and took him in her hand. Her light fingertips stroked the crown, clutched hard around the shaft, and moved down to the base. Again she stroked the shaft, reached beneath and cupped him. With a firmer pulse, she held him and moved along the length of him. He quivered and tensed as she repeated the caress. Her lips softly brushed against his aching flesh. Her mouth descended, engulfing him. He bucked wildly as he spewed his seed into the starched sheet that covered him.

They were watching, but he clung to the mattress and wept. The silence in his mind was unbearable.

"Gunter, how did the patient get to the roof?"

"Like I said, Doctor, somehow the door to her room was left unlocked. She wandered out and down the hallway to the stairs.

"And the lock on the stairway door?"

"Defective. Been defective for quite a while. If you push hard enough, it snaps open." Gunter gave the doctor a half smile. He knew that they were going through the motions. If the doctor actually meant to do anything, he'd have called the authorities a long time ago. The death certificate and burial had all been handled on the grounds. The girl's family had been relieved to know they were no longer obliged to send monthly payments to the clinic to keep the real heiress confined. And if the doctor were foolish enough to point an accusing finger at Gunter, he'd find that Gunter was not without his own weapons. Accusations could cut both ways.

"Gunter, do you expect me to believe that a child Lisbet's size could force that door? She weighed less than half what I do!"

Gunter smirked and rubbed his large, meaty hands up and down his thighs. He slumped comfortably in the chair, and Dr. Richmond was annoyed by his obvious confidence. After several nights of insomnia, the doctor had decided that he had to act on Dr. Flescher's annoying reports and conduct a formal investigation. He didn't actually expect to secure a confession from any of the attendants, but he intended to use the incident to instill in his staff fear and discipline. For too long the attendants had enjoyed autonomy on the floor, and excesses were becoming more frequent. Dr. Richmond was also concerned that incidents such as the unexpected death of a patient might eventually bring the local authorities to the clinic. He would not have outside interference.

Curiously Gunter was not cowed by his questions, nor had he offered an even remotely plausible explanation of how Lisbet had managed to make her way to the roof. At this rate, Dr. Richmond would hardly be able to convince Dr. Flescher that Lisbet met with an unfortunate accident.

"Your explanation is ridiculous, Gunter. I have to inform you that you have been accused of improper conduct with the patient and…"

"Accused?" Gunter rose from the chair, no longer nonchalant. However he wasn't exactly frightened either. He was infuriated. "What the…? Who said I touched the bitch?"

Dr. Richmond noted silently to himself that he had not specified the actual nature of the charge. Although he was somewhat unnerved by Gunter's threatening attitude, he kept his voice even and his face blank. He was adept at facing any number of emotions with a placid demeanor. "You don't need to know that."

"It was that bastard, that ugly bastard Costanzi, wasn't it? He said he'd…" Gunter ground his teeth, destroying the next words he might have said. He took several ragged breaths and relaxed his grimace into a cocky grin. "Well, no one believes a madman, Doctor, do they?"

"Gunter, this is a serious charge. You had opportunity. You were the one who took Lisbet to her room on several occasions. According to the log, you were nearby on each of the times that Lisbet became upset. And you were seen on the floor the night she fell. Dr. Flescher examined Lisbet just days before her death and found…"

"You can't hang this on me," he hissed, leaning over the desk and coming rudely close to Dr. Richmond's face. "That shit doesn't mean a thing except that she was a loon and a cunt." Gunter was a man with a large round face one would not call ugly or handsome. His features were nondescript. His nose was on the broad side, his forehead square, his eyes a color somewhere between gray and light blue. He had a large mouth with blunted, off-white teeth. He was not remarkable, except when he was crossed. Then his face took on the visage of a rabid wolf. At this moment, Gunter tried to hide his anger. He settled his features into a faintly obscene smile and added in a falsely pleasant tone, "You know, Doctor, I've had a conversation or two with someone we both enjoy."

Dr. Richmond was stunned when the man straightened before the desk and grabbed the front of his trousers, in a lewd gesture, cupping his genitals. "She's got a sweet one, that Celeste. Says you like it hard and dirty. Didn't know a gentleman like you would play that kind of game."

Richmond was going to be sick. The threat that hung between the two men gagged him. Even though he feared he'd retch if he opened his mouth, he somehow managed to dismiss the attendant.

As soon as the door closed, Richmond opened his collar. The muscles of his throat convulsed, and he bent over just in time to empty his stomach into the basket by the desk. He tasted Celeste's body on his lips as he wiped the vomit from his mouth. Her smell clawed at his nostrils. For one bleak moment, he understood why Gunter had thrown Lisbet from the roof of the building.

Costanzi's uncooperative manner made hypnosis unavoidable. Dr. Richmond realized immediately that it would be dangerous to be alone with the patient. Costanzi blamed him for the young girl's death. He hadn't protected her. Audrich and Himmel remained until, after several failed attempts, Dr. Richmond finally had Costanzi in a deep hypnotic state. Only then did he feel safe to dismiss the attendants.

"Erik, step through the door. Let's go underground to your world under the opera house." Was it relief he saw relax Erik's features? "Erik, are you happy deep underground?"

Erik nodded.

"Use your voice."

"Ssshhhh."

"What is it? Why are we quiet?"

"It's the music. I want to hear it. It's even nicer when you climb up to the catwalks and listen from above."

"Have you often gone up to listen?"

"Yes."

Erik had once revealed that he was forbidden to go up to the surface by the girl who saved him. "Why do you sneak around in the opera house? Is it because you're afraid of the policemen?"

"No, silly. There aren't any policemen at the opera."

"Then why?"

"I don't want to be looked at." The child's voice was tense, strained. "Madeleine says I'm safe down under the house."

Dr. Richmond studied Erik's disfigurement. It had been used for profit, its ugliness intensified by the circumstances of the fair. That world of the bizarre had determined who and what he was. Erik, like the crowds, had believed the barker as he described in grueling detail the hideous child of Satan.

"Is it your face, the disfigurement?"

"Yes." But Erik's tone suggested there were other causes that kept him buried alive for twenty years.

"What else keeps you from going upstairs where you can hear the music?"

...

"What is it, Erik, that you're avoiding?"

The child—for Dr. Richmond was sure that this Erik was still only a boy—shook his head as if he didn't want to speak. Erik, a grown man, drew his knees sharply to his chest and pulled himself into a protective ball.

"Tell me why you're afraid."

"Madeleine told me to hide. She said I'd be safe from him down in the vaults. He mustn't know I'm here. He never goes this far down into the darkness."

"Who is he?"

"He works up above the stage, in the rigging, with the pulleys and ropes. He stays in a little room in the back. Madeleine doesn't like him. She told me to stay away from him."

"Do you know his name?"

"Yes, and he knows mine."

"What's his name, Erik?"

"Buquet."

"How did he come to know your name?"

...

"Did he ever catch you, Erik, when you came up from the vaults?"

"Madeleine said I wasn't to come out of the darkness. I was to stay in the darkness."

Why was he crying?

"I thought you liked your underground vaults."

"Yes. No. Yes. Yes. NO! No, I don't want to stay here. I want to be safe, but I don't want to be here. It's…cold…so cold… I hear things in the night, things I can't see. I'm lonely. I want to come and watch the dancers, listen to the music. I told Madeleine I would wear a disguise. Then I would be able to come up and be with people. They wouldn't laugh or scream at me, if I had a disguise."

"Did she agree with you?"

"No. She said it wasn't safe. She wanted me buried alive. She regretted saving me. She wanted me to die down here and rot away so that no one would know she saved the Devil's Child."

"I thought you said she cared for you, Erik."

The anger had allayed the fear. He unfolded his body, but his conflicting emotions were evident in his agitation. He could not lie still. Finally one emotion must have won out over the others. "I'm sorry. I'm sorry," he moaned overcome with regret. "Madeleine only wants to protect me. She's right. When I'm big, I can come out. When I can protect myself against men like Buquet, I can come out."

"What is dangerous about Buquet?"

"He watches the dancers dress. He spies on the singers, too, in their dressing rooms. He hurt the little girl."

"What did he do to the little girl, Erik?"

"No, I don't want to talk about it. Please don't make me watch."

"Just tell me what he did. You don't have to describe it."

"He used her, did things to her to make her cry. He hurt her. He left her in the dark."

Dr. Richmond felt his stomach turn, a hard sharp pain seared up through his chest. He didn't want to think about the torment of a young girl. Lisbet's death was too recent.

"That's enough, Erik. You don't have to say any more."

Dr. Richmond wiped his face with his handkerchief. Slowly he recovered his control and asked, "Did this man ever hurt you, Erik?"

"He caught me watching the rehearsal. He grabbed me from behind and put a knife to my throat. When he saw my face, he almost let go. But then he laughed. He said he knew who I was. He'd seen me himself at the fair."

"So he knew you had escaped after murdering your father."

The child frowned. The child did not know he had murdered his father. Dr. Richmond spoke reassuringly. "Did Buquet threaten to turn you in to the police?"

"No, he just laughed. He stared at me. He was frightening."

"What did he do?"

"He dragged me down to a room, a storage room. He put me inside a trunk and locked it. It was cramped, dark. I couldn't breathe."

"What happened when he came back for you?"

"I was gone."

"How did you get out?"

"Madeleine came and let me out."

"Did Buquet go away then?"

"No." Erik bore a strange expression. His lip curled up on one side, but there was no mirth in the half smile.

A cold shiver of dread ran up the doctor's back as it occurred to him that Erik might have killed again.

"What did you do to Buquet?"

"I killed him."

"When you were a child?"

"No, I waited for a long time. I was a man when I killed Buquet."

"Why did you choose to kill him after waiting such a long time?"

"Because he would have done those wicked things to Christine! He was following her and watching her. He would have raped and maybe killed her."

"Who was Christine?"

"The woman I loved."

"But I thought you loved Meg?"

Erik did not want to think about Meg. The doctor noticed immediately that the patient was resisting. When Erik next spoke, it was with hesitation.

"That was later."

"How did you fall in love with Meg?"

"She saved me."

"From what?"

"From those who came down in the underground to hunt and kill me."

"Why were they hunting you, Erik?"

"Because I had killed."

"Buquet?"

"Because I had killed, and killed, and killed. Because I was a monster."

"Who had you killed?"

"Buquet and others."

"Why?"

"Because they kept me from Christine. Because I wanted Christine. Because…because Christine didn't want me, didn't love me."

Oh my God. Richmond couldn't take his eyes off the man who lay on the couch. "Erik, what is your real name?"

"My name is Erik," he shouted. "My name is Erik. I am a man, and I have a name."

"What else do they call you?" Richmond sat forward already divining the answer. He had heard the stories years ago. It had been a famous case, reported in all the gazettes in France and repeated in England. "What do they call you?"

"No, I don't want to talk anymore. I'm tired. Let me lie down and sleep."

"You must tell me the complete story, Erik. What do they call you?"

"Monster."

"That's not true. That's not what they call you. You must tell me."

"Je suis le fantôme de l'opéra, monsieur docteur. Le fantôme, c'est moi."

15 October 1888

Dear Edward,

    I regret that I must write this letter. I have not read your correspondence for several weeks due to the hectic schedule of my practice and the demands of the classroom. However, I recently reviewed all the letters you've sent me and have grown more and more concerned. Little did I think that you would take your fascination with Costanzi to such an extreme.
    I cannot be a party to your actions. Although we at one time spoke in hypothetical terms about an examination and study of a subject like Costanzi, I would never have sanctioned what you have done and are doing to this man. If you can find a way to restore him to his family, you must do so.
    If I have in any way unfortunately encouraged you in this obsession, you must forgive me. Upon the completion of my teaching duties, I intend to return to the Bragant Institute. I advise you to take another leave and to join me there. I believe the rest will do you good.
    Please accept my best wishes for you and take heed of what I say,

Your teacher,
Dr. Klinen

Dr. Richmond's journal. 19 October

I've completed a thorough history of the subject. I include it with these notes out of habit, but I don't think that they will ever see the light of day. Little did I know that I was interviewing a famous murderer. I can still hear those words, his confession: "Je suis le fantôme de l'opéra." A convicted and supposedly executed criminal, he admitted to having been the notorious Phantom of the Opera. Even though he was under hypnosis when he said it, I could hardly believe in the reality of what he told me. It was just too incredible.

Dr. Klinen advises me to close this case and release my patient, but under these circumstances knowing what I know of Costanzi's real nature and his past, how can I free this man?

Erik—if that is indeed his name—is still angry with me. I see the accusation in his eyes each time he has come to my office. Only when he is under hypnosis am I not afraid of him. And then, as he begins to unravel his story, my fear returns. This musical genius, this successful director and composer of opera, is a fiend! That would be the natural conclusion one would draw upon hearing of the Phantom and his trial. He is responsible for the deaths of several patrons of the opera. He was also accused of other crimes over the course of ten or more years in the theater district. According to the gazettes that I have investigated, he was found guilty of them all and hanged.

In our sessions, he has confessed to having killed Buquet, a man who preyed on the young girls at the opera house and may even have murdered. He has also explained an ill-fated passion that led him to sabotage the opera house. It is this final act that led to the deaths of eleven people in the amphitheater. Yet, horrendous as it might seem, I felt more compassion than horror at Erik Costanzi's story.

I cannot go on with this case. I cannot help him. I don't know how one could help him to carry this burden. Dr. Klinen offers no real solutions for me. Should I turn Costanzi over to the law? They believe he's already dead. Has he killed since? In self defense, he swears, and I have no choice but to believe him.

At our last session, I took him back to the cage at the fair. I told him that he was to remember all that he had shared with me before, all that would happen once he escaped the cage. I told him that he had revealed to me his true identity, this alternative personality called the Phantom or the Opera Ghost. I asked him what he felt, knowing that he would leave the cage and kill, knowing that he would commit other crimes. Then I asked him if he would choose to stay in the cage or leave it, knowing what he knows. He was the child in the cage and the grown man that he is today at the same time. He was aware that I had found all his secrets, and he was still under the power of hypnosis and could do nothing about it. He asked me if there was any way that I could make him forget what he had once been. I told him that I couldn't. I asked him again if he would choose differently if he were back in the cage and his father still lived. He begged me not to ask him to make that choice. I pushed him to answer. His emotional turmoil was almost unbearable, even for me. When the child killed the man who kept him in the cage, he hadn't known that this man Abel was his father. He hadn't foreseen that he would grow up in isolation and loneliness. In tears, he told me that if he could choose all over again, knowing what he knows now, he would stay in the cage. His exact words sent shivers down my spine.

"I would stay a beast and live like a beast. What good did it do to live like a man for such a short time?"

Should I feel absolved of my interference with this man because I have wrung from him a willingness to live like a freak, an animal, in order to avoid committing murder? Does this choice not show a higher morality, one that perhaps without my assistance he would not have reached?

I told him that it was for the best that he stay with us. For the first time since we have been working together, I saw doubt in his eyes. I believe I also saw a glimmer of trust. I ended this ordeal for the two of us with a posthypnotic suggestion. I told him he would remember our sessions. He will know that he shared this with me.

A master of illusion. An escape artist of the first caliber. The Phantom of the Opera had been a ghost who moved about the opera world at will. No one could trap him, and he could appear anywhere he wished.

It had been an easy matter to slip into the manager's office and leave a note, then slip out again. It only took a small explosion of smoke and light for him to take his place on the grand staircase amid his foes. Escape was at hand. The trap in the floor released the boards, and down he'd plunge into his world. A panel slid easily to the side, black against black, and he would vanish from a room, from a corridor. It had been nothing more than timing and trickery, clever deception and art. A shadow world of passageways and rooms that no one else knew let him navigate unseen throughout the inner sanctum of the opera house in Paris.

Here there were no hidden doors, no sliding panels, only locked doors and barred windows. The Phantom had no keys. He didn't know the secret skeleton of the building. It was the doctor who hid behind the walls, behind the mirror, and watched.

Erik stared at the large mirror that dominated the wall of his bedroom. Was anyone fooled into believing it was placed there for the patient's use? What need would one of them have to inspect his clothing? All the patients wore the same drab gray uniform. There was only one reason a mirror—especially one that size—would grace a prison cell. Erik sometimes stared so long that his eyes would dry and burn. He'd blink until the strain would go away. But if he looked long enough, in the darkness, eventually he'd discern a solid shape on the other side of the slick, cold surface.

Soon, he told himself. Soon he'd find a way to escape.

The doctor knew who he was, what he had done. He had used his tricks on Erik and made him reveal all his crimes. The doctor had no intention of ever allowing a crazed killer to roam free. Erik had sealed his prison door. Erik couldn't bear the smug look of righteousness on the doctor's face without wanting to retch. The doctor had unearthed the Phantom and erased everything Erik had done since that nightmare. He couldn't be Erik Costanzi, Director and Composer at the Teatro Dell'Opera. The doctor had found *who he really was*! He was the Phantom. He was a killer. He must escape.

Erik watched everyone, taking note of their habits, their comings and goings. He examined the pathways open to him, watched as the attendants would leave by a side door in the hallway. He'd steal a glance inside the open doorway to see another door opposite, a stairway that both ascended and descended. There were too many keys between him and freedom. He waited to find some other way. He calculated the relative security of the common room, his own cell, the hallway, the office attached to the doctor's office, the infirmary. Each day he watched and calculated until slowly in his mind he drew a more and more detailed map of the building.

He tried to remember the way they had brought him in that first day. He had been sick to the bone, dehydrated, dizzy from the long trip enclosed in the windowless box. The cool air on his skin revived him somewhat, but the path the attendants had taken was now a blur in his memory. He recalled more his bewilderment and fear.

How could she have done this to me?

He wouldn't think of Meg. He tried very hard to forget her. If he recalled her face, her voice, a horrid wave of anger and confusion washed over him. The strong emotions crippled him, made it impossible to bear his circumstances. But no matter how adamantly he closed the door, at night when he could stare no longer at the mirror he found his mind clinging to Meg.

He would get out. But he wouldn't think of Meg. It was not to run to Meg's arms. The Phantom was not Meg's husband, Erik Costanzi was. But Erik Costanzi was an illusion. He didn't exist. The Phantom had to escape. It was a matter of survival.

Someone was trying to kill him.

Infirmary 22 October

Treated: Erik Costanzi, possible food poisoning.
Notes: Costanzi was brought in shortly after the evening meal with severe abdominal cramping and vomiting. Stomach contents were evacuated. No unusual substances, no blood in contents. Slow hydration over the next hours. Patient fell into a deep sleep. Nurse reported Patient was anxious to speak with me. Costanzi has been strongly affected by the unexpected death of Lisbet Schneider.

Dr. Flescher wouldn't consign to paper what Costanzi had actually said. Anyone might read the log. The accusations the patient made fit the facts such as they were, and the doctor was prone to believe him. But what could he do? A madman made a poor witness. Dr. Flescher had already made his complaints to Dr. Richmond, who had done absolutely nothing. As far as Dr. Flescher could ascertain, Dr. Richmond's "investigation" had been little more than a brief talk with the attendants.

Shortly after Dr. Flescher had informed Dr. Richmond of Lisbet's condition, the esteemed director had had the nerve to instruct him to perform a procedure on the child. Dr. Flescher had listened to the cold rationale his superior had presented. The girl was too young to carry and bear a child without serious risk to both. The clinic had no provisions to care for an infant, and Lisbet was incapable of fulfilling the role of mother. The pregnancy itself—not to mention labor and childbirth—was a cruel torment to put a young girl through and might seriously aggravate her deteriorating mental health.

Flescher forced back a bitter taste in his mouth. Dr. Richmond was, of course, correct—correct for all the wrong reasons. Dr. Flescher had wanted to fling in his face the true motivation for such a procedure. The good doctor meant to erase the consequences so as to avoid dealing with the cause. He couldn't or wouldn't address the actual crime. Someone had raped—and raped again—a child. Eliminating the fetus did not ensure that the abuse would not recur.

The order had been given only days before the girl fell to her death. Even Dr. Flescher had to admit his own cowardice at the news of the tragic event. He didn't want to look further into the fate of Lisbet Schneider. She was dead, so was the unborn child. No one else could make her suffer. Not anymore. Now Costanzi stirred his indignation once more. The patient was convinced that the fall was meant to cover the original crime, to eliminate the only one who could accuse the rapist, the only true witness, because she was the victim of the crime. And Costanzi had given him a name. No longer a faceless animal, no longer an unknown, the man had been singled out from those who were suspects. Dr. Flescher could not justify inaction due to ignorance.

Did he trust what Costanzi said? Oh, yes. It had only needed to be said for Dr. Flescher to know that he, too, had already deduced who the assailant was. And now murder was heaped upon the other crimes.

Erik Costanzi had not eaten a bit of turned meat. No one else had gotten sick. Nor was it sickness that made him so violently ill. The doctor was afraid to conjecture in the log. Might it make matters worse? Dr. Flescher could go to Dr. Richmond and accuse Gunter Wassler of poisoning one of the patients. Richmond was no more likely now to act than he had been before. Would Dr. Richmond alert Gunter to the accusation? If that were to happen, then they might well discover Costanzi's drowned body in the baths after an unfortunate, but serious fall and blow to the head. No, there were too many ways for a patient to die in the clinic, and no one would even think to question it.

Patient 579, cell c, floor 3, Erik Costanzi. 23 October

Erik returned after lunch from the Infirmary. He sat in the chair where Lisbet had often sat. He rose and paced the perimeter several times but always returned to the same seat. Celeste has been frantic over the bust. "Y" picked it up and threw it on the floor this morning, and Celeste jumped on him, her fingers digging into his face. She nearly took his eye before we got her off him. She calmed once "Y" was removed. She picked up the bust and started to smooth and repair the clay where it had been damaged.

This afternoon Celeste left the bust and approached Erik as he was walking. She stood, barring his path, and stared at him. We were all on alert lest she attack Erik, but when she lifted her hands to his face, it was not to gouge out his eyes or scratch him. Erik didn't flinch or move away from her. She had both hands splayed across his face, her thumbs along either side of his nose, her palms across his cheeks, the fingers darting out across the rest of his face, exploring eyes, brows, forehead. Then her hands began to move, pressing on bones under the surface. She was very attentive to his deformity.

When at last she dropped her fingers from his face, Erik turned away from her and stared out the window. Celeste didn't immediately go back to the sculpture. She stood next to him for quite some time. Just before dinner, she worked feverishly on the bust.

Erik never looks at the work Celeste is doing.

At dinner, Patient ate the hard roll but left everything else untouched, including the water. H.--

Erik's hearing was sensitive. He stood stiffly by the windows. Wilhelm and Gunter casually chatted by the door. Gunter's voice rose and fell as he dominated the conversation. Distinctly Erik heard Lisbet's name pass between the men. Gunter chuckled as he told Wilhelm about a recent encounter with Richmond. He boasted that he had put the doctor in his place.

"He had the nerve to question me about the door to her room."

"Who was on duty that night?"

"Audrich."

They both were silent for a few moments. Then Wilhelm snickered quietly. "He's an idiot. Can't remember half the time to button his own pants after he takes a piss. He crawls up on the sofa in the back and sleeps most of his shift."

"If Richmond wants to ask questions, let him ask Audrich, not me. I won't put up with his lame threats."

"What does he think happened?"

"Oh, I don't know. I guess he wants to blame someone. I told him about the hallway door a thousand times. If he hasn't taken the time to have the lock fixed, he can blame himself for the girl's escape and death."

Erik tried to control the rapid increase in his breathing. This was it, this was the way. He slowly turned so that he could observe the two attendants. They were oblivious to him. Erik noticed the sly glance Wilhelm gave Gunter before he spoke again. "Too bad though."

Gunter cocked his head at Wilhelm's tone. He gave the man a darkly questioning look.

Having stepped over some imaginary line, the other guard blushed. "I mean she was a sweet thing." He rubbed his finger roughly under his nose as if to stifle a sneeze and glanced up to see if Gunter was placated.

Erik swallowed the rise in his gorge. Wilhelm knew what Gunter had been doing to the child. He knew and had done nothing.

In a cold, low tone, Gunter snapped, "Keep your thoughts to yourself, Wilhelm, if you know what's good for you."

"I wasn't saying anything," he hastened to cajole his colleague. Trying perhaps to set the man at ease, he returned to the idea of the doctor. "Guess you told him what's what, no?"

"Richmond?" Assuaged, Gunter relished sharing the memory of his victory over the doctor. "I just let him know that we see more here than he wants us to see sometimes. You get my drift?" He nodded toward Celeste who was engrossed in the details of the bust.

Erik could tell Wilhelm was surprised. Evidently he had not seen what Gunter had. Erik, too, couldn't help but glance in the direction of Celeste. She was a beautiful woman, powerfully made. Her arms and hands, after years of working clay and marble, were slickly muscled. Her eyes were intense, passionate, dangerous. Erik knew she would burn, go up in a moment of intense heat, if she were touched.

Unbidden his body surged with a current of passion, lust always just under the surface. Far, far back in his mind an image of a small blond beauty sparked, and he cruelly snuffed out its light. He would not think of her. Not ever, not ever again.

A way out. There was another way out. He would not have to leave this hell via the cemetery after all. All he had to do was reach the hallway.

Dr. Richmond signed the transfer papers for Celeste Renoit. Within the next several days she would be taken by train and steamer to England. She would be committed to the Bragant Institute under the care of another physician. Dr. Richmond hoped that the man was very old and nearly blind. Perhaps this new doctor would be able to resist temptation better than he had. Dr. Klinen was right. A physician needed to be married. It was not a profession for a single man.

If he got his courage up, he would write Dr. Klinen and confess his indiscretions. They would come out sooner or later in sessions with Celeste's new physician. Perhaps Dr. Klinen would be able to protect him by taking on the case himself. Whatever happened, Dr. Richmond would have the satisfaction of having done the right thing in this case. At least he stopped himself. Lord knows that he should never have started.

Raoul had returned to their rooms and had found Christine waiting for him, the porcelain tub filled with warm, sandalwood-scented water. The moment he entered, she cast aside her silk robe and stood naked. Raoul silently drank in her form. After the sadness and waste he had witnessed at the clinic, he had no words to express his gratitude for her love.

"Meg won't be back for more than an hour." Her intention was clear.

When she saw Raoul slump into a chair, she stooped and gathered her robe, clutching it to her chest. Something was terribly wrong. It was not fatigue that weighed him down. She put on the robe and stood before him.

Raoul reached out and took her onto his lap. He buried his face in her hair and breathed in the hint of her perfume.

"Erik...," he began to explain. His voice rumbled through his chest. Christine pushed away from him so that she could see his expression. Sadness, worry, weariness. Whatever had happened, it was too harsh, too grave to put into words.

"Don't. Not yet. Tell me…tell me when you've kissed me. After you've touched me." She pressed her lips onto his as if to stop him from speaking.

"Oh, Christine," he said as he broke the kiss.

For several moments they remained folded in each other's arms. He whispered words—soft and reassuring sounds that had nothing to do with Erik—until he felt her relax and lean against him.

Over the past few days, Raoul had told the two women the bits and pieces that he'd overheard at the clinic, carefully selecting what he wanted Meg to know and what he would only tell Christine later in the privacy of their rooms: Erik was mostly silent. He was surrounded by poor creatures who were genuinely incapable of living outside the institute. The worst part was that Erik clearly didn't belong there. It was even apparent to the men who worked there. All had not gone smoothly since Erik's arrival in Austria. There had been violent episodes. He had not been a cooperative patient.

But nothing compared to what Raoul had just witnessed.

"Is he…?" Christine's voice brought Raoul back to the present.

"He's alive." The rest would be more difficult. He must choose his words carefully to avoid the deep regret and shame that had latched onto him during the events of the early morning hours.

Raoul was not accustomed to failure. He'd spent months searching for Erik. Both women had looked to Raoul for reassurance and direction. And as long as there had been a clear path to follow, specific tasks to be accomplished, he had been purposeful and unflagging in his determination to restore Erik to his family. But seeing Erik in the clinic surrounded by men and women who were clearly demented and incapable of living independent lives had shaken Raoul. The initial relief of having found his friend had given way to the question of what to do next.

How was Raoul to free Erik?

Raoul couldn't begin to imagine how Erik had managed to get as far as he had in the attempted escape. When Gunter ordered Raoul to accompany him and the others in pursuit of the fugitive patient, Raoul tried to think of a way to prevent their success. Then the dogs had come! He'd never seen animals savage a man. Even now he could hear the sounds of ripping jaws, the wet throaty growls the beasts had made as they bit and latched onto Erik. Raoul shivered. Erik had not uttered a sound, not when they pulled the dogs from his body, not even when the orderlies kicked and struck at him with their fists.

Christine was ready to listen. She turned her face up toward Raoul's and waited.

"He tried to escape."

"Tried?"

"They let the dogs out…"

"They what?"

"He's alive. He's in the infirmary. They…they pulled the dogs off in time before anything serious happened." Raoul held back a description of particulars. Christine would only worry. Raoul consoled himself that Erik had suffered far graver injuries in the past. He was sure that he'd mend. "I…was one of the men who had to pursue him."

Christine was silent.

"I had no choice. All I could do was help get the dogs off him. I had to help them carry him in…"

"Carry him? He couldn't walk under his own power?"

"He'd lost some blood."

Raoul waited and let Christine absorb the facts. "Did he recognize you?"

"No."

So he was unconscious, thought Christine.

"The good thing is that Meg was still at work in the infirmary. So she'll have some time with him. She'll be able to tell better than I how serious his injuries are."

Christine was quiet for some minutes. Then suddenly in a small, frightened voice, she asked, "How do you think he'll react to seeing Meg?"

The question took Raoul by surprise. He'd assumed Erik would be relieved and happy to be reunited with his wife. But he caught Christine's meaning. He remembered how angry Christine had been with Meg when she found out her friend had agreed to commit Erik. Would Erik be angry, too?

"She'll explain. He loves her. He's…he's been through a horrible ordeal. I'm sure he'll be thankful to know we're here." They had to hope for the best. Erik needed their help to escape. If Raoul gave in to despair, Erik would end his days like the walking dead, locked away with those other poor shades.

That simply was not going to happen. Raoul wouldn't let it.

They both heard the clock strike the hour. "She should be back by now. I've not heard her come in. I'm going to check on her." Raoul was touched to hear the concern in his wife's voice. The two women had always loved each other. Christine would help Meg through this.

Raoul lay back against the soft cushion in the chair and dozed off immediately. He woke to Christine's worried voice. She was shaking him roughly by the shoulders. "She's not there. She's still not home."

"Calm down, Christine. I would bet you anything she's by Erik's side."

"You think so?" Less sure of herself than before, Christine thought Raoul's explanation might be correct. It had been months since Meg had last seen Erik. She would be beside herself with worry when she saw him carried in, mauled by dogs. It made sense. There was no way Meg could get word to them to tell them she had decided to stay with Erik. She probably couldn't force herself to leave him. "Yes, you're right. I imagine she's watching over him, taking advantage of these moments to tell him what we plan to do."

"Come here." Raoul held out his arms to her, and she came quickly to him. "I'll find a way to go to the infirmary."

"Don't do anything stupid. Don't hurt yourself to get sent there!"

"No, no I won't do anything stupid." Raoul squeezed her tightly forcing a slight, unfeminine grunt from her, as he laughed out loud at her concern. "I know! I'll play the love-sick swain. I'll pretend I'm sweet on Connie and sneak up to see her. What could be more natural? But now I have to get a few hours sleep."

Christine scowled silently for a moment, but she had to admit that it was a plausible excuse. "Just don't be too convincing!"

Hilda had spent more than an hour telling Meg about the disfigured man who had tried to escape.

"The first time he was brought in here when I was around was sometime in August. The whole cartload of them came limping and bleeding into the surgery. Dr. Flescher had no choice but to attend to the guards first. Gunter's nose was bleeding so badly we thought we'd all drown in his blood. Then one of them might have had a fractured head. The other had a broken finger. So we set about dealing with them. They sat and whined like babies. Don't you think all men are babies when they get hurt? God knows why they weren't made to have babies! The whole human race would have come to a crashing halt!"

"You were telling me about the patient." Meg gave her a gentle reminder. She was not interested in the attendants or their wounds.

"Oh, yeah. Well, like I said, this was the first time I laid eyes on him. I have to confess that I was startled when I saw it. You know." She circled her index finger over the one side of her own face. Meg smiled slightly noting that it was the wrong side. "It was kind of hard to look at, but then everyone was pretty messed up. So it didn't take much time at all for me to come to appreciate his other features." The nurse actually giggled. Meg wanted to slap her. But there was a part of her that warmed to Hilda and liked her the better for liking Erik. "Well, what really stood out about him was that he was so… so…quiet and scary. But he sat on the cot in the other room, on the other side of the window there so he could watch us patching everyone up. Himmel, that's the young one with the sweet smile, had to handcuff him to the bed because everyone was busy and wouldn't be able to watch. I glanced over several times to see if he was having trouble breathing or if he was going into shock. Each time I looked at him, he was sitting there…in the same position…his eyes fixed on Gunter and the rest of them. He wiped the blood from his nose several times, but other than that he gave no sign of being hurt. But he was awfully roughed up. Dr. Flescher had to bind his ribs. Then when the doctor was examining him, that's when I noticed he was sitting with his legs spread wide apart. Those guards had gotten him down on the floor and kicked him in the balls several times. One of them was so swollen and purple, Dr. Flescher told me later that he thought he might have to remove it. That was when I got my first look at his equipment. You snuck a peek, didn't you?"

Meg blushed crimson at the thought of sharing such an intimacy with a complete stranger. She stammered for a moment, and Hilda took that as a yes and continued. "He was so polite and sweet. I took to calling him my green-eyed monster! I think he liked it. He likes sweets, too."

"I know." It came out without Meg's thinking. Hilda looked at her questioningly, and Meg rushed to add, "All men are such babies, aren't they? They all like sweets."

Hilda laughed good naturedly and went on, enjoying the conversation. "Then there was the next time I remember he came in." Hilda's tone changed dramatically as if she were angry at something. "That Gunter did it, I would bet you anything. He's got a mean streak. Erik was brought in again, beaten soundly. Gunter said he had fallen. Dr. Flescher had to fix his nose. I suppose it was payback as far as Gunter was concerned."

Meg stood up and walked away so that Hilda wouldn't see how upset she was because of the list of injuries, evidence of blatant brutality that her husband had had to suffer. She felt nauseous.

"Dr. Flescher proved that he was an excellent doctor that day. You see, it's one thing to repair someone's nose when they're normal, but our stallion over there didn't have a normal nose. It was all messed up inside, and Dr. Flescher wasn't quite sure how to restore it to the way it had been. So he sat the patient up in a chair, sedated him as best he could. The trick was to keep his airways open while the doctor worked on the nose. He actually made some incisions and reworked the bone fragments into what he thought was the closest thing to a normal nose he could get. So my monster has actually become even more gorgeous under our care."

Meg smiled broadly at Hilda's kind teasing. Meg had noticed something different about his face. His nose was more symmetrical than it had been, the one side no longer flattened to his face.

"So has he been all right since then? Surely the director of the clinic has stepped in to protect him from continued problems with... Gunter?"

"Well, no. He was in again recently, just a few days back." Hilda dropped the comic tone and brushed her skirt down. Her quiet worried Meg.

"What happened?"

"He was just sick, real sick to his stomach."

"You sound like it was more serious than a stomachache."

"Well, it didn't make sense. The doctor thought it might be he ate something he wasn't supposed to eat."

"How could that happen?"

"Not likely in here. If that had been the case, we'd have been cleaning up vomit all over the place. The whole ward would have been ill. I think someone purposely slipped something into his food and his alone."

"You mean someone poisoned him?"

"I'm just a nurse. I don't know what goes on past those doors, but this man has been in here too many times. If you ask me, they're mistreating him." Hilda's smile returned as she looked at Meg out of the corner of her eye. "Don't get me wrong, I like seeing him. I've been tempted to give him a little extra comfort at night. You're a widow, right? So you know what I mean. It has to be hard on a man living this way, locked away alone, no one to care for him. He's a good patient. Barely asks for anything. It's sad. It's as if he doesn't expect anyone to be nice to him." Meg swallowed hard and forced herself to listen impassively. "One night I sat by his bed. I was curious and I put my hand on his face, along the side where he's disfigured. He pressed his face against my hand as if he couldn't get enough of it. Heard him say something, too, but he was too drowsy to make it clear."

"What? What did he say?"

"I couldn't make it out. It was a name, I think. Something short, something with an 'm,' but believe me he wasn't calling for his mother."

Meg grabbed Hilda and hugged her. "Oh, I'm silly. I just think you're a wonderful nurse to have taken care of him as well as you have. Forgive me. I've been very emotional since I lost my husband."

"That's all right, Connie. Does he remind you of your husband?" Hilda sounded skeptical.

"Oh, no. It's just that no one likes their loved ones to suffer."

"What did your husband die of?"

"He was lost. Lost at sea."

"So you never recovered the body?"

"No, not yet." Meg saw the peculiar look Hilda was giving her. "I just mean that he's out there somewhere. It's hard not to have found him."

Erik struggled to consciousness. His arms throbbed curiously. He couldn't understand why his arms would throb. He tried to lift his head, but couldn't. So he wrenched his eyelids apart and stared out through unwilling eyes. The light was dim, and for a moment he thought of the cavern under the Opera Populaire. In the large vestibule of his home, he had always kept a taper and candles lit. Their flickering light refracted off roughly hewn rock walls and ceilings and across the black surface of the underground lake. Whenever he woke or slept, he had sufficient light to discern the shape of things, the edges, the depths and shallows of his rooms.

The familiarity was comforting. For one brief moment, he felt safe again. Then the truth came to him. He was not in his sanctuary, the sanctuary that had protected and nourished him into adulthood. Nor was he in his home in Rome. He had failed to escape.

The clay he had taken from Celeste, the clay that she saw him take, had clogged the lock when Audrich turned the key. The lock had only imperfectly sealed, compressing the clay, but not engaging completely. Erik had grabbed the covers around his body in the bed and pretended to sleep, his back to the mirror. Then after several hours, hoping to have bored the observer into a dull repose, a half-sleeping vigilance, Erik rolled from the bed to the floor opposite the mirror. He left in his wake the covers mounded and shaped to his form, the mere illusion of a body. He slunk across to the door. He had worked out the specific angle of the door, the breadth of opening that would be outside the perimeter of the observer's vision from behind the mirror along the adjacent wall, if the observer trained his eyes on the sleeping figure in the bed. He pulled on the handle, but the door did not open. The lock was more solid than he had thought. Erik shifted his weight, lifting the door up, pressing it so that the lock came slightly away from the doorframe. The lock clicked open with a satisfying metal twang.

The hallway was deserted. Audrich was on duty, probably asleep as usual. Erik crossed the hallway and quickly reached the door to the back stairwell. He pushed his weight against the door. Gunter had not lied. The lock came loose, and he found himself in the stairwell. No more locked doors stood between him and the grounds.

He had almost made it to the oak tree. If it had not been for the dogs, for so many dogs, he would have reached the tree and climbed. He had studied the grounds for weeks. He had chosen the tree and the very limbs he would grasp to climb to the uppermost branches. These branches swept across the grounds, close enough to the wall and over it that Erik would easily get to the other side of the walled grounds. There was a chance that the drop would kill or cripple him, but he was willing to risk it, anything to die somewhere else or to have a chance to live. There was also a majestic elm on the other side of the wall, the branches of which mingled with those thin extremities of the oak. They would most likely not bear his weight, but he might use them to swing out to catch at a sturdier limb. He had always been excellent at moving across the flies in the theater, at maneuvering along the ropes, pulleys, and catwalks.

But they had sent the dogs after him. He had kicked one away and had torn away from a second, ready to run the dozen feet left to the oak. It was the third and fourth dogs that jumped and latched onto his forearms. The throbbing made sense. He had been pulled to the ground by the dogs' weight, and then the other two came rebounding back snarling, barking, and snipping at him, waiting their turn to dig fangs into resistant flesh, down through blood and bone.

He shifted his weight and searched the room for the doctor or his nurse. The light was just beginning to come through the windows from the east. He shook off the effects of the draught they must have given him. He needed to be alert. He heard feminine voices, one was Hilda's, the other sounded familiar.

He pulled himself painfully to a sitting position. Before he could call out, he heard the door close. The voices were silent. It couldn't be. His mind was playing tricks on him, cruel jokes. She was miles and miles away. Was it because he had thought to escape that her voice came to mind now? He had resolved to wipe her from his heart! He imagined a life without her. His escape was not a return to home. He had no family. He had gnawed at the ties that linked him to Meg and even to his children. They were never his. He wasn't part of that life. She had chased him away, and he would not crawl back to her. So why should he imagine her voice now?

Hilda came briskly round the corner toward his bed.

"Well, let's see who has an appetite for breakfast!" She fussed over him, as she always did. He watched her closely as she pulled the blanket up underneath his bandaged arms and patted the material flat and snug about him. "You look a bit down, my green-eyed monster." She teased him, taking his chin between her thumb and index finger and wagging it gently. "Seriously, you could have died out there. You mustn't put us through that fright again. The doctors will let you go home as soon as you're all well." Of course she wasn't referring to the canine rips and gashes.

"Who were you talking to just now?" he asked, never taking his eyes off hers.

"When? Just a while back?"

He nodded slightly, his heart in his mouth. For although he had reasoned it all through, there was such a longing to find himself wrong!

"Oh, you must have heard me saying goodbye to Connie. She stayed up with you last night. She's a sweetheart. But she's got too soft a spot for tall, good-looking men like you."

Erik looked away for an embarrassed heartbeat, but Hilda was not making fun of him. She patted him familiarly on the thigh, and he met her gaze again. "You know, since Dr. Flescher fixed your nose, you look quite distinguished."

"Perhaps I should go on the stage."

"Ah, that's more like my monster." She winked. She brought him his chamber pot and waited, her back politely turned, for him to use it and give it back to her. "I'll bring you something you like. Maybe some sweet cream with your tea? You rest." She took the chamber pot and left the room.

Cindy? No, she had said, 'Connie.' So it was only his imagination. He'd not succeeded there either. Meg still dwelt deep in his soul.

He had to find a way out. He would go to the ends of the earth. Perhaps there he could escape Meg's voice.

Raoul slipped into the infirmary easily. No one was really watching. It was just past dawn, and the next shift would be coming soon. Those who worked the nightshift were tired and impatient to return to their homes.

He glanced about, but he didn't see Meg. There was a man's overcoat hung by the door. Beside it was a woman's coat, but it was maroon. Meg's was a deep blue. They must have just missed each other.

Quietly he made his way to the main room where he hoped to catch a moment alone with Erik. Upon entering, he saw that there was only one occupied bed.

"Erik?" he whispered.

Erik lifted himself painfully in the bed when he recognized Raoul. He stared perplexed at the man's attire until it dawned on him that Raoul was disguised as a guard. Before Raoul could say another word, Erik slid his legs to the ground and stood. There were supplementary uniforms for the patients folded in the cabinet. He had seen them before. Soiled clothing was taken away, but fresh uniforms were always on hand. Erik rifled through several until he found one that should fit.

"Erik, we've got a plan," Raoul said in an attempt to get Erik's attention.

But Erik interrupted him before he could explain.

"You're the guard. I've overpowered you. You have keys and can get me out of here. Once I'm out, you can do what you like. They can't do anything about it or to you." He threw the uniform to Raoul. "Take your clothes off." Erik stripped off the hospital gown.

Raoul scowled, but he didn't hesitate to do as Erik demanded.

"Did you see Meg?"

Erik's fingers tightened fiercely on the shirt Raoul had exchanged with him. His demeanor became guarded, sullen, closed. Raoul felt a plummeting sickness in his gut. He'd never seen Erik look like this—not in relation to Meg. Erik pulled the shirt over his head and tucked it into his trousers.

"Where will we meet?" the count asked. He could tell there was no use arguing with Erik to delay his escape or to rethink his plan.

Erik's eyes—green fire, ice hot—stared into Raoul's clear blue eyes and said nothing. Raoul sighed audibly, a bitter dread itching under his skin. He wanted to yell at Erik, to shake him. They were alone. There was only this moment, and if they weren't careful the chance would pass them by. It was time for action, let the consequences be damned. Quickly he told Erik where he, Christine, and Meg were staying, several particulars about the inn, their travel arrangements, all in as succinct a manner as possible while they finished dressing.

Erik seized some object from the cabinet and grabbed Raoul by the neck. He loosened his grip somewhat when he felt Raoul tense and heard him sputter a complaint. They began to move out the door into the hallway. At the double doors at the end of the hallway, as Raoul fidgeted with the keys to turn the lock, Erik hesitated. In the opposite direction, he would find Gunter, he was sure, getting ready to wake the patients. It would take no time to rush up behind him and slit his throat.

"What is it?" Raoul whispered through tightly clenched teeth at Erik's delay. He could feel Erik's indecision. "We have to go!"

Erik took a deep breath as if to calm himself and pushed Raoul through the open door.

Behind them they could hear Hilda's stunned voice, raised in alarm. "What are you doing out of bed? Where are you? Dr. Flescher, Erik's gone!" Erik tightened his grip under Raoul's chin. Raoul felt something hard, cold next to his throat.

"That's not a blade, is it? One slip and you could really end my singing career."

Erik pushed him more quickly down the hallway. "Your voice isn't that good, mon ami. But don't worry, it's only a dull letter opener, and the sharp edge is pointed away from you." Of course Erik was lying. The scalpel had no edge that wasn't razor-sharp. But Erik would not spill a drop of Raoul's blood, even if he had to crush the blade in his own hand to keep it from cutting his friend's throat.

At that moment, Gunter stepped out into the hallway from Frieda's room. Taking in at a glance the situation, he came rushing toward them.

"Stay back. He's got a knife," Raoul warned, genuinely tense and worried about the potential for error.

Gunter reluctantly came to a standstill and watched for an opening.

"Oh my Lord," screamed Hilda, suddenly aware of the sharp instrument Erik held to the attendant's throat. She and Dr. Flescher had come out into the hall to look for their patient. Seeing the double doors in the middle of the corridor ajar, they had both come rushing through into the next hallway. They joined Gunter.

Erik waved the scalpel in plain view of the three of them. "Don't move or I'll cut him."

"Erik, you're making a big mistake. Give me the scalpel." Dr. Flescher raised his hand as if to approach, but the fierce look Erik gave him stopped him in his tracks. Raoul, for one moment, sincerely wanted to struggle against Erik's hold.

Erik counted the rooms, found the one he wanted, had Raoul open the door, the door to Laurent's room. "Get inside. Move now or I'll cut him open from ear to ear!" Gunter wanted to rush him. Erik could see him balance his weight as if to jump, but Dr. Flescher restrained him and forced him into the patient's room.

Laurent was startled by the intrusion and sat up in his bed. From the doorway, Erik called to him. "Laurent, come with me."

The man Raoul saw could be anywhere between thirty and fifty. His fine blond hair hung in long strands past his shoulders, disguising a receding hairline. His eyes were a watery blue, large and set far apart. His wide mouth dominated the lower half of his face, but his lips seemed thinned by the effort to clamp them shut.

Grabbing his sheet, Laurent pulled it more tightly under his chin. "Damn, damn, damn, no, nuts, nuts, nuts, nuts and cock, nuts and cock, can't go, shit, shit, shit, sick, sick, sick in the ass, ass, asshole, head!" He further made it clear that he would not leave with Erik by pulling the sheet up over his head. Erik waited for a moment in spite of the fact that he had clearly understood Laurent.

Without another word, Erik closed the door and locked it from the outside. Fists pounded on its surface, but the door was meant to withstand much more than this. Even Gunter's shouts of alarm were muffled.

At the end of the corridor, Erik released Raoul, and the two of them ran toward the stairs.

"Wait! I have to do something." Erik halted at the top of the landing. He didn't wait for Raoul's agreement. He ran back the way he had come and turned down the east wing.

"Erik, what do you think you're doing? You can't go about trying to release all the patients." Raoul cursed, frustrated that Erik would put his escape in jeopardy. Clearly these people needed to be confined! "Now what?"

"Wait." The door to Dr. Richmond's office was not locked. Erik opened it and beckoned Raoul to follow.

"Erik, we don't have time. The next shift starts soon. Wilhelm and Himmel will be here." Erik paid no attention to him. Instead he opened each drawer of Dr. Richmond's desk, one by one, and rifled through their contents. Finally he found what he was looking for. He crammed the file inside his trousers, in the back, as snuggly as he could. He nodded to Raoul, and they rushed from the office and down the hall.

It was curiously calm. Patients had not yet been roused. Staff were concentrated in the kitchen and the staff rooms, preparing to start the morning rounds. Raoul and Erik made it outside without obstacle.

Just in case, Erik pulled Raoul back into an arm lock. Awkwardly they made their way to the front gate. Raoul's horse was tethered a short distance away in the copse of trees, well hidden from the grounds. Gilbert walked to work. The count rode on horseback.

Suddenly a pistol shot rang past their ears. They stopped just inside the compound, looked back at the figure fast approaching. It was Gunter. Behind him, Erik could see several figures, among them Drs. Flescher and Richmond.

"Stop right there, Costanzi!" Gunter shouted. He slowed, bringing the gun up into firing position.

Raoul felt Erik tense, but his only thought was that he was about to die. Gunter could not hope to shoot Erik without the risk of killing Erik's hostage. The second report of gunfire shocked him. The sound clapped like thunder and then echoed against the forest beyond them. Raoul didn't feel anything. And as he thought to turn to see if Erik had been shot, he saw Gunter instead collapse to his knees, roll to the side, and grab his leg tightly to his chest in pain.

Dr. Richmond strode forward, a smoking pistol in his hand, and gave Gunter only a cursory glance before he approached Erik and Raoul.

"Erik. Erik, listen to me. Let the man go."

Raoul was momentarily confused until he realized Dr. Richmond was referring to him. Erik tightened his hold to make a point.

"I won't stop you. You're free to go," Richmond added. "We'll not follow."

"Why should I trust you?"

"You have little reason to, I suppose, from your point of view. I won't keep you here any longer. It doesn't make sense to keep you here."

"I can't stay," Erik said. Raoul wondered at the curiously flat tone in which Erik had spoken.

"I know."

"Gunter?" Erik growled, anger taking the place of the formerly flat, neutral tone.

"He won't be able to do anything."

"That's not what I mean!" Erik hissed. Raoul felt Erik's moist breath on his cheek. He felt as if he weren't really there between the two men, as if they didn't realize he was there. He was in the middle of some conversation they had started sometime before he'd arrived that morning.

"You were right. But only partially. He'd taken her to the roof. Afterwards, he dozed off. When he woke, she was already gone."

"Afterwards?"

Dr. Richmond blushed scarlet.

"It doesn't matter. He killed her! He did it as surely as if he'd pushed her off himself." Erik was unappeased.

"But he didn't, Erik. He didn't. I'll see that he pays for what he's done. I promise I'll see to it."

Dr. Richmond had spoken with the other attendants. Slowly the pieces fell into place with a deafening finality. Wilhelm confirmed that Gunter had sexually abused several of the patients but chiefly the girl. Then, fearing he'd be blamed as an accomplice, Audrich confessed that he'd seen Gunter hanging about the ward that evening and that he himself had lain down to rest since everything was quiet. Something woke him, and he saw the doorway to the roof partially askew. Curious, he went to investigate. Gunter was asleep when he found him on the rooftop. The girl was nowhere about. She was already dead.

Erik stared at the body on the path between him and the prison he'd just escaped. Gunter had passed out. His knee, shattered by the bullet, still bled. He would carry the consequences of his crimes with him.

But would they make sure that he would never do to another what he'd done to Lisbet?

"Just let the man go. No one will stop you."

Erik didn't comply. He kept the scalpel dangerously close to Raoul's carotid artery. "Who will stop you, Dr. Richmond?"

The doctor rubbed his hand roughly over his face and looked out over the grounds. No one else was within hearing distance. Everyone else hung back, waiting.

"I will. I give you my word, Erik. I'll return to England. I'll place myself under my former teacher's guidance. He'll supervise me and make sure that I keep to the straight and narrow. I might still be of use. I can work at the Bragant Institute, quietly, carefully. I was wrong to do what I did, but Erik you must know that you have a good many dark secrets. They won't always stay buried."

"But they're mine, Doctor. They're the only thing I have to hold onto now."

Dr. Richmond bowed his head in defeat.

Slowly, Erik released Raoul and stepped back. Richmond walked to the gate, took out his own keys, and opened the lock. He pulled at the heavy iron bars, and the gate slid open.

Erik gave Raoul a slight push forward, away from himself. Without a glance backward at either of the two men, Erik ran through the gate and dashed into the forest. Within moments, he was swallowed by the dense blackness.

Raoul rubbed his throat as if Erik had held him too tightly. Dr. Richmond watched the woods for several moments. Then he turned to Raoul.

"Are you all right?" he asked, sincere concern in his tone.

Raoul nodded.

"Go help Dr. Flescher with Gunter."

"Yes, Doctor." Before Dr. Richmond walked away, Raoul called to him. "Dr. Richmond, do you mean to keep that promise?"

Scowling, as if he just then realized the new attendant was a witness, he replied, "Yes, I do. What concern is it of yours?"

"Well, I guess I'll have to look for another job then."

"Perhaps not. We don't necessarily have to close the clinic. There are several competent doctors who can take over the directorship. I daresay we might entice Dr. Vernon to return. He was always eager to reform the clinic. He'd be thrilled to replace me. He will do a better job of it than I have. In the meantime, I'll need a replacement for Gunter, and there may be a few other vacancies as well."

CHAPTER 7

❀

The Rape

> *--I will do such things,--*
> *What they are, yet I know not: but they shall be*
> *The terrors of the earth. You think I'll weep*
> *No, I'll not weep:*
> *I have full cause of weeping; but this heart*
> *Shall break into a hundred thousand flaws,*
> *Or ere I'll weep. O fool, I shall go mad!*
>   *King Lear, William Shakespeare*

Erik knew where she was. He knew how to find her. The moment he had tasted freedom, the moment Raoul had told him she was here, not in Rome, not in the past, not hidden and locked away somewhere deep, somewhere soon to be forgotten, in his mind, Erik had known what must be done so that she couldn't hurt him again.

 He found the black gelding, a regal, straight-limbed beauty, hobbled near a brook. The horse whickered suspiciously when Erik drew near. Erik spoke the words that soothed—would he use them to beguile the yellow-haired demon?—and laid his hands on the shivering flank—would he touch her skin and risk burning forever?—and seduced the beast.

 It was daybreak, the sun barely filtered through the forest canopy. Around him were all the living things of the world. Erik sank for a moment to the dirt. The horse snorted, puzzled by the stranger with hands that pleased, large, square hands that stroked and calmed.

Erik placed those bare hands on the root-gnarled ground, brushed aside acorns, thistles, and twigs, and listened to the thrum of the earth. Cool to the touch, it eased his pain. He listened to breaking twigs, knowing without seeing, that a doe and her faun were grazing off tree bark not too far away, listened to a pair of chipmunks chasing each other over mushroom caps and up stately oaks, heard the caw of a crow bouncing on the thin upper branches. He smelled the composting of former forests laid low so that these trees and plants might scale the heights and cradle sunlight in their leaves.

He dug his fingers into the moist soil. Slowly he grew roots. Tendrils burrowed downwards from his knees and shins. The palms of his hands sank like bulbs into the earth to germinate and bring forth tall stalks of crimson buds. His skin turned a dark green with sap. From his limbs, branches knotted and corded, stretched and spread up towards the sky, searching for the darting rays of sun through shivering late autumn foliage. He felt his own leaves unfold and buds unfurl releasing honey sweetness. Nectar dripped down his branches and pooled at his roots. But as he gloried in the verdant fruit of his changeling form, pain stippled across the long green stems. Thorns erupted, curved scimitars, slit the air that caressed him, shredded the breeze that wafted by.

No, he cried out, but to no avail.

His petals leaned, to mourn their virgin fate. No one would taste his nectar; none but the wind would caress his leaves.

Erik rose from the ground. His skin prickled as if thorns had indeed sprouted from his skin. He lifted his head and stretched his throat with a gut-wrenching cry of anger. He was not soothed. The earth had not cooled his fevered rage. A murderous desire swelled in his black heart, even against his will, even in the face of his longing for solace.

She was here. *She* had come to the clinic. Raoul had said that Meg had been with him through the night. To what purpose? To see her handiwork with her own eyes? To ensure that the madman was indeed chained? Even if it had been to cry over lost love, Erik would not forgive her. She had done to him what no one else had. She had opened him up from stem to stern and exposed him. She had known who he was and had cast him out. She had told him she loved him and forsook him, handed him over to his enemies. She had called him husband and sent him away to become the beast.

He couldn't wait until the daylight passed. The horse skittered, frightened by the burning eyes of the monster who mounted him. Erik dug in his heels and spurred the animal on recklessly through the dense forest toward the yellow-haired demon's den. He would not rest, could not, until her eyes no longer watched him, until her voice was silenced, until her breath was gone.

When Meg returned to the rooms at the inn, she found Christine waiting, already aware that Erik had been taken to the infirmary. Meg told her how she had watched over Erik throughout the night, how terrified she had been to see him so vulnerable, knowing how near she had come to losing him forever.

Christine explained that Raoul had rested a few hours and set off again for the clinic not an hour ago. He had worked out a possible plan to sneak Erik out, but it would take a few more days.

Meg was not sure she could bear to wait.

"I have to lie down for a while. I haven't slept all night."

"Raoul will find a way to get a message to Erik. There's nothing either of us can do at the moment. Rest. Do you want me to wake you?"

"In a couple of hours. I need to be back by midday. Erik might have awakened by then. I want to be there."

Meg slipped into her bedroom and shut the door behind her. Dr. Flescher might find it odd to see her back so soon, but Meg was resolved to be near Erik. She removed the starched nurse's uniform and laid it to the side, intending to lie down for just a little bit.

Already she felt his absence like a festering wound. She couldn't tell where the pain was. It permeated her entire body making it difficult to breathe except in ragged bursts and sobs. She found herself crying without ever meaning to. She'd found him. She should rejoice. Raoul had devised a plan they would put into action in the next few days. They would only have to wait until Erik was healed. But soon, very soon, she'd have him back. Yet she still felt as if the earth were about to swallow her whole. The tears kept up their steady course. She couldn't stop thinking of what Hilda had said. He'd been in the infirmary several times already.

Hilda, sweet, sweet Hilda! Meg was glad that Hilda had been there with Erik, that Hilda had teased him, had brought him sweet tea and sugary cookies, had even touched him, perhaps giving him some pleasure. She wouldn't think about that.

Meg cracked the window in her bedroom to let in a hint of fresh air but pulled the drapes to keep out the early morning rays. Clad only in her chemise, she lay down and closed her eyes. She imagined being in the infirmary again. In the dreamlike fantasy, it was nighttime, and Erik lay sleeping.

She softly stepped to his side. He rested, calm, his lips parted. She ran her fingers over his face, over the coarse stubble of his beard, to his mouth. Softly, gently, she slid one finger inside the moist opening and glided over the sharp edge of teeth, across a wet, textured tongue. Removing her finger, she rubbed the slick surface over her parched lips, tasting him, remembering him. His eyes opened. There were green stars in the darkness. His hands opened the panels of her gown and brushed across her skin. Heat pooled in her depths, between her thighs. His palms, his fingers kneaded the softness, cupped the round heaviness of her flesh. His voice rumbled against her body, a shocking scorch of warm air as he spoke her name, "Meg." The tongue she'd touched touched her. It laved her breast in broad, wet strokes, air cooling against a trail of saliva. She could feel the pulsing in her swollen sex and cried out to him in a sigh of longing. "Erik," she called to him.

She found him naked, the curls of hair across his chest soft and springy. She rubbed her fingers over the contours of his muscles, over his chest, and down his belly. She stroked the taut muscles of his abdomen, briefly stopped at his navel, circled it until the tips of her fingers felt his muscles ripple in response. But she wanted more. She wanted all of him. Her fingers combed through the thickening patch of wavy hairs. He shifted his pelvis, wanting her touch, inviting her to take and weigh him in her hand, to cup him, to stroke silky hardness.

She couldn't breathe from his kisses. His tongue did to her mouth what she wanted him to do between her thighs. He lifted her so that she knelt over his body. Deliciously his large, strong hands guided her as she took inside her the length of him. He filled her, stretched her to a wonderful tautness.

Unbidden she began to move. She grabbed the sheet in fists on either side of his face. Her knees flexed as if she were riding a horse, a stallion, black and sleek, wet with sweat, wild with the lust of muscles working, blood flowing. His eyes, green fire, fixed on her, and his mouth parted as he breathed in time to the pulsing work of their hips. He drew her down to lie against his chest and took her mouth hungrily. Slickness in mouth, in her pulsing depths, burning along the pathway to the swollen nub of flesh as her pubic bone found solid resistance in his body. Her knees locked against his sides, her body surged and retreated until the firing of nerves sparked and burst, and she screamed and captured him in a frantic series of thrusts along hard, slippery flesh. The currents of pleasure rippling inside her spread, engulfing them both, as she pulled and clutched at him, gripping him deep inside, feeling him throb with each explosive surge of his seed splashing against her womb. She gloried in his gasp, his tightly woven embrace, the painful ecstasy on his face as he spilled his last drops.

The fantasy was too vivid, almost unbearable, as she collapsed against empty sheets. She wondered that she could survive such an onslaught of longing, was amazed at the savagery of her need of him.

Erik stroked the sweaty flank of the gelding as he examined the hamlet. The inn where she slept was surrounded by flower gardens. It was a two-story building. They had conveniently placed trellises along the southern and eastern walls, but Erik might not find them strong enough to bear his weight.

"I have need of you, my black beauty. You'll do my bidding, won't you?" He crooned softly, seductively to the gelding. All the while, he leaned into the horse's side, laid his ear against his barrel to marvel at the resonance of the animal's beating heart, stroking long caresses along his black fur, slicking off the film of sweat cooling in the autumn air. Erik could feel the horse's rapture as the blood tingled through him after the precipitous and dangerous race through the woods. "Yes, that's right, mon petit cheval. Tu as le coeur tres fort et courageux." He praised the animal, its strength, its courage, its nocturnal beauty. "Tu es beau, beau comme la nuit." Erik clicked, and the gelding fell easily into step behind him.

A man, a man dressed like other men who worked, a man like other men except for his face, except for the reddened, angry thing that ate most of the right side of his face, walked slowly, leading a sleek, black gelding, down the dirt road of the hamlet. A man who was a stranger passed a handful of residents on their way to and fro. The passersby glanced, then turned quickly away, stunned by the unexpected ugliness on a form so proud, so well-formed.

Erik pulled his mount off the beaten path. No one paid heed. No one followed. Erik wound his way to the back of the inn. A bank of windows looked out over a garden of dormant azaleas toward the eastern horizon. In all but one, the heavy drapes were pulled aside to let in the light. Raoul had described the layout of the rooms. Erik pictured stately bedrooms on either side of a sitting room. Beyond one of those windows he would find Meg Giry. She would have returned to rest. He would gamble on the window whose drapes were still drawn, the only one that locked out the rays of the morning sun.

"Come." He clicked to the gelding, bringing him directly underneath the window. As he suspected the trellis was not made to bear a man's weight. However at a distance above his head, an iron spike had been hammered into the wall to fix the trellis in place. That was all he needed besides the cooperation of the gelding. "Sssshhhh," he comforted the beast as he removed his shoes. He placed them in the saddle bag. Then he mounted the horse. Swiftly he raised himself in the saddle, his knees dead center on the horse's back, then brought his knees up to position his feet flat beneath himself. The gelding whickered at the strange sensation and shift of weight, but he was large and strong enough to support the burden. Erik whispered encouragement to the animal, who had pawed the ground indecisively but was immediately calmed by Erik's voice. "Bon, mon ami."

Erik grabbed at a roughened and gouged indentation in the surface of the wall and hoisted himself until he managed to lift his foot to the iron stud. It was barely enough for his toes to settle on, but enough if he kept himself in motion. Stretching out he reached the bottom of the window. It was cracked open only an inch or so—enough for Erik to cup the bottom and push it up. A pang like a ghost crossed his chest. He had always insisted on leaving the window open, even if only an inch, even on the coldest nights in winter, thirsty for the fresh air. Meg complained sometimes of the cold, but she relented, knowing he needed that one assurance of freedom.

The opening was just enough for him to enter. He lifted himself onto the window ledge and slid head first through the aperture. The curtains brushed his face and draped his shoulders as he landed on the floor. The room was gloomy, but the figure on the bed tossed fitfully, perhaps disturbed by his entrance. Erik came to his feet and waited for his eyes to adjust to the dimness. His heart was beating from the climb, he told himself, from nothing more than the exertion of having scaled the wall and breached the window. He stared at her. Her chemise had ridden up along her thighs. Her vulnerability was shocking. The gaping wound of her sex was hidden by the soft dark blond curls at the juncture of her thighs. She stirred, curling onto her side. Her face, soft and smooth, rested on one small hand. The other hand fell across the covers as if she were reaching out to caress a lover. He had been that lover. He had awakened to the touch of that hand thrown across his chest in slumber, her fingers pressing for reassurance along the flat of his stomach, her fingers with a knowledge all their own.

How could she look so innocent?

There were things that had to be done first. Erik slipped to the connecting door and cracked it open to look inside. It was a small sitting room. No one occupied it at the moment. He stepped inside and went to one of two other doors. Inside he saw Christine. She wore a robe hanging loose at her sides. He caught a glimpse of her small bosom barely covered by a silk negligee. He held his breath.

He knew he should not watch, but he needed to know where she would be for the next few minutes. She sat at the dressing table and brushed her long brown curls. He felt himself aroused in spite of his shame, his resistance, his irritation with himself for reacting to Christine with remembered passion. Finally, she finished. She set the brush aside and rose. She went to another room. Erik saw a flash of modern plumbing. He heard the water.

Quickly he went inside. Next to the large wardrobe were several empty suitcases. He took a small one and filled it with clothing from Raoul's side of the wardrobe. Opening several drawers, he took other essentials, just the bare necessities. One pair of shoes he particularly liked he held up to the bottoms of his feet. They were more or less a fit. He dropped those, too, into the black satchel. He found a comb and a razor. He stole a bar of soap and several small towels that had been laid out recently by the maids. He looked round the room to make sure everything seemed in order.

Then he heard the water stop. Taking large, silent strides, he went to the door, but her voice brought him to a sudden halt. Christine was singing. He straightened and turned toward the bathroom door and listened. Music! He had not heard music for days, for weeks. He no longer heard the cascade of sounds in his mind. He bit down hard on the inside of his mouth to quiet his gasp of pain and ecstasy. He couldn't stay and listen. He mustn't. He still had to pack for Meg. He had to take Meg away. They would try to stop him if they knew what he planned.

Reluctantly he slipped out and closed the door silently behind him. In the parlor he took a sheet of stationery and quickly wrote for a brief few moments. This missive he took with him back to Meg's room where he would leave it for Raoul and Christine to find. Once there, he found a similar satchel for Meg. With less hesitation, knowing his wife's articles better than he had known Raoul's, he packed several garments into the small bag.

He lowered the suitcases through the window to the ground. Before he could turn, he heard the covers rustle. He was at the bed before she could speak. When his hand pressed hard across her mouth, her eyes grew wide with shock. For one moment their eyes met. It was enough to freeze Meg's heart.

He released his hold on her mouth. Her lips trembled. Before she could struggle, he wrapped her tightly in the yellow blanket, pinning her arms to her sides and trapping her legs. Speechless, she stared at him. But he could not trust her. On the bedpost hung a silk scarf that she must have tossed aside the night before. Erik grabbed the silk and gagged her with it, tying it in a knot behind her head. Then, without so much as a second glance at her frightened expression, he took the loose end of the blanket and folded it over her head and face.

He hoisted her easily to his shoulder and slipped out into the hallway. No one was about, and he made his way down the stairs to the back entrance and out of the inn in no time. The black beauty waited nervously for him, smelling at the two satchels that had fallen from the sky. Erik leaned Meg unceremoniously against the wall while he attached the satchels to the saddle. He draped Meg over the gelding's withers and mounted behind her. With one hand on Meg's back and the other on the reins, he spurred the gelding back into the dense forest. He would find someplace where he and Meg could be alone, someplace where no one would hear the yellow-haired demon's pleas for help.

"Where is he?" Raoul asked as he burst through the door.

Christine sat in a chair by the window, trying without much success to read. She had not expected Raoul to return until the early evening. She rose from the chair and went to Meg's door to listen.

"Sshh! You'll wake Meg."

"He's not here then?" Raoul searched the room for a sign of Erik's arrival.

"Who?" She turned to see Raoul. He was wearing a strange gray uniform. "Why are you…?"

"Erik, for God's sake. Who else?"

"What happened?"

"He escaped." Raoul pulled at the buttons on the uniform, without caring that they flew hither and thither onto the floor.

Raoul had not remained at the clinic. Once the others had come to carry Gunter inside, Raoul slipped away to return to the inn. There was no reason to keep up the charade. But first he checked the glade where he had tethered the gelding. Needless to say, the animal was gone. Raoul wasn't surprised. Erik had taken it, as they had originally agreed. So Raoul had no choice but trudge the several miles into town. He expected to find Erik near the inn, waiting for him. When he arrived and saw no sign of the gelding or Erik, Raoul went quickly to the suite of rooms he had rented thinking Erik had not been able to wait and had rushed up to be reunited with Meg.

Mostly to himself, he muttered, "Where the devil could he be?"

Christine followed Raoul to their bedroom. She watched him undress, dropping the garments as he walked. As they fell to the floor, she grabbed at them more from curiosity than anything. They were plainly stitched, a dull gray, a blend of linen and cotton. She hadn't seen them before so she surmised these were the clothes worn by the patients at Dr. Richmond's clinic.

"You're sure he got away?"

"Yes."

"Were these his?"

"We switched clothes." Raoul grabbed his robe and jerked it on. He stopped dead and whirled round toward Christine. "He's got my purse."

Both of them arrived at the same conclusion at the same time. Raoul easily reached Meg's door before Christine did. Without a thought to impropriety, he pushed the door open and stepped inside.

The bedspread had been pulled from the mattress and was gone. The drawers were half open, articles of clothing hung haphazardly over their edges. Christine reached out and took the note that lay on the pillow while Raoul uselessly searched out the open window.

"He's taken her." Christine tried not to sound worried.

Raoul and Christine,

My wife and I have not had much time together recently. So I intend to take her away with me. Please do not trouble yourselves about us. I have taken the liberty of stealing a good deal of your money, leaving sufficient funds for you to bide the time until you can secure more from your bank. I have also borrowed a few other items that I will need. Forgive the inconvenience.

I'm not sure when we will be going home. There are many things we have to discuss and do, Meg and I.

Do not follow us.

Accept my fond regards and warm appreciation for your assistance in reuniting me with my wife.

The Phantom

"Somewhere private, you say?" The old man rubbed his eyes and squinted at the tall man who blocked the warm light from the chimney. The gleam of several gold coins, however, shone through quite well.

"Yes." Erik tapped the purse on the pocked surface of the desk. "I also need a wagon, horses, and supplies for a few weeks."

"Uh, well, there is a cabin a way from here. I can give you the directions. It might take you a bit to get there. It's about a mile or so up the side of a hill, surrounded by pine, fir. Good hunting in the area." The old man winked at the blurry face before him. There was a strange irregular color to the stranger's features, but the old man couldn't make out details anymore.

Erik understood what "hill" meant. It was in the mountains. It would be cold. He would need blankets. "Is there a source of water?"

"Oh, certainly, sir. There's a brook that runs down by the cabin. Plenty of firewood in a lean-to nearby. It's a hunter's lodge, but

I can let you have it for the month." The old man stared down at the coins. He touched one with the tip of his finger and looked up meaningfully at the stranger.

Erik opened the purse and added two more coins, doubling the original offering. "Now where are the wagon and the horses?"

"Right this way, sir."

"The road is in good enough condition for the wagon?"

"A small one with team of two would have no problem. The rains have stopped. The road is packed solid. I'll fetch supplies for you. Won't be more than a few hours."

Enough time for Erik to check on his captive bride.

"I'll be back. I expect everything to be ready."

Meg shook her head in annoyance. The insect had crawled across the bridge of her nose several times. Her scream of frustration was muffled by the hardened slick ball of silk that still gagged her. She couldn't touch her face with her hands so she rubbed her nose gingerly against the hard, dry bark. Erik had torn strips from the cover. Then he had lifted her to the fork in the massive trunk of the oak. Stretching her limbs to the point of pain, he had pulled her arms and legs on either side of a thick branch and used the strips of cloth to bind her at the wrists and ankles. He left her there several feet above the ground. She supposed that he had meant to keep her safe from the ground vermin.

Or perhaps he thought she liked sitting in trees?

She tried not to panic. Erik wouldn't harm her. Her certainty was shaken by the fact that he had galloped away from the inn with her lying like a package across the withers of the horse. Each bounce pushed the air from her lungs in a gush. Her stomach was as sore as if he had pummeled her with his fists. Her mouth was ragged, her lips taut and dry. She could tell that her mouth would be tender.

In spite of her resolve to remain calm, she was frightened. He hadn't said a word to her the entire time. Given the gag, she had made as much noise as she could, but he had not even looked at her again. Even when he lowered her from the horse, lifted her to the fork in the tree, and then tied her, he had avoided her eyes. She knew she must look insane. Curiously, he did not. He had seemed cold and calculating as he adjusted the restraints. Then he turned without so much as a goodbye and galloped off with that demon horse of his.

How long had he been gone? She thought hours. Hadn't the sunlight been brighter? She glanced at the ground and tried to distinguish the shadow of the oak compared to the other shadows on the forest floor. Wasn't the shadow longer? The sun must be setting. Then she felt them again, the burning tears, the swollen and runny nose, the pressure building behind her cheek bones and eyes. She could so easily give in to despair. Why was he doing this to her? He had to be mad. He had to be.

An insect buzzed about her eyes and nose seeking the moisture. She screamed and tossed her head until she was dizzy. Exhausted she let her head fall forward onto the branch of the tree and closed her eyes.

She must have slept.

Warm, thick cloth brushed by her, sealing her eyes shut, blocking out even the dim moonlight. She jerked her head away from the restraining touch but found resistance. Moist exhalation dampened her cheek. He had returned for her. She smelled his breath. Swallowing raw, ragged breaths, she tasted him. Large hands yanked at her, pulled her roughly from the perch in the bent fork of the oak. She fell for an instant to land against a solid wall of muscle.

Erik? her mind screamed. A man's body—how could she mistake the long, hard bulge that pressed into her stomach?—slammed into her, driving her back against the trunk of the oak tree. Rough bark scraped her shoulders and buttocks. His hands squeezed her through the material in which she was still wrapped. Fingers searched and pulled, unwinding layer after layer, unbinding her breasts barely covered by her thin chemise. A hand cupped her rudely, vulgarly, hungrily, and she stifled a gasp behind knotted silk.

What was he doing? Was he a stranger? Could someone have happened upon her in the woods? Terror drove her to fight against the wall of muscle, against the winding sheet that restrained her limbs. Her struggle excited him. She felt him bend his knees and grind his hips into her in response. As his face drew near, she felt his breath quicken next to her cheek. He laid his on her shoulder, turned his mouth toward her neck. Teeth scraped her skin, a tongue smoothed away the pain.

She tried to think, to hold on to rational thought. She tried to convince herself she was not about to be raped by a stranger. This was *his* touch, his rough, savage demand. *His* need, ugly and searing, a need he could not let her see! Willing herself to cling to the belief that Erik held her captive, she stilled, housed between hard abrasive wood and hard electric tissue.

"Is it you, Erik?" she asked. But as the sounds gurgled in her throat—the inarticulate sounds dampened by knotted silk—she felt ashamed to hear the note of desperation. She was growing small, smaller. She couldn't hold herself erect in the face of such violent possession. She couldn't bear not knowing who touched her with an enemy's strokes. *Let it not be Erik,* she begged. *Let it not be.* But in the same breath, she prayed, *No, let it, please, let it be Erik.* Unsure what to ask for, she pleaded for the moment to pass quickly. Then as his hand pushed at the material and wedged its way between her thighs, she screamed in her mind, *God, please let it not be Erik!* Not this, not this cruel, frightening monster. She stiffened, unable to breathe, and then fell limp against him. As soon as she stopped struggling, he, too, stilled. His hand withdrew. He held her so that she wouldn't fall to the ground. Then she began to tremble. Shivers wracked her.

His hands wrapped the cover around her tightly, covering her exposed breasts, tightening the knot at her wrists. The hands spread round her back, pulling her away from the trunk, lifting her into the bough of strong arms. She lay, incapable of voluntary movement. She was aware of being carried. Several feet from the tree, he stopped and lowered her to the ground. Then she was alone.

She almost called out to him. She felt as if she were sinking into the ground unable to tell if she were prone or hanging upside down, still or falling. Where were his hands? She was numb with cold. She had to pee. Her mouth was dry, sore. Again the footsteps drew near. Would he crush her under his foot? He stopped so near her face. His hand lifted her head and laid it back again on a soft bundle of cloth.

She heard the muffled smack of cloth against air as he shook out a blanket and laid it over her.

He did not touch her again. She listened to the sound of crickets and knew it was nighttime. She smelled the fire, felt the warmth, heard the crackle of burning wood, and slept.

When she woke, Erik was looking down into her eyes. He moved away from her immediately. He had removed the blindfold. She was lying on her back on hard boards, not on the ground. Her hands were still tied, but more loosely. The gag was not in her mouth, but she was stunned to find she was afraid to speak. She was relieved to see him, relieved to know that the man who had touched her had been Erik.

She could sense he didn't want her to speak to him. He wanted her to lie submissive and quiet. The relief she had momentarily felt upon recognizing Erik died. She felt his anger. It roiled over her through the air. She must be cautious. She would wait and watch and listen to find out what he had in mind. Perhaps her calm would calm him. She remembered the rough way he had pressed against her, the sharpened edges of dry bark, the hardened length of him demanding, surging against her belly. His need she could understand and welcome. She, too, needed. But it wasn't only the need to make love to her, to be held and loved that she recognized in his body, in the brief glimpse of his eyes. There lay something dangerous, something she must find a way to soothe or dispel, or the two of them would be lost.

She felt a jerk forward. Then the floor beneath her began to rock and sway. She lay in a wagon. They were moving. It became clear that they were ascending, following a road that curved endlessly upward. She raised her head to see herself surrounded by boxes and cartons, two dark satchels, a saddle, a mound of blankets, pails, a rifle, a shovel, an axe. Just over a pile at her feet, she spied the black muzzle of Raoul's gelding. He was tied to the back of the wagon and trod behind them. Reason had it that Erik was driving the team. She lay back and sighed. He had a plan. What it was, she couldn't guess.

Her mother had cautioned her, and she had been right. Meg had betrayed Erik. What had it been like for him? Since the beginning of August, Erik had been locked away as a madman. Meg had fallen asleep each night remembering Erik's eyes, what she had thought was the madness in them, but also the sheer terror and disbelief as the metal doors slammed shut on him. She must find a way to reason with him. No doubt she would have to beg him to forgive her.

Later, much later, the wagon came to a halt. Through the back of the wagon, Meg saw only the sloping grade of the dirt road that curved and disappeared among the firs and pines of the mountainside. It was late October, nearly November. There was a smell of snow in the wind. She shivered under the blankets. During the long ascent, she had found herself to be more mobile than she had expected. She had curled into a ball, trying to forget how thirsty she was. Now that they had arrived at their destination, she pushed herself up into a sitting position.

Erik appeared at the back of the wagon, blotting out all light. He hesitated as if he hadn't expected to see her awake, alert, sitting, waiting for him. He unlatched the backboard and pulled out the supplies that lay between him and her. Then he disappeared. Meg slid herself carefully along the wood to the edge of the wagon, her legs spilling over the lip. She was still clad only in her chemise, but she held the layers of blankets around her. Erik returned. Without a word, he grabbed her bound hands, bent, and gathered her over his left shoulder. She grunted with the impact of sore muscles on hard bone.

"Please! I have to pee!" She hadn't meant to say anything. She knew he wanted her silent. But the plea escaped with the gust of air expelled involuntarily from her lungs. Her voice was scratchy. The pressure on her lower abdomen was unbearable. He dropped her feet to the ground and took the blankets from her. He waited, his eyes averted, and she realized he meant her to squat right there and do it. She was too desperate to argue. She lifted the hem of her chemise out of the way and squatted by the nearest tree and peed. It took a long time to empty her bladder, and when she was done she smiled with momentary pleasure.

Erik grabbed her and settled her once more over his shoulder. He didn't slow his pace until he reached the door to the mountain cabin. He bent to clear the door frame and gently set Meg down on her feet inside the room. For a moment, neither of them moved. She drank him in with sad eyes. He loomed over her, his back to the dim light that filled the open doorway. Inside the dark room, he was black in shadow, a silhouette. He grabbed her hands and yanked them forward. Bent over her, he worked at the knot to free her wrists of their binding. She raised her hand to touch his face.

He jerked away from her, stepped back, and froze.

She, too, froze, her hand caught in an empty gesture.

He turned and left her. Surely he had gone to empty the wagon of the other supplies. Meg rubbed at the soreness around her wrists. A keg lay on the table. She uncorked it and held her mouth under it, drinking and sputtering until she choked.

Erik slammed a cup down beside her. The sound startled her, and she jumped. He turned and left again.

For several moments Meg wondered if this might be the day that she would die. She would never have thought him capable of harming her, not even in anger. She considered fleeing. Could she run from him? He was faster, stronger. She might slip away in the night, if he hadn't yet strangled her and if he didn't tie her up again.

It was insane! He was her husband. He wouldn't hurt her. He loved her. She loved him. But he didn't believe she loved him, not after what she had done. How was she going to convince him?

The sound of his entrance interrupted her thoughts. He went directly to the fireplace and dropped the firewood in the rack next to the hearth. Stooping, he set about making a fire. Once the kindling had caught and the wood began to burn, Meg drew near. She held her hands out over the blaze. She hadn't expected him to move as quickly as he did. He whirled round and caught her. His hands dug into her forearms. In a cool, dispassionate corner of her mind, she noticed the bandages wrapped round his own forearms, the stains of dried blood from the attack of the dogs. Yet there was no abatement in his strength. If the wounds bothered him, he refused to let it show.

He forced her back to a chair at the side of the room. Roughly he pulled her arms behind her and expertly using the rope—for he must have included rope among the other supplies he had purchased—he bound her wrists to the chair. Then he roughly spread her thighs and tied each ankle to a separate chair leg.

"Erik!" she found the courage to say. "Erik, you must listen to me."

He crushed her face in his one hand. His thumb dug into the soft hollow of her cheek, his fingers splayed on the opposite side. His face inches from hers, his green eyes alive with hatred—or was it agony?—his mouth twisted cruelly as he answered, "Don't call me that! I'm not Erik!"

As quickly as he had grabbed her, he released her. He stood over her, panting, poised to do she couldn't guess what.

"I was with you last night." She kept her voice soft, quiet.

"Last night you were tied like a Christmas turkey on the ground."

"I mean the night you tried to escape. I was with you all night long."

"Am I to thank you, my love? Am I to kiss your dainty foot and thank you for watching me sleep?" His tone was heavy with sarcasm. He spoke through clenched teeth, his body strangely, dangerously still.

"You're angry with me, I know." She would try to reason with him. He had every right to be angry with her. She would take his anger.

"Angry?" He returned to the fire. He took a poker from a stand of tools, stirred the fire, moved the logs. The blaze rose, licking the tops of the blackened stones. With his back to her, his tone was softer, less wild. Yet there was a calmness to it that disturbed Meg. "Yes, I am angry."

"Erik, I…"

"I told you not to call me that. There is no Erik." When he turned toward her, the lights from the fire danced across his face, changing his features, distorting them into an uneven and flickering mask of light and shadow. The effect unsettled Meg almost as much as his denial. "It's not my name."

"Of course, it is," she snapped. "You're my husband. I damn well should know your name."

He sneered at her, the corner of his mouth twitching without mirth. "Your husband, Madame Costanzi? Your husband died. He expired one night in his own vomit and filth. He lay down and begged, like a dog." He walked toward her, each step deliberate. "Do you want to know what he begged for?"

"Stop it, Erik. Please, stop it. I'm so sorry that…"

"He begged. He begged…for a candle, a small glimmer of light. He begged…for a drop of water. He begged…he pleaded…with… There was no one there to hear him. He was trapped in a black box, and he soiled himself and wept and begged like a dog!"

Meg couldn't breathe. She felt her ribs expand and contract, but she couldn't feel the air. She held his gaze.

"Erik died. Good riddance."

"Then who are *you* if you're not Erik?" If he spoke, perhaps it would all come spilling out. If it all came spilling out, perhaps he would lose the anger as well. If she let him rail at her, would he eventually come to her arms and seek her comfort? "Who are you?" she asked again.

Erik turned so that Meg could see only his profile, exposing only the reddened and irregular surface of his deformity.

"You may call me Phantom, Mme. Costanzi." His voice was low and even, but his words chilled her.

"The Phantom died a long time ago, Erik."

He raised his hands and inspected them. Then he rubbed them down his chest even as low as his groin. "I don't feel dead, Madame. As a matter of fact I feel quite…vibrant with health. I'm surprised that you don't recognize me."

"Erik, you're talking as if you were mad!"

"Mad?"

The space between them disappeared. He reached out his hand, and Meg flinched away from him. He saw her fear. Instead of grabbing her by the throat, he touched her cheek with his fingers.

"Such a lovely face, Meg. The Phantom loves beauty. He would like to have beauty around him always." He withdrew the fingers after they had barely brushed Meg's skin and straightened over her. He cocked his head to the left as if to study her better. "But only true beauty touches him. Not the lie, not the pretense. He knows when beauty is a lie, Madame. You are no beauty."

Meg knew it was foolish to be hurt by his insults. She blinked back tears and took several deep breaths to compose herself. She didn't speak again for several moments. She merely watched him as he unpacked supplies. He disappeared into one of the bedrooms with the satchels. He came out with a large folder filled with papers and laid it on the table. She thought perhaps he'd begin to prepare them something to eat. She was famished. And unless he had eaten in town when he left her in the woods that time, he had to be as hungry as she was.

"Erik, I'm hungry. I've not eaten for days."

Erik sat in a chair across the room from her. He slumped as if tired, but his eyes were trained on her. "Hungry?"

"Yes. I've not eaten for two or three days. I suppose that even the Phantom gets hungry?"

"How do your days compare to my months? I've a hunger that will take a lifetime to satisfy. Perhaps your lifetime, Madame."

"Erik, please untie me." She waited for him to scream at her. His silence was more effective. She recognized the anger as it churned in the pit of her empty stomach. "M. Phantom, we've met before. You remember, don't you?" How could she help but let a bit of her own sarcasm rise to the surface. "I was the ballerina, third from the left. Mme. Giry, my mother…"

"Another traitor," he snapped coldly.

Meg pursed her lips. She knew Erik had forgiven her mother years ago for trying to separate them. "Yes, she couldn't understand how I could love a monster." If he insisted on playing the monster, so be it. She saw the tightened expression around the corners of his mouth and his eyes. She'd hit her mark. "I'm hungry, M. Phantom. You've brought supplies, so I daresay your plan is not to starve me to death."

She didn't know how it was possible, but he crossed the room and stood in front of her before she saw him move.

A whisper was all it took because his face was next to hers. He knelt between her thighs, spreading them even farther apart. His hands braced the back of the chair as if he would fall if he didn't grab hold of something to steady himself.

"I told you, ma petite, your hunger does not compare to mine. J'ai faim. A hunger you cannot imagine. A hunger you don't want to know." His tongue came out and licked her lips. His eyes blazed with a cold fire, studied her, waited to see terror in hers.

There was no fear in Meg's eyes, only desire. She licked her lips, savoring his taste.

For one moment she saw shock. Then she could see nothing because his mouth came down hard on hers. He pierced her with his tongue at the same time that his hand roughly spread her labia. He inserted one finger, then the second, into her vagina. She gasped but was unable to pull away from his kiss or touch. She was already wet. In spite of her fear, in spite of the heartache he inspired in her, she felt drawn to him even now. His kiss paused, but his lips remained on hers, leaving barely the space necessary for their breath to come and go. His forehead leaned against hers, his eyes—heavy lidded—looked into hers. His exhalation, soft and sweet, fanned across her tongue, her mouth. Was he shocked, too, to find her soaked and swollen, anxious for him to make love to her? Had he expected to enter her dry? To stretch and tear her with his thrust? There was no pain. He had stunned her by his blatantly violent possession, but she yearned for him to insert a third finger, for his hand, for his cock. She began to move her hips. She wanted more, more of him, and she wanted him to know how she burned for him.

He withdrew his fingers. He stood and stared down at her. His breath ragged, his emotions torn. He brought his fingers to his face and smelled her, his nostrils flaring. Like an animal, thought Meg. Then he licked them, tasting her. Meg gasped at the naked sensuality of his act, at the sight of his red tongue laving the cream from his fingers. Never had she imagined wanting him so badly. If he touched her, she would come. She would burst into a thousand stars if he touched her lips. She saw his arousal. He strained to be released from the dark trousers. The fabric pulled at the buttons along the fly. She held her breath as he lowered his hand and offered his fingers to her. Meg took them into her mouth, her strange taste on his familiar skin, and sucked them.

He bent his knees and knelt again before her, his hips wedged between her legs. She closed her eyes.

She licked and sucked at his fingers and imagined the bulging member freed. She felt him pulling her bottom forward on the chair. She saw, felt, imagined him—hard and silky—slide inside her. The hard wood of the chair pressing from below, the hard bone of her pubis pressing from above. And she came.

He took his fingers away. Pulled them forcefully away, raking them over her teeth. Eyes open, she convulsed in his embrace, and he held her together so that the pieces would not fall to the ground. Then he kissed her. He kissed her as if she were drizzled in honey, kissed her as if she were his sustenance.

Then, as the shudders in her body subsided, she began to cry. She recognized her sobs as if they didn't belong to her. For he hadn't taken her! He knelt in front of her, but the silky hardness inside her had been his fingers. He had held back, away from her, his own pleasure. He had driven her forward with his need, his demand. She had wanted all of him, but he had not shattered with her.

"Little Meg. Little Meg, envious little Meg who stole down to the black pit in search of a monster." His voice was soft and sweet at first, as if he were telling her a nursery rhyme. "She wanted to hold the monster in her hand. She wanted to touch him with her golden locks and make him bow down to her sweet light. Little Meg, little Meg asked the beast to pretend to be a man. She said, 'I'll make you a man. I'll take the beast away and make you a man if you bow down before me and worship me.' The beast liked the taste of little Meg. He might have eaten her, but it was so tempting just to nibble, to taste her, to lick from time to time. And as he licked the licorice from her nether lips and drank the honey from her mouth, she stole round his neck a collar, spiked with diamonds and nails so that she could lead him, her beast, where she wanted them to go. But he thought she had performed the miracle. He thought he was a man. Poor monster, little Meg wanted the beast. Little Meg had lied, lied, lies. And one day, little Meg tired of sharing her bed with a beast who thought he was a man. And she told him, 'Beast, leave my bed. You dirty my sheets and your claws tear my pillows. You scratch the wood on the bedposts, and you leave your smell everywhere you lie.' The beast protested, 'But Meg, you are my wife. I am a man, not a beast.' 'Beast,' she answered, 'you can't believe that I would marry you. A woman does not marry a beast. You are not a man.'"

Meg's sobs had faded as she listened. The pleasure was gone. His body was cold like lead against her. The Phantom kissed her lips chastely, stood, and walked away.

It was a meager meal, but it would keep them alive. Erik knelt beside Meg and raised the spoon to her mouth. She jerked her head away and pursed her lips against his offering.

"You said, Madame, that you were hungry."

"I can feed myself, Monsieur," she replied testily.

He rose so abruptly that she turned to look at him. He set the plate down on the floor and went to the table. There he picked up a serrated blade, the one he had used to cut the dried, salted pork. Meg could see the opaque gleam of grease on the blade as he held it tightly in his grip. She searched his eyes, biting her tongue to keep from screaming. When he drew close enough to strike, she couldn't help but close her eyes and look away. She felt the tug and grind of the blade on the rope that bound her left hand to the chair.

She was sure he heard her audible sigh of relief as he passed to the other side and cut the rope that anchored her right hand. Kneeling once again, while Meg rubbed the bruised lines across each wrist, Erik released her ankles from their bondage. Without so much as a word, he went to the door, grabbed the coat from the hook, and walked out of the cabin, closing the door behind him.

She sat watching the door as if he might turn around and come back in. She imagined him rushing to her side and begging her to forgive his roughness, his silent torture. Nothing happened. Time continued to pass, but the door remained steadfast in its immobility.

Her foot touched the tin plate, and she remembered her hunger. She lifted it and smelled the salty pork. Her mouth was awash in saliva, and she took the spoon and shoveled the mash inside until her cheeks were bulging. She made small animal noises of pleasure as she swallowed. It was quite good, rich and savory. But anything would taste good to her after having tasted silk for so many hours and nothing else but her husband's anger.

She disguised her burp of satisfaction with a useless "excuse me" and took the plate to the basin to wash. Still the door remained stubbornly unresponsive to her anxious gaze. Her hand was trembling, she noticed, as she wiped the plate and set it on the counter. Behind her on the table, she saw a second plate filled with food. Erik's. He hadn't eaten yet. Why was she concerned for him? He was obviously quite capable of taking care of himself. He had for many years without her help.

For a moment she considered the hypothetical life he might have led under the Opera Populaire had she not ventured down into the vaults and found the doorway to his second sanctuary. She always assumed he'd have died if she hadn't insisted on finding him. If she hadn't given him something else to live for. If she hadn't intruded on his life. What if she were wrong? He had gotten a fever. But wasn't that after she had fallen into the well and he had rescued her? She had lain for a couple of days with a fever. Afterwards he had caught it perhaps from her. Then there was no reason to believe he would have gotten ill if she hadn't come searching for him.

He would have grieved. He might have languished. Yet he himself had often said that his body betrayed him. Even when he had wanted to die, his body resisted death. She felt the tears burn her eyes. She had prided herself on saving him. She had dragged him into the light, hadn't she? Had it been cruel?

"I won't regret it. I can't," she said out loud to no one in particular.

Her muscles ached from long hours of rough travel followed by hours of forced immobility. She stretched. It felt so good to have eaten and to be able to move again. There was a nice space between the counter and cupboard along one wall and the table. She listened for him but heard nothing. So she decided that her body needed exercise more than rest. She had had enough of rest lying across his horse and then on the floor of the wagon. She had spent hours tied to the chair while he settled them into the cabin and meditated on her fate.

Meg stood with her left hand poised on the counter and began to stretch. She rose sur la demi-pointe, repeating the movement several times until she felt her tendons accommodate the stretch. She progressed to la pointe and held the pose, counting in her head to ten, then to fifteen, and so on. She bent from the waist, her legs straight, feet in first position, then second, and so on. She continued with a series of pliés. She was beginning to sweat, feeling the burn in the back of her legs all along her sides, even in the buttocks. Then she struck an attitude, her leg raised behind her, knee bent at a ninety degree angle and foot sur la pointe. She performed several repetitions. Suddenly she felt light. She raised her arm en l'air and made small circles and then large circles and reversed them. After each set of exercises, she switched her pose and balanced her other hand on the counter.

She had forgotten about the door. A cold blast of frigid air struck against her unprotected limbs. When she turned and saw him standing in the doorway, his stillness was so complete, so menacing, she gave a small yelp of surprise.

"Erik! You scared me."

His face was very red from the cold, and there were snow flakes on his shoulders and hair.

"I often have that effect," he said dryly.

How long had he been out there in the snow? Meg noticed through the window the eerie whiteness. The darkness was dispelled by a thick layer of new snow.

"Will we be able to get out?"

"There is no getting out of here, Madame." He kept his back to her.

She ignored the implications of that statement.

"You can't mean for us to stay here in the middle of nowhere, Erik."

"I told you Erik is dead!" He shouted at her, his face contorted with anger. "Stop calling me that. Stop talking altogether."

Several moments passed without either of them speaking or moving. Finally, in a small voice, very calmly, Meg said, "Your food is cold. Do you want me to heat it up for you?"

Erik looked down at the tin plate on the table. Quietly he answered, "I'm not hungry."

Meg started to take the plate away. The quickness of her movement must have triggered an automatic response in Erik. He grabbed her hand and took the plate from her. The contents swished messily onto his hand, but he didn't seem to notice. He retreated to the chair where Meg had been tied. He sat and eagerly ate.

Meg turned back toward the counter to hide her smile. He would be easier to talk to once he had eaten. The man had the willpower of ten. He was perfectly capable of killing himself by starvation if he set his mind to it.

"You haven't asked about the children," she said, hoping to change the subject and to remind him of what they shared.

Something whizzed by her head, narrowly missing her. Bits of gravy sprayed her before the plate clanged against the wall and fell to the counter. She jumped, her hand pinned to her chest.

Erik took her by the throat and stretched her neck. He pushed his thumb hard against her chin to tilt her face up to meet his. She rose on tiptoe and for one giddy moment thought he might lift her off the ground. She clawed uselessly at his hand. He lightened his grip just enough so that she could breathe, but her eyes were wild with panic.

"I have no children, Madame."

He released her throat and grabbed her by the arm. He dragged her to one of the doors. Inside the small room was a bed. He threw her on it. Dust rose from the impact. She caught herself before she might have tumbled to the other side and onto the floor. Righting herself, she called to him just as he turned to leave.

"Erik!"

"You killed Erik!"

"Then kill me, too!" she answered in desperation.

He took several steps toward the bed, but stopped when he saw her stiffen.

"Would you die with me, Meg?"

"Yes!"

"If I were to take a knife and slit my wrists, would you slit yours?"

"I don't know if I would have the courage to do it. But I would offer you my wrists and ask you to do it for me."

He studied her as if trying to gauge if she were sincere or mocking. He took another step forward, paused, then rushed to her. He bent over the bed to look down at her. When she didn't move away from him, he cupped her face in his hand. Slowly he lowered her to the mattress, hovering over her, his weight braced by one arm, his hips resting solidly against her.

"You and I could die together. We could lie together in death. I would take you, Meg. We would join our two bodies." He kissed her parted lips. His were still cold from the time he had spent outside. His fingers, too, were cold on her cheek. His breath was warm. "I would love you," he nuzzled her cheek with his nose, "to death." He bent her head to the side and kissed her throat, planting a series of warm, wet kisses from her jaw to her collarbone. He licked the bruised flesh where he had bitten her in the forest. "We could open our veins and lie afloat in our blood." His hand brushed down her throat and stroked the smooth muscles of her arm. He drove his hand between her and the mattress and lifted her toward his chest, bringing her closer still to his body. "Would you die for me?"

"Oh, God, Erik, I would so much rather live for you."

She tried to hold him, locking her arms around him. But he broke away from her. His green eyes stared down at her, their surfaces flat.

"Meg, only the dead lie with the dead."

The room darkened, and Meg's heart forgot its rhythm.

He left her. He closed the door behind him and left her lying on the bed. The reflected light from the snow cast a white mist inside the room. That was her only light. She wondered how she would reach him. How could she save a dead man?

Raoul squeezed Christine's hand. Squinting at them, the old man confessed that a stranger had indeed passed through the town. He protested that he couldn't see very well anymore, and unfortunately he had been quite alone when the stranger came in.

Earlier Raoul had questioned the stable boy. The boy remarked that the man hid his face. He had stood in the darkening shadows of early evening, his coat collar high, his profile barely visible. The boy thought he had seen something strange about the man's face, but he couldn't explain what it was.

"Was he accompanied?" Christine had asked the boy, unable to resist seeking more information, worried as she was for her friend.

"No, it was just him."

Raoul had given Christine a meaningful glance. Erik might have asked Meg to wait somewhere for him, somewhere outside the town limits. Perhaps he had meant to throw them off the trail if he came into town without Meg.

"Did he give you any indication as to his destination?" Raoul asked the old man.

As if trying to recall some long distant memory, the old man rubbed the stubble on his chin.

Raoul reached into his new purse and drew out a gold coin. The old man blatantly sneered. Obviously Erik had been quite liberal with Raoul's money. Raoul scowled but dipped his fingers inside the small purse and drew out several more newly minted coins he had attained at the bank in Linz. That had delayed them already several days. The old man nodded in approval.

"He didn't seem to have one."

Raoul's hand slammed down over the coins just before the old man could brush them off the counter into his own.

"Where did he go? Do you have anything else to offer for these coins?"

"All right, milord. No need to get testy. I was going to tell you. Although mark my words, I wouldn't, except that I need the money. I've got a lame son, and I'm not going to be here forever to help him make his way. So I hope it's worth the risk. The man you're looking for made it clear he wanted no one to follow him or to know his whereabouts."

"We know him. He won't feel the same about us. I assure you. You'll come to no harm." Christine spoke with such confidence that the old man visibly relaxed.

"Well, that's different. That does settle a man some to know that the other won't sneak back and cut our throats in the night. 'Course he was a right serious man."

"Yes, he has that effect on people," said Raoul, dryly.

"He wanted someplace to hole up for a while. Had a list of supplies he wanted…"

"Do you have the list?" interrupted Christine. Raoul gave her a puzzled look.

"Come to think of it, it might be over here. We reuse paper. The backside was clean, I believe." The old man picked up a bundle of loose sheets and held them so close that the tip of his nose brushed the surface of each one.

"May I?" Christine held out her hand, and the old man handed the pile to her.

While she searched for the list, Raoul reminded the old man that they needed to know where Erik was headed.

"I told him of a cabin, a hunting lodge, up on Mt. Bauer. It would take the better part of a day to get there."

"We'll set out tomorrow."

"Won't do you much good. It's snowing. The road won't be passable in a couple more hours. You'll never make it up the hill."

Meg was sleeping. He had barricaded the door to her bedroom and left her alone in the dark. He had heard her crying for a short time. But he had heard grown men crying at night at the clinic. A stab of anxiety forced him to the cabin door again. He opened it wide. Icy crystals of snow melted as they touched his skin. A gust of frigid wind blew through the room. The papers he had been examining flew from the table. Quickly he closed the door and stooped to gather the lost sheaves.

Strangely it was as if he picked up his own mutilated corpse. Pieces of his soul, too, lay scattered among the black ink words that were his and not his.

He had stolen the file because he feared anyone knowing his secrets. He knew that within those papers lay the truth of his past. They were his confessions, so to speak, and he had revealed that he was the Phantom of the Opera Populaire. He could never leave the clinic if he didn't steal or destroy Richmond's notes. Once he had gotten clear of the clinic, it occurred to him to burn them.

That first night in the forest with Meg, he had built a fire and had removed the file from the satchel where he had kept it. He opened it and took out several sheets of paper. He held them out over the flames only to jerk them away and stamp out the small sparks that had caught the corner of one. He shuffled through them, admiring the exact handwriting, the neat and precise organization. He caught his name peppered throughout, but he feared reading the text itself.

Instead of destroying the file, he had returned it to the satchel and had brought it with them to the cabin. But he had resisted examining it. The words were about him. Therein lay his secrets. Yet the words were Dr. Richmond's. He wasn't sure that he could bear reading about himself through the discourse of his enemy.

Was he a coward? He laid the papers on the table. He chastised himself for the delay. Chilled to the bone, he went to Meg's door to listen again. She was asleep. Was she dreaming of him? Were they nightmares? Or was she dreaming of escaping from him? She had come to save him. Raoul had told him as much. It hadn't made a difference at the time. Erik had been beside himself with anger.

But he had watched her from the window. He had made the mistake of touching her. Again.

On the table, the papers mocked him. He was not a coward.

He sat down in front of the file. The light from the oil lamp was sufficient to read. He rubbed his hands along the tops of his thighs, summoning every ounce of his courage. Finally he opened the file, took the first page, and began to read.

"I have to pee."

She startled him. She stood like a child in the doorway. He quickly covered the papers he had been reading. He had forgotten to put the barricade back when he last stole in to check on her. She had been so quiet that he had needed to see her, to make sure she was breathing.

"Go back to bed," he replied sternly.

"I can't. I have to pee, and I can't find the chamber pot in the dark."

She had always hated to rise in the middle of the night to use the chamber pot. She tried to wait until dawn. Then she would hasten from the bed and use it quickly only to clamber back under the covers again, placing her cold feet against Erik's legs.

Reluctantly, Erik brought the lamp to the room. Meg stepped back so as to allow him to enter. She looked up at him so earnestly he was momentarily at a loss. As he suspected, a chamber pot lay just under the lip of the bed. He pulled it out and handed it to her. She had always had a dread of the darkness under beds, too. He watched her as she went to the opposite corner of the room. Instead of lifting the bottom of her chemise, she dropped the garment from her shoulders and stepped out, in spite of the cold, naked into the golden light. As he admired her hourglass figure, she slowly turned to face him. Even after three pregnancies, she had a taut body, all curves and smooth flesh, perhaps a bit riper, more generous around the hips. Her bosom had always been large for her small stature, but now her breasts were full and voluptuous in a mature way that pleased him greatly.

She squatted over the chamber pot, and still he couldn't look away. He watched and listened to her pee, the sound loud in the cavernous porcelain vessel. There were pieces of newspaper on one of the tables, and Erik took one to her so that she could wipe herself. She thanked him as she stood and turned toward him. He looked down at her, he completely clothed, she completely naked.

When she reached out her hand, Erik reluctantly stepped back a half step, enough to tell her that she mustn't.

"Stay with me. I'm cold."

He shook his head, not trusting his voice.

"Give me your hand. Feel me. I'm cold to the touch." She reached out and took his hand. He pulled it away as if it burned.

"Go to bed, Meg. Tomorrow night I'll build you a fire. I'll bring another blanket."

He started to leave, but she wasn't giving up that easily. "But there aren't enough blankets, and you'll be cold in the night. Come sleep beside me. We could put one of the blankets between us if you prefer."

"I have a fire going in the next room. I won't be cold."

"Do you still like to sleep naked?"

"Madame, in the clinic, each patient is expected to wear regulation uniforms during the day. At night, too, we have a regulation uniform."

"But we're not in the clinic anymore, thank God. You're a free man, Erik."

"Erik, indeed, is free. Nothing can hurt him. I don't think you want the Phantom to come to your bed."

"What if I do? What if I desire the Phantom? What if I feel naughty and dangerous and want the Phantom to hold me, naked like I am now?"

Erik hesitated. He had never seen her so brazen. He couldn't play this game with Meg. It was all unraveling. She knew him too well.

"Don't," he pleaded. "I can't."

"Why can't you, Erik?" She sounded concerned, sad.

"Because you might touch me."

"Why can't I touch you? I'm your wife."

"Because I might…I might…hurt you."

Quickly before she could question him further, he left the room and closed the door.

He had tarried too long. He might have done it in the forest. She had been blindfolded. He could have killed her with a rope. He had almost raped her. He pulled away just in time to control himself. Among the supplies, he had bought rope. The noose would have fit neatly round that long neck of hers. He could have thrown the other end over the thick branch at the fork in the tree and dragged her from the crook and left her to dangle, her ballet feet making those little twittering steps in a perpetual jetté. He imagined her body forever suspended between heaven and hell. But it would not have been such a pretty dance.

Every day since their arrival it had snowed. It had taken him nearly an hour to push the door open inch by inch, digging the snow away with his hands, then with a cup. Finally there was enough room to wedge his shoulder through the narrow gap and crawl out on top of the snow bank. They still had half a bucket of water, a circular lid of ice along its surface, inside the cabin. There was also plenty of firewood, but he hadn't started a fire. He had watched the snow fall, saw it accumulate, knew it would block the door, making it impossible for them to leave. He could admit it now that he was outside knee deep in freshly fallen snow. He had panicked to think that he was trapped again. It didn't matter that there were no guards, no chains, no bars. He couldn't bear to be enclosed. So he had worked at pushing the door open and digging the snow away little by little until he was free.

He used the shovel to clear a path from the door. His breath came out in little spurts, frozen clouds. The fever of his exertions slowly dissipated, the sweat turning to crystals in the cold. The world slept. He was surrounded by silence except for the brittle clacking of overhead branches. He saw tracks like hieroglyphs round a tree trunk, a squirrel he surmised.

It was good to stand alone under the clear sky. It would not snow today. It felt good to be cold. He had been so hot in the cabin, wild with impatient anger. Reluctantly he admitted himself wild with longing for the yellow-haired demon, his demon, his tormentor, his Meg. He tried to dispel the memory of her heat, her wet heat on his hand, her live flesh milking his fingers. He felt a stab of longing in his groin, a responding twitch of his own flesh against the tight fabric of his fly. He swallowed the sudden rush of juices to his mouth. Meg. He had rarely passed a night without her touch. He had assumed their passion would cool over time, but it hadn't. Not until she sent him away. And then it had seared him like a hot brand, filled with anger and pain as well as desire.

Prim, proper Meg. Not so prim and proper in his bed! His body was alive with the memory of her mouth, her tongue, her delicate fingers. He had taken that body, the body of a dancer, and bent it one way and another. He had nibbled every inch of her and pierced every orifice. And he had made her beg him to stop and then not to stop. As petite as she was, she had had him on his knees, his heart in his mouth. He could have died happily tangled in her limbs, joined at the belly and groin, buried deep inside her warmth. That would have been heaven.

The image of her slight body swaying at the end of a rope assaulted his senses. Not pretty. The rope would have cut into that creamy white skin. The blood would have stilled and turned purple, then black. Her tongue would have swollen and protruded from her blue-lipped mouth. She would have evacuated her bladder and bowels, soiling her naked legs.

He had been fooling himself when he said he wanted to drag it out, when he protested that death at that moment, in the forest, would have been too soon, too easy. He had vowed that she had to pay for her betrayal. He saw it now for what it was—the ravings of a madman.

Even though they had sufficient water, Erik had taken the extra pail and wandered down the path to a clearing among the evergreens. He stood over the brook where the surface of the water had frozen to a glassy sheen. Just under the cap of ice, he could see the stream running over smooth, polished pebbles. Looking at an angle, to avoid the monster, he brought the edge of the shovel down hard on the ice to break through to the cold mountain water beneath and dipped the pail into the stream.

His forearms ached from the exertion of the morning. He had removed the bandages. The wounds had healed nicely, leaving only tenderness in their wake. He lifted the pail of water and trudged through snow, sinking deeply with each step. He cursed that he hadn't thought to buy snowshoes. Perhaps he could find some in the stable. Later he would check on the horses and look to see if some hunter had left snowshoes among the odd assortment of equipment. He might try to set some traps for small game somewhere off among the trees. He was not a hunter, but fresh meat would be a welcome supplement to their supplies. He had no idea of how long they might be stranded on the mountainside. He hadn't expected such a heavy snow so early in the season. He had never been at the mercy of the elements before. He had come thinking only of revenge and exorcism. But he tired of the intensity of his own anger. He didn't want to feel anything ever again. Yet he could not go on with the burden of what Meg had done to him, the fear of what she could still do to him.

As he approached the cabin, he saw movement inside. It was Meg. Starved for activity, bored by his silence and neglect, she had taken to doing her ballet exercises. She had tied her hair up with the knotted silk scarf he had used to gag her. He snorted a quick laugh at her ever practical nature. She stood in her chemise. He'd not thought to mention the clothes he'd packed for her. She was using the edge of the table as if it were a bar. Bending, curling, she stretched and worked the large muscles in her legs, her arms, her back. She stood sur la pointe. He remembered her telling him the term for the impossible position—all one's weight resting on the tips of one's toes. Her chest thrust forward, her torso extended, he admired the taut flatness of her stomach. A flash of pain crossed her face, and she leaned forward. Erik dropped the bucket beside the window into the snow and raced inside. He grabbed and lifted her into his arms, thinking she was about to fall.

She grunted from his sudden embrace, annoyed and puzzled. He set her down in a chair.

"Oh no, Erik, not again!" she groaned. "I won't let you tie me up." She began to struggle, but his hands held her down. He scanned her body until he found the source of her pain. Her toes were bloody. She didn't have her ballet shoes, and like the stubborn woman she was, she had tried to stand on the very tip of her toes without proper support or protection.

"Be still," he demanded. He took her foot, but she squealed and pulled it away from him in reflex. Struggling to keep his hands away from the most ticklish part of her body, she kicked her foot out in a straight line into Erik's face. The flat of her foot hit his nose soundly with a hard thud. Swallowing a curse, Erik cupped his nose in his palm. His eyes watered.

"Oh my God, Erik." Meg tried to remove Erik's hand from his face to see the damage. "You tickled me," she protested. "I didn't mean to…"

"Leave it. It's fine."

Meg was relieved to hear his voice level and calm. If he had cause to be angry, certainly being kicked in the face would only add to it. The fact that he wasn't screaming at her or striking her was obviously an encouraging sign.

"Sit back, and let me see," she said, coming forward onto the edge of the seat and still trying to get Erik to lower his hand.

Erik had fallen back onto his haunches when she hit him. Now he sat on the floor, surprised more than injured. She examined him as if she were in charge. He felt the sharpness of the blow receding fast. The tears that had welled into his eyes were simply a result of the blow and where it had landed. Her small hand pulled at his, and he let her remove it. He studied her faun-brown eyes. They were far too large for such a small face. It made him giddy to look at them. If they were only smaller and crooked. And if they were dull instead of a rich brown, like chocolate, he might have looked away.

His nose was not bleeding. Meg ran her fingers over the strange surface of it. Dr. Flescher has smoothed and opened the one side which had been somewhat flattened and collapsed. He had created a more symmetrical effect that made the disfigurement recede from the nose. It was more…common…more normal in appearance in spite of the fact that it was still not exactly right. Meg hadn't been sure how to react to it. As she studied his face, he gave her such a strange look. Then she recognized that look. It was woeful and full of wanting.

Without thinking, she kissed him. She held his face in her two hands and kissed him. Lips touched lips. A sweet kiss it brought them together as if they had been two stray pieces in a puzzle. Then she lifted her lips to his nose and kissed it very gently, too. She felt him move his face in her hands, tilting his head so that her lips grazed his forehead. She slid from the chair onto his lap, her knees straddling his body. Her chemise rose from the action, leaving her bare and open to him, shockingly open.

"Meg," he whispered. His eyes were closed; his hands lightly touched her shoulders. He leaned into her kisses, silently leading her to his cheek.

She kissed the corner of his mouth instead and flicked her tongue into the crevice where his two lips came together. She angled her way to the sad twisted surface, near his cheekbone. She had long lost any revulsion, if ever she had felt any, for the strange landscape of her husband's face. Her fingers and tongue knew every crevice, every protuberance. The skin along his disfigurement was very sensitive, as if it were tissue of a different sort. He liked the feel of her hand, especially the touch of her lips along the side that he usually kept hidden. She pushed his long stray hair back away from his face and kissed the caracole of his ear. Then she found herself swaying in his lap, responding to a desire that would not leave her. She rose slightly and brought his face to her chest, wanting him to take her breasts. Willing to be led, he nuzzled her. His hands had traveled to her bottom. He cupped her buttocks, round and full but all muscle, and he shifted her so that she came down hard against the growing bulge in his trousers.

"Oh my God, Erik. Please, please," she began, then hesitated. She couldn't bear it if he pushed her away now. But the pain welled up inside of her and spilled over into trembling lips and tear-burnt eyes. "Please, please forgive me."

He froze. His hands clamped tightly on her bottom held her motionless in his lap.

"No, no, no, no, no, no," she wailed, sensing he was about to push her away. She lifted his face from the soft place where he had rested it. She glared at him. She felt like a demon ready to throw a lightning bolt at his heart if he didn't obey her. "I was wrong. I made a terrible decision, and it was wrong. Don't tell me that you've not made mistakes, M. Phantom!"

She felt him shift under her. His hands left her bottom, and she knew he would set her aside. She clung to him, wrapping her arms around his neck, sliding her legs around his hips. She pressed her knees hard against his sides as if he were a recalcitrant stallion.

"You must. You must forgive me, or we're both lost! Listen to me!" she shouted by his ear. "I love you! You love me!"

Somehow Erik rose, bringing Meg with him. She hung on for dear life. Instead of pushing her from him, he settled her on the rug before the fire she had lit upon waking to a cold, empty cabin. He fell heavily on top of her, but she didn't complain. His hands began to pull at her chemise, and she helped him push the fabric up and off. She worked at opening his shirt and pushing it out of her way, as he fumbled in a wild panic with the buttons on his trousers. When she felt him naked and engorged between her legs, she squirmed until he was at her opening and then pushed until she felt him sink deeply inside her. She came instantly. Unabashed, she screamed and twisted under him. She demanded, begged that he thrust hard, harder. She remained at the pinnacle of a long coasting ride of pleasure and then impossibly soared again into a second, even deeper orgasm. She wanted to taste him, to swallow him whole. She feared she was bucking so violently perhaps she'd fling him from her body. But then she felt him anchor her hard against the floor with his own dark, pulsing need. She opened her eyes and saw his—green and fiery—staring down at her. Without breath, he whispered huskily to her, "Come, Meg. Come again for me." She did. She reeled out of control, her body demanding, grabbing at him, pulling and throbbing so hard that she thought they'd become locked together, unable to ever separate. Then he gasped and cried out, "Oh Meg, come with me. Oh God, Meg!" And she felt filled with him, awash in him, pierced through to the heart by his passion. The waves broke and broke again. He folded himself over her as if he'd wrap her in his embrace forever. She squeezed his tense body inside and all around her. There was nothing that could come between them, not a whisper of air, not a thought.

They must have slept. When Meg woke, Erik lay to the side, his body partially covering hers. Her naked, exposed skin was warmed by the dying embers of the fire. She smiled at the intimate feel of his now quiescent flesh on her thigh, but she scowled to realize that he was almost fully clothed. That had been the only thing to mar an absolutely perfect coupling. She hugged him, enjoying the soft innocence of being trapped in his embrace. Her head had been lodged in the semi-circle of his throat, his chin lost in her strands. She placed her hand on his chest to feel the steady beat of his heart. Should that heart ever stop, she couldn't go on. Should that heart ever truly stop loving her, she'd wither like those silky roses he used to pluck and dress in black ribbons for Christine. Long dead, those fatal black-edged crimson buds!

She kissed his Adam's apple and smiled to feel him swallow. He began to stir, twisted away onto his back. His arm, however, clasped her and scooped her to his side. She curled to him, her head on his shoulder. He was awake. He squeezed her arm gently. She pressed herself harder against him. She didn't want the moment to pass.

He cleared his throat and slowly left her. She almost protested, but thought it was better there were no words between them. What if he took back with sharp, biting accusations what they'd just shared? She wouldn't risk it. They had slept the morning away. For her it was the first dreamless sleep she'd had in a long, long time.

Erik stretched and went directly to the larder. He pulled out apples and what was left of the bread. It was hard and stale, but he cut off several slices and brought them to the table. As Meg looked for her chemise, he spoke.

"In the satchel, you'll find several changes of clothing."

Meg had thought that the satchels held clothes only for Erik. He had changed already several times. She smiled knowingly at him. His eyes flickered briefly with satanic glee.

"I suppose you liked seeing me day in and day out in only this thin chemise. Is that what a husband secretly desires?"

"Come eat something," he said instead of answering her.

They sat and ate their apples noisily. Meg chose the chair next to Erik so that she could press against him. He didn't seem to mind.

On the table the edges of several sheets of paper peeked out from the file Erik had taken from Dr. Richmond's office. Meg slid one out, waiting for Erik to protest. When the sheet was more than halfway out of the protective folder, Erik placed his hand softly over Meg's. He wasn't ready. Not yet.

"I could gather snow and melt it. You could bathe," he suggested, as if the papers didn't exist.

"Are you trying to say I smell?"

"No more, no less than I do, I'm sure."

"Would you bathe with me?" she teased.

"I would if the bath were big enough, but I'm afraid we'll have to do with a half barrel. I, myself, may have to bathe standing up."

"I love you," she whispered. She couldn't help herself. The sweet calm of the moment made her long for his forgiveness.

He sighed. "Everything…has…changed."

His lack of emotion worried Meg. "Have your feelings for me changed?"

"How could they not?"

Meg swallowed the panic rising in her breast. "Yes. Yes, I suppose it was foolish to think… I read too much into it. It felt like love."

She started to rise from the table, but he took her hand and held it. "Don't."

Meg waited to hear more. She slowly sat back down even though he said nothing. They remained shoulder to shoulder for a long time. Finally Erik began to speak again. "It was. It was love."

She wished he'd turn to look at her. He held her hand. He threaded his fingers with hers, but his face was slightly turned away.

"Will you come home with me? The children miss you."

His hand left hers to join his own. He pressed both to his face. His shoulders sagged. She wrapped her arms around his body and held him until she felt him calm. His voice was strained when he spoke again. "What you said—before they locked me away in the wagon—was it the truth? Was it, Meg?"

He turned earnestly toward her.

"What do you mean, Erik?"

"You spoke of…the children. You spoke as if…"

"Oh, Erik! You don't still believe Mario's dead, do you?"

"Isn't he?"

"No! I told you. I told you he…"

"Don't lie to me, Meg! I swear I'll strangle you if you lie to me about this. I can't imagine anything but that day. He was bloody. His body was all disconnected, loose. He was dead. I held him in my arms, and he was dead!"

"No, you were wrong. He was badly, badly hurt, but he'll recover. Erik, listen to me. Listen to me. His leg and ribs were broken, but even before I left home he had already started to walk on crutches. Erik? Are you listening?" He had gotten up and was pacing the room, from the hearth to the door. "Erik, he told me to come bring you back. François, Laurette, both are worried about you. François knows how serious the situation is. Laurette just thinks you're away because you needed to rest. The twins keep asking for you every day."

"He's alive. He's alive. He's alive." Erik repeated the words as if they wouldn't make sense until something clicked into place. Then he dropped to his knees. Meg rushed to him. He pulled her down into his arms. "Oh, thank God, Meg. I thought he was dead. He ran after that boy. All because of a stupid mask. Because I wasn't brave enough to face others' shock or revulsion. Mario, mio piccolo, I almost lost him."

"I know. I know."

"No, you don't. Mario was the one that made up for all the others. If…if…if I couldn't save him, I couldn't save myself. But he's alive. He's going to be all right? He'll be able to walk? What's happened won't make him a thing like me?"

"A thing? Don't, don't ever talk about yourself that way! I won't have it! What did that man do to you?"

Erik squeezed her tightly. She couldn't see his expression, but she could hear it in his words. He shook the defeat from his voice. The tension melted away. He rocked back and forth as if she needed the soothing instead of him.

"No, it's all right, Meg. I'm all right. That doctor almost stole my soul. I was about to leave my body completely, like those soulless bodies that simply live. I'd started to disappear. I would pace or sit and stare out the window hour after hour." Suddenly he pushed Meg back a little so he could see her face. Without a hint of humor, he said, "I met an angel, you know." Meg gave him a cautious look. "No, I'm not insane, I swear. But there was a young girl. Her name was

Lisbet. I could see it in her face. If there are angels that walk this earth, she was one of them."

"What happened to her? Is she still there?"

"No," he whispered, "she got away from them all."

They were quiet for a long while.

"Meg, I want you to read Dr. Richmond's journal and notes. I've been thinking about it. I need you to know what he found."

Several hours later, Meg came out of the bedroom with Dr. Richmond's notes. Her eyes were red. Erik felt a pang of remorse. He also felt strangely uncomfortable, embarrassed. Surely all or most of it Meg had already known.

"Erik? Did he…? Do you still hear music?"

"No. It's gone."

Before she crumpled to the ground, Erik went to her.

"Oh, oh, oh, oh, God, no! It's not. It's not all right!" She shouted the same cry over and over again. She fought his arms. She beat his shoulders with her hands.

"No, it's not all right," he said sternly. Her sobs struck his heart, made it impossible to breathe. He shook her, trying to quiet her. Then he pulled her back into his arms where she began to calm. "You're right. It's not all right. I…may…never…get it back." He soothed his hands down the slope of her back. "You will have to be my music. You, Meg." He kissed her. He wiped the salty tears from her cheeks. "You, Meg, are my music." He kissed the trembling flesh of her mouth. Her lips were hot. "You will be my music, my love."

He lifted her, cradling her in his arms, and took her inside the bedroom.

CHAPTER 8

❀

The Rescue

True, we love life, not because we are used to living, but because we are used to loving. There is always some madness in love, but there is also always some reason in madness.
    — *Friedrich Nietzsche*

Raoul and Christine had taken rooms at the small tavern. They were cramped and drafty, but neither one of them was willing to give up and return home until they knew the gruesome truth. Christine insisted that Erik would never harm Meg, but Raoul wasn't so sure. He had seen Erik at the clinic. Raoul had been forced to stand aside, after the dogs had been restrained, while Gunter and Audrich beat Erik into submission. Then he had helped the attendants drag an unconscious Erik to the infirmary. Raoul had listened to Himmel, who didn't like the way the patients were treated, tell about Gunter's irrational antipathy toward Erik and about certain suspicious things that had happened. Raoul hadn't been able to find a way to speak with Erik. He had only seen him from a distance. Even the time Raoul was instructed to help bathe the patients, it was the ones who couldn't bathe themselves. So even then, he had been nowhere close enough to make his presence known, much less to speak with Erik.

But the times he caught glimpses of him, Erik had been eerily quiet and still.

Christine and Raoul argued about what they might possibly find once the snows stopped and a way was cleared to the cabin. Having taken the slip of paper that Erik had given the storekeeper, Christine ran her finger down the rows of supplies, looking for some clue to Erik's state of mind. Had he been thinking of Meg and her needs? All the provisions were staples that anyone might have stocked. But Raoul's eyes halted at the one purchase, towards the end, that had particular significance in his mind—a long cable of rope. When Christine's eyes met his, she wadded the scrap of paper and threw it into the fire.

Raoul prayed that Erik wasn't insane. In spite of the list, Christine swore that they would find them well and content to have had the time to work things out. Raoul hoped she was right. He couldn't think what he'd do if he came upon Erik, a crazed killer, leaning over the bloodied corpse of his wife. Would he have to kill Erik? Would he be forced to return him to the clinic as a patient? How would he and Christine live with themselves if Erik and Meg had destroyed each other? Raoul had helped Erik escape. Whatever had happened in that cabin over the last several weeks, Raoul and Christine would have to bear some responsibility for the consequences.

Finally the weather broke. Several days of sun bode well. The snow on the road was packed down, and the old man's sons had returned from their hunting. They were willing to take the Chagnys up to the cabin if they were prepared to go on horseback.

The going was slow. It took the better part of the day to arrive at the base of the path that led up the mountain. There was a small shelter left for travelers where the party camped that night. The next morning, they would reach the lodge.

The first time Erik had read through the entire file, he had tried to discount the doctor's conclusions. What did Richmond know of him? Erik preferred to think the exact and careful markings on the paper were nonsense. But he kept going over again and again the tedious details of the hypnosis, the childish subterfuges, the misguided inquiries. Richmond himself had to revise his thoughts on more than one occasion. The doctor went deeper and pressed harder until Erik had confessed that he was the Phantom of the Opera Populaire. Was that the sum of it? Was that what the doctor had wanted? It wasn't what he had expected. But it was the final entry that tore at Erik. A summation of sorts, it dismissed Erik, his case, his history. It sealed the file. Treatment was a failure. Erik could not be saved. Diagnosis: Bleak.

Erik had shared the file with Meg, even the final entry. They had made love and eaten a light repast. Meg was asleep in the bedroom, a cozy fire burned steadily in the fireplace. Erik sat at the long table in the main room and opened the file again. He went to the final pages. They had been written the day before he escaped. There was a finality about it that was ironic. Little did Erik realize what a lost cause he had been when he decided to take his chances and escape that night from the clinic.

Dr. Richmond's journal. 23 October

I have read over my case notes several times and have begun to see a shape to this man's life. I believe there might be a key buried deep inside his mind. Erik Costanzi doesn't evidently recall much that transpired before his life in the cage at the fair. His childhood is marked, irreparably, by this cruelty. I've come to realize that he doesn't really believe he's anything more than an animal or a freak. Curiously he rarely speaks of himself as a freak, and yet that is what he was, a curiosity, a biological mistake. He was a fortunate source of revenue for Abel who marketed his son, whom he must not have really considered a son. In practical terms, Abel surely saw Erik as a misshapen product of an illicit love affair, not as a child so much as a thing. He would not be able to lead a normal life. Abel may have assumed—as many do in similar cases—that Erik was of subnormal intelligence. He may even have concluded that the child lacked a soul. So he decided that the boy's only future lay in the fair as a curiosity, an exhibit. The malice Erik attributes to his father is mythic. Abel was simply a heartless businessman.

Any departure from the expected, that is to say, any indication that his "property" had a soul, a will of its own, or any intelligence approaching normal must have disquieted Abel. His reaction was to brutalize the boy in order to best make Erik conform to the role he, as father and owner, thought to be his son's destiny. The mother evidently had known Erik's potential and had tried to protect him. At least this is what Erik believes and what he has told me. Although under hypnosis, he will not allow me to push him back to those moments that predate his life in bondage. But since the mother died in an accident—according to Erik in free discourse with me—she failed to persuade Abel that Erik was, except for the facial deformity, a normal child. Abel would not have wanted to listen to her. He didn't want a son, he wanted an "act." Erik Costanzi has continued to live as if the "act" were indeed his reality. For all intents and purposes, Abel convinced his son, as well as the audience, that Erik was a monster, not a human being.

Given his resistance to going beyond the fair to explore his life with his mother, there is little or no chance that he will ever be able to escape the delusion that he is masquerading as a man. His character is a loosely woven series of masks. Whenever he is confronted with a major crisis, the tenuous and false nature of his assumed identities becomes just that, a masquerade. The only solid bedrock that he can return to is the manufactured and marketed identity of the Devil's Child.

His father's abuse was so successful that Erik fears disobeying him still. Unfortunately, Erik killed his father at such a young age that the child was unable to crawl out from under the threat of punishment from the father figure; the father looms as gatekeeper still. That is to say, Erik has never succeeded in getting free of the cage. He's continually in danger of being pulled back to this original trauma at any moment. On some level, in his mind, he lives there even now. His father may have died, but FATHER continues to dominate his core personality, threatening him and pushing him to act out the role of monster, of Devil's Child. Although he has layered his identity by creating other masks, he has not been able to eradicate this first imposed identity. It lies just below the surface, and its effects can be discerned in his subsequent attempts at a normal life.

The door to memories perhaps of a healthier kind is barred by the father's law. Erik sees blood and becomes extremely frightened and belligerent whenever we approach that threshold. In spite of what he has since been told by someone who knew his parents, his only actual memory of his mother is one of betrayal. He remembers holding onto the hem of her gown. He recalls the day she delivered him up to the father. His fate was doubly sealed by his mother's unspoken demand that he obey his father and by his father's obvious power over him. The reaction of the spectators daily reinforced the truth of the father's implied will. Their acceptance of the identification of monster inscribed that identity on the child's mind in spite of the fact that he was growing stronger physically and manifested a superior intelligence and an extraordinary talent. The incongruity further split his personality, forcing him to develop unusual ways of dealing with his own dilemma and with all future crises.

Unfortunately Erik doesn't trust me. Therefore, I cannot make him go past that door. If it were possible, it would take years of work. Only with his trust and cooperation might I help him to breach the law of the father and find something prior to the cage. Of course there is a risk that we would only find more horror. Erik clings to the hope that his mother loved him. He has learned as an adult a few facts, enough that he has constructed a consoling fantasy of pure maternal love around the missing mother. Would it perhaps be more devastating to push him farther beyond the door and find a mother who must disappoint him? The real mother cannot live up to the fantasy he clings to. What if the one memory of her delivering him into bondage is the truth of her? Perhaps she did despise him. Might he have been the product of a rape? It would be natural for the young woman to reject an offspring of such a violent event in the best of situations. But in the case of a disfigured child, would it be so strange if she couldn't love him and refused to raise him? Indeed it may be best to keep that door locked. It's the only way to leave intact the illusion of a consoling mother.

If we undermine too drastically the compensating fantasies upon which his current persona is based, we might find a man without any identity at all except that which his father foisted upon him.

Meg rested in the bedroom. She had read the file. It hadn't changed what she felt for him. Marks on paper, she had said. But Erik had fought the rising sensation of nausea in the back of his throat.

Now alone in the silence of the cabin, Erik straightened the pages and returned them to the folder. It was not easier to read them a second time. He imagined it might have been better had he not read the final entry. Peeling away all Erik's masks, Richmond had thoroughly summed him up: a poor mistake of nature, an unwanted child rejected by his parents, a commercial bonanza—no, not even that—just one of many exhibits, just one of a handful of freaks, outcasts.

Every triumph, every success he had achieved seemed irrelevant. Nothing that he had done since the cage, since his years haunting the Opera Populaire, was of interest to Dr. Richmond. The doctor saw only the pain, the years over which Erik had had no control, the reality from which he had spent his whole life running.

This is what you are, the papers said. *This is what you'll always be,* he heard whispered around him.

No!

He bolted from the table. He kicked the chair which went skittering across the floor. He grabbed a coat and stepped out into the winter wind. It was snowing again.

Blinded by the swirling white wind, he trudged forward to the first of the trees. The dog bites had healed. But they were still sore when he banged his fists and arms against the trunk of the tree, trying to blast the doctor's words from his mind.

A solid clump of snow, from an overhead branch, fell heavily onto his head and trickled down the gap between his collar and the back of his neck. As the snow slid along his bare skin, he shivered from the shock and shook like a dog in an effort to dislodge the icy clumps from his body. He cursed the snow, the trees, the ground he stood on, and then without warning he felt the absurdity of it all and laughed insanely. What was he doing beating his hands against a tree trunk? His laughter reverberated against the snow-wrapped landscape. He took in several wet lungfuls of air and let them tumble out in a thunderous roar of laughter. It felt good to give himself over to the giddy riot of sounds, to the convulsive power of his lungs, to the defiant grin that he couldn't restrain.

The words in the file would not change. They would tell him again and again the same story. But that was not the end of the story, not *his* story.

The good doctor spoke of him as if he had never had any choice but to be what he was, what his father evidently had made of him. What was shall always be!

It wasn't true. Choices! By God, he had choices. He had always had choices. If he had never escaped the cage at the fair, he had certainly bent the bars.

Erik took a deep breath of the cold, wet wind. Snow flakes melted on his eyelashes, on his lips. When a new wave of frigid air hit his lungs, he coughed. It felt good to be surrounded by snow. It felt good to stretch his muscles and hit only empty air. No bars. There were no bars here. He'd have no bars in his mind either. He had choices. He had always had choices. And he had always lived by his decisions. He'd not hide any longer, not from a phantom!

"Erik, when are we going to go home?" Meg licked Erik's finger. He dipped it once more into the honey and sucked off the velvet sweetness.

The saucer of honey lay on Meg's naked belly. Erik had insisted on eating in bed. He stared up at her from the level of her hip, nuzzling the top of her thigh with his cheek. He coated his finger again with the sticky mess and offered it to Meg.

"I've had enough," she said as she rubbed her hand up along the inside of Erik's thigh to his groin. "You're wicked."

Erik wiped the honey onto Meg's abdomen, just above the blond curls of her mons. He pushed himself up on one elbow and flicked his tongue over the honey trail. Meg moved the saucer to the table beside the bed and sat up. She leaned back on the palms of her hands to see him better. Erik took advantage of the position to fix his sugared lips on her nipple. For a moment, she closed her eyes and enjoyed the pull of his mouth. She felt the warm, wet tug of his suction, the swirl of his tongue down to her swollen center. But then she moved away, forcing him to release her.

"We've been making love for days. I'm sore and worn out."

"That's why we did what we did," he smirked. "Surely you found my honey treatment soothing?"

She glanced out of the corner of her eye and noticed that he was stirring yet again. "How can you be aroused after all the lovemaking we've done?"

"I have a wager for you. You act as if it's somehow unusual or unnatural for me to desire you. You're sated. You've had enough. You can't imagine wanting more. But I can prove to you that it's quite simple. I bet you I can make you wet without even touching you."

Meg blushed down to her ankles. "That's no wager that I can win, and you know it. I have no doubt whatsoever that you can make good on your word. Although I'm a bit skeptical about the part about not touching me. But as far as the physical effects of arousal, men are not like women."

"Oh really? I hadn't noticed," he teased. He slipped his hand down toward his groin and caressed himself.

Meg's eyes could not resist watching him.

"I mean that men usually make love once, perhaps twice, and then they have trouble arousing themselves." She smiled at him as if she knew he didn't expect her to be so plain-spoken.

"I didn't know you knew so much about other men." He raised a skeptical eyebrow.

"I don't know in the way you mean." She feigned annoyance. "But women do talk."

"God forbid." He chuckled. "Well, whatever you've heard from…" He squinted his eyes at Meg. "Oh please, dear God, tell me it wasn't from Carlotta!"

Meg laughed out loud.

Relieved, Erik continued, "Whoever passes information on to you, doesn't know *me*. You, my dear, should know better than to question my gifts."

"Oh, is that what you call your insatiability? A gift?"

"No, that's my curse, I'm afraid. I call it a gift that I am usually quite ready if the need arises."

"So I see!" Meg glanced down at her fully aroused husband. "But I'm afraid that I'm a bit worn out. And although honey is glorious to the taste buds, I don't think it makes a meal."

"But the honey was dessert."

Meg giggled. "You can't have gotten as much as I did out of this meal."

Erik's mouth curled up on one side. "I told you that you didn't have to swallow."

"It was swallow or drown."

"We could start all over again. I could lick your toes if I didn't fear you'd kick out my teeth, and then I would kiss my way up to your knees, especially that tender spot where your leg bends, at the back. I find that most sweet. Then I would take my hands and push your thighs to either side until you felt a burning at your joints. I would take my fingers and spread your lips apart. I would look at you, the soft blond hairs, the rounded lips, the scarlet secret of you. I would smell you. I love your smell. There's absolutely nothing like it, not among the flowers, not among the fruits. I would slip my tongue inside between your lips and trail a kiss up to the top where that naughty little nub hides. I would slide one hand under your bottom and squeeze hard. Then I would kneel between your legs and bring my..."

"Stop it! You win! I'm...I'm aroused."

"Wet, you mean?"

"Wet!"

"Dripping with cream?"

"Erik, for goodness' sake, stop. I can't get any redder or my blood vessels will all pop!"

"Do you want me to take advantage of the situation?"

"Can you describe what you're doing as you do it?"

"I can try. But at a certain point, I don't think I'll be able to put two words together. Will it be all right if I grunt instead at that point?"

"Yes, yes. I like grunts and groans. I like it when you moan in my ear."

"Perhaps you should do the talking."

Erik kissed Meg, and neither one could speak for some time.

They had eventually come out in need of something more substantial to eat and a bit of fresh air. Erik brought several buckets of snow, and they melted it in the large cauldron by the fire. Erik let Meg take the first bath. They both felt itchy and smelly, sticky with honey and their own secretions. Meg was truly sore, and Erik would never admit it but he, too, was raw and irritated. Meg was small enough to bend her knees to her chest and sit in the barrel and soak. She kept making loud sighing noises of pleasure. Like a cat, she slowly raised one arm, then another, and stretched. Erik was anxious to get in, too, so he felt it easier to pass the time if he helped bathe his wife. He took the bar of soap that he had used in a basin to wash and shave. He lathered his hands with it and washed her everywhere she might have had trouble reaching and many places just for the fun of it where she could easily have done it herself. He helped her wash her hair, and he rinsed it for her with some of the warm, clean water that he had kept aside.

Eventually he pouted so sweetly that Meg stepped out into a large blanket to dry, leaving the barrel free for Erik. Since the barrel wasn't big enough for him to sit, he stood and took large handfuls of water to dump over his head, shoulders, chest, and arms. Meg complained about the mess he was making. Water went everywhere around them, landing on the floor and drenching a few of the articles of clothing they had taken off recently. He didn't apologize. There was little he could do about it. After he was cleaned and rinsed, he stepped out and unwrapped some of Meg's blanket and wrapped it around himself. They both huddled together before the fire, shuddering from the cold.

"I love you, Meg."

"I love you."

"I have something I have to discuss with you though. It might not make you happy. But I've thought about it for a while now and think it's what I must do."

Erik unwrapped himself and grabbed the fresh clothes he had put to the side. He dressed while Meg sat on the rug, still wrapped in the blanket, waiting for Erik to continue.

"I wanted to kill you when I realized what you'd done to me. I thought it was the worst thing anyone could ever have done to me. And I thought it was completely without reason. But that was unfair. I have managed very well over the past years. You've been the major reason I've not spiraled down into madness." Erik paused, trying to gather his thoughts about him and to find the best way to say what he meant to say. "I hated reading those notes about me. I hated it, because the man I saw—that Richmond saw—was me. I wanted to think it wasn't, but it was."

"Erik, you're not mad!"

"No, I'm not. But I might be. I could be."

"What are you trying to say?"

"I need help, Meg. I can't go back home. Not the way I am now. I know how tenuous my grip on reality is. I've clung to a façade of power for so long that I forgot that it was a façade."

"Are you saying that the man I love doesn't exist?"

"No, that's not what I'm saying." He dropped to his knees beside Meg and settled on his heels. He caressed her cheek with one hand. He could see she was worried. "I'm yours. You know me. You've always known me. Since that day you saw me in the mirror in the dressing room, you saw the man behind the mask and knew he wasn't the Phantom."

"Then what are you going to do? If you don't go home, I won't either. I'll follow you wherever you plan to go. I won't be left behind. I can't…I can't…"

"What? And leave our children orphans?"

"Maman and Marcelo will look after them," she said in a small, high pitched voice even she didn't recognize.

"You aren't serious." He scowled at her. "Besides it won't be necessary for you to consider such a sacrifice. And that's what you're trying to make. I want you to go home."

"No!"

"Yes!"

"I won't and you can't make me."

"Meg, be reasonable."

"What are you planning on doing?"

"All right. If you must stay, then stay. But know this. I plan to go back. Back to the clinic."

"What?"

"I think Richmond's the only man who can help me. I want him to take me to the door. I have to see what's on the other side, Meg."

Trudging up the mountain road was exhausting. The old man's sons were used to such travel, but Raoul and Christine were tense with every step the horses took. The snow was deep and crusty, lying a foot or more at the base of the mountain but growing deeper as they climbed.

But it was more than the snow that worried the two foreigners. Christine had stubbornly insisted on being hopeful, but Raoul saw the creases around her mouth, the furrows etched in her forehead. Finally he broached the subject quietly so that their guides wouldn't hear.

"Are you prepared?" he asked. He didn't need to explain. The worst was on both their minds.

It almost seemed that Christine wouldn't answer she waited so long. "I just can't think Erik would do anything so sad. But if we find them…dead, then I think my heart will break."

Raoul felt unsettled by the thought. Even though he had been the one to entertain the grim possibility, the image of blood and carnage seemed unreal to him. He tried to picture Erik mad, violent.

That was no problem. All he had to do was search his memory. Erik dressed in his most somber, most regal attire, as if he were a dark prince attending a gala performance with heads of state, climbed among the flies in the opera house hell-bent on blood, on Raoul's blood. No, that was chillingly real. But the image of that same man choking the life out of Meg just struck Raoul as obscene and fantastic. It didn't fit. It shattered against everything Raoul knew of the relationship between Erik and Meg.

Out of nowhere came the memory of Erik's frustration with Meg the night she had convinced Raoul to sneak her into Erik's prison cell. It was supposed to be their wedding night. Raoul hadn't been fooled. He knew Erik and Meg had already been intimate. But Erik was soon to be executed, and Meg had begged Raoul to slip her into the prison. Raoul couldn't say no. At first Erik had been furious and had demanded that she go. Their loud voices brought Raoul back toward the cell, ready to protect Meg in case Erik became violent. He saw Meg in tears start for the cell door. He also saw Erik's face as he stopped her. Raoul saw the gentle way he held her. He could tell Erik restrained himself. He could have so easily hurt Meg. Instead, it had been a revelation to watch as Erik lifted Meg and laid her on the bare cot. The man might have crushed her, broken her with a single blow, but his hands touched Meg with gentleness that even now stirred Raoul. Raoul had slipped away to allow them their privacy once he knew Erik would not do anything foolish.

"If we find them both dead," Christine broke into Raoul's thoughts, "what shall we do? Will we bring them back to Rome? To Paris?"

"Arrangements will have to be made. I can instruct the solicitors in Linz to deal with the details. I imagine the best would be to have them taken to Rome. Marcelo and Madeleine will be devastated. I'm sure Marcelo wants them buried in the family crypt."

"We'll have to lie to the children, Raoul. Marcelo and Madeleine will have to know, but we can't do that to Erik's children. They can't grow up knowing Erik killed their mother. We'll say it was a fall, while hiking in the mountains."

Raoul saw how difficult this was going to be for his wife. She loved them both. Meg was like a sister to her. And Erik was…well,

Raoul was never sure how to describe the bond that linked Christine and Erik.

"Yes, I agree." Raoul was lost again in memories. Once he happened upon them in the parlor in each other's embrace. Erik's head was on Meg's lap, his face turned towards her, lying on his side, his arms tightly wound round her waist. They were fully clothed, yet it was intimate. He noticed her hand was stroking the length of him, down his side, along his hip. Then for one moment, he saw it disappear from view. Raoul regretted interrupting, but he coughed loudly so that they would know he was present. He remembered how Erik tumbled to the floor and Meg turned a bright crimson. It was rare and delightful to see Erik look foolish.

"What are you smiling about?" Christine asked.

"Oh, I was remembering catching Erik and Meg together, you know, on a couple of occasions. Just tender moments, private ones."

"Raoul, if he's…if you're right…if Erik has gone mad and…"

"Don't think of it, Christine. I take it all back. I can't imagine Erik harming her. And if he did, I can't imagine him living on afterwards. We'll either find them both dead or both alive."

"But if we're wrong?"

Raoul understood Christine's need to prepare for the worst. "If we're wrong, then the man we find will not be Erik. Erik would never do something so vile. And we'll have to restrain him."

"Do you think you can? Do you think you can restrain him? Wouldn't it be better to kill him outright?"

Raoul was shocked. His wife had always been so tender-hearted, especially where Erik was concerned. "Why this sudden bloodlust?"

Christine didn't flinch. "I know him. It would be a mercy to kill him. If the madness is passing, he'd suffer incredibly if he had to live with Meg's death on his conscience. I think he'd rather be dead. And if he's truly mad, I think he'd rather be dead than live the rest of his life in an asylum."

"Christine, what you're saying is…"

"What I'm saying is that you're his friend. You're the closest friend, the only friend he's ever had who can help him. You're the only one who he would trust to be merciful. He'd expect it of you. As do I."

Raoul looked away and was silent. How could she lay such a heavy burden on him?

"Raoul, he loves you."

Again Raoul looked at her in shock. He knew she left unspoken the other part of that truth. Raoul loved Erik like a brother. He didn't know why he was so moved by the man, but he was.

"Christine, I don't know if I can," he confessed.

"Promise me, you'll do what's best. You'll try to be merciful to him."

Raoul couldn't speak. He only nodded. Christine gave a great sigh of relief. Only then did Raoul see the tears run down her cheeks.

"If Marcelo and Madeleine agree, I want to raise the children. If not, then I want to be close to them. They could come and visit often. I want to be a part of their lives. For Meg." She couldn't say more.

"Of course," Raoul replied. He, too, could say no more.

"Nothing?"

"Nothing," he answered.

"No melodies?"

"None."

Meg could tell he didn't want to talk about it. So she dropped the subject for the moment. They had both bathed, and Erik had already dressed. Meg opened the satchel and pulled out a stunningly incongruous selection of clothing. She laid the garments side by side on the bed and stared at them in disbelief. Nothing matched.

"Did you pack in the dark?" she asked as she held up a green bodice and a red skirt to her body.

"If you recall, my dear, I had thought that you'd have little or no use for clothing where I meant to send you."

"Did you really intend to kill me?" She tried to keep a playful tone, but Erik wasn't fooled.

"I don't know anymore," he answered truthfully. "I honestly don't know."

"Why pack clothes at all?" she offered.

"I meant to…make you suffer." It was as if Erik were trying to reconstruct the thoughts he had had at the time.

"Well, you kept me for days in my chemise. Did you want to withhold the mismatched clothing as a final torture?" She threw the articles on the bed and tried to find something more suitable. "I think you weren't as determined as you'd like to think."

Of course, she knew what he'd like to think. She had understood that Erik wanted to believe he'd not really contemplated and even planned to murder her. Meg left the doubts to do their magic.

Erik smiled at her and said he liked being dramatic. Of course, at the time, he had been so angry with her that he had wanted to hurt her. Kill her? Now he doubted it more and more. Not Meg, not his Meg, but the Meg who had betrayed him, the one he feared no longer loved him. He had wanted her to disappear. He hadn't been sure that the other Meg, the one who loved him, still existed.

Meg threw up her arms in despair and put on the red velvet skirt and the taffeta green bodice with the under shirt of deep purple. She looked like a clown!

Erik pulled her to the sofa in the main room. The overstuffed piece of furniture smelled of mold and gave off great puffs of dust when they fell onto it.

Gently Meg stroked Erik's cheek and jaw. She kissed him on the neck. He pushed her away and kissed her soundly on the mouth. "It tickles," he said in way of explanation.

"Erik, try again, won't you?" she coaxed. "You've always had melodies tumbling around in there."

He stiffened as if to pull away from her. She tried to hold him, but he was too strong.

"I told you. It's gone. Silence. That's all I hear." He sounded more tired than angry.

Meg gnawed at her lip in consternation and dread. Music had always been a part of him, of both of them. Would he never compose again? Would the silence eat at him until there was nothing left?

"You seem to be dealing with it well." She pretended to a casual tone neither of them believed.

"I try not to think of it."

"Is that why you won't let me rest?" she teased. Their lovemaking had not abated. It was as if he needed to be constantly with her, intimately connected. If they were not actually making love, they were touching hands and bodies in sweet tender ways. The afternoon of the previous day, after they had made love several times, even exhausted as they had been, Erik held Meg, naked, on his lap in a slow, erotic caress that went on for hours. It finally erupted into another heated coupling after which they fell into a sleep that lasted more than twelve hours. They had awakened this morning, famished, realizing they had not eaten for more than a day and had completely lost track of time.

Erik looked at her sheepishly. "It makes the pain go away."

Meg's veneer of playfulness cracked. She pulled him down to lie in her lap and kissed him sweetly. "Let me take it all away, Erik. I don't ever want you to suffer, my love."

"Sing for me, Meg." It was the first time he'd asked. He had told her that she would be his music. She had waited for him to ask her to sing or for him to sing to her. But it was as if music had ceased to exist between them.

She began with a love song from *The Stranger*, but he stopped her.

"No, not mine. Sing something else, something different."

She cleared her throat and waited for the ache of disappointment to fade, then she sang some folk songs, songs all French children learn, songs she and Christine and other girls in the ballet dormitories used to sing together or in rounds. The tension in Erik's face melted away. After a few bars of one song, she was pleased to hear a low, soft hum rise from Erik's throat. He smiled up at her. When she finished, he kissed each of her fingers.

"Do you suppose that this is normal?" he asked.

"What?"

"Do you hear it all the time in your head, Meg?"

"Music?"

He nodded.

"Sometimes. Not usually. A lot of the time I'm thinking of things I'm doing or about to do. I don't think I hear music all the time."

"I did. Sometimes other things interfered."

"Such as?"

"Anger. Mostly rage and fear. Then it would abandon me. It was always a relief when the sounds came back. But now, it's gone. I…I…have to force myself to remember music. It doesn't just happen anymore. It's the memory of music lost, gone. I don't know if I can explain it, but it feels different. It's dead. I think something has died inside me." She pulled him tightly to her. His hands clutched and squeezed the fabric of her gown. He was a block of hard, tensed muscles. She began to sing to him, songs of innocence, children's songs, to frighten away the monsters.

"Don't stop, Meg. Please."

"Do you hear? Stop! Stop!" Christine reined in her mount and cocked her head toward the sound.

Raoul heard the wind whistling through the upper branches of the forest. Then he noticed.

"It's Meg. She's alive! She's alive!" Christine shouted. She spurred her horse ahead, past the others.

Soon they heard the greeting of other horses, the ones Erik had taken. The animals had caught the familiar scent of the approaching party. Around the bend, nestled among fir trees, in a small clearing was the cabin. Set off away from the cabin was a structure that served as stable. Smoke curled lazily above the chimney, and the notes of a comic song from an opera by Verdi rose sharp and clear.

Raoul motioned the guides to wait while he hurried up a narrow path that had been dug to the door. The singing had stopped well before Raoul reached the door. Without knocking, he swung the door open to find Meg standing, feet splayed, dressed in a hideous combination of green, purple, and red. At her shoulder was the butt-end of a rifle, her head was tilted, one eye screwed shut, her finger on the trigger.

"Oh my God!" she cried as she lowered the weapon. "I might have shot you!"

Behind him, Raoul heard the horses snort and whinny in fear as someone hit the ground heavily. Then Christine's voice broke through. "Erik! Stop!"

Raoul and Meg both ran out to the side yard where Erik held one of the young guides in a deadly arm lock. His visage was wild and threatening. But quickly he realized who had come upon them. He loosened his grasp on the young man and let him drop to the ground.

Everyone stood frozen for several heart beats, then Erik addressed the guide. "Sorry. My wife was alone. I didn't expect company."

Raoul stepped forward and offered the boy an arm up.

"These young men offered to bring us up the trail. We were worried about you."

Christine slid from the saddle unassisted and ran to Meg. The two women were talking loudly and with obvious delight, as if they had made previous arrangements to holiday together at Mt. Bauer.

Erik grinned at Raoul's discomfort. "I left you a note," he said.

"Indeed," scowled Raoul. But he accepted Erik's hand. He clasped it firmly, holding on a bit longer than necessary.

Erik could tell Raoul was relieved. The letter Erik had left had hinted at the dreadful purpose he had had in mind when he stole Meg from the inn. The sarcasm had been a taunt, but it was also an entreaty. And his friends had answered. There was no sarcasm when Erik whispered to Raoul, "Thank you. Thank you for coming."

Raoul sent the young men down the mountain, saying that the four of them would depart the next day. There had been a break in the weather, and it promised to continue for the next few days. The two couples ate the simple fare Erik had brought, supplemented with fresher foods from Christine's and Raoul's provisions. The conversation was awkward at first, but after a few glasses of brandy, they eased tremendously.

Christine could tell Meg wasn't telling everything about the last several weeks. She saw the veiled looks exchanged between Erik and

Meg. There was discoloration around Meg's wrists, and Christine made a mental note to draw her aside when the opportunity presented itself to ask her about it.

It was sooner than she had thought. Raoul suggested Erik join him for a smoke after checking on the horses. Although Raoul didn't indulge often, he enjoyed a good cigar.

Christine cleared the table and began to do some last minute packing. As soon as the men were gone, Christine took Meg to the bedroom and asked in a stern voice, "What did he do to you?"

Meg's mouth dropped open. "Nothing," she snapped. "At least nothing I didn't want him to do."

Christine crossed her arms over her modest chest and waited.

Meg sighed. "Oh, all right. You want the truth?"

"You know I do."

"At first I thought he might hurt me. He was incredibly angry."

"The bruises around your wrists? What happened? Where else did he touch you?"

Meg burst out laughing. Christine was scandalized. She stared at Meg as if she had lost her mind.

"I'm sorry," Meg said, trying to control her laughter. "It's just such a strange question to ask me."

"I don't see why."

"Well, there's barely an inch of me that Erik hasn't touched, Chrissy! After all, we're married."

"That's not what I meant, and you know it."

Meg calmed down and looked a bit sheepishly at her friend. "Yes, I'm sorry. I know you've been worried about me. He tried to be mean to me. I think he was seriously thinking of…" She broke off. She could see the effect her honesty was having on Christine. "He was furious, but he was also in pain. I signed those papers, Christine. He wanted to hurt me. But he couldn't. It was actually quite sad how badly he failed. He growled and threatened, but he couldn't stop touching me. And these days we've spent up here have been incredible. He has loved me so, so…" She sighed. "I can't tell you how wonderful he's been."

"I told Raoul that I didn't think he'd go through with it. He left a letter that was very strange. It sounded like the ones he used to write the owners at the Opera Populaire. Raoul thought he might do something rash. Is he all right?"

Meg's smile wavered. "He's better than one might expect after spending months locked away in a lunatic asylum. But…"

"But what? You can tell me."

"I know. I know I can." Meg took a deep breath and continued, "The music is gone. He's lost it."

Outside the air was refreshing. Both men were a bit tipsy so they relished the shock of the cold. The horses were warmly settled for the night. Everything was ready for the trip down the mountain. They would leave the wagon and travel on horseback.

Erik asked how Raoul had found them, and Raoul explained that it had not been too difficult. If it hadn't been for the need to travel to the bank in Linz and for the early snow, they'd have arrived just shortly after Meg and Erik had gotten to the cabin. Erik silently gave a prayer of thanks for the delay. The last few days, in particular, had restored his faith in Meg and in his own sanity.

Raoul offered him one of the cigars, but Erik had never taken to the habit. He waved it away and watched as Raoul worked to light it from the lantern. The silence was comfortable between them, and Erik was reluctant to break it.

"Is Richmond still at the clinic?"

"I wouldn't know. I left the same day you did, but I imagine it takes time to hand over control of an institution that size to another director. He might still be there."

Again the silence stretched between them.

"I need your help."

Raoul answered easily, "Of course. What is it?"

"Take me back."

"That's why we're here, Erik. We have every intention of escorting you home."

"No, you don't understand. I'm not going home. Take me back to the clinic. It's my only hope."

"You can't be serious."

"I'm deadly serious. I think I went a little mad. I'm just so relieved that I came to my senses in time. When I kidnapped Meg from the inn, I wanted blood. I wanted to… It wouldn't have been quick or merciful."

"Erik, you were upset."

"For God's sake, Raoul, don't be patronizing! I expect better from you. You've seen me. You know how I can be."

"But that's the past."

"The Phantom is not in the past. Richmond, he found him. He's here." Erik pounded on his chest with his closed fist. Slowly he opened his hand and rubbed in small circular movements as if to ease a pain. "The Phantom wanted to rape Meg until she begged for death. The Phantom was…is…still aroused by…blood, by scenes so repulsive I can't even whisper the truth to you. Richmond did something. And now the music doesn't play in my mind. If I could hear it, I would feel calm. I don't know if I can go back home without it."

"But how would going back to Richmond's care be the answer?"

"I read the files he wrote. He transcribed in detail all our sessions, including the ones when he hypnotized me. I didn't know." He stopped speaking. Raoul waited, hearing the strange hitch in Erik's breathing. After a moment, Erik spoke again as if nothing had happened. "It was agony to read them. I told him things I haven't told anyone, even Meg. It sounded as if I relived them."

"But still, Erik, even more so, why would you trust the man?"

"I don't. That's why I need your help. I want you to be present, to protect me, to listen so that he doesn't tell me lies or keep things from me. It has to be Richmond. I won't go through this all over again, and I won't share my secrets with anyone else. He can take me to the door."

"What door?"

"There's a door, a barrier, in my mind. Richmond could never get me to go beyond it. Once he found out who I was, he was afraid to push me. Under hypnosis, I introduced myself as the Phantom."

"How far back did you go?"

"Back to the fair. You knew about the fair? The cage?"

"Madeleine told me the story. She told me how she met you and why she brought you to live in the vaults."

"When was it that she told you?"

"About the time you delivered *Don Juan Triumphant* to the managers of the Opera Populaire and challenged everyone to stage it."

Erik looked away. There was a cold blue light on the snow.

Raoul reasoned that he shouldn't need to justify himself, but he did. In spite of the sad story Madeleine had told him of the Phantom's childhood, Raoul had felt no pity for him at that moment.

"That was just after you had murdered Buquet in the middle of *Il Muto*. You remember what you said when you threw the score at the owners' feet? I don't think I'll ever forget it. You ripped the engagement ring I had given Christine from the chain around her throat and told her that she belonged to you."

"And I would have killed you, my friend, in the hall of mirrors had Madeleine not saved you." There was no irony in Erik's confession. "True. You had no reason to pity me and a thousand reasons to want to see me destroyed."

Raoul tasted the smoke bitter and hot, as he exhaled. He tossed the barely smoked cigar out into the snow. "Things have changed."

"But people don't."

"You really believe that?"

"No, it's what I fear as well as what I hope. Behind the door, my earliest memories are waiting for me. Perhaps, too, there's some other child, not the one who lived in the cage, not the one who murdered. Richmond will keep my secrets. I won't trust anyone else with them. And then you're my insurance."

"And you trust me with your secrets?"

"I trust you, Raoul. I trust you with my life and with my soul. Because that is exactly what is at stake."

Erik offered Raoul his hand to seal the bargain. If Raoul accepted, then there would be no holding back. Raoul didn't accept Erik's hand. Instead he quickly embraced him and as quickly released him. The two men stood silently, near but not touching, gazing out at the dark stiletto branches of the trees that clattered and wove above them against a clear, moonless sky.

CHAPTER 9

❀

Laurette's Story

> *What, art mad? A man may see how this world goes with no eyes. Look with thine ears: see how yond justice rails upon yond simple thief. Hark, in thine ear: change places; and, handy-dandy, which is the justice, which is the thief?*
> *King Lear,* William Shakespeare

Richmond stared up at a nightmare. It was the middle of the night, and he had awakened to find a demon looming over his bed. Erik's unmasked face was so close the doctor could see the faint remains of an old white scar across the red disfigured tissue of his face.

"What?" he gasped in fear.

Hands, more than one pair, dragged him from the bed and forced him to his feet.

"Put this on." Erik threw the robe to the doctor who stood in a flimsy nightshirt.

As Dr. Richmond gathered the sides of the robe and tied the sash, he recognized the other man as one of the employees, the one Erik had used as a hostage. But this man was dressed in elegant doe-skinned trousers, a fine white silk shirt, a waistcoat elaborately embroidered with gold and silver thread, a wool coat with gold studs. Erik, too, was dressed in similarly rich fabrics, like a gentleman.

"This is my friend Raoul, Count de Chagny. He has agreed to be witness." Erik introduced Raoul to the befuddled doctor.

Raoul raised a pistol in his right hand and flicked the trigger without engaging it as if thus he confirmed his role as "witness."

"But you're the…"

"Gilbert, Dr. Richmond. As you see, I was never really in danger."

"But why are you here?" Dr. Richmond summoned all his professional skill in order to keep the fear from his voice. "I've kept my promises, Costanzi. Dr. Vernon has agreed to direct the clinic. He'll be here within the fortnight." His efforts to defend himself struck even his ears as weak.

Raoul worried as he saw the glint in Erik's eye. He edged closer so that he'd be within Erik's line of vision, gambling that his presence would remind Erik of the purpose for their return to the clinic. With some difficulty, Erik relaxed the tension in his limbs. He backed away half a step.

"It's not what you think." Erik's voice was smooth as honey, low and somber.

"I turned Gunter over to the police. He's in prison." The doctor was not reassured by Costanzi's calm. The memory of the Phantom's revelations was too fresh in his mind for him to forget just how dangerous Erik Costanzi had once been.

Erik sneered at the man and looked around the bedroom as if searching. "And Celeste? How is she?" His tone was mocking.

"She's gone," Richmond said quietly. "I had her transferred to another facility."

Erik's sharp gaze demanded an explanation.

"To a hospital in England, under the care of another doctor," Richmond rushed to clarify.

Erik's dark expression softened into a sarcastic grin.

"You sound disappointed, Dr. Richmond. Could it be you miss her?"

Dr. Richmond wouldn't answer. Erik studied him for a moment, then decided to let the subject drop. "This is why we've come back. I want you to continue with my case, as my doctor."

Shock couldn't be more obvious on the doctor's face. "You must be joking."

Erik scowled dangerously at the man. "Do I look as if I'm joking, Doctor?"

Raoul stepped in, hoping to smooth the process. "Dr. Richmond, Erik has read the file you kept on him. He thinks you were close to a breakthrough that might be important to him."

Raoul and Erik could tell the doctor understood what they meant. "I can't possibly."

"Raoul will keep me from killing you, Richmond. If that's what you fear."

"That's only part of it. Such a process requires months, if not years, of intense work."

"I'll give you until the end of the month."

"Impossible," sputtered Richmond. But when he saw that Costanzi was serious, he tried to explain. "The barrier you've erected is there for a reason, Costanzi."

"Erik, Doctor. You must call me Erik. Remember the contract."

Annoyed by Erik's sarcasm, the doctor struggled to find a professional distance. He forced his expression into neutrality. "Erik, it's ill-advised. If I push you to open a door that you've put in place because you *can't* deal with what's behind it, we could do far more damage than you can imagine."

"I don't care," said Erik without thinking.

"Wait," interrupted Raoul. "I would like to know the risks."

Erik turned on Raoul savagely. "It's not your risk or your decision."

Reluctantly, Raoul closed his mouth. He turned and walked to the window where he stared blindly out into the darkness.

"I won't be held accountable if..." the doctor started to protest.

"Not to worry, Dr. Richmond. I accept the risks. I want to know what I might have been. I need to see behind that door."

What he didn't say—but it was obvious to Richmond if not to Raoul—was that Erik needed to remember a beginning untouched by sorrow. He wanted to remember his mother. Whatever was left of those memories was buried behind the door. Be they black as sin, steeped in blood, Erik was determined to have them.

"You know she might be very different from what you imagine."

Less sure of himself than before, Erik argued, "I've been told something about her."

"Others often think they know, but it's all supposition. You might find it hard to meet your real mother. We're not any of us simple."

Erik raised one mocking eyebrow and smiled at the doctor. "Please, Doctor. I think we'd better start before I lose the little respect I still have for you."

"Remember your promise. Don't leave me. Whatever happens, I want you here." Erik held Raoul's hand in a death grip and spoke in a hurried whisper.

"You have my word."

Dr. Richmond had stepped out of the room for a moment.

"No matter what you hear." For a moment, Erik regretted that he'd not allowed Raoul to read the notes in the doctor's file. He wasn't at all sure just how much the count really knew about his past. He certainly had the large brushstrokes of the picture. But when they spoke of the night the Phantom had given *Don Juan Triumphant* to the managers of the Opera Populaire and had challenged them all to stage it, Erik had realized that Raoul viewed those events from the vantage point of an adversary. Hypnosis brought back more than the memory, it placed Erik within the skin of his former selves. When he spoke of the past, he was who he had been. Not who he had become. Not who he was at present. Would Raoul be shocked by what Erik might say during the session? Would he be appalled to hear the Phantom rage against destiny? Might Raoul withdraw his friendship?

"Erik, what do you fear? That I'll find out that you're a monster?" Raoul mocked him. "I already know what you've been and what you've become."

"So you really think I've changed?"

"Don't you?"

Erik didn't have time to answer. Dr. Richmond came back into the room with a needle and a phial of amber-colored liquid.

"Take off your coat and roll up your sleeve. I need you to be relaxed." The doctor inserted the needle into the phial and began to pull the plunger out to fill the cylinder.

"No. No drugs."

Dr. Richmond paused to argue, but he could tell it would be useless. "Very well then. But it may be more difficult to put you under without the tranquilizer."

"Just get on with it," Erik snapped.

It took Richmond more than ten minutes to put Erik under, at least three times as long as it should have taken. But he finally saw Erik sink deeply into a hypnotic trance. Erik's friend sat, anxiously watching, in a nearby chair. He was in reach if there were any need of him. Richmond led Erik down the same path they had taken, session after session, through one door to the next, not letting him linger at any point along the way.

"Erik, what do you see?"

"They're dancing."

Raoul tensed and gave the doctor a questioning look.

"The opera house. Judging from his tone, I'd say he's fairly young," whispered the doctor. Turning again to his patient, he asked, "Who's dancing?"

"Madeleine. She's so light. She flies like the trapeze artists."

Dr. Richmond rubbed his hand across the line of his jaw. Yes, it was the early years at the Opera Populaire. Again and again Costanzi returned to the same sanctuary, the same prison.

Unbidden, Erik continued, "She's going away. She's going with him. She'll marry him."

Intrigued, Dr. Richmond leaned forward and asked, "How does that make you feel, Erik?"

"Sad. Sad and…angry. She should stay with me. It's safer."

"Why would you worry about her safety?"

Erik struggled. He didn't like the question. "I'm very tall for my age. I am strong. I could pick Madeleine up like the man on stage is doing."

"Why should she stay with you?"

"I can protect her. I wouldn't let anything bad happen to her."

"Erik, why do you fear for Madeleine?"

Reluctantly he whispered, "He might hurt her."

"But doesn't he love her?"

"*I* love her. *I* will protect her."

"Husbands love, Erik."

Raoul shifted in his seat, uncomfortable with the direction Richmond's questions were taking. Erik's intense reaction to Madeleine's marriage evoked scenes of an incestuous nature. If such had been the relationship between Erik and Madeleine, Raoul preferred not to know.

"Erik? Is it not the role of a husband to love and protect?"

"No!" Erik's voice was deep and gruff. The ferocity of his reply startled both Raoul and Richmond.

"Why do you distrust husbands?" Richmond suspected a link to an event that Erik had not yet disclosed.

"I think he'll hurt her."

Dr. Richmond sat back and thought for several moments. He could feel Raoul's eyes on him. He tried not to be distracted. Annoyed, he whispered to the count, "He might be responding to the trauma of a previous experience. In that case, I suspect Madeleine represents his mother."

Raoul felt instantly relieved. The hint that Erik's interest in Madeleine had been carnal had unsettled him.

The doctor eased his chair closer to Erik. In a stern voice, he ordered Erik to go to the next door.

"Not forward, Erik. We're not done. You want to go back, before the years in the cage."

Years? Raoul sat forward, stiffly in his seat, and studied Erik. He had not known how long Erik had been caged and abused. He had always assumed it had been only a brief time, mere days or weeks, not years.

Erik began to move turning slightly away from the doctor's voice, rubbing his leg against the back of the couch. Raoul couldn't exactly tell what was going on until Erik turned full onto his side away from them and buried his face into the cushions. Then he heard a low moaning.

"Erik, you mustn't be afraid of the door. It's the last door. We've been here before. You want to know what's behind it. You need to know."

The agitation and moaning increased.

Dr. Richmond turned to Raoul and said, "I dare not force him. It's useless. The prohibition is too strong."

"What prohibition?" asked Raoul.

"The father's. He fears the father."

Such bald emotion must indicate how close Erik was to discovering what he had successfully buried away for years. Raoul was deeply affected by Erik's obvious fear. He had never seen Erik in the grip of terror, his vulnerability undisguised, unmitigated. Even in the Parisian cell, at the mercy of Leroux, Erik had struggled to maintain his dignity.

In his most authoritative tone, Raoul insisted, "Dr. Richmond you have to go on. Erik read the file. He needs to know the missing pieces."

The doctor scowled. *Of course, he had read the file. Having stolen it, the patient could not resist. But that only complicated matters even more.*

"If I force him, it could send him over the edge. I want no responsibility."

Raoul was sure the blood had left his own face and plummeted to his feet. On the verge of backing down himself, he watched Erik writhe on the couch, obviously frightened, unable to mask his raw emotions. Contagious, Erik's fear reached out to Raoul. He fought the urge to tell the doctor to desist, to bring Erik back to the present, his secrets buried forever in the past. But he had promised Erik.

"Proceed, Doctor."

Dr. Richmond wiped the sweat from his brow and steadied himself before he spoke to the patient again. "The door is in front of you. Erik, what do you hear?"

"Voices."

"Whose?"

"Their voices. Inside. They're angry. She's always angry or sad when the man comes."

Something was different. Dr. Richmond sat forward, attentive to what Erik was experiencing. When Richmond had asked about the voices, he had given Erik another way to pass through the barrier. Erik had followed the voices and had sidestepped the door altogether. He had not gone directly but via a less frightening path. But he was, Richmond believed, experiencing memories that had been closed off from him until this moment.

"Is one of the voices a woman's, Erik?"

"Mama is talking to the big man."

"Who is the man?"

Richmond felt the electric shock that ran through Erik. Quickly he steered the patient to safer ground. "Don't think about the man for a moment, Erik." They must proceed cautiously, or Erik might close the door again. "Tell me where you are."

"Outside the door."

Puzzled, Richmond wrote something on the tablet that lay across his knee.

"Which door is it?"

"The door to our room. I have to sit here in the hallway when Mama's friends come."

"Are the friends all men, Erik?" The doctor studied the man's face. His intuition was correct. Erik, the child, didn't understand, but Erik, the man, did.

Raoul leaned his face against his opened palms as the truth hit him. *Why did Richmond have to make it any clearer than it was already?*

"Yes. Mama stays inside with them for a while. Then we can go eat at the bakery. But I have to sit in the hall. One time I came in while Mama was lying down with one of her friends. He didn't like my face. So Mama makes me wait outside."

"What is the hallway like? Are you frightened to sit outside by yourself?"

"No. There's a kitten I play with. I draw. I have to draw quickly because the people pass by without stopping. I say hello to them, but they try to hide from me."

"To hide?"

"They…don't like…to look at me."

"Erik, do you know what you look like?"

Erik's voice was small and sad. "Yes."

"Does your mama not like to look at you?"

"She cries sometimes when she looks at me. She took the mirrors away."

"How did that make you feel?"

"Scared. I can't see my face anymore."

"Why do you need to look at your face in a mirror?"

"I can't see if it's getting worse."

"Oh, God," Raoul moaned. Dr. Richmond turned toward him with a warning look. "Erik, how do you feel toward your mother?"

"I wish we could go back to the opera house."

Raoul noted again the fast scrawls as Richmond jotted something down on his tablet. "We can't go back to the opera house, Erik. We must stay with your mother for a bit longer."

"Mama used to take me to the opera house."

Richmond paused as if confused. "Erik, why did she take you to the opera house?"

"She used to clean. She put me inside her bag of rags. She told me to keep the rags over my head so no one could see me."

"Was it because of your face?"

"No, that's stupid. I had to hide because they didn't want her to bring me to the opera house. I got into things."

"So your mother worked at an opera house, but she wasn't supposed to bring you along. She didn't want to leave you at home. What did you do while she worked?"

"I hid from the people. I climbed the ropes to the wooden bridges and walked above the stage. I watched the dancers and listened to the music. I was faster and more clever than the men who worked above the stage. They never caught me."

"Did you enjoy these trips?"

"Yes." Erik's voice was softly laced with tears, a child's tears.

"Tell me about the opera house."

"I listen to the music. They practice the same songs over and over, and I memorize them. I sing them to Mama when we're home alone. The men who come don't like me to stay in the room. I sing sometimes in the hallway, if no one comes by. Mama says I shouldn't make a fuss or draw people's attention. I disobey. I don't mean to, but I say hello to whoever passes by."

Suddenly Erik began to sob.

"Why are you sad?"

"We can't watch and listen to them sing anymore. Mama coughs too much. She has to be quiet. The stage manager says she bothers the singers. She has to clean after everyone goes home. It's quiet when we come to the opera house. There are only a few people left in the whole building."

"You don't like it anymore?"

"I liked it better before. I liked watching the people dress up and make believe on stage. The music filled the house and demanded that everyone obey. The music told them what to do. But now I can play the instruments in the music room. The first time Mama caught me in the music room, she spanked me. She said I might break something, and we can't afford to pay for the instruments. But I begged her to let me show her."

"What did you show her?"

"I played one of her favorite songs on the violin. It was easy. But I can play many more songs than the ones I played for her. So she lets me visit the room when she cleans."

"Erik, why did you stop going to the opera house?"

Erik quieted. Richmond could sense that he resisted being drawn back to the hallway outside his mother's room.

"Mama's too sick. That's why more of the men come now. It makes Mama tired and sad."

"Erik, tell me about the angry voices."

"No, I don't want to. I think I'd rather play with the kitten and my monkey. Mama made it for me." Again the doctor wrote something on the paper. "He's the monkey just like the one the organ grinder has."

"Go on," said Richmond. He continued to take notes.

"I wanted to play the organ, but the man was mean. He called me names and pushed me. I tripped and fell in the gutter. Mama told me I couldn't go outside anymore without her after that. She yelled at me. She was angry." Erik's voice trembled. "She said I was ugly and people would be cruel. She hurt my arm. She pulled me and held my face over a puddle in the street and pointed to the ugly thing in the water. Then she started to cry. She scared me. She locked me in the room and went away. I thought she wasn't ever coming back."

"How did you feel, Erik?"

"I thought she'd leave me. I thought I'd done something horrible to make her not love me. It was my face. No one wanted me around because it was sickening to look at me."

"Was that the last time you saw her?"

"No! No, she came home. She came back. She wasn't angry anymore. She kissed and hugged me. She brought scrap material, and she made the monkey doll for me. She used the hem of her best gown to make its clothes. She called me her little monkey and… and…she said I was beautiful."

"Did you believe her?"

Erik didn't speak for a long while. Then he quietly answered, "No. But she said it was a miracle. She said that inside the room I became beautiful. Then she asked me to sing."

"Erik, I think that's enough for today. I want you to step back through the door."

"No, I don't want to leave her. She's coughing so badly. She takes the medicine the man brings, but it doesn't stop the coughing. When I sing, she lies back on her pillows and soon she closes her eyes. Let me stay and watch over her while she sleeps."

Raoul fought a wave of intense sorrow as it washed over him. He felt as if he were there with Erik in a squalid little apartment. The whole scenario came shockingly into focus: Erik as a child alone with an ailing mother who was barely more than a child herself. At the mercy of poverty and disease, the young mother cared for a child, knowing that he would surely be left to die in the streets when she was no longer well enough to fend for him.

"Dr. Richmond, could you ask him to describe his mother?" Raoul interrupted.

The doctor considered for a moment the request, then he spoke to Erik. "What does your mother look like? Can you describe her?"

"Pretty. She's very, very pretty. But I wish she would eat more. She's pale and very thin. She has large brown eyes and brown hair that's always getting in her way when she bends over. She says my eyes are my father's. She sounds sad when she says it. But she laughs when she tweaks my ears. She says one of my ears is hers, and the other one must have fallen under the wheel of a carriage before God strapped it on. I wish she'd laugh more, but she can't. She always starts to cough, and then there's blood on her lips."

Raoul stood and went to the window. Dr. Richmond could see that Erik's story had affected him. The doctor was as exhausted as Erik. He'd not push him farther today.

"Erik, step back through the door. It's time to wake. I want you to remember what you've seen today."

"But I want to stay with Mama," he said. In his voice persisted the plaintive note of the child.

"I want you to remember your mother. I will count backwards from five, and when I reach one, you'll awake, refreshed and relaxed. Five, four, three, two, one…"

The session had ended. Erik rose from the couch and staggered to the door. Raoul helped steady him. Without a word, Erik pulled away and went down the corridor alone toward the exit. Raoul stayed only long enough to tell Dr. Richmond that they'd return the next day.

Outside the grounds of the asylum, Erik mounted the gelding. Raoul had given up his claim to the black horse and had purchased a beautiful chestnut mare for himself. Erik spurred the gelding forward, and Raoul and he cantered back to the inn. When the two men arrived, a boy from the stable came up to them and took charge of both mounts. Normally Erik would have seen to the gelding himself. But, to Raoul's surprise, Erik surrendered the lead to the boy. Without a backward glance, he entered the inn and climbed the stairs to their suite of rooms. Once inside, Erik greeted no one. He went straight to the bedroom, closing the door behind him.

Meg cast a quick glance at Raoul who tried to smile encouragingly, and then she followed after Erik to their private rooms.

"How was it?" asked Christine.

"Grueling. I need a drink." He plopped down on the sofa and closed his eyes. He opened them only when Christine placed the tumbler of brandy in his hand. "Thank you." After taking several sips, he sighed and spoke again. "Actually I think Erik was right to return. But it's not all bright and shiny."

"The doctor warned him, didn't he?"

"Yes, but it's something Erik needs to do." He set the half-empty tumbler on a nearby table and patted the cushion next to him. Christine sat and leaned in against him. Raoul draped his arm around her shoulders in a familiar gesture of intimacy, bringing her in closer still. "He remembers his mother now."

"Was it terrible?"

"Terrible?" He pulled back a little to look into her eyes. "Oh, I see what you mean." He relaxed and squeezed her arm gently, in reassurance, in understanding. "No, not in that way. I got the impression that his mother truly cared for him."

"In spite of…?"

"Well, yes. It was clear that she had accepted the deformity, but she must have been very young. She didn't know how to protect him."

"So is it over?"

"Afraid not. There's still something very dark lurking in the shadows. I think I already know what it is. But Erik hasn't faced it yet."

Before Christine could ask any more questions, Meg came into the parlor.

"He's sleeping." Meg walked across the room and sat near the fireplace. She hugged herself as if she were cold.

Christine sensed Meg was worried. "He must be exhausted, Meg. It's good for him to sleep."

When Raoul said nothing, Christine nudged him in the ribs. He scowled down at his wife. Christine nodded toward Meg. There, sitting near the hearth, so small and alone, Meg stared into the flames of the fire that had been set to ward off the growing chill of the afternoon.

Raoul cleared his throat to get her attention and added, "Dr. Richmond said that Erik might need to be alone for a while. He tells him to wake refreshed, but even so it drains him. It must be difficult for Erik to sort through all these new memories and feelings. Even I was exhausted at the end of the session. I can't imagine how worn out Erik must be."

Meg bit her lip but was quiet. Her mind was on Erik. Christine and Raoul were silent. Finally Christine left Raoul. She sat down on an ottoman next to Meg's chair. She took her friend's hand in hers. "Are you all right?"

Meg smiled. "Yes, I'll be fine. I miss my children. I wonder how Mario's healing. He could have a limp, you know."

"He'll be fine. That won't stop him."

"Yes, he's strong," she said as if a hundred miles away. Then, changing her tone, she rushed to add, "He's quite like Erik, you know. Actually it just struck me how both boys are just like Erik in their own individual ways. François has his dark seriousness, his genius, his intensity. But Mario is the clever survivor. He lives by his wits, but he hides, too. Mario's mask is different from Erik's. I see now why Erik protects him so fiercely. He sees himself in that boy."

"He doesn't favor Mario over the others, does he?" asked Christine.

"No. No, it's not like that. It's just different with Mario. He's cautious, tentative with François. I almost think he… Oh, I don't know. I think his relationship with François is difficult because François is so similar to him."

"Perhaps he fears François will suffer as he has."

"Yes, it's possible. But there's something else. It's as if he doesn't trust himself as a father to François." Meg was quiet for a moment. No one spoke for a while, then Meg took a deep breath and said, "Erik saw his mother. I think it was hard for him. She's gone, and this is all he'll ever have. It's as if he just lost her again." She was glad to have Christine by her side.

A loud crash stunned them. Before Raoul could reach the door to Meg's and Erik's room, it flew open and slammed against the wall. Erik stood, his arms flung from one side of the doorway to the other, half dressed. His shirt was undone and lay open, revealing a chest dusted with dark hair. His trousers hung low on his hip, and Christine tried to look away from the line of hair that disappeared below the slanted waist. He was barefoot, but what most shocked them was his obvious distress. He looked round the room wildly. Once his eyes fixed on Meg, he could see no one else in the room. He wrenched himself away from the doorway and marched over to where she sat. For one moment, he hesitated. Then he reached out, grasped her by the hand, and pulled her up into his arms.

"Where were you?" he hissed.

Raoul stepped forward and placed his hand on Erik's shoulder. Erik spun on him, flinging off Raoul's hand. "Don't touch me!" Then he turned again to Meg and steered her towards their room.

"Let her stay with us, Erik," Raoul warned.

Meg glanced quickly over her shoulder as if to discourage him from interfering. Raoul made as if to follow them. "I'll be ...," she said. But Meg didn't have a chance to finish because Erik pushed her forward into the room and slammed the door shut behind them.

Christine rushed to the door. She was about to pound on the surface with her clenched fist when Raoul held her back. He put his finger across his lips in sign that she should be quiet. Then he pressed his ear to the door and listened. After a few moments, Raoul gave Christine a reassuring smile and stepped away from the door. Then he led his wife to their adjoining rooms.

Once the door was closed and they were safely inside the bedchamber, Erik released Meg. He fell heavily onto the bed and closed his eyes. Meg sat next to him and cautiously laid her hand on his bare chest. Immediately she felt him calm. He opened his eyes lazily and studied her.

"I woke, and you were gone. I couldn't think. I didn't know where you were. I panicked." The madness was gone. "Touch me," he whispered. Meg leaned forward and kissed him. "No, not like that. Touch me."

"What do you want, Erik?"

"Take this off." He pinched the fabric of her dress between his fingers. "Lie with me. I need you," he whispered huskily. His hand skimmed under her hair and pressed against the back of her neck. He drew her down. Gentle at first, the kiss deepened, became raw and hungry.

"But it's the middle of the afternoon, and Raoul and Christine are next door." Her words, wet and breathless, were swallowed by his kiss.

"I'll die if I can't touch you, Meg. Take this off," he pleaded. He fixed her with his stare. "I want to feel you. I need you to touch me or I'll disappear."

Meg slowly pulled away from him. Helplessly, she looked at the thin door that separated their room from the parlor and back at the man whose eyes were green lightning. His hand lay softly over his groin. She could see how aroused he was. Her own desire unleashed rose in response to his. She lifted her eyebrow in mock disapproval.

"You're naughty, Erik. You know that, don't you?"

He answered her with a small grin. It helped to ease the tension.

"Very well," she said. "But you must be quiet."

She began to unfastened the buttons along her bodice. Erik watched with eyes that eerily did not blink. As she disrobed, she felt his gaze as if it were the weight of his hand upon hers. She removed her garments one by one, folded them, and set them aside. She wondered at his patience given the panic she had before witnessed. She approached the bed, her hips swaying gently, resisting the urge to cover herself in the afternoon light, for she knew that he liked to watch her. Having pushed the covers aside, Erik lay back against the pillows naked and fully aroused. All her inhibitions melted, ice turning to liquid fire.

As she straddled her husband's hips, she hoped, but doubted, that she, too, could be quiet.

The sound of the piano woke her. Meg felt the empty side of the bed and knew it was Erik. She slipped out of the covers. She was still naked. They had spent the entire afternoon in bed. They hadn't even excused themselves to Christine and Raoul, but somehow Meg knew that their friends had wisely retired to their own private rooms to give Erik and her some privacy. She grabbed the robe and tied it tightly about her.

In the parlor with a lone lamp fighting the darkness, Erik sat at the small pianoforte and played. His brows were knit, almost as if in anger, but she knew that it was only the intensity of his concentration. He played the same motif over and over. It sounded vaguely familiar. When she was only inches from him, he caught sight of her and demanded, "What is this?" He played the melody yet again, this time going on to another verse or two, then back to the beginning.

"I don't know. I don't recognize it."

"It's 'Rossignolet du bois,'" came the answer. Christine stood in the doorway from the second parlor that adjoined her and Raoul's rooms. "It's a traditional song my father used to play. The youth wants to learn how to woo the songbird's mistress, so he asks the nightingale to teach him how to speak like the nightingale and how to make love."

"Sing," he demanded and returned to the keyboard.

Meg nodded to Christine, who stepped barefoot into the center of the room, just to the side of Erik. She missed her entrance, and Erik stared up at her with a scowl. Then he started again.

Rossignolet du bois
Rossignolet sauvage
Apprends moi ton langage
Apprends moi à parler
Et dis moi la manière
Comment il faut aimer
Comment il faut aimer

"It's beautiful!" exclaimed Meg. Erik didn't even look up. Instead he started to play another melody. "I know this one, Erik," she said with delight. She waited for the cue and sang a verse.

Derrière de chez mon père
Il y a un moulin
Le meunier qui l'habite
Est un joyeux blondin

Christine joined her for the chorus.

Revenez-y donc ma jolie demoiselle
Car il est, car il est en train mon moulin
Revenez-y donc ma jolie demoiselle
Car il est en train d'y moudre

As the two women sang and Erik played, Raoul stepped out into the parlor and waited for the music to end. This song, too, was a traditional folk song but far less romantic than the first. In its many verses, a miller calls to a young girl who lives nearby and asks her to come grind her corn at his mill. The ribald meaning of the song is barely disguised when the young miller refuses to grind an old woman's corn. His mill won't grind her corn; she is far too old. Both Christine and Meg encouraged each other to remember other verses that accompanied the refrain.

Suddenly there was no more music. Meg and Christine were laughing over the puns, but they both came to a dead stop when they saw Erik bent over the keyboard, his head against the keys, his arms crossed tightly over his chest. He was so bent that for a moment Meg thought he had collapsed. She went to him. He was barely breathing. He turned his face and whispered, "These are my mother's songs. She gave them to me. She sang them to me." He cleared his throat roughly and took several large gulps of air. Then he sat up stiffly on the bench. "Leave me alone, please. I want to play."

Erik finished the final touches of yet one more portrait. Richmond and Raoul waited. Several charcoal sketches—some more detailed than others—lay on Richmond's desk. In each one, the face belonged to the same girl. Her hair was wavy and long, her eyes the most prominent feature, her bones delicate. The expression varied from one to the other, as did the angle. The last portrait was in three-quarter profile, and the girl—who couldn't have been more than seventeen or eighteen—had just the hint of a smile.

"May I?" asked Richmond. He held his hand out to take the sketch that they had been waiting for Erik to finish.

Erik had brought six sketches with him to show Richmond. Raoul thought it was just an excuse to keep them with him. They had awakened late—due to the events in the middle of the previous night—only to find Erik at the table next to the windows, catching the morning light, feverishly drawing.

Reluctantly, Erik handed the drawing to Richmond. Raoul looked over Richmond's shoulder. There was a distinct similarity, perhaps the mouth or perhaps the underlying bone structure, between son and mother. But Raoul couldn't help but think that the differences were equally striking. Of course, that would suggest that Erik took after someone else, most likely his father.

Erik scowled and searched in the tablet for one more sheet of paper. The tablet was empty. Before Erik could complain, Richmond suggested they needed to talk.

"Talk? There's no need. Just hypnotize me." Erik sat back in readiness.

"Not yet. Perhaps tomorrow."

Erik flew off the couch, his hand braced firmly under Richmond's chin. "There's nothing to talk about, Doctor. Take me back!"

"Erik, release me now or the sessions are over."

Raoul was amazed at Richmond's tone. For one moment, he thought he might have to intercede to keep Erik from murder. The fury was palpable, like waves shimmering off Erik's skin. Richmond held Erik's gaze. Then, suddenly, the tension was gone. Erik's hand dropped. He stepped back and sat on the couch, his eyes still focused on the doctor's.

"That's better. I want you to tell me what you've learned about your father."

Erik scowled. "Nothing."

"Don't be coy, Erik."

"I remember my mother. I didn't see my father." Erik looked over at the drawings.

"You drew some beautiful sketches, Erik," said Richmond.

Raoul saw Erik's hands tighten into fists.

Richmond continued as if he had not noticed Erik's increasing anxiety. "You are drawing her because you are looking for something. What are you hoping to find?"

"I don't know what you mean."

Raoul stifled a twinge of anxiety. It had not escaped his attention that the girl in the charcoal drawings bore a modest resemblance to Christine. *Had Erik noticed?* Raoul wondered.

"Why so many pictures, Erik?"

"One won't tell you what she looked like."

"Why do we care what she looked like?"

"I care!" Raoul tensed as Erik answered. There was a warning in Erik's voice.

"Why?"

"Because she's my mother, you idiot! Why else?"

"Why is it necessary to keep drawing her? One would suffice if you meant to show us what she looked like. What are you looking for?"

A long forgotten conversation recurred to Raoul unexpectedly as he scanned the numerous sketches of Erik's mother. Christine had described the rooms to which the Phantom had taken her. It was the first time Christine had glimpsed the world the Phantom had created in the vaults beneath the opera house. She had been amazed and somewhat frightened to see her image strewn over various surfaces, fixed to the sides of mirrors and furniture, even nailed into the stone wall of the cavern itself.

"Why do you need to keep drawing your mother over and over again?" the doctor insisted.

Erik frowned and hesitated. He glanced at Raoul, at the doctor, then at the charcoal images. Lines, thick and thin, shadows and smudges against empty fields, strokes on paper were all they were. His lips thinned in a tight-lipped scowl.

"What face are you trying to forget? Whose face do you erase each time you draw your mother's? Whose features, Erik, keep coming in the way?"

"No one's," he growled.

"Whose features do you have that you keep searching for when you draw her brown eyes?"

"Don't," he said. He bent slightly at the waist as if he'd been struck by the doctor's fist.

"Whose is the angry voice inside the room?"

"No, no, no, no. Don't." Erik doubled over and rocked, his head bent toward the floor.

"Who is the man who yelled at you to go away while he lay with your mother? What do his eyes remind you of?"

A flash of a hideous face in a murky puddle, the distorted features in a warped mirror at the opera, the eyes of strangers passing him in the street. "Mine! They're mine! Damn you! His eyes are mine!"

"Whose?"

"My...father's. The big man who pushed me aside and yelled at her. I struck him. I took the fork from the table and stuck it in his leg! He hit me with his fist. Oh, God, oh God, I...I...want to go. I have to go..." Deathly pale, Erik rose quickly from the couch, upsetting the table whose surface was cluttered with the empty sketch pad and blunted charcoals. They tumbled to the floor. He groped his way past Raoul in search of escape. Raoul grabbed him and held him firmly, blocking his retreat.

"Erik, you can't run away. You wanted to know about your past," Raoul reminded him.

"Not that. Not my father. I don't need to remember him. I see him every time I look into a mirror!"

"Sit down," demanded the doctor. His tone was stern but even, as if he had no doubt that Erik would obey. "We have a lot to talk about."

Erik pleaded with Raoul silently. Although Erik's struggle had abated, Raoul could sense the remnants of fear and disgust in Erik's ragged breathing. He loosened his grip on Erik, but he did not let go. "No lies, no hiding," he whispered to his friend, their faces close, their eyes locked in wordless intimacy. Then Erik slowly nodded, broke their hold, and turned back to Richmond. Raoul waited for Erik to resume his seat before he went back to his by the window.

"She's beautiful, your mother. All mothers are beautiful to their young sons. You loved her."

"Yes," he said quietly. "I loved her, but she was weak."

"She was ill. She was poor."

"No. She was weak. She…let him come back."

"Your father? Was your father the 'men' you spoke of?"

Erik furrowed his brow as if confused. "No," he whispered so low that Raoul wasn't sure he had heard properly.

"Then your mother was a whore."

The shock in Erik's face was only surpassed by his pain. He bent his head into his hands and broke into loud, painful sobs. Raoul rose to go to him, but Richmond waved him back. They sat and listened to Erik as he cried out his shame. Eventually, he quieted, but he kept his eyes averted.

"You hated her for sleeping with that man, didn't you, Erik?"

"Yes. I wanted to punish her. She closed the door, but I could hear them. The people passing in the hallway could hear them, too."

"They were disgusted by those noises more than by your face, weren't they?"

"Sometimes. Yes. Sometimes they said things."

"What did they say?"

"They called me a freak, a bastard, a whore's son."

"Is this necessary, Doctor?" Raoul asked, clearly angry that Richmond was tormenting Erik. "This isn't what he remembered yesterday."

The doctor glared at Raoul. "You must not interfere. Yesterday, he opened the door. Other memories follow inevitably. The child doesn't understand and can't tell us what the man knows. Don't speak again."

Raoul clenched his jaw, annoyed that the doctor was clearly in charge.

"What are you looking for in the picture?" The doctor resumed.

"I want to see how much I look like her. I want to see where it hides. I need to know where did it come from."

"What is 'it,' Erik?"

Erik pointed at his right cheek, the side blighted by his deformity. His tone had softened when next he spoke. "I don't…judge her." He took one of the drawings. "It can't touch her, not her soul. She had to feed me. She whored because she didn't have the strength to work anymore at anything else. But she wasn't ugly. Words, ugly words. Looks, the way the women looked at her. She wasn't any of that. The words were wrong. No one helped us. They turned away. The respectable people turned away. They looked at me and thought she didn't deserve their pity, their help."

"Go on, Erik."

"I didn't understand what happened behind the door when she pushed me outside. She'd give me my doll and a piece of apple or bread, if we had any food. I worried that the men hurt her. So sometimes, when I heard things, I got scared and knocked loudly for her to let me inside. She told me she'd hit me if I did that again or she'd take me somewhere far away and leave me." Erik couldn't go on for several moments.

"Do you think she meant it?"

"At the time, I thought she did. She did eventually, didn't she? But it was later, later that she took me to the fair and left me. With him."

"Do you remember that or do you remember being told about it?"

"I remember."

"We have to deal with the other face, Erik, the one you keep erasing when you draw your mother."

"Please, please, don't make me remember him," he pleaded.

Raoul consciously relaxed his fists. They had gripped the arms of the chair, his knuckles hard and white.

"You look like him, don't you? How do you resemble him?"

Raoul wondered how the doctor could be so placid, so merciless.

"The eyes." Erik picked up another of the drawings and touched his mother's dark eyes, smearing the line inadvertently. "Her eyes were brown, a deep soft brown."

"Would you draw him, Erik?"

"No!"

"All right. You don't have to. It might help, but perhaps later you'll do it."

"No, I won't! I want him out. Out of my head, do you hear? I want him gone!" Erik was very angry. But he didn't move from the couch.

"His eyes were…green. Is that right? In what other way do you see yourself in him?"

"See myself?" Erik stared at Richmond. Suddenly he sat back and sighed. "I know what you're doing, Doctor, but it won't work. He was a monster. I have eyes like his. I'm…built like he was."

"Your mother let him share her bed, didn't she?"

Erik's nostrils flared. Raoul prepared himself to come between Erik and the doctor, but Erik didn't move.

The doctor continued, "Come now, Erik. Tell the truth. Your father—the monster—was one of the men who came to the apartment."

…

"You saw him. Yesterday you saw him in the apartment with her. He was one of the angry voices. You tried to protect her. You took the fork and stabbed him. But that was not the first time or the last time that he came to your mother's room, was it?"

Erik shook his head but remained silent.

"What was the argument about?"

"She…wouldn't let him take me." Erik sat forward and grabbed the doctor's hand. "Please, don't. I don't want to remember. I can't remember."

"Tell me what you fear?"

Erik was crying silently now, his eyes riveted on Richmond. "He was shouting. He…said it wouldn't matter to me. He said that I was just an animal, not a human being. He said that I was his, and he could do whatever he wanted with me. She said I was a child, but he laughed at her. He didn't think I could understand. I was afraid of him. He pushed her back into the dark place where her bed was. She begged him to let her put me outside. But he laughed and said I didn't know what was happening. He thought I was simple. He took his clothes off, and…"

"Erik? Did he take you away that day?"

"He told her, afterwards. He said something. I can't remember. He tossed coins on her stomach. Before he left, he bent down and looked at me. His face was so close I thought he might bite me. He… I can't remember. I can't."

Richmond slipped his hand from Erik's. He studied Erik for several moments.

"All right. I think that's it for today."

Erik didn't move.

"She was innocent. She was ill. She…did what she could." Erik spoke as if to defend his mother against an unspoken accusation.

Richmond wasn't paying attention. He was writing several notes in his tablet.

"What are you writing? What is it?" Erik lunged for the tablet. Richmond tried to keep it but wasn't quick enough. Erik scanned the strange marks on the paper. He couldn't make any sense of it.

"It's shorthand, Erik. It comes in handy. It's a faster way of writing, using special symbols. And as you see my patients usually can't read it."

Erik stood and threw the tablet at Richmond. He stormed out of the office.

"Erik, I think this will be our last session. I want to hypnotize you and take you back to the angry voices, the last time your father comes to visit. I want you to step inside the room and tell us what you believe is happening. Do you understand?"

"I'm not an idiot, Dr. Richmond. You should know that already."

"Erik, this is not a matter of intelligence."

Erik sighed and looked away in annoyance. "I think I know everything I need to know. My mother was a whore. I was born a freak. My father thought I was little more than an animal."

"Is that how you see it?"

"It's difficult to see it any other way, isn't it?"

"This is not you talking, Erik. It's what you imagine anyone else would say. You were there. You knew her. She wasn't a whore, not in the scornful sense that you mean it."

"Let's just get this over with, shall we?" Erik sneered.

Richmond was tempted to remind Erik that it was he who had insisted on continuing with the sessions. On the other hand, he realized that Erik's belligerence was a sign that they were close to something particularly painful that Erik was reluctant to face. It was, thus, an indication that his own conjectures were correct. They'd open the final door today, or it would remain forever closed.

Erik fell easily into a hypnotic trance. He lay back on the couch, his arms limp by his sides, the features of his face smoothed into a mask of complete calm. Richmond took him back deeper and deeper. As they approached the final threshold, Erik's calm was marred by the deepening lines of concern that emerged near the edges of his mouth, along the plane of his forehead, at the corners of his eyes.

"You're outside the door, Erik, and you hear your father and your mother arguing inside. Take the knob and open the door. They won't see you."

"No, it's locked."

"It's not locked. It's just stuck. Push it, and it will easily come open."

Erik's breathing came in quick, shallow gusts. He began to rock his head gently back and forth on the cushion. "I don't think it will open."

"Trust me, Erik. It will. You're a strong boy. Like your father."

Raoul jerked his attention to the doctor as he heard the last statement. He couldn't imagine why he'd say something that was sure to hurt Erik.

"You're not like your mother, are you Erik? You're not weak. Your voice is strong and clear. You can breathe without choking. You can sing without stopping for breath. You won't be at anyone's mercy like she has been, will you?"

"No," Erik answered. "No, I won't be. They won't be able to hurt me."

"Not like they hurt your mother. Not like your father hurts her?"

"I won't let him hurt her."

"You can't protect her outside in the hall, Erik. Can you?"

"I pushed the door open."

"Good. Now you must listen to what they are saying. You will tell us what they are arguing about."

"Me. They're talking about me. He shouts at her. He says that I'm in the way. I've always been in the way. He says she should have gone through with it like he told her to. She says that I'm a normal child, like other children. She says he should love me. He's my father, and he should love me."

Erik liked that the dark man brought them food sometimes. He tried to like the dark man. His mother told him he should love him. The man was his father, but Erik didn't understand. He had no father. He only had a mother, and he was all his mother had. They were better off without the dark man who stood like a giant in their small room, sucking up the air, taking away the space. Erik would stop eating. He didn't need to eat. That was the only reason for the man's visits. He brought food. Erik would prefer not to eat if it would make his mother sing again.

She used to sing, but she stopped when the coughing came. Erik stared at the brown dots that had dried on his monkey.

He looked up at two giants on either side of a wooden table in the center of the one room that was his world. Behind them was the dark alcove where the small bed had been crammed in, filling the space. A curtain of sheer blue material had been tacked to the edges of the opening to give the appearance of a separate room. That was where she slept. That was where sometimes she let Erik sleep with her, like a puppy dog, curled in the soft hollow of her body, the softness from which he had come, she told him. The larger man, a giant, kept his back to Erik. But Erik knew what he looked like. He looked like the future, dark and large and strong with deep green eyes that hurt when they fell on Erik.

She argued with the giant, saying that Erik was just a baby and that she needed someone to look after him.

"You're his father. You have to take him!" She had tears in her eyes, but they didn't spill down her cheeks. She stared through them, bloody spit sat in the corner of her mouth, and her hands were tightly closed and

pounded on the table to emphasize her words. "I can't take it anymore, Abel. I can't."

"I told you to get rid of him. There were ways to do it. You didn't have to birth it. Nothing had to change, Laurette. You let it happen. You let that thing change it."

Then the giant did something that made Erik's heart stop beating. He went round the table and crushed his mother in his arms. Erik listened for his heart to start beating again, but the silence was only broken by the strange sounds coming from the man and the woman. The man was so large that Erik couldn't, at first, see his mother. She had gone!

Even though Erik desperately wanted to find his mother again, he didn't want to see her arms curve around the giant's back. He tried to look away, but the doctor wouldn't let him. He wanted to think the giant was eating her, cracking her ribs, but the doctor made him understand. He had to understand. The voices had stopped. The silence was shocking.

Then her voice came so softly. Erik couldn't see his mother's mouth, but he could imagine it next to the man's. "Please, please, Abel. If you ever loved me. I'm dying. I can't feed him. He's down to skin and bones. If I die, he'll be alone. No one will take him in. Not the way he looks."

"You should have taken him to the river and drowned him, Laurette. How could you have nursed that thing?"

"He's my baby, ours. You mustn't think that way about him. He's so sweet, Abel. You should hear him sing."

"Don't be stupid. He's a half wit."

"No, you're wrong. He's very bright. He can play music. He's not even four years old, and he can play the violin like a virtuoso."

"What violin? Have you gone mad, Laurette? Look at him!"

The giant man turned, and Erik wanted to sink into the ground. He felt his pants grow wet as he lost control of his bladder. The man's lips, full and dark, twisted in a half smile that was not tender or funny. His large, square hand pointed at Erik's face. "He's killed you. You were healthy before you gave birth to this." Erik saw the eyes consider him. The man was lost in thought. He was thinking, and the thought was scuttling back and forth as if trying to find someplace to rest. Then the eyes changed. They widened and fixed upon him as if the giant had, for the first time, noticed his presence. "But then again," the man whispered. The voice drifted down *like vapor from a dragon's mouth. Erik smelled garlic and fetid meat. He tried to shrink away so as not to see the strange smile on the man's face.*

His mother stood beside the giant. She didn't look at Erik. One hand lay on the giant's coat sleeve, the other caressed his dark oily curls. She couldn't reach the man's face, but she kissed his shoulder through his coat. Her eyes were large brown, wet and sad, entreating. "He's all I have in the world. You have to take care of him."

The giant stiffened, his eyes locked onto Erik. "Bring him this Friday to the fair."

"Then you will?" Her fingers trembled as she brought them to her lips.

"Put a bag over that face. Do you hear me? If you show up with him like that, I'll throw you both out. Mark my words, Laurette. Cover his face. Bring him to my tent at noon. And bring your things, too. You should never have run away from me."

"Yes, Abel. I'll do anything you ask. Just promise me you'll be kind to him."

"Just do what I say. Or you can both go to hell."

The giant pulled away and went to the door, but Erik's mother called after him to wait. Erik clasped his hands tightly over his mouth as he watched his mother pull the dark man down and kiss him on the mouth. For one moment, Erik saw the green eyes soften. The large, square hand touched his mother's face. Then the man looked at Erik. All the tenderness was gone.

"Erik, what did your father mean to do with you?"

"He wanted her, not me. He never wanted me. He thought he could have her, that I took her from him."

"She left Abel because Abel wanted her to abort you, didn't she?"

"Yes."

"What did your father mean to do with you when she brought you to him? Do you think he meant to keep his promise to your mother?"

"No, I don't, I don't, I can't, I can't remember. Damn you, I didn't want to know! Not this!"

"What? What is it, Erik?"

It was early in the day. Erik's stomach rumbled from an unbroken fast. His mother pulled the mended sweater over his head, kissing him on his nose when his face poked free of the material. When she knelt, as she now did, Erik could look her in the eye without tilting his head. He felt older, bigger, stronger.

"Now you need to listen to me, Erik." She began to explain to him about his father. "He'll take care of you, my love. Your father will take care of you when I can't."

Erik could feel his lips tremble and his vision blurred in a sea of salt tears.

"Remember the opera?" she asked, her voice too loud and too gay. "You'll grow up to sing at the opera. You'll sing for them, all the proper gentlemen and their grand ladies. You've got a beautiful voice. It won't stay this way forever. But you have perfect pitch. You won't lose that. And when your voice matures and deepens, it will be like magic. When you're a man, you'll write music. You'll learn to play more instruments. Which one will be your favorite, Erik?"

Caught up in the plans his mother drew like pictures in his mind, Erik answered, "The piano, Mama, the piano and the violin and the viola and the organ."

"All those instruments?"

"The organ is easy, and the oboe has a nice sound. I will play them all, Mama," he promised. She smiled broadly, and he knew he'd said the right thing.

"Will you make music for me, my little angel?"

He nodded. Suddenly, the tears were back. "I want you to sing, too, Mama. I'll bring you to the opera house to live, and you'll sing on stage like the fat lady."

"I'll sing to you in here," she said as she touched his chest. "Oh my sweet, I wish... I wish..." but she never finished her wish. She couldn't get her breath. The coughing didn't stop, and she placed Erik on his bed and went to sit on her narrow cot behind the blue gauze, her back rigid against the wall, the white handkerchief darkening against her mouth.

Was it the next day she took him to the fair?

She led him by the hand. He tripped over the discarded boxes, papers, and other debris left from the night before on the ground. He could barely see through the two holes she had made in the burlap bag. He had resisted when she tried to put it over his head the first time. She had had to explain that it was a game. He had wanted to believe her. He would have continued to struggle against the bag except that he sensed the urgency and panic in her voice as she invented one excuse after another for him to put it on.

She was walking too quickly, and he was tripping to keep up. He watched the hem of her dress through the oblique angle of one of the holes in the burlap. The stripes waved as she walked. He held his monkey. She had told him to hold the doll tightly. In the satchel that she carried were the few articles of clothing that were his. They were going to the fair. His father would take care of him—of both of them. She had added herself only as an afterthought when he had begun to whimper.

Just outside the main tent, she stopped and knelt in her very best gown. Erik didn't want her to dirty her skirts. He tried to make her stand up again. She held him for several moments without speaking. He cried silently under the burlap bag. She lifted the edge just enough to kiss him on the lips. Then she stood and pulled him roughly behind her.

The man, his father, waited inside. Erik heard her thank the man. She didn't look down at him anymore. She was walking out of the tent, but the man stopped her and turned her around. He kissed her. She pushed away and began to cough violently. She rubbed her hand across her mouth, smearing the bloody spittle. The man took some coins from his pocket and tried to press them into her hand. She shook her head violently back and forth. She said she didn't need the money. He asked her when she would come back. She stared at him without answering, then quietly she mumbled that she'd return later that day. Erik felt better knowing that his mother was to return. They were both going to live at the fair with the dark man.

Erik waited by the opening to the tent for his mother to return. His father came and went, never saying a word to him. Erik carefully stayed out of the man's way. Later, the sun was beginning to set, and Erik could tell the man was waiting, too. The man—Erik didn't like to think of him as his father—was nervous and kept looking out into the distance over the crowds that were surging onto the fair grounds. Then he left Erik in the dark. He was gone for hours. Still waiting for his mother's return, Erik lay down in the straw near the entrance to the tent.

The man's loud noises woke him. A single light on a table lit the man's terrible face. The sounds were coming from the man's mouth, painfully as if they were part of him. He poured from the half empty bottle into the glass and upended the dark liquid into his mouth. Erik looked about the room for his mother. She was nowhere to be seen.

"You killed her! You freak, you monster!" The man's face was directly above his. Erik smelled the alcohol thick on the giant's wet breath. "You worthless piece of shit! She never meant to come back. Do you hear me? Can you even understand? She stepped out onto that street in the path of the carriage."

Erik couldn't breathe. He panted. The burlap bag lay on the ground next to him. He grabbed at it to pull it down over his face, to make the giant disappear, to block the image of a carriage rushing down a muddy street. But the man grabbed the bag and crumpled it in his hands.

"She left you. She's given you away to me. She expects me to take care of you. Says I'm your father. You don't have a father. You're not a child."

When he took hold of Erik's collar and began to drag him, Erik wailed in fear. He called for his mother. He screamed. That was when his father struck him. Erik tasted blood. His head was woozy. His father picked him up and threw him inside the cage.

The panther was old, tired. The cat sniffed at the child, the scent of fear momentarily sparking his interest. He growled at Erik. Erik stood and froze, his back against the bars of the cage. The panther pushed his head against Erik's body and bared his teeth.

"Back, Balthazar! Back, you damn carcass!" The dark man stepped inside the cage and flicked the sharp whip at the panther who arched its back and raised its front paw—claws ground to the nub—in an empty show of menace. The animal went to his corner and growled resentfully as Abel stared at Erik. "You might be worth something after all. A monster, instead of an aging panther."

He grabbed Erik by the arm and pulled him from the panther's cage. He brought him to a smaller enclosure that also smelled of Balthazar and flung him inside.

"Monster child. No, that's not right. Let's see. Freak child." The man's eyes were glazed over. He was having trouble focusing on Erik. He mumbled incomprehensibly. The sounds were slurred.

Erik thought perhaps he was talking to someone. But they were alone in the tent.

"Devil. That's what I am," his father said more clearly, raising his voice and spitting at Erik who squatted in the corner of the cage, trying to disappear. "That's what she'd call me. A devil. Lucifer. Laurette, the little angel. I've played the devil to her angel. Why not continue the farce?" The man reared back and struck the bars with the thick pummel of the whip. "Well, you're mine now." Spittle flew from the ugly mouth as the man spoke.

Erik didn't flinch. He began to hate the giant, the dark man, the man with green fire in his eyes.

"That's it." The dark man laughed, his whole body shaking. "The Devil's Child. I was wrong. You're not worthless. You'll earn your keep. I daresay you'll make me a comfortable living."

"Erik, you will remember everything you've heard and seen. I will count back from five, and when I reach one, you will wake up, refreshed and alert. Five, four, three…"

CHAPTER 10

❃

The Beginning

There was never a genius without a tincture of madness.
Aristotle

"What can they be doing? They've been locked away for two days." Christine whispered, even though she and Raoul were several rooms removed from Erik and Meg.

Meals had been delivered, empty trays removed. Since the two men had returned from the last session at the clinic, Erik and Meg had exchanged no more than a few words with Raoul and Christine. Last night, a bedraggled couple, with dark circles under their eyes, had indeed joined Raoul and Christine for a walk through the hamlet. They spoke of returning to Rome. Meg repeated their original invitation, insisting that the Chagnys remain through the coming holidays, even though they were a month away. Erik was mostly quiet, but he smiled tenderly whenever Christine directed a question his way. Raoul watched his friend, noting the calm that had finally installed itself, permanently it would seem, in Erik's soul.

"Do you think they're...?" asked Christine with a slightly scandalized gleam in her eyes.

Raoul scowled at her as he loosened his cravat. "Christine," he said, his tenor deepening to a low, stern baritone. He pulled his cravat from his neck and dropped it on the floor.

Christine made as if to pick it up, but Raoul cleared his throat and shook his finger at her. Then he raised one eyebrow and demanded, "Come!"

Christine hesitated, then she giggled and slowly stepped forward into Raoul's embrace. He kissed her soundly.

"I'll be damned. It works." He smiled as he bent to kiss the rise of her bosom over the edge of her gown.

"What do you mean?" She laughed as she leaned back and invited him to kiss a trail up her long, lean neck to her lips.

"Erik told me to try it," he answered, blowing softly on her skin. "Evidently Meg likes him to take command of a situation."

"Oh, my God. Don't tell me you and Erik are exchanging hints on making love?"

"No, we were talking about how to train disobedient wenches."

"I think it's time that we returned." Erik moved his knight across the board, taking Raoul's queen. If Raoul didn't move his king, he would lose in the next round. His queen no longer protected his king. "Check," Erik said, smiling crookedly at the last pieces on the board.

Raoul studied the board for options. If he moved to the left, Erik's rook would have a free path to his king. If he moved forward one space, he could take Erik's knight, but the bishop would then take Raoul's king. To the right was no better than to the left, and he couldn't go backwards. Raoul sighed loudly and gently toppled his king. "Good game."

"Thank you," said Erik, pleased with himself. The game had lasted long into the evening. On several occasions, they had suspended play in order to listen to Christine read from a lovely volume of poetry she had found in the inn's library.

"Now what?" asked Raoul. "Oh yes, you said we should set out for home? You're sure you don't wish to meet one last time with Dr. Richmond?"

Erik's smile faded. "No. I think that I want to close this episode of my life."

"I was under the impression that things had gone rather well and that you were pleased to have followed through with the sessions. Have you changed your mind?"

"No. Not at all." But he didn't elaborate. Instead he watched Meg who, across the room, next to Christine, was talking animatedly about something. The men couldn't hear them. He smiled broadly.

"Things are back to normal between you and Meg, I see," teased Raoul.

Erik caught Raoul's light tone and lowered his eyes. Raoul could swear that Erik had colored slightly. "I'm very content. I'm anxious, though, to get home. I want to see Mario for myself. I miss them all. I'm sure they've been worried even though Meg has sent several letters home explaining why we've not yet returned. They'll be expecting us soon."

"What then?" Raoul asked.

Erik didn't answer. Instead he rose from his seat and went to the piano. He stood admiring the highly polished surface. It was a good piece, nicely tuned. The owners of the inn catered to royalty and nobility from all over. He sat on the bench and opened the keyboard.

Everyone waited, expectantly. Meg and Christine stopped their playful banter and waited for Erik to play. But Erik didn't play. He swept his fingers lightly across the keys, admiring them. When he became aware of the silence, he looked round the room at the others. "What?"

Meg sighed in exasperation. "We're waiting for you to play, isn't it obvious?"

Christine and Raoul kept their tongues.

"Well, perhaps I don't feel like entertaining you. Perhaps I like the silence now that the two of you have stopped your incessant chit chat and giggling."

Christine sputtered, and Meg glared at him. "We don't expect you to entertain us. Surely if you play one of your modern pieces, you'll only succeed in annoying us."

Erik wasn't fooled. The corner of his mouth rose only a bit, but he chuckled softly. He lifted his fingers and poised them over the keyboard. The room disappeared and only his hands and the white and black keys stood out against the darkness. Erik heard it just a hummingbird's wing before his fingers set down and began to play it. The long note that he imagined sustained in the graceful stance of a ballet dancer. Meg's body. He saw her stretch and lift her leg at an impossible angle and grasp lightly the toe of her slipper as she held the note. Then all of his fingers began to play across the surface. *When you're a man, you'll write music. You'll sing for proper gentlemen and their grand ladies. You'll play your own compositions. Sing for me, my little monkey, play. You'll find your soul in your music; you'll hear my voice in your song.* Erik stopped. His fingers had begun to tremble.

"Erik? Are you all right?" Meg came behind him and laid her hands firmly on his shoulders.

"She stepped out into the road, Meg. I'm sorry." He shook the sadness as best he could from his body. He patted Meg's hand. He could tell Christine and Raoul were also concerned. "Really, it's all right. It just hit me for a moment while I was playing. I wish I could have had her for a little while longer. But I have the music. She's there, too."

The notes rocked him. Gently they wafted through his dreams. Rossignolet apprends moi comment il faut aimer. Lightly in a beautiful soprano, she sang to him. His mother carried him on her hip and sang to him. They walked along the Parisian streets and entered the boulangerie. They stepped up to the counter, a large glass display of pastries, rolls, croissants, loaves of bread. The people around them smiled until their eyes lit on him. She sang, apprends moi à aimer, apprends moi à chanter. *He rested his head on her shoulder, his fingers twined in her brown hair,* teach me to love, teach me to sing, *the smell of fresh baked bread so thick in the air that it folded over him and sank into his pores. The people looked away, then looked back again. She whispered in his ear to sing with her. Very quietly he opened his mouth. The warm scent of baked bread rushed inside, and he swallowed the taste of it with pleasure. The skittish, down-turned eyes of strangers in the bakery glanced up at him. He sang softly along with his mama. The guarded reserve receded; smiles came to their eyes. They all commented on how beautifully his mother sang. They all remarked that the child had the voice of an angel. He was beautiful. An old lady, large and round, with sad watery eyes and scanty gray hair hidden under an elegant but worn wide-brimmed hat, reached up and touched his cheek.* Oh poor little angel, God must have known you would be special. *His mother tightened her grip on him, rubbed his back with the palm of her hand. It hurt in a good way, he thought. He stopped singing and kissed his mother's wet cheek.*

Erik woke. The milky pre-dawn haze was just spilling into the room. He wiped the dampness from his face. She had done the best she could. But she had broken his father's heart. If his father had had a heart. Erik knew that the most difficult truth that he had to accept was that his father had indeed been a man, not a monster. But his father had only loved one person, Laurette.

Erik turned onto his side toward the messy bundle of covers next to him in the bed. The days were cold now. Winter was firmly in place. He found what he thought was Meg's waist. Her back was to him, her knees drawn up. He slowly and carefully slid her toward him as he found a way to touch her. He laid his head on her pillow just over the tangle of blond hair and settled in to wait for the true light of dawn. His mind wandered, and he thought of his children. He ached to return to them. They proved that life went on, that love endured and was ever born again. They completed him. A lone violin played in his mind. The music had never gone. His mother whispered to him still. *It's here in your heart.* It had only been silenced behind a wall of fear and anger. The music was alive again. All he had to do was remember. All he needed was to forgive and remember.

Meg moaned and stirred. Selfishly Erik held her more tightly, keeping her pinned to his body. She quieted again. He listened to the music as it built, flowed, and filled the empty silences. The violin was not alone anymore. The window through which a tenuous and diffused light drifted became a stage. The whisper of a story took hold, and Meg and the company began to spin round the stage, their costumes changing as quickly as the story and its characters changed in Erik's mind. Words, the verses of an aria, at first indecipherable grew crisp and clear.

He had to commit the notes to paper, but Meg was so soft and warm in his arms. She had completely surrendered to his will. Reluctantly, Erik slipped from the bed. He listened to her regular, deep breathing. A slight nasal flutter threatened to become a snore. The sound made him smile.

At first he played quietly, not wishing to wake them. But the music had its own demands. The dynamics changed, and Erik followed suit. He forgot the passing of time. He became oblivious to the presence of the other occupants in the suite of rooms they occupied. He saw movement from the corner of his eye, and for a moment he thought of the fact that he wasn't properly dressed. The thought wasn't important and worried him only briefly. He let it fall away. He madly transcribed the score, jotted notes about verse and scene in the margins. He had had to draw the staff lines on blank paper. When he was almost done, he found he had run out of paper. He checked the sheets to be sure he'd used both sides. Every inch was filled. Wildly he looked about, and his eyes lit on one of the many sketches he had drawn of his mother. Without hesitation, he turned the sheet over and jotted down the remaining notes of the first movement.

Suddenly the room was brightly lit with sunshine and filled with faces. Erik realized that Meg, Christine, and Raoul were chatting at the table near the windows. They were having breakfast. Erik became aware of a hungry twisting ache in his stomach. He was famished. How long had they been there?

"Good morning," he said, tentatively.

Raoul swallowed what he had been chewing and answered for the party. "You were right, Meg. He is alive! We weren't sure, you know."

"Come have something to eat. There are still some rolls and wonderful cream filled pastries. Come before the tea gets cold," Christine urged while Meg patted a seat next to hers.

"We've not eaten it all, yet. But I make no promises," warned Raoul.

Erik looked wistfully at his pages and pages of notes. He must have been at it for hours. It was morning. The sun had long cleared the horizon and sat high in the eastern sky. Everyone had risen languidly and taken their time before they assembled in the common parlor for breakfast.

"It's beautiful," Meg said as Erik took a seat.

"I'm not dressed," he said. It sounded silly. He pulled the robe securely closed, suddenly aware that he was practically naked underneath. In contrast, everyone else was perfectly outfitted, ready to leave the rooms, if they wished.

No one ventured a remark. Raoul handed him a cup of tea. Christine passed him the honey, and Meg poured a liberal dollop of cream into his cup as he stirred the aromatic brew. Hungrily Erik chose a pastry iced with melted sugar and apparently filled with a dark purple marmalade.

When Christine asked him if he was serious about leaving soon for Rome, he couldn't answer, for his mouth was stuffed with the sweet gummy mess.

Finally, he licked his fingers rudely, only mildly embarrassed, and said, "I want to leave immediately."

The others stopped in mid-sip and mid-bite, having expected he would have given them more notice.

"I want to go home," he added as if there might be doubt as to why he wanted to leave.

Raoul spoke up for the three of them. "I thought as much since we did discuss our departure just the other day. I *have* made arrangements for a carriage comfortable for the four of us. As long as the weather holds, we should be able to complete the journey over the course of a few days."

"No," interrupted Erik. "A carriage is too slow, and the weather is more likely a hindrance on the roads. I've decided we're taking the train. We will go by carriage to Linz and take the train from there. We'll be home much sooner." Erik downed his sweet tea and held the cup out for more. Christine hid her smile as she served him. "Make the arrangements." Everyone sat silently staring at him. "Please," he added, as an afterthought.

Raoul laughed out loud.

Erik blushed, but he laughed, too. "I'm sorry. It's easier to bark orders than to make polite requests."

"Clearly. Don't worry about it, Erik. Some things just don't change. I'll send someone to Linz for the tickets if you're sure that's how you wish to travel." Raoul sobered and cast a cautious glance at the women.

"Why wouldn't I? It's the fastest way. Everyone marvels at the speed and reliability of rail service."

Meg laid her hand softly on Erik's knee under the table where no one could see it. He turned toward her. She was willing to broach the subject that their friends were reluctant to raise. "The carriage is so much more private, that's all."

Encouraged by Meg's opening, Christine suggested, "I suppose we could send our man to find a mask for Erik?" She directed her question to Raoul.

"There's no need, Christine." Everyone waited for Erik to explain. "I realize the train stations are crowded, as are trains." Erik hesitated. Suddenly he wasn't as sure as he had been when the idea had taken root in his mind. He rose and searched the room until he found what he was looking for. A long, rectangular mirror hung on the wall by the exterior doorway. Certainly it was meant for ladies who would check the position of their hats before leaving their apartments. The mirror extended from the low table at its base to the level of the transverse beam of the doorway. Within its gilded frame, Erik could see the reflection of his upper body and his unmasked face. There he was—the illusion of presence—looking back at himself. He stared into his eyes, eyes that he now knew would forever link him to his father. But above all else, they were *his*. They belonged to *him*, as did the rest of his life. Gradually his gaze moved along the plains of his face. For several seconds, he examined the strange, irregular surface of his disfigurement. Then he turned toward the others and asked, "Is it really so hideous that I can't walk outside like any of you unless I cover it?"

"Of course not," answered Meg, but then she'd become intimately accustomed to him.

Christine was next to speak. "We only thought that you would be uncomfortable surrounded by strangers if you didn't have a mask. But it was only your comfort that we had in mind."

Raoul said, "Frankly, Erik, people will stare, and some might simply shy away. But damn them anyway. There's absolutely no reason you should hide. So you're not pretty. So what?"

"He is too!" protested Meg.

Erik laughed. "Stop. Raoul's right. I am a strange looking creature." He looked again at his reflection. "With a face only a mother could love." He smiled at himself. "Damn the rest," he repeated Raoul's oath. "I've given it a lot of thought. There are many who are more unfortunate than I. Just look at your husband, Christine." He winked. "He's got that nasty slice down his cheek from playing with knives and pretending he was something he wasn't."

"Whoa. Just one minute there. Weren't you the one who said this scar—which I got trying to save your worthless hide—would make me look dashing?"

"I lied," Erik replied. Meg and Christine both burst out laughing at the men.

"I suppose we should pity ourselves, Christine, for having married such ugly men." Meg couldn't resist joining in on the fun.

"Thank goodness we're so beautiful no one has eyes for anyone else when we're around," added Christine in collusion with her friend.

"True. All very true," shouted Erik above the laughter. "Seriously, my friends, I know that this," and he pointed to his face, "will never be anything better than an ugly misfortune." Everyone quieted to listen. Erik sat again at the table. "But I've gotten a glimpse into what my life might have been like if my mother had not gotten ill." Meg took Erik's hand in her own. "She—my mother—didn't cover my face. She carried me with her just as other mothers carried their children through the streets of Paris, into shops, amid crowds of people. She wasn't ashamed of me, but she was protective. I had thought she was the one who forced me to wear a mask. But it wasn't she. She expected me to grow up and learn how to live with my deformity. It was simply a part of me, like Christine's dimples—which are beautiful—or that tiny brown mole at the base of Meg's throat—which is so dear to me—or Raoul's eyes—which are set far too closely together and make him look rather like a half-wit."

Raoul struck Erik a mock blow on the shoulder as the women looked at Raoul's eyes to see if indeed Erik was right. "I'd rather look a bit silly than frightening."

"Frightening can have its advantages," Erik defended himself. "The point is I don't have to hide behind a mask. I realize that it has taken a good deal of my energy to continue the masquerade. Some people, I'm sure, will be cruel. What do I care? You accept me. My family accepts me. Deformed though I may be. Imperfect as I certainly am. Then, by God, the rest of the world will either put up with me or they can all go to the devil."

Arrangements had been made, and they were about to depart. Erik made one last-minute request. On the way out of town, they would pass the clinic. Erik wished to stop briefly before they continued on to Linz. Dr. Vernon had arrived and was eagerly carrying out improvements to the procedures and care of the patients. He had hired twice the number of staff, added several doctors, one to assist Dr. Flescher. Dr. Vernon also included more women among the staff, arguing that a feminine presence served to humanize the institution. Dr. Vernon, along with Dr. Richmond, greeted Erik at the door to the common room. Erik was impressed by Dr. Vernon's compassion. It was clear that his motivation was solely the comfort and wellbeing of the patients. Dr. Richmond was preparing to leave for the Bragant Institute the next week.

Erik asked if he might have a few minutes inside with the patients who had shared his trials. The moment the door opened, Heinrich scurried under the table. Only when he recognized Erik did he come out. Erik greeted those who were aware of his presence. He lightly patted the hand or touched a shoulder as he made his way through the room. For a moment, Erik thought of Celeste. He would have liked to have taken his farewell of her. But hers wasn't the only absence. Erik checked his wayward thoughts. He would not wish to see Lisbet's ghost trapped between these four walls.

Erik made his way to the bank of windows where Laurent stood, nervously shifting from foot to foot. "Laurent, I've come to say goodbye." Erik held out his hand and waited for Laurent to take it. The man clenched his jaw shut to keep from barraging Erik with a line of filthy invectives. Erik regretted that Laurent would most likely remain in the institute the rest of his days. The world could be a small and mean place with little room for compassion.

It took too much energy for Laurent to hold his tongue and to accept Erik's hand in any but an awkward gesture. He shook it roughly. A rush of air burst forth, and Laurent couldn't stem the flow of curses. "Cock shit lucky shit bastard shit lucky damn asshole cock shit bastard!" Laurent paused to breathe.

"It's good to see you, too, Laurent," Erik calmly answered.

Laurent let out a sigh of relief.

"Dr. Vernon's a good man. Things will be better here."

"Sssshhhit..." Laurent bit down hard on his tongue and groaned. "You...got, shit, damn fffff..., got out! Good cock codpiece, bodkin, shit eating...oh God!"

Erik smiled. Laurent relaxed. "Take care, mon ami. Sing, Laurent, sing or hum. It's harder to curse in rhythm to the music."

The last stop Raoul and Erik made was to the infirmary. Erik owed Dr. Flescher a debt of gratitude. The physician had attended to his injuries on several occasions. He had also believed Erik when he insisted that Lisbet was in danger. Flescher had done what he could to protect the child. Even so they had both failed to save Lisbet and would share the regret.

Before he could depart, Erik asked to have a word with Hilda. Her teasing ways had eased his pain and loneliness. Just inside the doorway to the common room, Hilda waited, never taking her eyes off Erik. He took his leave of Dr. Flescher and walked over to the nurse.

"Thank you for the sweets," said Erik. He bent and brushed his lips across her cheek. Unable to muster the words, Hilda reached up and pulled Erik down. She kissed him full on the mouth. Dr. Flescher cleared his throat, but Hilda was oblivious. Erik gently broke her grip on the back of his neck and stepped out of range. Smiling, he bowed at the waist, expressed his gratitude, and bid farewell to both Hilda and Dr. Flescher.

But just as he was about to leave the infirmary, he couldn't resist adding, "My wife—Connie Boncoeur—sends her regards to you both." He smiled a crooked smile and left.

"I thought something was peculiar about that woman." Dr. Flescher glanced at Hilda who had turned a bright pink. He disguised his chuckle with a discreet cough and went back to his duties.

Dr. Richmond joined Raoul and Erik as they made their way toward the front doors of the asylum. Raoul walked ahead to allow them some privacy. Neither Richmond nor Erik spoke until they were nearly at the carriage door. There the two men stopped.

"Will you find Celeste at the Bragant?" asked Erik.

Dr. Richmond grimaced at Erik's uncanny insight. "She is a patient. She's under my mentor's care."

"Is your mentor as unethical as you?"

"Direct, Erik, you're nothing if not direct."

"Well?"

"Dr. Klinen is a teacher and scholar. He would never put anything before the patient's wellbeing."

"So I have your word that you won't…"

"What? At a loss for words, Erik?"

"You may call me Sig. Costanzi, Dr. Richmond. I'm no longer a patient here."

"Sig. Costanzi, for what I've done to you, I ask your forgiveness."

"It has been…enlightening."

"But as far as the situation with Celeste is concerned. It's… complicated."

Erik's brows furrowed. He examined the doctor. "Do you have feelings for her?"

For a moment, Erik thought Richmond would refuse to answer.

"I can't stop thinking about her." The doctor could not sustain Erik's gaze. Instead he stared out toward the park beyond the asylum gates. "I abused my position. I have no right to expect…"

"If you care for her, you should be by her side. You must find a way to help her. But beware, Dr. Richmond, that you mustn't press your attentions on her if she doesn't return your affection. I know from experience that you can't force someone to love you."

"Advice from a former patient. The world is changing."

Erik paused. "I...do owe you something. For my mother, I thank you." Erik stepped up into the carriage. Without looking, he called back to the doctor, "I hope we never meet again, Dr. Richmond."

Home! Erik rushed inside far ahead of the others. The servants greeted him warmly, and a buzz of voices swept through the rooms, from servant to servant, that the young Costanzi had returned home.

"Erik?" Madeleine approached from one of the side parlors.

Before she had taken more than two steps outside the parlor, Erik met her and lifted her in his arms. He twirled her around until she began to shout, "Put me down! You're making me dizzy!"

Erik lowered her carefully to one of the chairs along the wall in the foyer.

"Where's Mario?" he asked even before she had gotten her breath back.

"I say, Erik, you might wait and greet me." Marcelo slapped Erik fondly on the back. Erik turned toward the older man. Marcelo smiled and held his arms open wide. Erik stepped inside the man's embrace. He buried his face against Marcelo's shoulder. The two men stood, frozen in time. Madeleine kept wiping her eyes. The moment was broken when the hallway filled with the sounds of the others' arrival. Erik stepped away, his eyes averted, and composed himself.

"I must see Mario. The children?"

Madeleine saw the glistening sheen in Erik's eyes. "Upstairs. Mario and François are in the game room. The twins are with the nurse. I'm not sure where Laurette is."

But Erik wasn't listening. He was already halfway up the stairs.

Erik stood in the doorway to the game room that Mario and François shared. There the two boys leaned over a game of chess, arguing. Erik stepped forward over the threshold. Two pairs of eyes lifted in his direction. One boy rose and with the barest of limps came quickly to Erik. The other remained fixed to his spot at the table. François watched as Mario hugged his father tightly round the waist. Erik fought to beat down the hurt to see his firstborn son hang back.

"I thought you were dead, Piccolo." He kissed Mario on the top of his head. "I don't know how you survived that accident. But you're tougher than I thought."

François listened. Erik smiled at him. François looked away.

"I've missed you all terribly. I didn't want to go away." He held Mario tightly to his chest, but his eyes were trained on François.

"We know Maman signed papers letting them take you away." François stood stiffly in defense of his mother. "She thought you were mad. It wasn't her fault. It wasn't. You were acting like a madman again."

"François, your mother had cause to worry. You're right to defend her."

Mario scowled. "But…"

Erik whispered to Mario, "She didn't understand, Mario. She was trying to do the best for us all. You mustn't judge her. She's your mother. No matter what she's done, she loves you. She loves me, and I love her. It's all right."

François still stood, his knuckles white, his hands in tight fists. Erik recognized the green morass of his son's eyes as if he were gazing into a mirror. Erik also saw the angle of his son's body. François leaned forward as if his feet were nailed to the floor and they were the only thing holding him back, keeping him from flying to Erik's arms. Gently, Erik separated from Mario and approached the table. But he stopped when he saw his son's eyes flare in anger.

"Come here, François." Erik reached out his hand toward his son. "I'm your father. For better or for worse, I'm in your blood. Even if I'm mad, I'm your father. And no matter how angry you are with me, I love you."

"You lost control. You can't do that. You were acting…acting like a madman, like you did with Leroux. I hate you. I hate that you can't control yourself."

"François, I think I'm showing tremendous control at this very moment, for I am tempted to whip you for disrespect. But as you see, I'm holding out the olive branch. I know you're upset with me. I'm your father. I'm also a man, and I'm flawed like all men." Erik's voice had thinned. He clenched his jaw against the rise of emotions that threatened to overwhelm him. Although he felt the sting of tears at the back of his throat, he had to reach François, to make him understand. "Do I have to be perfect for you to love me? Do only the beautiful, the straight, the successful ones deserve to be loved?"

François ignored the tears that spilled down his own cheeks. He still could not move. "I don't want you to ever go! Not again."

Erik's heart felt as if it would break. This had not been the first time François had lost his father. "François, you're so brave." It wasn't the first time that his son had been forced to be brave.

"No, I'm not," François cried, but no longer in anger. "I'm a coward. I was afraid when they took you away that I'd never see you again. And I'm not ready to be a man."

Erik reached out to Mario and led him to the opposite side of the table. He squeezed his arm and told him to sit down. Then he went over to where François still stood rigid and shivering with mixed emotions.

"I will come to you, if you can't come to me." Erik stopped just inches from his son. He bent his head only slightly, for François had grown so tall that he was nearly his father's height. Slowly, Erik raised his hand in supplication, in hope, palm up, his fingers extended. He wasn't sure that François was capable of forgiving him. But he could not bear to witness his son's grief. Erik brushed the tips of his fingers across François's wet cheek. The boy fell into his father's embrace and buried his sobs against his vest. All his anger, as well as his sorrow, flowed out with those tears, leaving behind only his love for his father. Erik returned in equal measure the strength and ferocity of François's grip, an embrace that neither broke for some time.

"I have such amazing children. I, who have no idea why I've been so fortunate. It's going to be all right, I swear. If it's within my power to make it so, it will all be all right."

Erik lingered in the game room with Mario and François. They spoke in quiet tones about what had transpired at home in Erik's absence, about Mario's recovery, about the opera house, about François's newest compositions. After he was sure that his sons were once more on an even keel, Erik suggested that they resume their chess game and watched over the final moves of their match. Eventually he left them.

Erik had not yet seen Laurette or the little ones and was anxious to see them. A few months meant a lot more with children as young as Raoul and Etienne. They changed nearly by the minute. Mario had mentioned that the twins were likely with the nurse. Erik headed down the corridor toward the nursery.

Meg was already in the room. The twins, Raoul and Etienne, were clinging to her skirts, and she was laughing with them.

"Maman! Maman!"

"Oh, my little monkeys." Meg caught sight of Erik in the doorway. "And look who I brought back?" She picked up little Raoul who immediately grabbed a fistful of her hair in his chubby hand and was pulling it toward his mouth.

"Papa, Papa!" Etienne stretched out his arms to Erik who picked him up and kissed him soundly on his dirty cheek.

"He's wet." Too late, Erik held the child out and away from his vest.

"Well so is this one." Raoul squirmed in Meg's arms. She rescued her strand of hair from his mouth and turned to Erik. "Here, hold Raoul, too, while I go find the nursemaid." Erik had just enough time to shift Etienne to one arm and accept his twin in the other.

"My God, you smell!" Both boys wove their arms around Erik's neck as if they were considering climbing up to his head. They stretched and kissed him on either cheek. Erik tried not to breathe.

"Drat and double drat!" Laurette slapped both hands soundly on the keyboard.

Erik cleared his voice roughly behind her.

"Papa!" Laurette ran the short distance and jumped into Erik's arms.

He easily caught her and twirled her around, her skirts flaring out as she went round and round the room. For a moment, he held her at arm's length in the air above his head. He took his time examining her. She had large brown eyes.

"Are you not mad anymore, Papa?"

"Yes, I'm not mad anymore. At least not today."

Laurette's smile threatened to collapse. Erik rushed to reassure her. "I'm not mad. I promise. If I start to act strangely, it's only pretend. Our secret. Agreed?"

Laurette nodded. "Papa?"

"Yes, ma petite?"

"Put me down. I'm too big to be treated like a baby."

"Oh, right." Erik forced his face into a serious expression that did not at all correspond to his feelings. "I forgot. You're all of nine."

"I'm nine years and eight months. I'm nearly a woman."

"Yes, quite." A smile tickled at the corners of his mouth, but he resisted.

Laurette examined him carefully. Erik furrowed his brow in an imitation of a barrister he had once seen. Appeased, she brightened. "I missed you, missed you, missed you, so, so, so, so, much!"

"But I was here all along."

"Where?" She looked around the room. "Oh, silly! I know what you're playing at. You were gone. And I'm angry with you."

"Is that why you were treating me so badly?"

"What?"

"When I came in, you were hitting me." Erik glanced across the room. "You smacked me soundly."

Laurette glanced back at the piano and blushed. "You wouldn't make the right sounds. You were being naughty."

"If you were perhaps a bit more patient, I promise you that I'd make the most beautiful music you could imagine." He bent close to her face and brushed back her brown curls. "Ma belle, I have a present for you."

"Oh, give it to me! Give it to me now, Papa." She started to go through Erik's pockets, searching for some treasure or other.

As if by magic, Erik drew the papers from behind his daughter's ear. "Why here it is. You were hiding it in your hair. You must have all kinds of things in there. By the way, have you brushed it today at all?"

Laurette jumped up to grab the papers. On the third try, Erik let her reach them. She stared at the sheet music, her eyes traveling over the notes, quickly turning the sheets until she reached the end.

"Oh, Papa, this is beautiful. This is quite the nicest. And you named it after me!" She hugged him, her arms encircling his hips.

He didn't correct her. It was after all her name, too. She sat at the piano and began to play, "Laurette's Aria."

"The holidays are going to be wonderful this year, aren't they?" Meg had come up silently behind Erik. She wrapped her arm around his waist and whispered so as not to distract Laurette.

"Yes, they will be. Raoul and Christine are settled in with the children?"

Meg nodded. "Elise wants to be an opera star. Raoul is beside himself with worry. Victor went up to officiate between Mario and François. He's quite the negotiator, it would seem. Erica took Roland up to the nursery. She says she's the only one who can take proper care of the three boys. She asked if she can take Etienne and Raoul home with her after the holidays. What do you think?"

"Well, it would be quieter, I suppose."

Meg laughed into his coat. "By the way, Raoul wants to fence with you this evening or tomorrow morning."

"I'll convince him he needs this evening to practice alone before we spar. We'll have a go at it tomorrow."

"It's almost time for the children's dinner. We adults will dine later."

"I'm not hungry." Erik brushed the hair back from Meg's forehead and kissed her. "Not for food," he whispered near her ear.

"Maybe we should rest a bit. So that we're fresh for dinner?"

"How long would we have?"

"Oh, I think we wouldn't have to come down for a while. Do you think we could rest enough in two hours?"

"It might be sufficient. But I think we will have to rest more than once."

Meg's brows rose in surprise. "Well, as long as I can lie back on the bed for some of the time."

"That sounds like a perfect idea. Let's go up and start now."

"I think we've already started."

"I stand here! This is the center. You don't put me behind a well. No one can see me behind the well. They come to see me, not the well! It is too tall, too big! Who built this well? Tell him it is too tall. He will cut it down."

"But, Carlotta, you're not supposed to be behind it." Rinaldo rubbed his forehead to quell the increasingly painful thud of a headache. "You're to the side."

"I don't want to be beside the well!"

"You're drawing water for God's sake for the horse."

"Ah hah! That's another thing. The horse she smells. She wants to eat my hat! She almost steps on my feet. I don't want the horse."

Rinaldo muttered several curses sotto voce as he turned his back and went to the assistant. He took the score from the boy and thumbed through his notes.

"All right. All right. We can have the young man offer to…"

"Young man? And why does he have to be a young man?"

"Because he's your son, Carlotta. Remember? He's the child you gave up, and you don't know him."

"Why can't I be his sister? The mama she dies, and the sister she's just a child herself. She takes the brother to the convent and leaves him because she's only three or four years old and can't take care of him. That's much better. I like it. We will make the changes."

"Certainly not." The voice was unmistakably *his* voice. Carlotta spun around ready to fight. She scanned the house for the mask.

"Where? Where is he? You, Sig. Costanzi, you leave us for months. You take your holiday and expect us to work, work, work. Rinaldo has been impossible." She stamped her foot soundly on the stage. Startled, the horse reared at the sudden outburst.

Erik raced up the stairs and took Caspiano's lead. "Whoa, there." He rubbed his hand soothingly along the horse's neck down to his crest. The animal quieted, flicked his head back to nuzzle against the man's shoulder.

Everyone on stage stopped what they were doing. The only sounds were those made by the horse and Don Erik.

Then the whispers began.

"Oh, my God. Do you see…?"

"What do you suppose did that?"

"That's why he insisted on the mask."

"Ugh. It's awful."

"It's just the one side."

"It's so sad. He's actually quite…"

"Why'd he take it off?"

"Bravo for him. Why should he…?"

"Maybe it began to hurt."

"But it's just one side."

"I knew it all along. Saw him once with Meg."

"She doesn't mind sleeping with that?"

"He's still a handsome man."

"Do you think it's just the face or…?"

"What do I care for his face? He pays me well enough."

"I think he's rather brave to come without it."

Erik ignored the murmurs.

"Quiet!" Carlotta's voice reverberated round the enclosure. Stunned the company ceased their muttering and waited to see what the demented diva was up to. "Sssshhhh. Ssshhh. Sshh!" Then she pushed the fake well out of her path with a jerk of one hip and strode over to Erik. In a theatrical stage whisper, she said, "Costanzi, you maybe dressed too quickly this morning and forgot something? Eh?"

Erik looked down at his clothes, running his finger across his buttons, pausing in particular over the fly of his trousers. Finding nothing amiss, he shook his head.

"Ha ha. Funny! You make like the clown. Ha. Ha." Carlotta pointed with both her index fingers at her own face.

Erik smiled. He knew exactly what she meant. "No, Carlotta, I have not forgotten. Jacopo, can you take Caspiano?" The scene shifter stepped forward and led the horse from the stage. Erik held out his hand for the score. Rinaldo readily handed the loosely bound pages to Erik and retreated. To the rest of the company, Erik shouted, "Take ten minutes."

Except for a few who splintered off from among the chorus and dancers, most of the performers lingered, refusing to leave the stage. They wanted to be there when the fireworks began. They relaxed against props and sat upon the floor and waited.

"Well, perhaps you're right Carlotta. Maybe we need an older actress for the part of the mother." Erik thumbed through the notes Rinaldo had already jotted in the margins of Erik's new opera.

"What?" She dropped her fists from her hips and stepped forward to stare over Erik's left arm at the sheets of paper.

"If you think you can't do it." Erik cast a quick glance at Carlotta out of the corner of his eye. "If you're too young, then I suppose Signora Lamberdini might be wooed away for a season from the Teatro Regio. Rinaldo." Erik left Carlotta center-stage, where she liked to be, and went to confer with his assistant by the wings. Rinaldo had nearly pushed his way through a bevy of ballet dancers near the exit in a vain attempt to escape before Erik roped him into the discussion. "Rinaldo, come here." The young man froze and slowly returned to the stage. Erik almost pitied him. "We need to recast the role of the mother."

Carlotta's voice commanded attention, especially when she sang. And that's exactly what she did. She lifted her chest and pointed her arms at an empty house and sang the words of the mother who comes in search of her missing son. Erik folded his arms over his chest and listened, keeping careful track in his mind of what needed to be modified or corrected.

The final note faded so gradually that Erik could still follow its strain. Several in the company applauded the diva. But Carlotta faced Erik, consciously or unconsciously mirroring his own stance, her arms folded neatly under her bosom.

"Do I take that to mean you've changed your mind, Signorina Venedetti?"

"Humph." She glared at him. "I will do the part."

"I'm pleased. It was written with you in mind." Erik handed the opera—his first since he'd returned from Austria—to his assistant. Rinaldo let out the breath he'd been holding, it seemed, for the past several weeks.

Carlotta wasn't sure whether she liked the fact that Erik had written this particular part for her. She didn't want to be old enough to have a grown son. On the other hand, the arias he'd given her character were stunning. And it would be nice to be in an opera where none of the main characters died for a change.

"Don Erik, there's someone who wants a word with you." Rinaldo whispered in Erik's ear. The young man kept glancing back over his shoulder toward the wings. "It's the reviewer, Ricci."

Erik noticed Carlotta straining to see past them to the wings. When she recognized Paolo Ricci, she scowled.

Rinaldo had not left Erik's side. "He keeps hanging about. Since you got back to Rome, for the past two months, he comes almost daily."

Erik ignored Rinaldo and spoke to Carlotta. "Then we will leave the score as it is, Signorina. I would suggest, though, that you go over the second movement again. Perhaps Sig. Bianchi can play it for you so you know how it's *supposed* to go."

Paolo Ricci was flirting with one of the chorus girls and didn't hear Erik approach. The girl, however, caught sight of Erik at the last minute. Her eyes became saucers, and she gasped. Without a word, she curtseyed and scurried away. Annoyed by the interruption, Ricci prepared to give the intruder a tongue lashing. When his eyes fell on the reddened and irregular surface of the formerly masked artistic director's face, Ricci forgot how to speak and just stood, his mouth agape.

"You've always said that you wondered what I hid under my mask, Ricci."

The journalist swallowed and cleared his throat. He pulled his eyes away from the disfigurement and searched madly for his pad and pencil.

Erik didn't budge. He waited, his hands clasped behind his back.

Finally Ricci raised his pencil over the blank page in his notebook. His hand trembled slightly, but his voice seemed unaffected. "Sig. Costanzi, this interview has been long in coming. Why do you consent to speak now to your public?"

"You misunderstand, Sig. Ricci. I speak to my public through my work. That is all that I have to offer. The rest is of little importance to them."

"I see. But people are curious."

"*You* are curious, Sig. Ricci, and your articles and reviews plant questions in the public's mind that they might never have thought of themselves." Before Ricci could ask another question, Erik asked one of his own. "Do you enjoy opera, sir?"

"Of course."

"Then why don't you write about it?"

"Why, I do."

"No, you don't. You write about masks and egomaniacs and bad seating and overpriced tickets. You do *not* write about opera."

Ricci fidgeted and pretended to write down what Erik was saying.

"Do you know what opera is?" Erik cocked his head so that his deformed side was even more prominent.

"I have been reviewing the opera season for…"

"Do you know what opera is?" Erik purposely drew closer to the man.

Ricci could not avoid seeing the deformed side of Erik's face. Erik stared at Ricci. In turn, Ricci forced himself to focus on Erik's green eyes. Unfortunately, it did not make him more comfortable to do so.

"What is opera?" Ricci repeated Erik's question, cursing himself that his voice was so quiet.

Erik's green eyes sparked, delighted by Ricci's prompt. "You must listen to me closely. It is here that you will learn what opera is." Erik's hand lay, fingers splayed, across the vest where Ricci's heart pounded in a mixture of fear and anticipation. "It is the cry of a child, the answering song of a long-lost mother, it is the fire of lust that burns both the lover and the beloved, it is the sound of water to a thirsty man, it is the death of a robin and the birth of a dove, it is a kiss that changes the beast into a man, wakes a sleeping princess trapped amid thorns, and betrays the lamb for slaughter. It's not the mask, Ricci. It's what lies beneath the mask."

"Erik?" Meg held back, seeing the two men intimately close.

The spell broken, Erik withdrew his hand from Ricci's chest and stepped back. "It's been a pleasure speaking to you, Sig. Ricci. I do enjoy your column. You've a gift for sarcasm. Please stop by the office before you leave. I'll have a season pass made ready for you. Box seven should be adequate?"

Meg raced behind Erik as her husband set off for the stage. "Well?"

He stopped so quickly she landed in his arms. He chuckled with the unexpected weight of her against him. Instead of answering, he kissed her. Then he kissed her again, allowing his tongue to glide over her painted lips. When he drew back, he saw he'd smudged the bright red coloring. With his thumb, he rubbed the stray smear, trying to repair his damage, but Meg slipped his thumb into her mouth and sucked on it hard. He felt an immediate sympathetic response, but he pulled the digit free and pressed it over her closed lips. "Not now, ma petite. It's time for the canary to sing."

He pulled her behind him to the stage. The company strained to see the beautiful chanteuse, Il canarino, in the arms of the beast. Already most were finding it less shocking to see the maestro without his mask.

When Carlotta, who had leaned against Rinaldo and had been fiddling mercilessly with his buttons, saw Erik return to the stage, she pushed herself back from her lover's arms and waved him away. He sighed and shook his head as he went to stand beside Erik.

"Sig. Bianchi." Erik nodded to the conductor who waited in the orchestra pit for instructions. "Let's begin with Meg's aria, Act II. Then we'll proceed to her duet with Signorina Venedetti." Then Erik spoke to the entire company. "Positions, please." Feet shuffled and clicked across the dusty surface. Sig. Bianchi raised his baton, his eyes on Erik. Erik scanned the stage until he was sure everyone was on his mark. Meg smiled at him. He gave her a reproving glance, and she settled her features into a mask of seriousness.

"Maestro." Erik turned to the orchestra pit. "Shall we begin?"

Afterword

❀

Although the events in this novel predate the rise of psychoanalysis as described by Sigmund Freud, certain practices and concepts that form the bedrock of later developments are already widely known in the 1880s. In *Freud: Darkness in the Midst of Vision* (John Wiley & Sons, 2000), Louis Breger affords a fascinating and readable introduction to the emergence of psychoanalysis. Of particular interest for my readers are the experiments and experiences of Jean Martin Charcot and Josef Breuer.

Charcot dealt with a wide range of conditions that were collectively diagnosed as hysteria—symptoms with no apparent physiological cause—at the Salpêtrière Hospital in Paris. By 1885, when Sigmund Freud met him, his hypnotic demonstrations were famous. Using hypnosis to induce his patients to recover lost memories, Charcot's work already suggested the existence of an unconscious. He postulated the concept of a post-traumatic 'hypnotic state' to explain the "blotting out of consciousness of events and emotions associated with traumatic events" (Breger 81). However Charcot showed little or no interest in the details of his patients' lives. It was Josef Breuer's treatment, from 1880 to 1882, of Bertha Pappenheim ("Anna O.") that best exemplifies what we associate with psychoanalytic therapy. "The talking cure," as the patient herself called Breuer's "cathartic method," encouraged the patient to recount memories and to experience the emotions associated with them. Hypnosis was sometimes used.

It's evident that fundamental concepts of psychoanalysis were current in the 1880s. A wide range of psychological problems or conditions were acknowledged as the result of the breakthrough of "damned-up, unconscious traumatic memories and emotions." The manifestation of these buried memories and emotions in physical symptoms were symbolic of the original trauma. Treatment involved unlocking these traumatic memories so that the emotions could be unblocked (105-106).

A great deal of poetic license has gone into the creation of Dr. Richmond and his particular use of hypnosis in my novel. But then again early psychoanalysis shares much in common with the literary imagination. All inaccuracies in the depiction of psychological concepts or practices are solely those of my character, Dr. Richmond.

S. M.